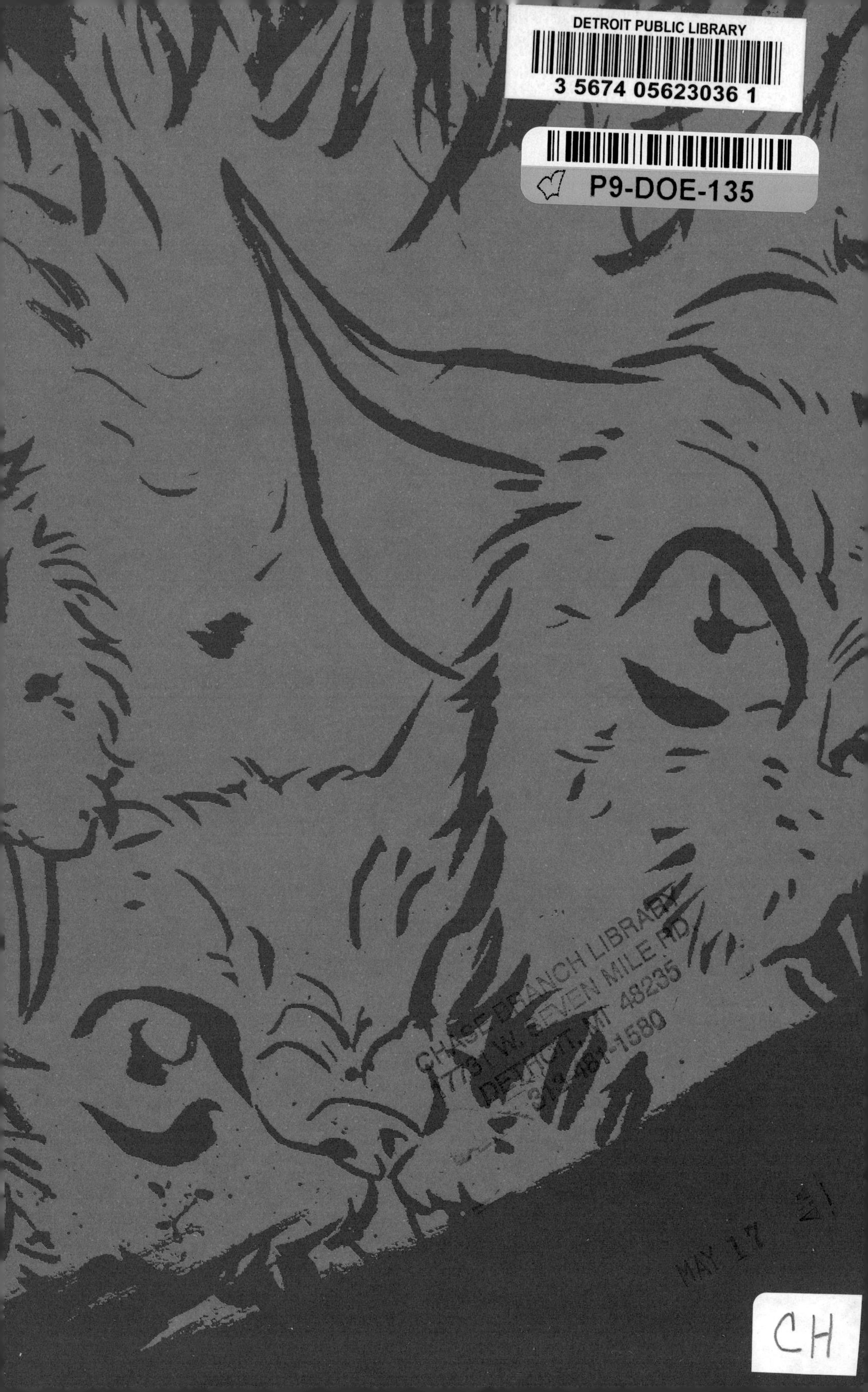

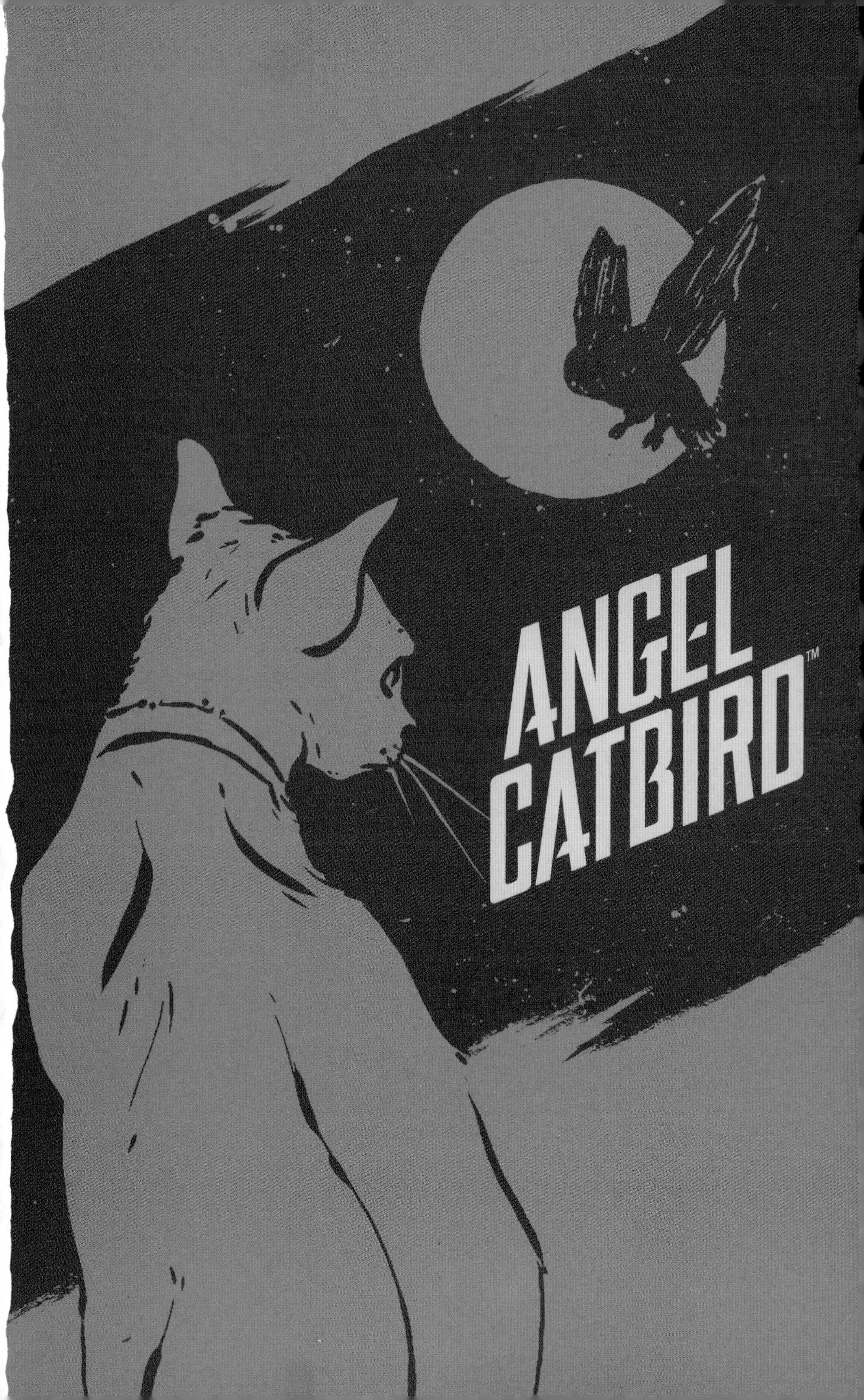
ANGEL CATBIRD™

ANGEL CATBIRD™

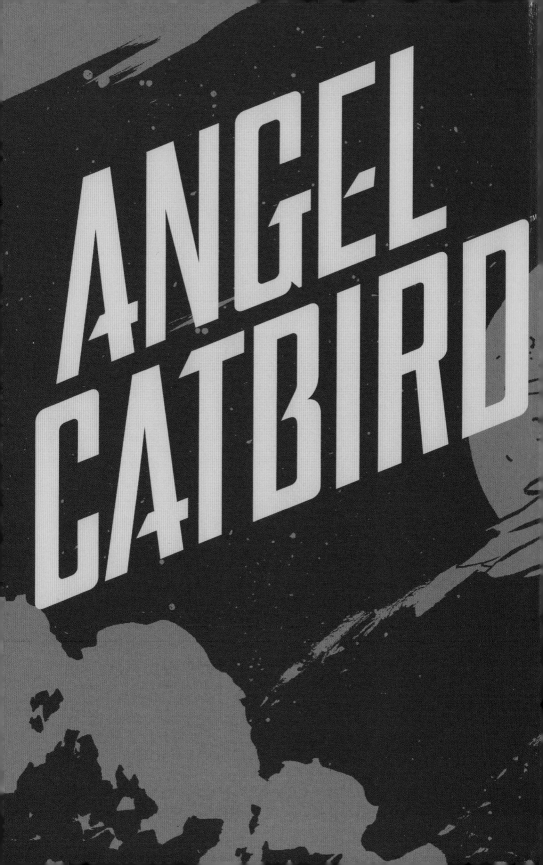

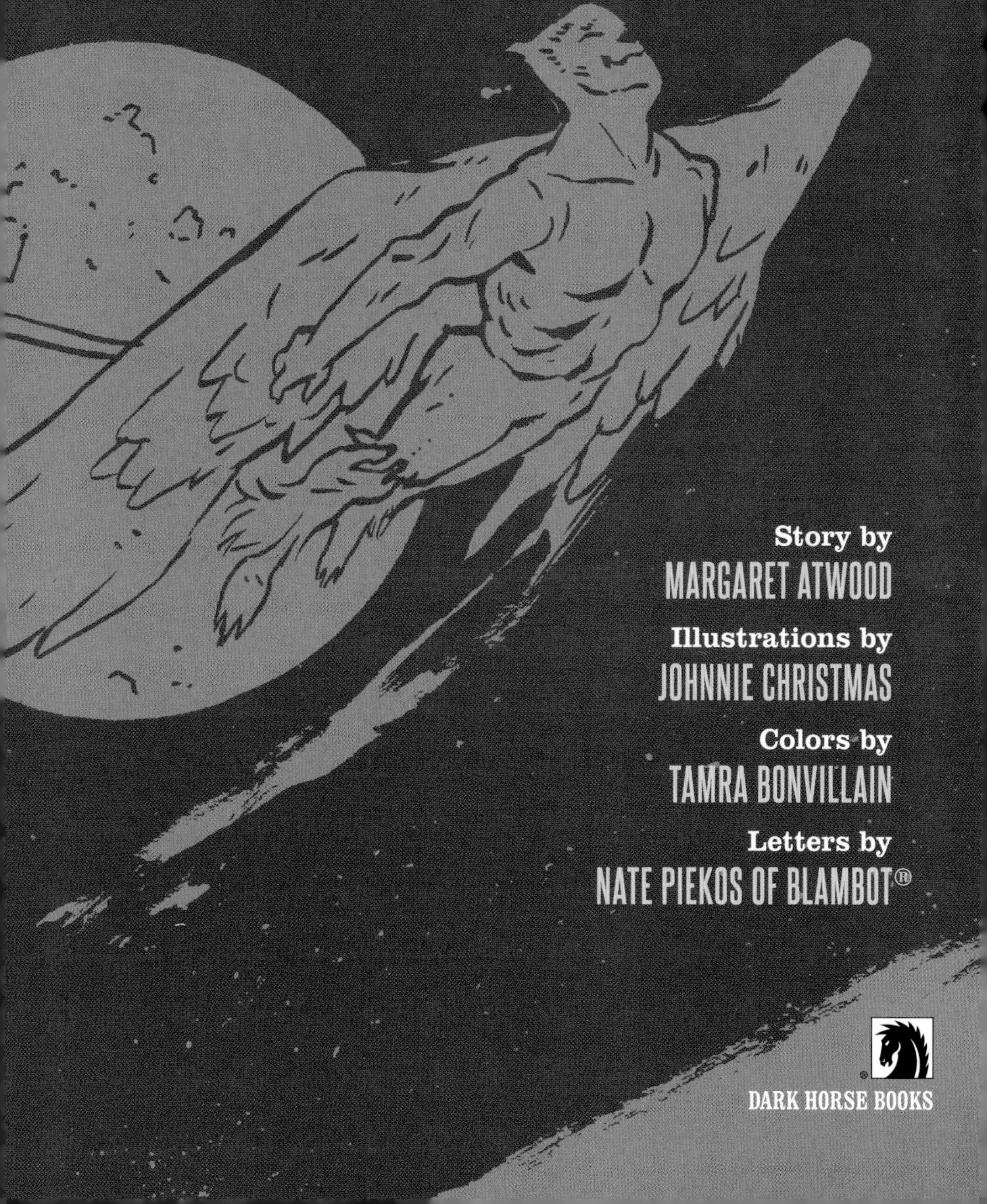

Story by
MARGARET ATWOOD
Illustrations by
JOHNNIE CHRISTMAS
Colors by
TAMRA BONVILLAIN
Letters by
NATE PIEKOS OF BLAMBOT®

DARK HORSE BOOKS

President and Publisher MIKE RICHARDSON

Editor DANIEL CHABON

Project Adviser HOPE NICHOLSON

Assistant Editor CARDNER CLARK

Designer CINDY CACEREZ-SPRAGUE

Digital Art Technician CONLEY SMITH

Special thanks to SARAH COOPER

NEIL HANKERSON Executive Vice President • TOM WEDDLE Chief Financial Officer •
RANDY STRADLEY Vice President of Publishing • MICHAEL MARTENS Vice President of
Book Trade Sales • MATT PARKINSON Vice President of Marketing • DAVID SCROGGY
Vice President of Product Development • DALE LaFOUNTAIN Vice President of Information
Technology • CARA NIECE Vice President of Production and Scheduling • NICK McWHORTER
Vice President of Media Licensing • KEN LIZZI General Counsel • DAVE MARSHALL Editor
in Chief • DAVEY ESTRADA Editorial Director • SCOTT ALLIE Executive Senior Editor •
CHRIS WARNER Senior Books Editor • CARY GRAZZINI Director of Print and Development
• LIA RIBACCHI Art Director • MARK BERNARDI Director of Digital Publishing • MICHAEL
GOMBOS Director of International Publishing and Licensing

Published by Dark Horse Books
A division of Dark Horse Comics, Inc.
10956 SE Main Street
Milwaukie, OR 97222

First edition: September 2016
ISBN 978-1-50670-063-2

10 9 8 7 6 5 4 3 2 1
Printed in China

International Licensing: (503) 905-2377 | Comic Shop Locator Service: (888) 266-4226

ANGEL CATBIRD VOLUME 1

Library of Congress Cataloging-in-Publication Data

Names: Atwood, Margaret. | Christmas, Johnnie, illustrator.
Title: Angel Catbird / story by Margaret Atwood ; illustrations by Johnnie
   Christmas ; colors by Tamra Bonvillain ; Letters by Nate Piekos of Blambot.
Description: First edition. | Milwaukie, OR : Dark Horse Books, 2016. |
   Summary: "On a dark night, young genetic engineer Strig Feleedus is
   accidentally mutated by his own experiment when his DNA is merged with
   that of a cat and an owl"-- Provided by publisher.
Identifiers: LCCN 2016010286 | ISBN 9781506700632 (hardback)
Subjects: LCSH: Graphic novels. | CYAC: Graphic novels. |
   Superheroes--Fiction. | Genetic engineering--Fiction. | Adventure and
   adventurers--Fiction. | BISAC: COMICS & GRAPHIC NOVELS / Superheroes. |
   COMICS & GRAPHIC NOVELS / General. | FICTION / Action & Adventure.
Classification: LCC PZ7.7.A896 Ang 2016 | DDC 741.5/973--dc23
LC record available at https://lccn.loc.gov/2016010286

MARGARET ATWOOD

INTRODUCTION

Some find it strange that a person known for her novels and poetry would take to writing comic books, especially comic books called *Angel Catbird*. Why is a nice literary old lady like me—an *award-winning* nice literary old lady—a nice literary old lady who should be resting on her laurels in her rocking chair, being dignified and iconic—why is such a nice old lady messing around with flying cat-owl superheroes and nightclubs for cat people, not to mention giant rat men? Strange.

But I myself don't find it very strange. I was born in 1939, and was thus of a reading age when the war ended and colour comics made a booming comeback. Not only did I read masses of comics in magazine form, I could encounter many of the same characters in the weekend newspapers, which had big spreads of colour comics. Some of the comics were funny—*Little Lulu*, *Li'l Abner*, *Mickey Mouse*, *Blondie*, and so forth—but some were serious—*Steve Canyon*, *Rip Kirby*, and the unfathomable *Mary Worth*. And some were superheroes: Batman, Captain Marvel, Wonder Woman, Superman, Plastic Man, the Green Lantern, the Human Torch, and their ilk. Some were even aimed at improving young minds: the *Classic Comics* series had an educational bent.

And some were just weird. In this last category I'd place *Mandrake the Magician*, *Little Orphan Annie*—in which nobody had pupils—and *Dick Tracy*: surrealist masterpieces, all of them, though somewhat disturbing for children. A criminal who could assume anyone's face, behind which he looked like melting Swiss cheese? It was alarmingly close to Salvador Dalí,

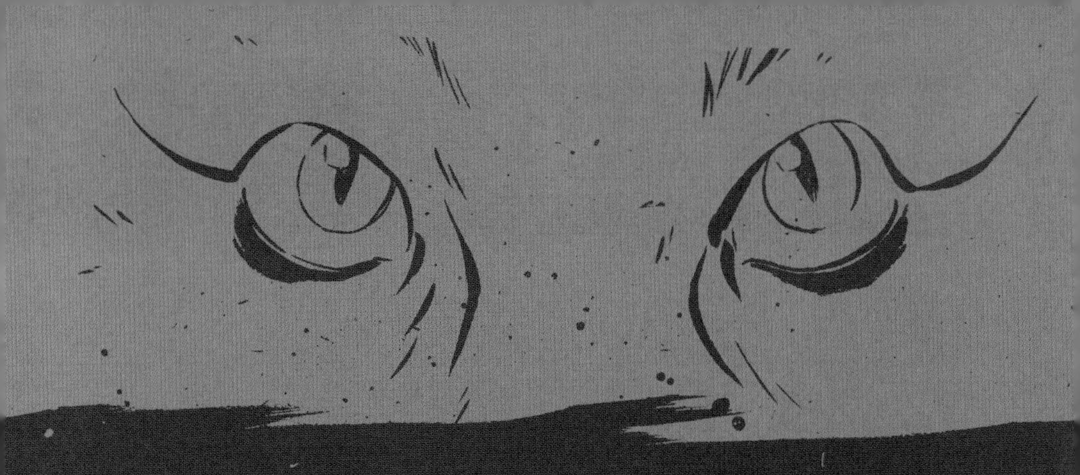

and kept me awake nights—as did Salvador Dalí, when I came across him years later.

Not only did I read all of these comics, I drew comics of my own. The earliest ones featured two flying rabbit superheroes, somewhat too jolly and fond of somersaults to be considered heavyweights. My older brother had a much larger stable of characters. They had more gravitas: they went in for large-scale warfare, whereas my own superheroes just fooled around with the odd bullet.

Along with the superhero rabbits I drew winged flying cats, many with balloons attached to them. I was obsessed with balloons, as no balloons were available during the war. So I'd seen pictures of them, but never the actual thing. It was similar with the cats: I wasn't allowed to have one because we were up in the Canadian forests a lot. How would the cat travel? Once there, wouldn't it run away and be eaten by mink? Very likely. So, for the first part of my life, my cats were flying dream cats.

Time passed, and both the balloons and the cats materialized in my real life. The balloons were a disappointment, liable as they were to burst and deflate; the cats were not. For over fifty years I was a dedicated cat person, with a few gaps here and there when I was a student. My cats were a pleasure, a comfort, and an aid to composition. The only reason I don't have one now is that I'm afraid of tripping on it. That, and of leaving it an orphan, so to speak.

As the 1940s changed into the 1950s and I became a teenager, the comic that preoccupied me the most was Walt Kelly's *Pogo*, which, with its cast of swamp critters combined with its satire of the McCarthy era's excesses, set a new benchmark: how to be entertainingly serious while also being seriously entertaining. Meanwhile I was continuing to draw, and to design the odd visual object—posters, for the silk-screen poster business I was running on the Ping-Pong table in the late fifties, and book covers, for my own first books, because that was cheaper than paying a pro.

In the seventies I drew a sort-of political strip called *Kanadian Kultchur Komix* for a magazine called, puzzlingly, *This Magazine*. I then took to drawing a yearly strip called *Book Tour Comix*, which I would send to my publishers at Christmas to make them feel guilty. (That didn't succeed.) It's no great coincidence that the narrator of my 1972 novel, *Surfacing*, is an illustrator, and that the narrator of my 1988 novel, *Cat's Eye*, is a figurative painter. We all have unlived lives. (Note that none of these narrators has ever been a ballet dancer. I did try ballet, briefly, but it made me dizzy.)

And I continued to read comics, watching the emergence of a new generation of psychologically complex characters with relationship problems (Spider-Man, who begat Wolverine, et cetera). Then came the emergence of graphic novels, with such now-classics as *Maus* and *Persepolis*: great-grandchildren of *Pogo*, whether they knew it or not.

Meanwhile I had become more and more immersed in the world of bird conservation. I now had a burden of guilt from my many years of cat companionship, for my cats had gone in and out of the house, busying themselves with their cat affairs, which included the killing of small animals and birds. These would turn up as gifts, placed thoughtfully either on my pillow instead of a chocolate, or on the front doormat, where I would slip on them. Sometimes it would not even be a whole animal. One of my cats donated only the gizzards.

From this collision between my comic-reading-and-writing self and the bird blood on my hands, Angel Catbird was born. I pondered him for several years, and even did some preliminary sketches. He would be a combination

of cat, owl, and human being, and he would thus have an identity conflict—*do I save this baby robin, or do I eat it?* But he would be able to understand both sides of the question. He would be a walking, flying carnivore's dilemma.

But I realized that Angel Catbird would have to look better than the flying cats I'd drawn in my childhood—two-dimensional and wooden—and better also than my own later cartoons, which were fairly basic and lumpy. I wanted Angel Catbird to look sexy, like the superhero and noir comics I'd read in the forties. He would have to have muscles.

So I would need a coauthor. But how to find one? This wasn't a world of which I had much knowledge. Then up on my Twitter feed popped, one day, a possible answer. A person called Hope Nicholson was resurrecting one of the forgotten Canadian superheroes of the wartime 1940s and fundraising it via Kickstarter. Not only that, Hope lived in Toronto.

I put the case for *Angel Catbird* to her, we got together in a strange Russian-themed pub, and lo and behold, she came onboard and connected me not only with artist Johnnie Christmas, who could draw just the right kinds of muscles and also owl claws, but the publisher, Dark Horse Comics. The Dark Horse editor of the series is Daniel Chabon, who from his picture looks about fifteen. I have never met him, nor have I met Johnnie, nor the excellent colourist Tamra Bonvillain, but I am sure such a meeting will take place in the future.

All of these collaborators have been wonderful. What more could an illustrator manqué such as myself possibly ask for? What fun we have had! At least, I have had fun. Watching *Angel Catbird* come to life has been hugely engaging. There was, for instance, a long email debate about Angel's pants. He had to have pants of some kind. Feather pants, or what? And if feathers, what kind of feathers? And should these pants be underneath his human pants, and just sort of emerge? How should they manifest themselves? Questions would be asked, and we needed to have answers.

And what about Cate Leone, the love interest? Pictures of cat eyes flew back and forth through the ether, and at one point I found myself scanning and sending a costume sketch I had done. What would a girl who is also a cat wear while singing in a nightclub act? Boots with fur trim and claws on the toes? Blood-drop earrings?

Such questions occupy my waking hours. What sort of furniture should Count Catula—part bat, part cat, part vampire—have in his castle? Should some of it be upside down, considering the habits of bats? (Count Catula is important in his own right, for bats are in a lot of trouble worldwide.) How to make a white Egyptian vulture look seductive? (You know what they eat, right?) Should Octopuss have a cat face and tentacle hair? Should Cate Leone have a rival for Angel Catbird's attentions—a part girl, part owl called AtheneOwl? I'm thinking yes. In her human form, does she work at Hooters, or is that a pun too far?

So. Like that.

There is, of course, a science-and-conservation side to this project: it is supplied by Nature Canada, who are not only contributing the statistics that can be found here and there in the book in the banners at the bottoms of the pages, but are also running a #SafeCatSafeBird outreach campaign to urge cat owners not to let their cats range freely. The mortality figures for free-range cats are shockingly high: they get bitten, hit by cars, eaten by foxes, and that's just the beginning. So, it's good for cats and good for birds to keep the cats safe, and in conditions in which they can't contribute to the millions of annual bird deaths attributed to cats. On CatsAndBirds.ca, cat owners can take the pledge, and as the pledges mount up, we can hope that there might be an uptick in the plummeting bird counts that are being recorded in so many places. It may also result in better conditions for stressed forests, since it is the migratory songbirds that weed insect pests out of the trees. Cats aren't the only factor in the decline of birds, of course—habitat loss, pesticides, and glass windows are all playing a part—but they're a big factor.

There used to be an elephant who came around to grade schools. He was called Elmer the Safety Elephant, and he gave advice on crossing streets safely and not getting run over. If your school had managed a year without a street accident, Elmer gave you a flag.

In my wildest dreams, Angel Catbird and Cate Leone, and maybe even Count Catula, would go around and give something or other—a flag, a trophy?—to schools that had gathered a certain number of safe-cat pledges. Who knows, maybe it will happen. Before we act, we imagine and wish, and I'm wishing and imagining a result like that. If it does happen, I'll be the first to climb into my boots with claws on the toes, or maybe sprout some wings, in aid of the cause.

Meanwhile, I hope you enjoy *Angel Catbird* as much as my partners and I have enjoyed creating it. It's been a hoot!

Or a meow.

Or both.

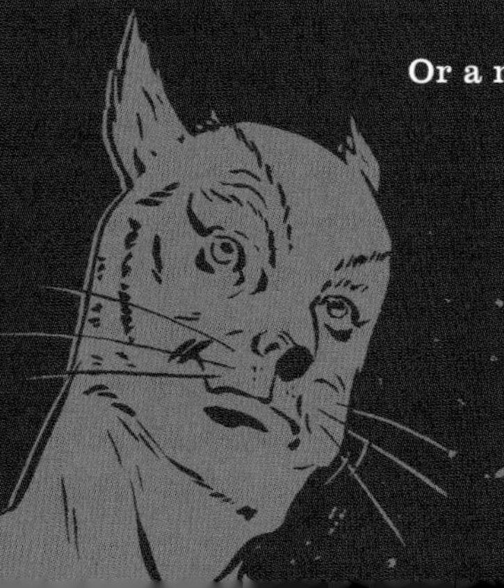

Margaret Atwood

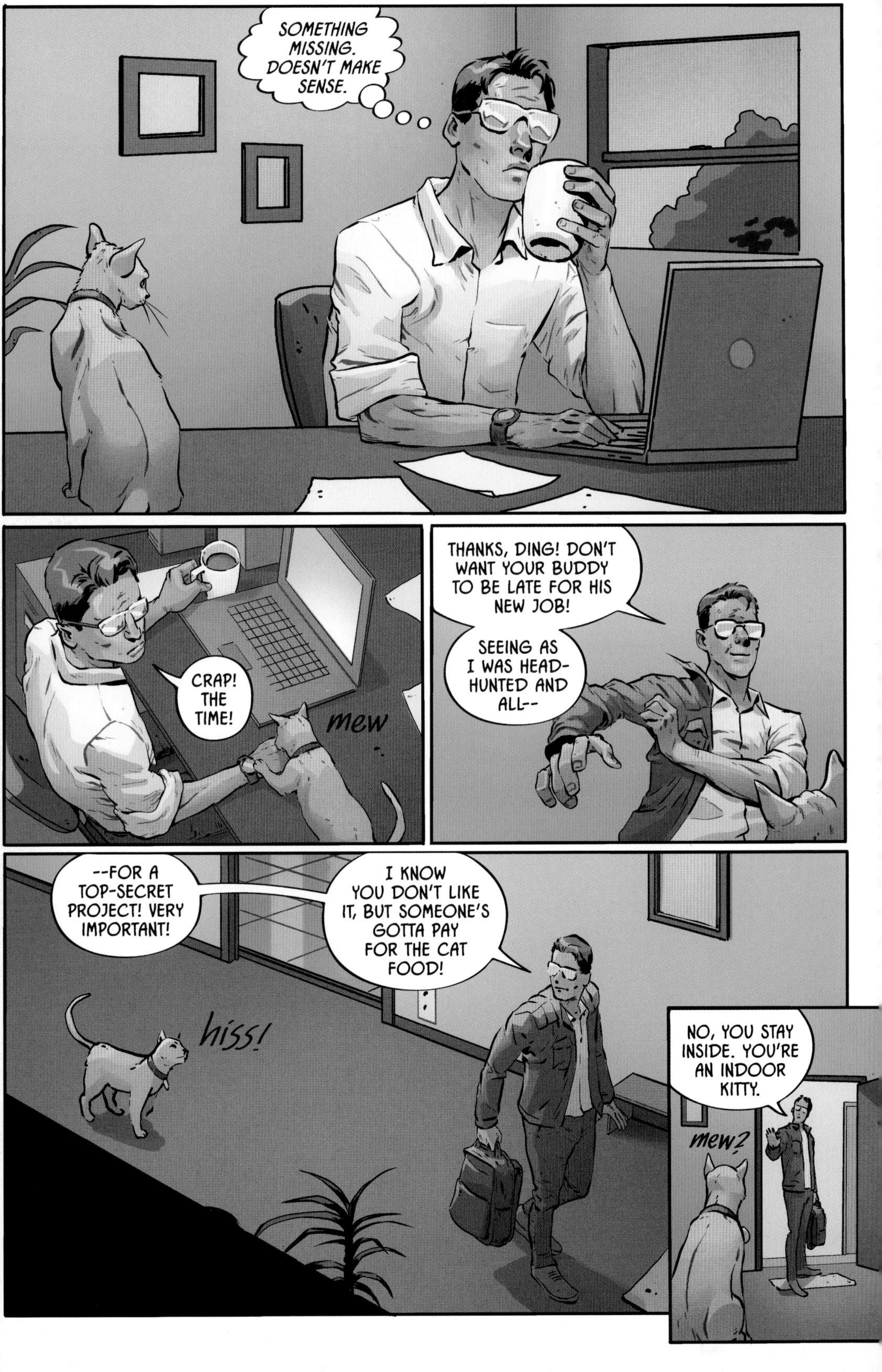
SOMETHING MISSING. DOESN'T MAKE SENSE.
CRAP! THE TIME!
mew
THANKS, DING! DON'T WANT YOUR BUDDY TO BE LATE FOR HIS NEW JOB!
SEEING AS I WAS HEAD-HUNTED AND ALL--
--FOR A TOP-SECRET PROJECT! VERY IMPORTANT!
I KNOW YOU DON'T LIKE IT, BUT SOMEONE'S GOTTA PAY FOR THE CAT FOOD!
hiss!
NO, YOU STAY INSIDE. YOU'RE AN INDOOR KITTY.
mew?

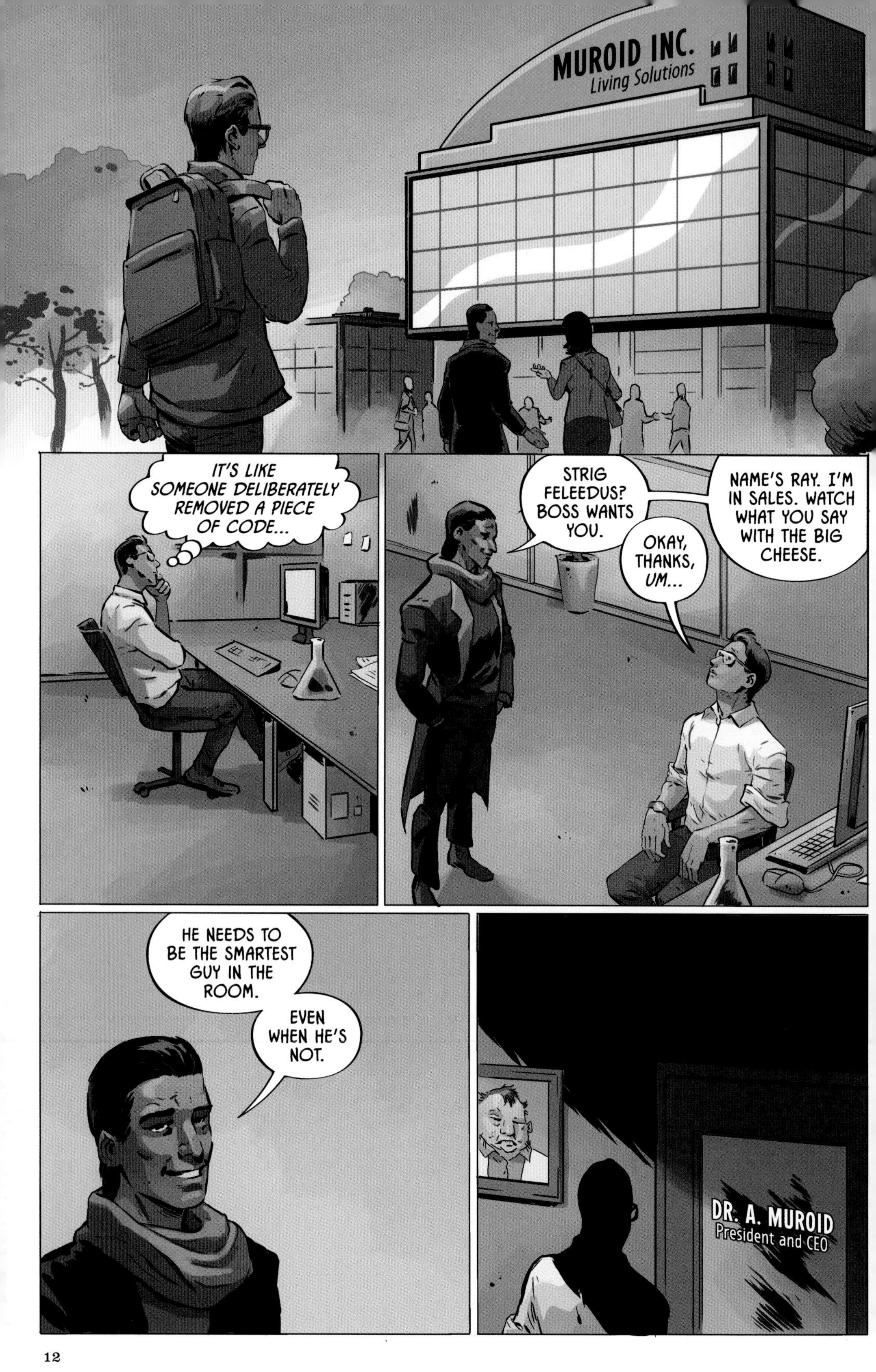
MUROID INC.
Living Solutions
IT'S LIKE SOMEONE DELIBERATELY REMOVED A PIECE OF CODE...
STRIG FELEEDUS? BOSS WANTS YOU.
OKAY, THANKS, UM...
NAME'S RAY. I'M IN SALES. WATCH WHAT YOU SAY WITH THE BIG CHEESE.
HE NEEDS TO BE THE SMARTEST GUY IN THE ROOM.
EVEN WHEN HE'S NOT.
DR. A. MUROID
President and CEO

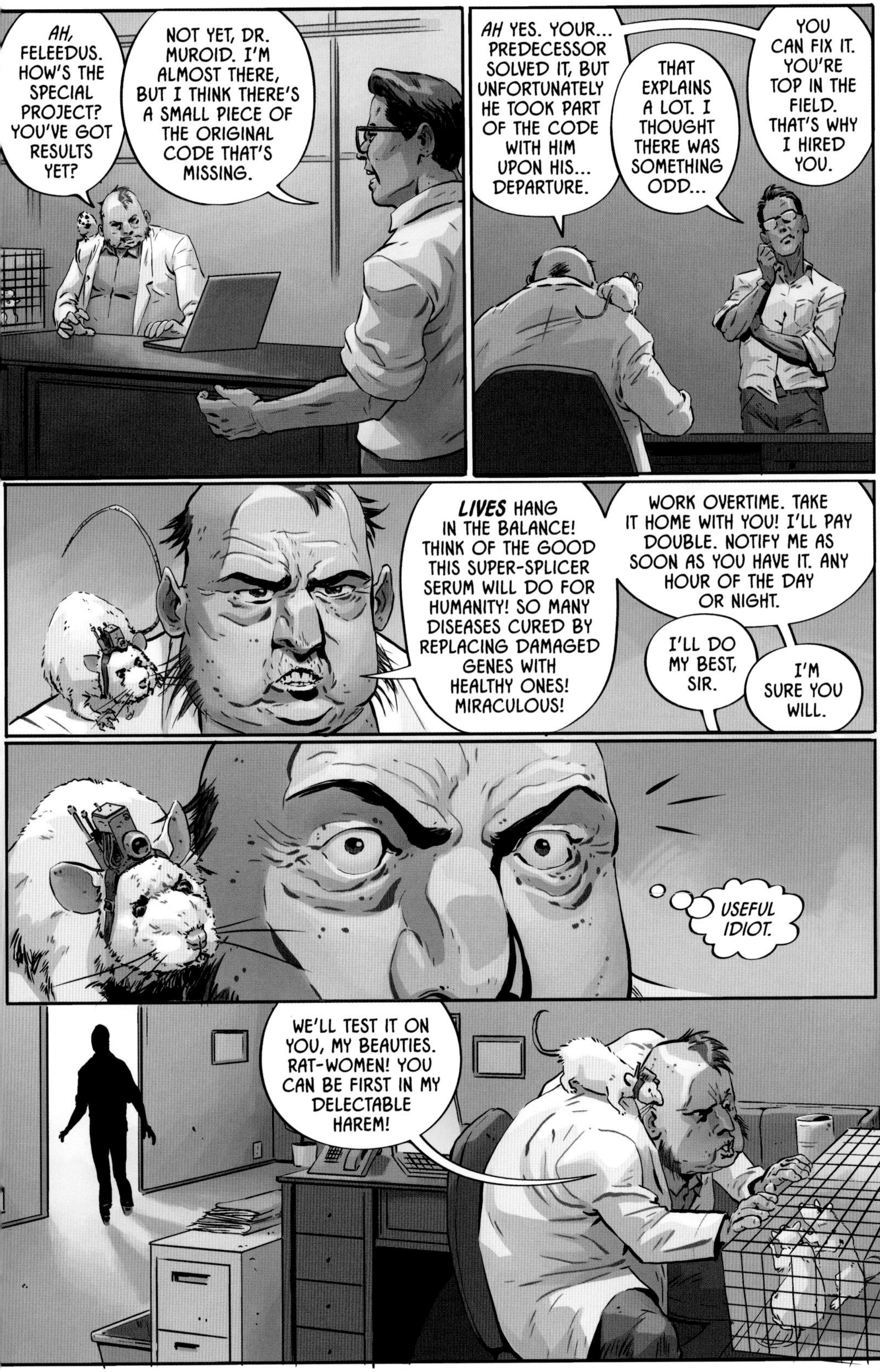
AH, FELEEDUS. HOW'S THE SPECIAL PROJECT? YOU'VE GOT RESULTS YET?
NOT YET, DR. MUROID. I'M ALMOST THERE, BUT I THINK THERE'S A SMALL PIECE OF THE ORIGINAL CODE THAT'S MISSING.
AH YES. YOUR... PREDECESSOR SOLVED IT, BUT UNFORTUNATELY HE TOOK PART OF THE CODE WITH HIM UPON HIS... DEPARTURE.
THAT EXPLAINS A LOT. I THOUGHT THERE WAS SOMETHING ODD...
YOU CAN FIX IT. YOU'RE TOP IN THE FIELD. THAT'S WHY I HIRED YOU.
LIVES HANG IN THE BALANCE! THINK OF THE GOOD THIS SUPER-SPLICER SERUM WILL DO FOR HUMANITY! SO MANY DISEASES CURED BY REPLACING DAMAGED GENES WITH HEALTHY ONES! MIRACULOUS!
WORK OVERTIME. TAKE IT HOME WITH YOU! I'LL PAY DOUBLE. NOTIFY ME AS SOON AS YOU HAVE IT. ANY HOUR OF THE DAY OR NIGHT.
I'LL DO MY BEST, SIR.
I'M SURE YOU WILL.
USEFUL IDIOT.
WE'LL TEST IT ON YOU, MY BEAUTIES. RAT-WOMEN! YOU CAN BE FIRST IN MY DELECTABLE HAREM!

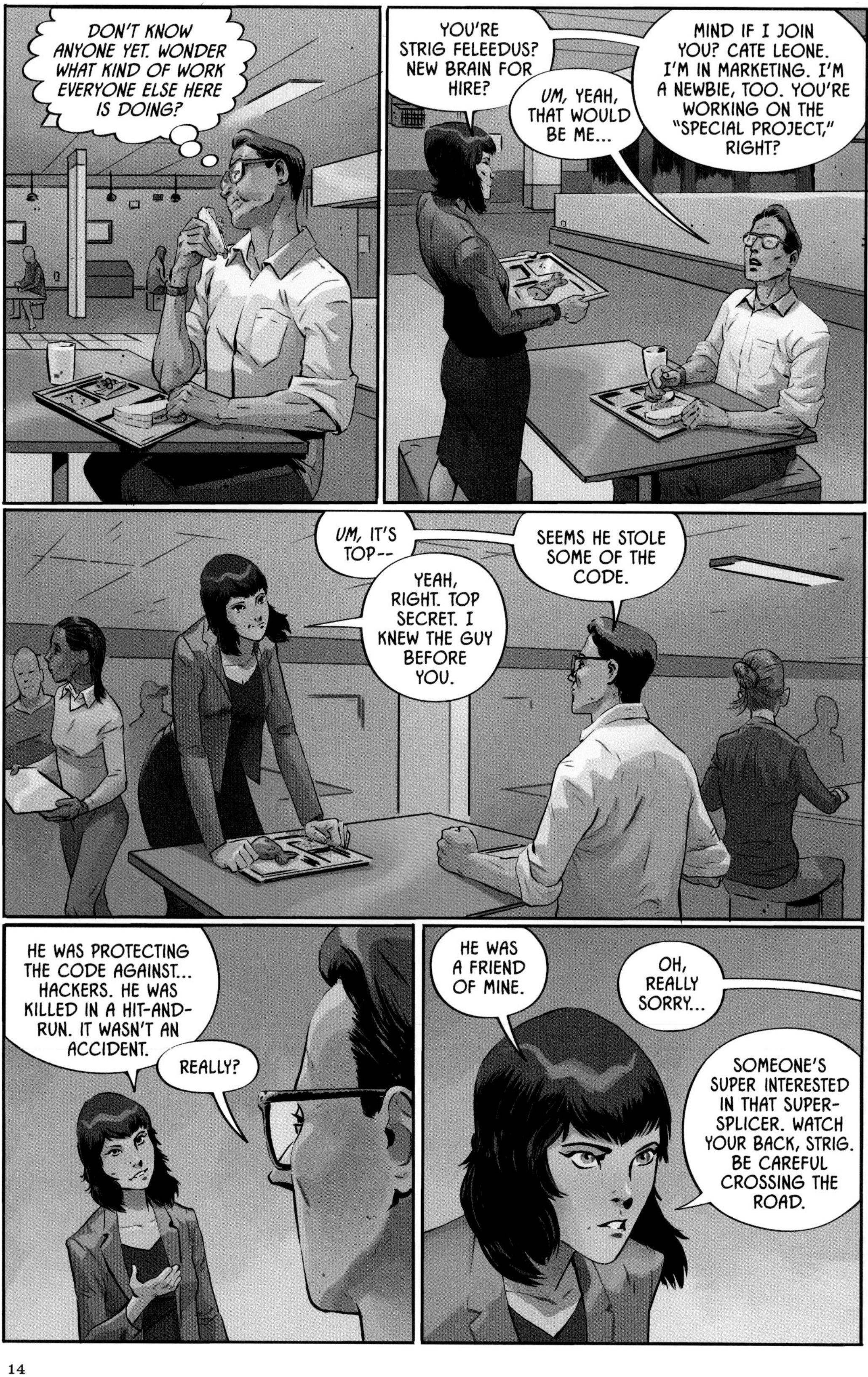
DON'T KNOW ANYONE YET. WONDER WHAT KIND OF WORK EVERYONE ELSE HERE IS DOING?
YOU'RE STRIG FELEEDUS? NEW BRAIN FOR HIRE?
UM, YEAH, THAT WOULD BE ME...
MIND IF I JOIN YOU? CATE LEONE. I'M IN MARKETING. I'M A NEWBIE, TOO. YOU'RE WORKING ON THE "SPECIAL PROJECT," RIGHT?
UM, IT'S TOP--
YEAH, RIGHT. TOP SECRET. I KNEW THE GUY BEFORE YOU.
SEEMS HE STOLE SOME OF THE CODE.
HE WAS PROTECTING THE CODE AGAINST... HACKERS. HE WAS KILLED IN A HIT-AND-RUN. IT WASN'T AN ACCIDENT.
REALLY?
HE WAS A FRIEND OF MINE.
OH, REALLY SORRY...
SOMEONE'S SUPER INTERESTED IN THAT SUPER-SPLICER. WATCH YOUR BACK, STRIG. BE CAREFUL CROSSING THE ROAD.

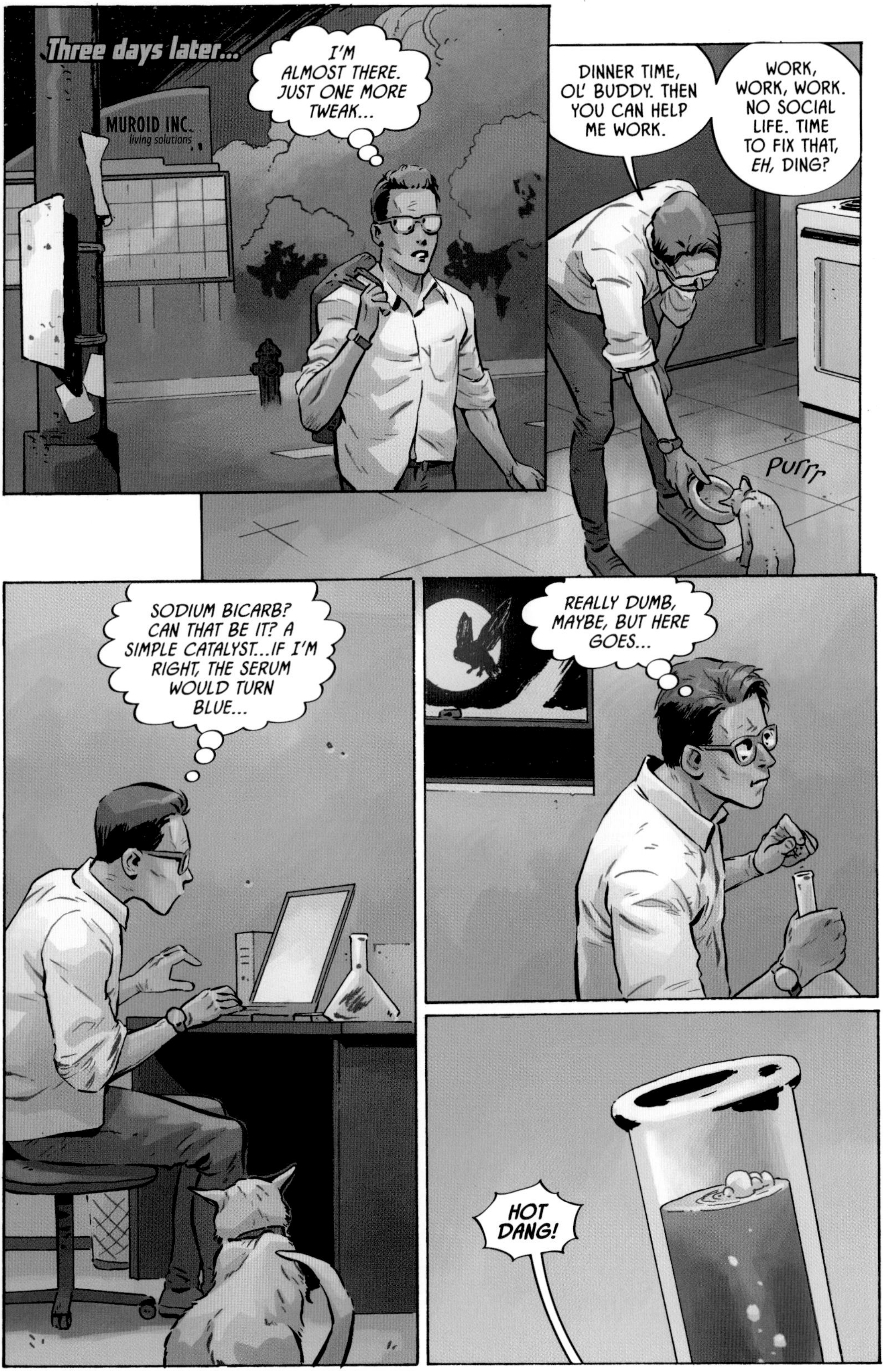
Three days later...
I'M ALMOST THERE. JUST ONE MORE TWEAK...
MUROID INC.
living solutions
DINNER TIME, OL' BUDDY. THEN YOU CAN HELP ME WORK.
WORK, WORK, WORK. NO SOCIAL LIFE. TIME TO FIX THAT, EH, DING?
PURRR
SODIUM BICARB? CAN THAT BE IT? A SIMPLE CATALYST...IF I'M RIGHT, THE SERUM WOULD TURN BLUE...
REALLY DUMB, MAYBE, BUT HERE GOES...
HOT DANG!

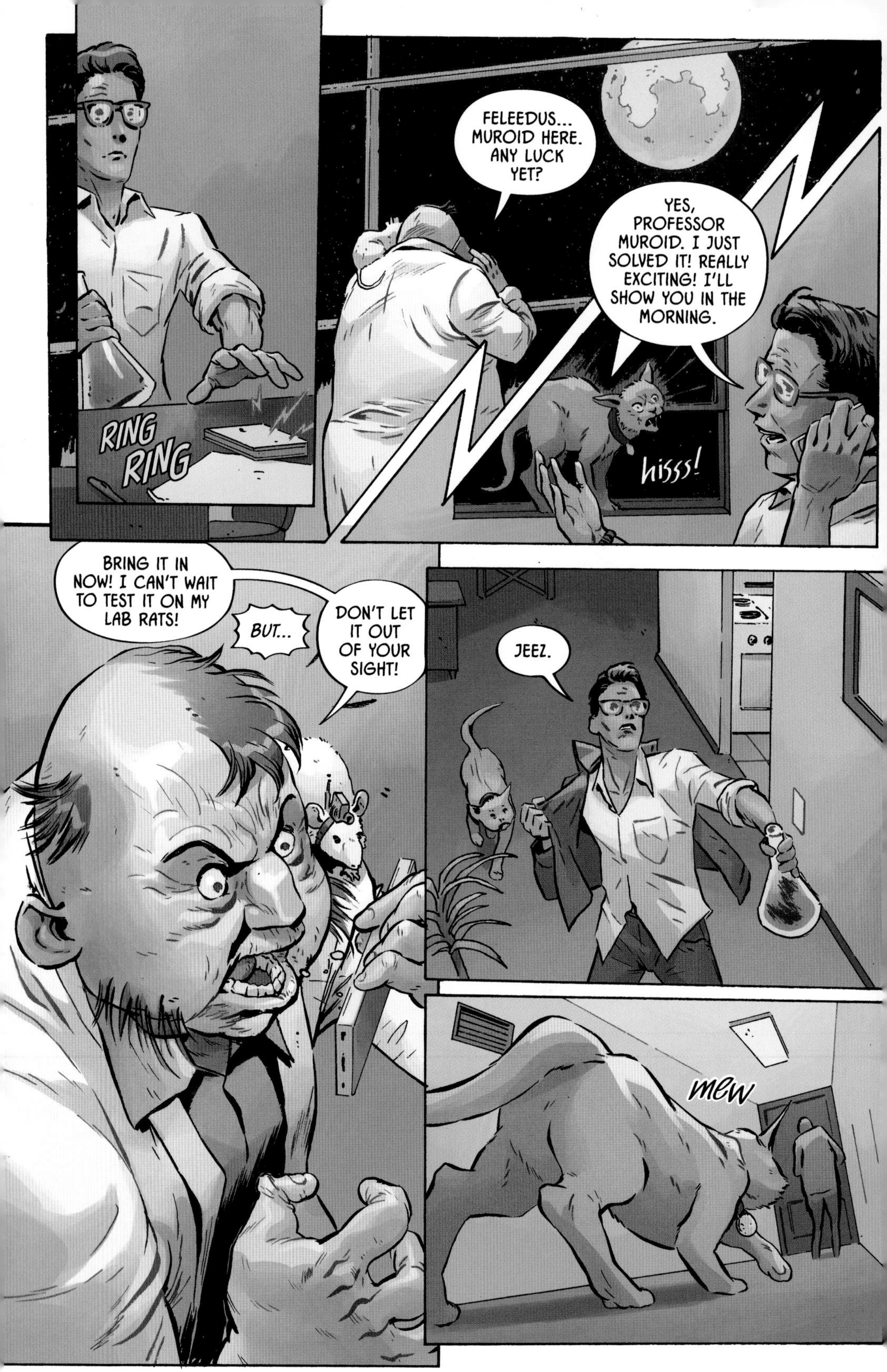
RING RING
FELEEDUS... MUROID HERE. ANY LUCK YET?
YES, PROFESSOR MUROID. I JUST SOLVED IT! REALLY EXCITING! I'LL SHOW YOU IN THE MORNING.
hisss!
BRING IT IN NOW! I CAN'T WAIT TO TEST IT ON MY LAB RATS!
BUT...
DON'T LET IT OUT OF YOUR SIGHT!
JEEZ.
mew

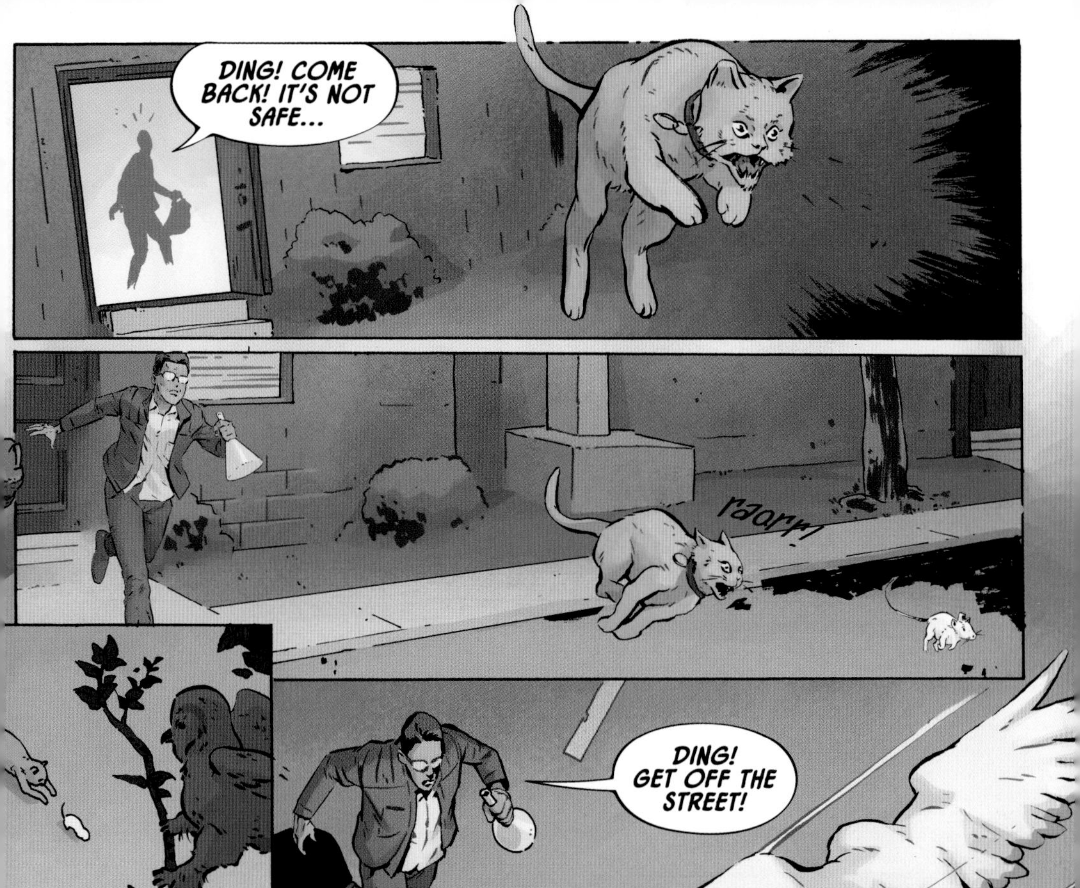
DING! COME BACK! IT'S NOT SAFE...
raorrr
DING! GET OFF THE STREET!
SKREEEEEEE

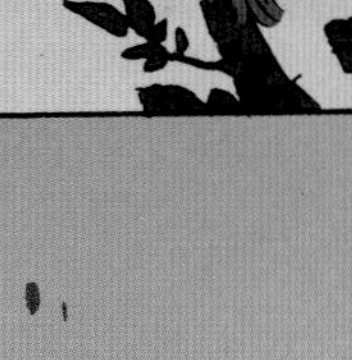

THERE LIES DANGER

Outdoor cats live a fraction of the lifespan of indoor cats: as low as a third. They frequently get hit by cars and are at much higher risk of contracting diseases, getting lost, fighting with wildlife and other cats, poisoning, and parasites. http://catsandbirds.ca/blog/keep-cats-safe/

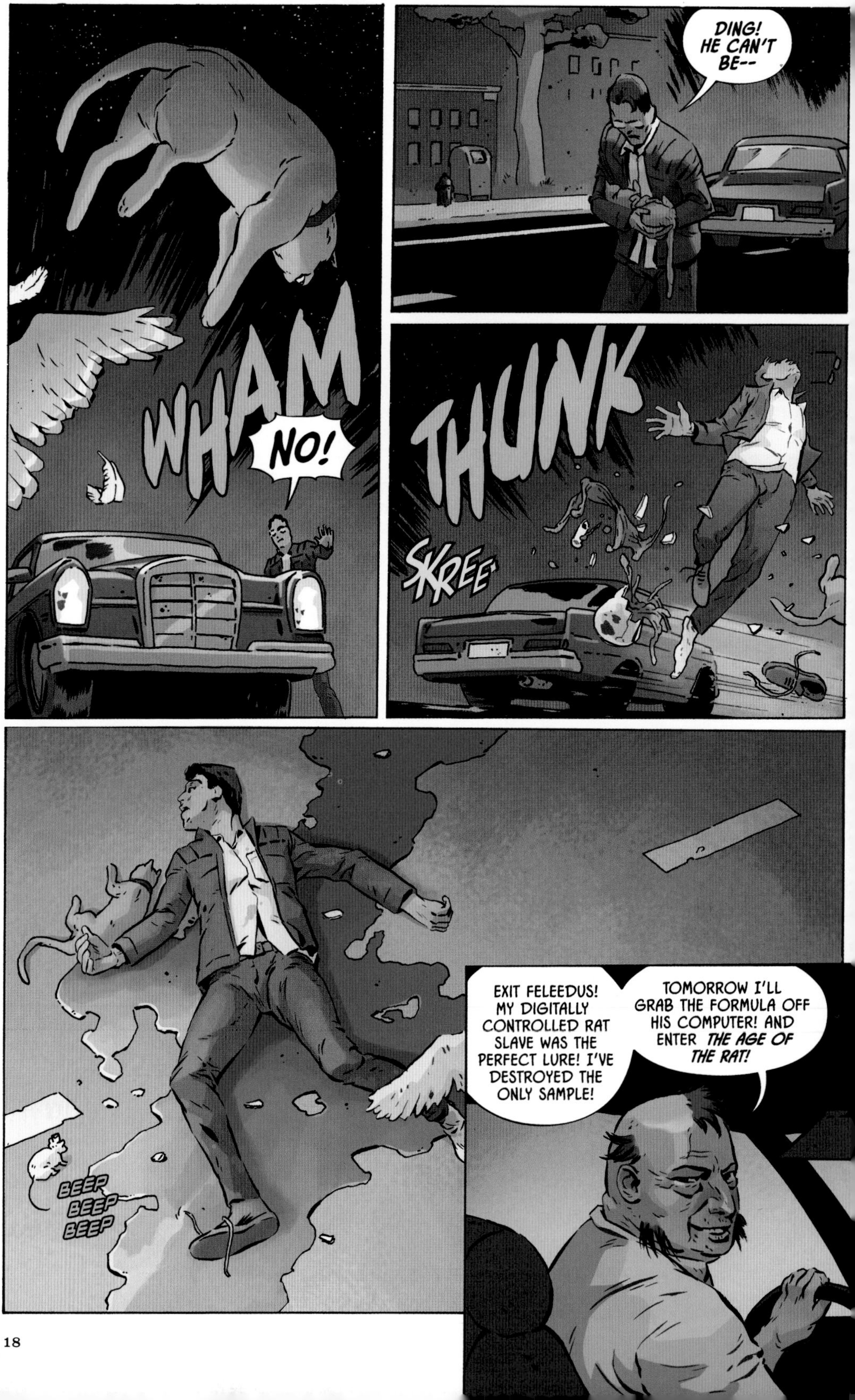
DING! HE CAN'T BE--
WHAM
NO!
THUNK
SKREE
BEEP BEEP BEEP
EXIT FELEEDUS! MY DIGITALLY CONTROLLED RAT SLAVE WAS THE PERFECT LURE! I'VE DESTROYED THE ONLY SAMPLE!
TOMORROW I'LL GRAB THE FORMULA OFF HIS COMPUTER! AND ENTER *THE AGE OF THE RAT!*

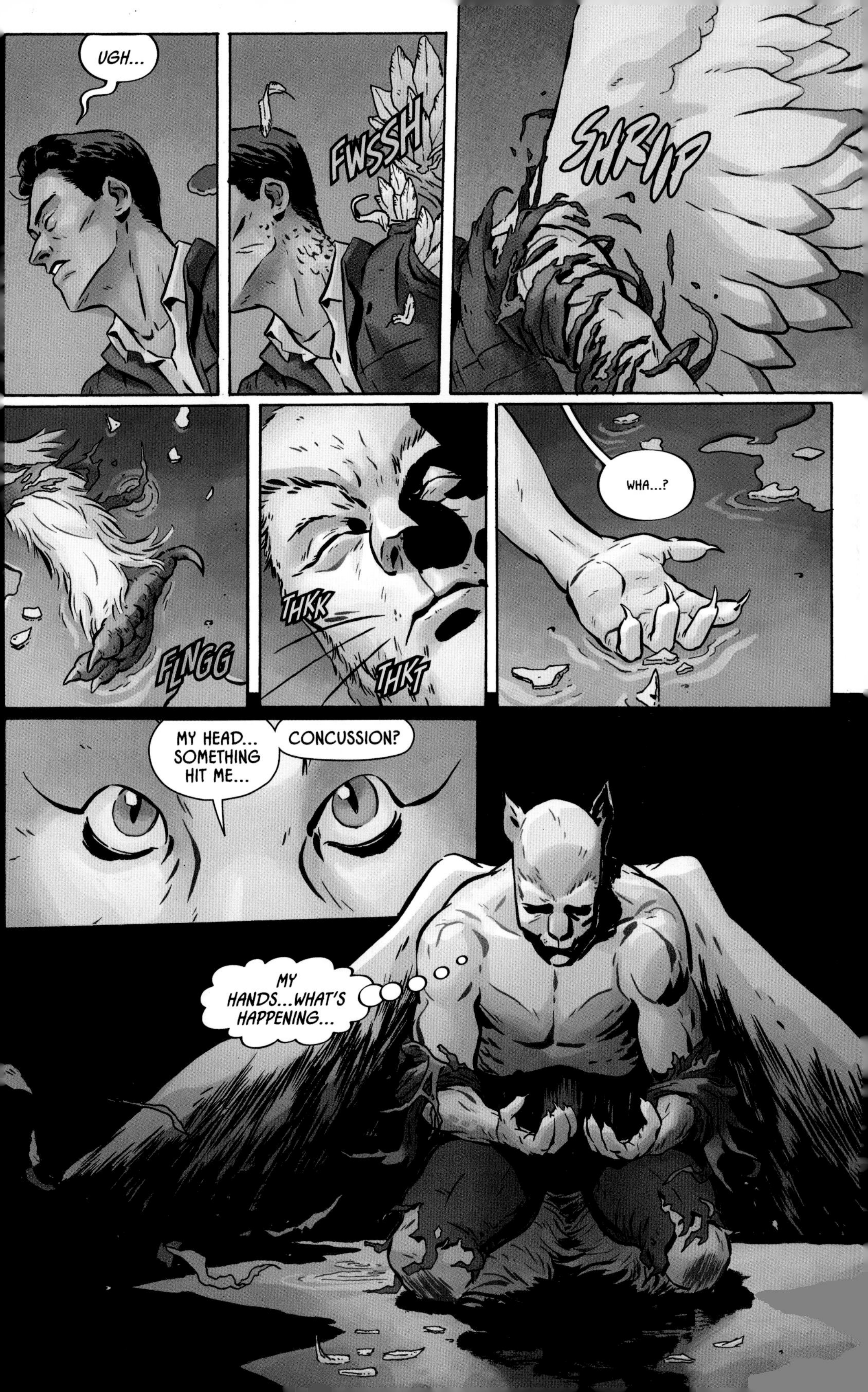
UGH...
FWSSH
SHRIIP
FLNGG
THKK
THKT
WHA...?
MY HEAD... SOMETHING HIT ME...
CONCUSSION?
MY HANDS...WHAT'S HAPPENING...

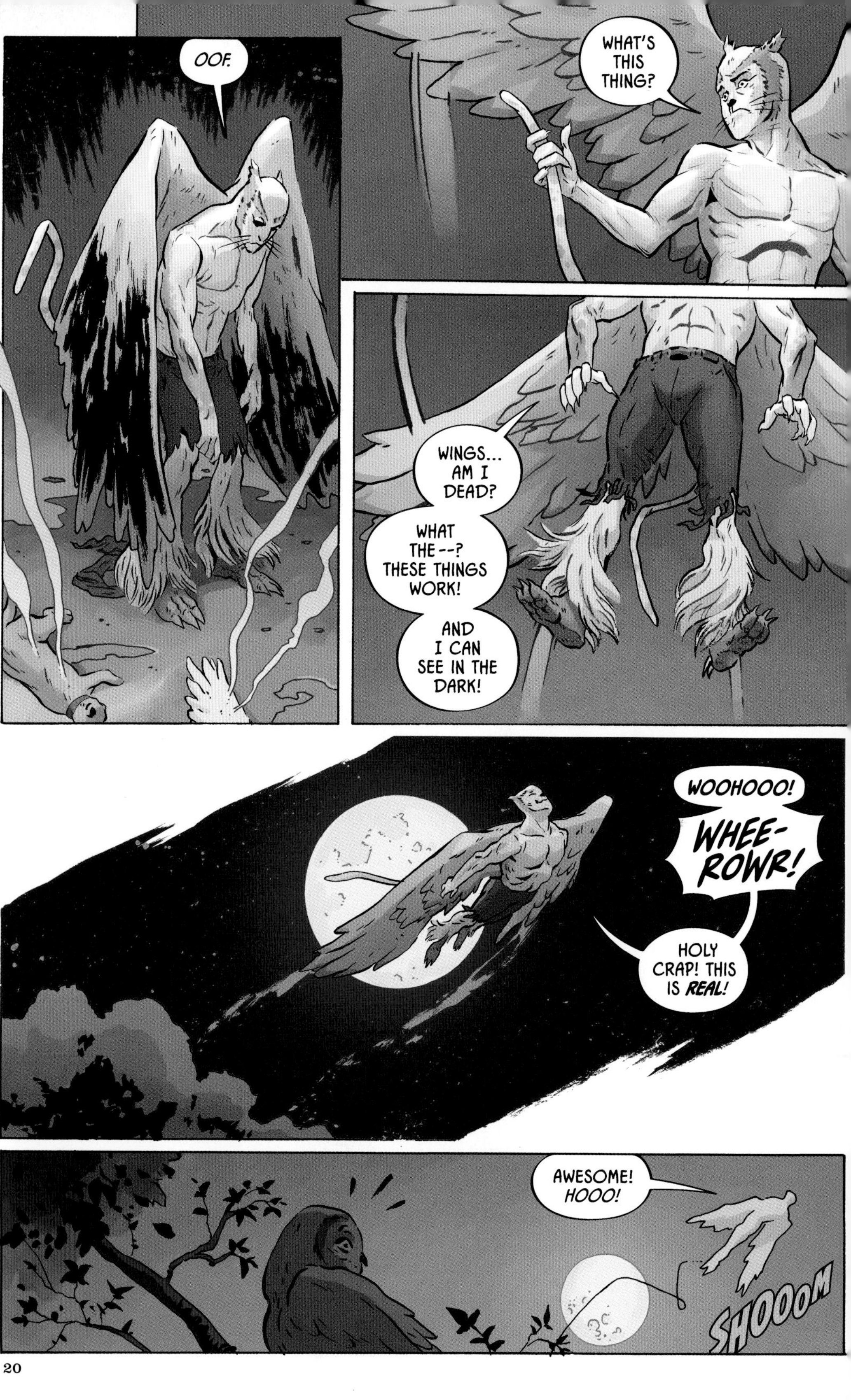
OOF.
WHAT'S THIS THING?
WINGS... AM I DEAD?
WHAT THE--? THESE THINGS WORK!
AND I CAN SEE IN THE DARK!
WOOHOOO!
WHEE-ROWR!
HOLY CRAP! THIS IS *REAL!*
AWESOME! *HOOO!*
SHOOOM

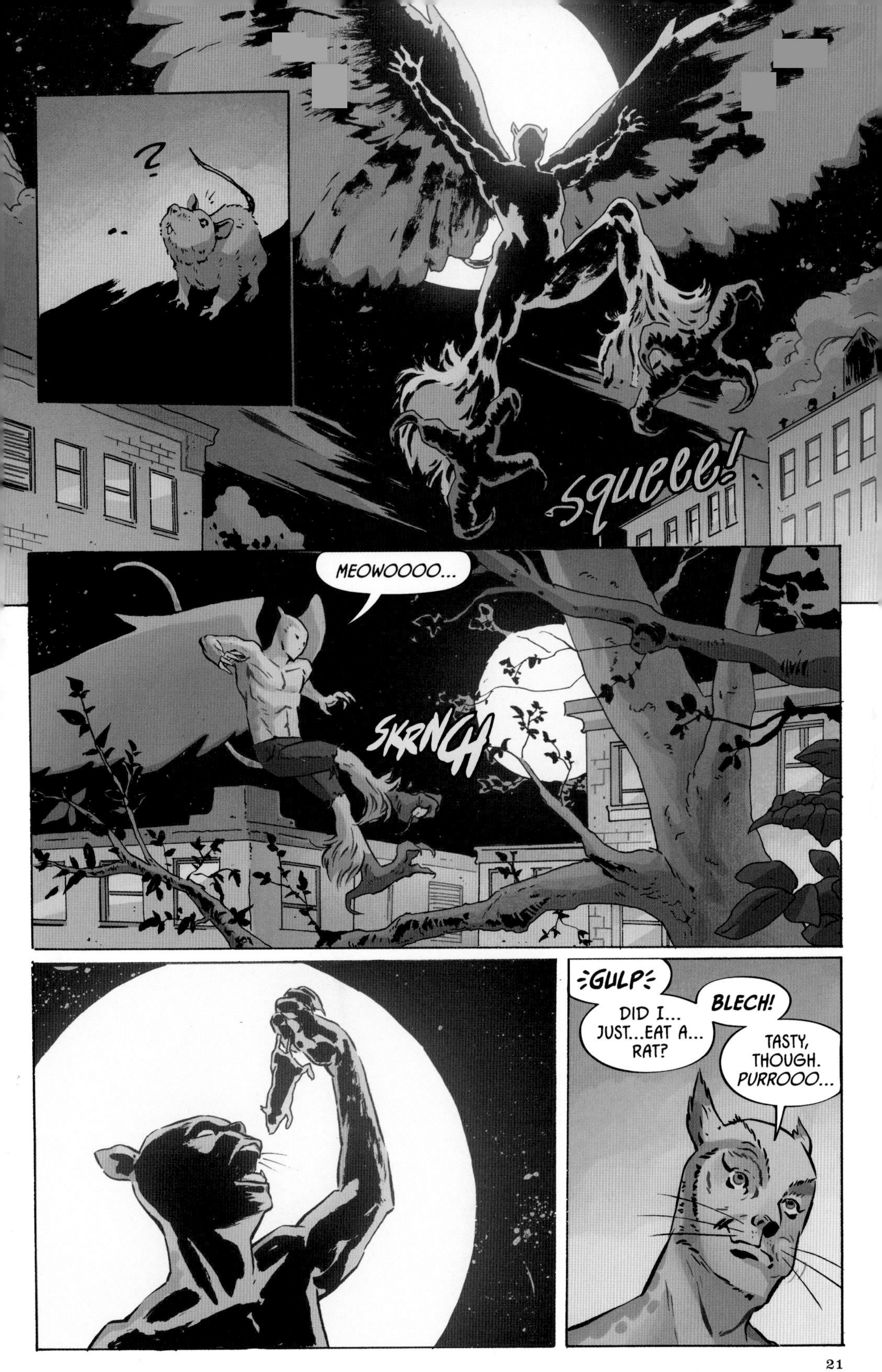
?
squeee!
MEOWOOOO...
SKRNCH
GULP
DID I... JUST...EAT A... RAT?
BLECH!
TASTY, THOUGH. PURROOO...

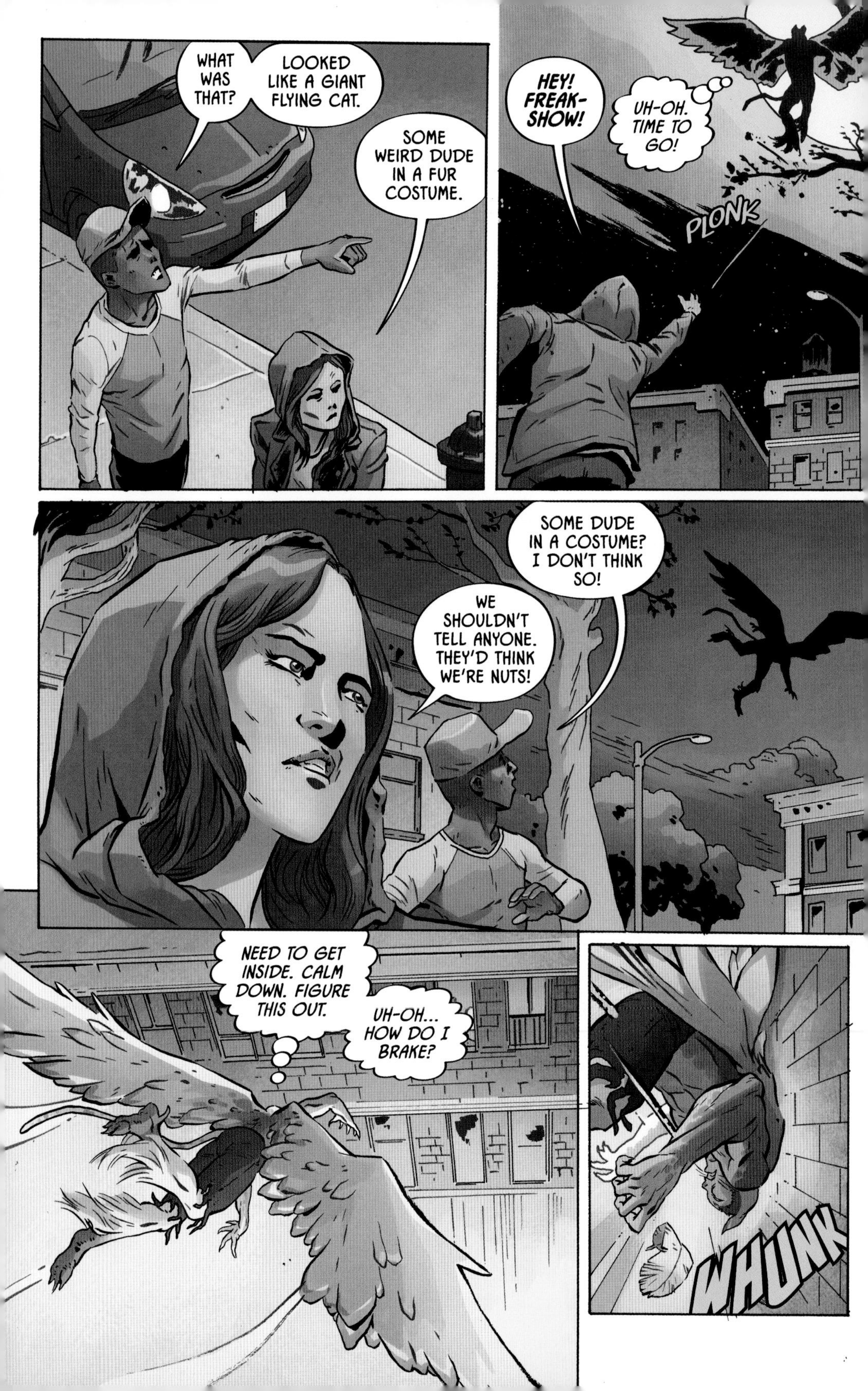
WHAT WAS THAT?
LOOKED LIKE A GIANT FLYING CAT.
SOME WEIRD DUDE IN A FUR COSTUME.
HEY! FREAK-SHOW!
UH-OH. TIME TO GO!
PLONK
SOME DUDE IN A COSTUME? I DON'T THINK SO!
WE SHOULDN'T TELL ANYONE. THEY'D THINK WE'RE NUTS!
NEED TO GET INSIDE. CALM DOWN. FIGURE THIS OUT.
UH-OH... HOW DO I BRAKE?
WHUNK

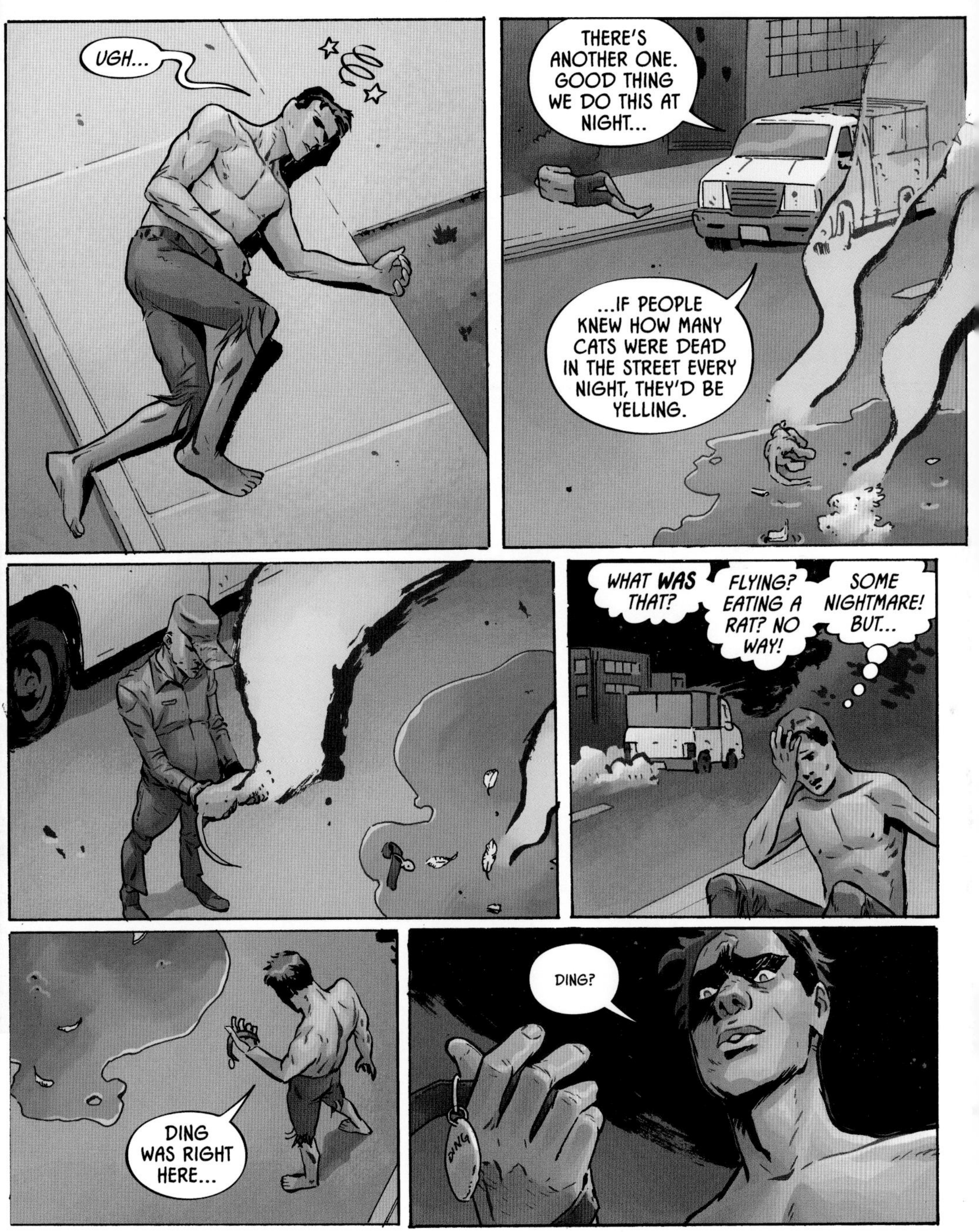
UGH...
THERE'S ANOTHER ONE. GOOD THING WE DO THIS AT NIGHT...
...IF PEOPLE KNEW HOW MANY CATS WERE DEAD IN THE STREET EVERY NIGHT, THEY'D BE YELLING.
WHAT WAS THAT?
FLYING? EATING A RAT? NO WAY!
SOME NIGHTMARE! BUT...
DING WAS RIGHT HERE...
DING?
DING

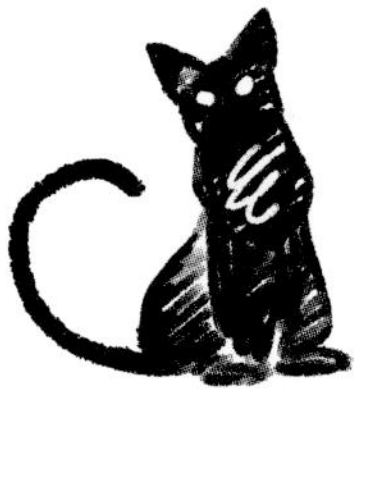

CATS AREN'T SO STREETWISE

Cars are a leading cause of sudden cat death, more so for young cats. In one study, 87% of trauma-related deaths were caused by cars. In the UK, an estimated 230,000 cats are hit each year. In the US, it's as high as 5.4 million. In Canada, about 200,000 cats die from car accidents every year.
www.catsandbirds.ca/blog/healthy-alternatives-to-free-roam

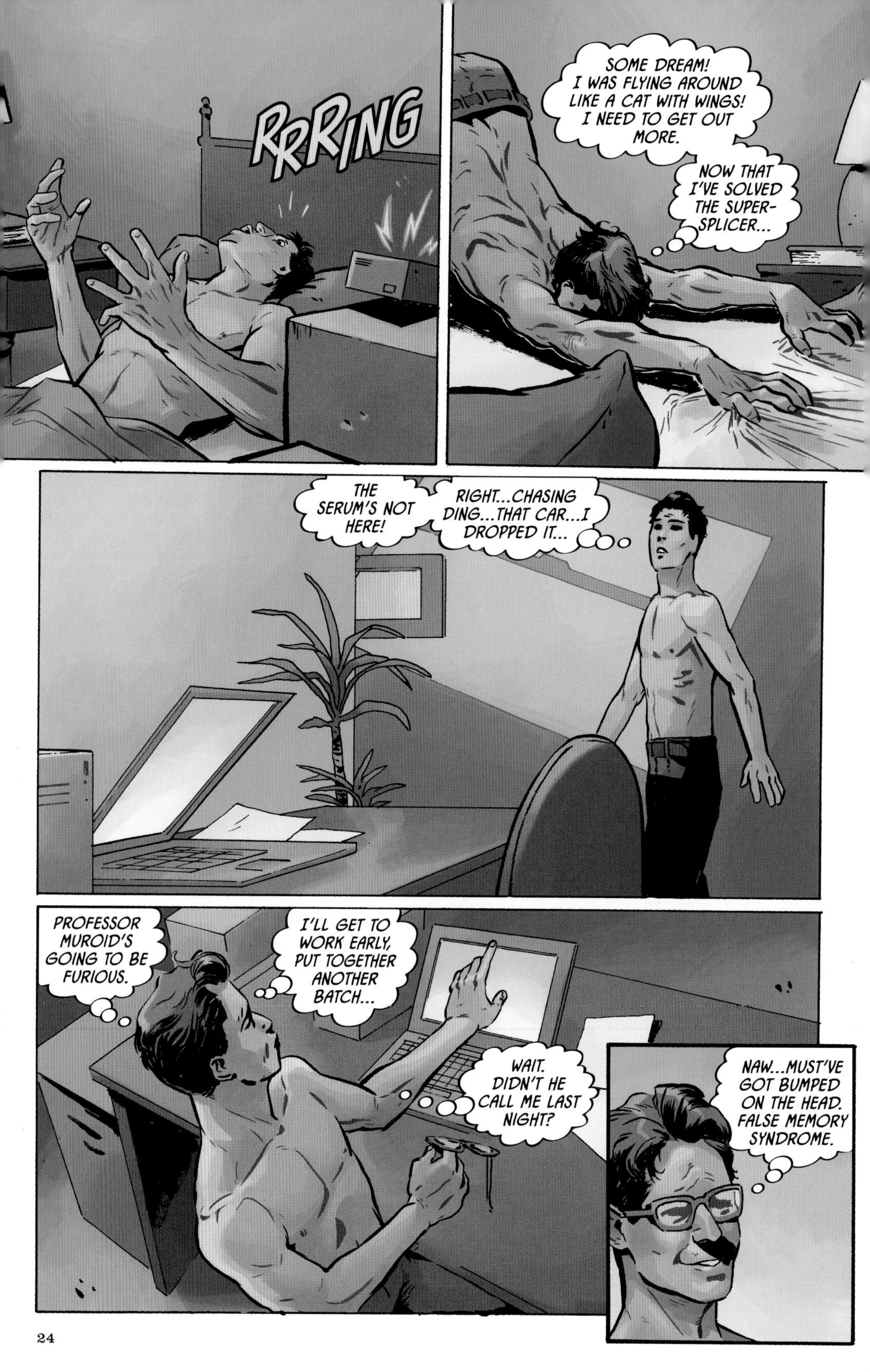
RRRING
SOME DREAM! I WAS FLYING AROUND LIKE A CAT WITH WINGS! I NEED TO GET OUT MORE.
NOW THAT I'VE SOLVED THE SUPER-SPLICER...
THE SERUM'S NOT HERE!
RIGHT...CHASING DING...THAT CAR...I DROPPED IT...
PROFESSOR MUROID'S GOING TO BE FURIOUS.
I'LL GET TO WORK EARLY, PUT TOGETHER ANOTHER BATCH...
WAIT. DIDN'T HE CALL ME LAST NIGHT?
NAW...MUST'VE GOT BUMPED ON THE HEAD. FALSE MEMORY SYNDROME.

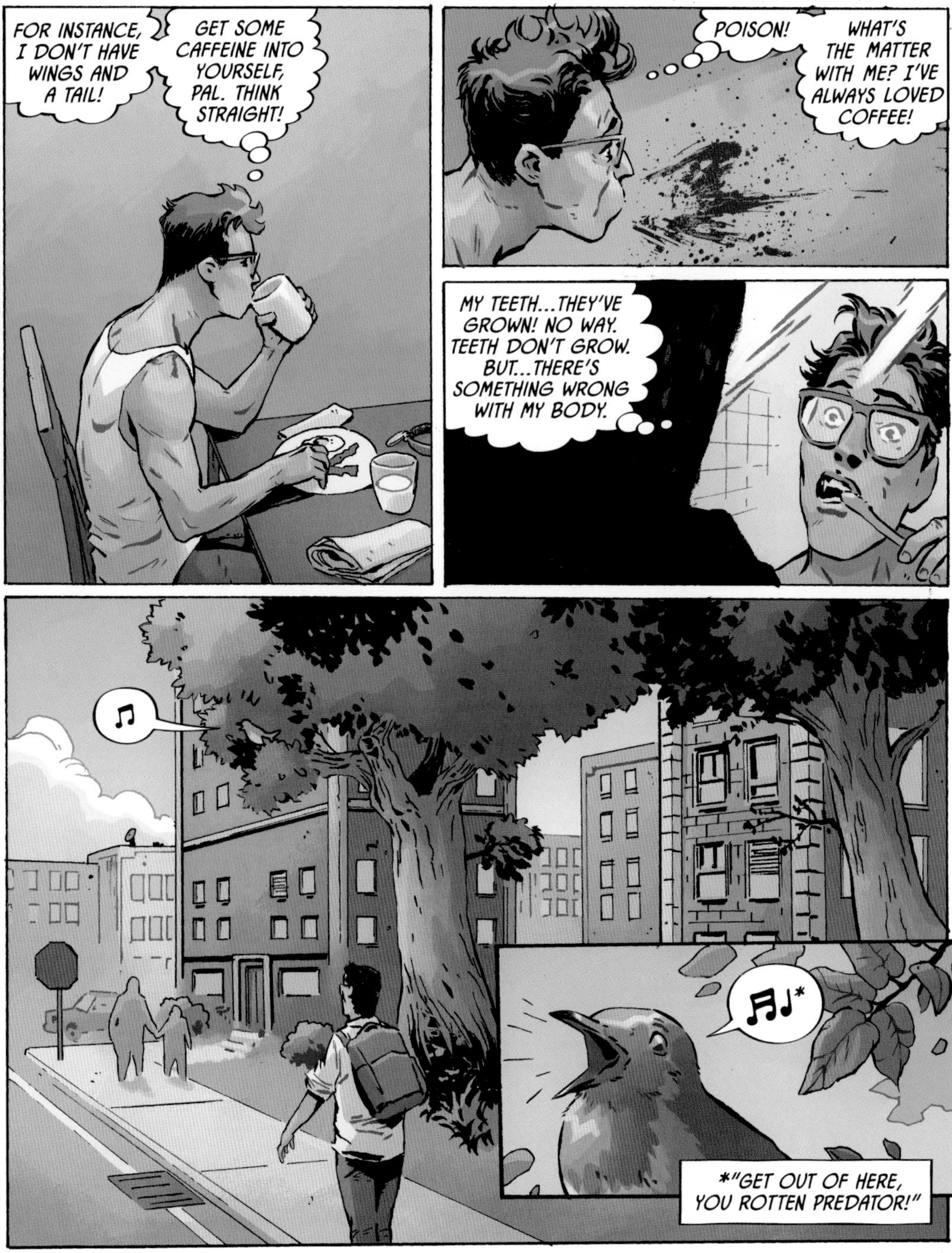
FOR INSTANCE, I DON'T HAVE WINGS AND A TAIL!
GET SOME CAFFEINE INTO YOURSELF, PAL. THINK STRAIGHT!
POISON!
WHAT'S THE MATTER WITH ME? I'VE ALWAYS LOVED COFFEE!
MY TEETH...THEY'VE GROWN! NO WAY. TEETH DON'T GROW. BUT...THERE'S SOMETHING WRONG WITH MY BODY.
♫
♬♩*
*"GET OUT OF HERE, YOU ROTTEN PREDATOR!"

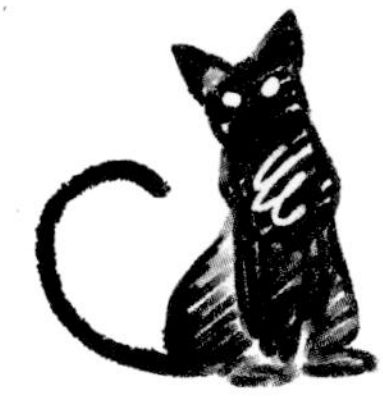

POISON, POISON, EVERYWHERE

Many human foods are toxic to cats: chocolate, coffee, onion, garlic, and tomato. Other poisons include common garden plants such as lilies, tulips, and begonias, as well as antifreeze, insecticides, and pesticides. Symptoms of poisoning include loss of appetite, vomiting, diarrhea, and loss of coordination. If your cat has eaten something toxic, contact a vet immediately.

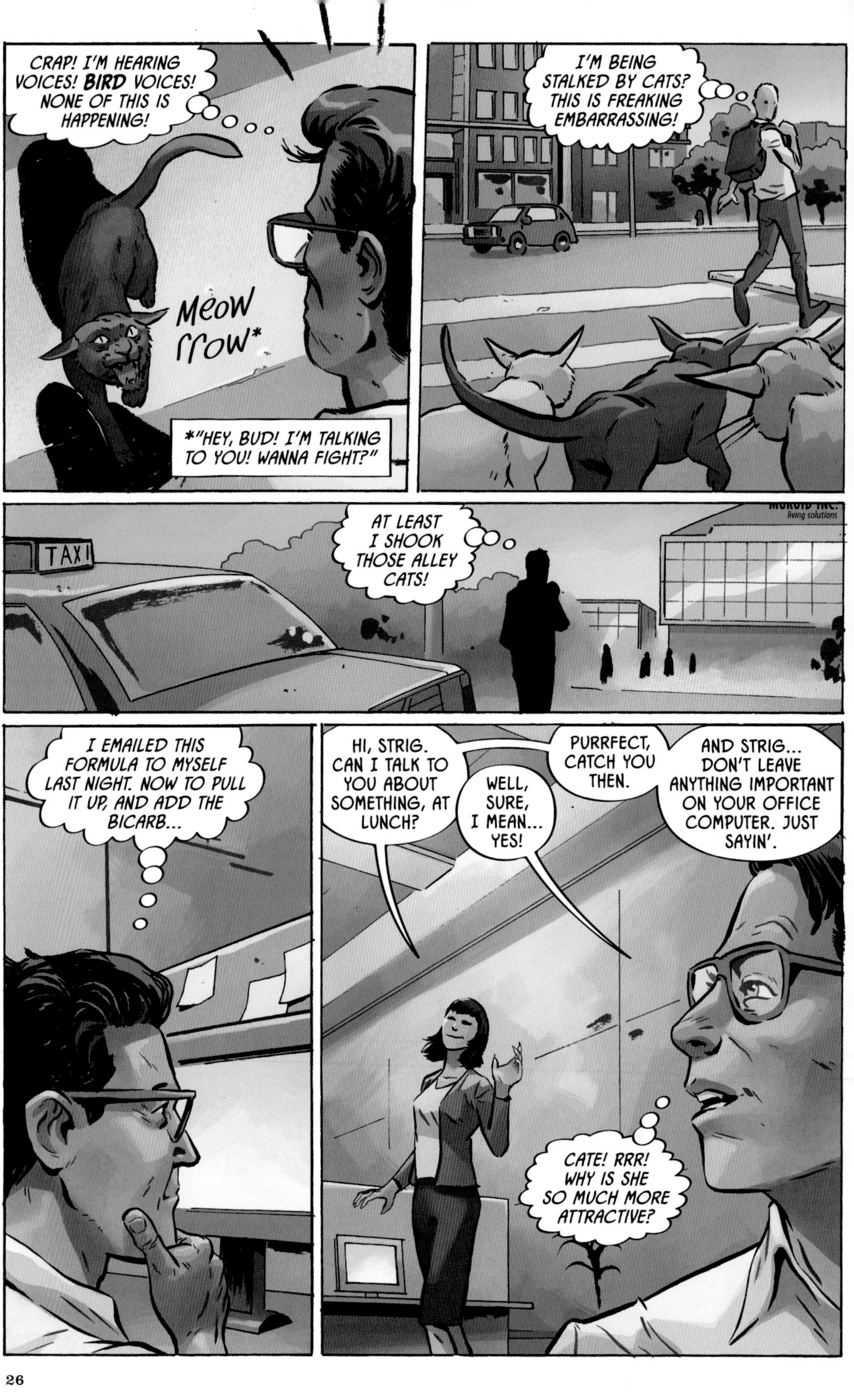
CRAP! I'M HEARING VOICES! BIRD VOICES! NONE OF THIS IS HAPPENING!
MEOW RROW*
*"HEY, BUD! I'M TALKING TO YOU! WANNA FIGHT?"
I'M BEING STALKED BY CATS? THIS IS FREAKING EMBARRASSING!
TAXI
AT LEAST I SHOOK THOSE ALLEY CATS!
living solutions
I EMAILED THIS FORMULA TO MYSELF LAST NIGHT. NOW TO PULL IT UP, AND ADD THE BICARB...
HI, STRIG. CAN I TALK TO YOU ABOUT SOMETHING, AT LUNCH?
WELL, SURE, I MEAN... YES!
PURRFECT, CATCH YOU THEN.
AND STRIG... DON'T LEAVE ANYTHING IMPORTANT ON YOUR OFFICE COMPUTER. JUST SAYIN'.
CATE! RRR! WHY IS SHE SO MUCH MORE ATTRACTIVE?

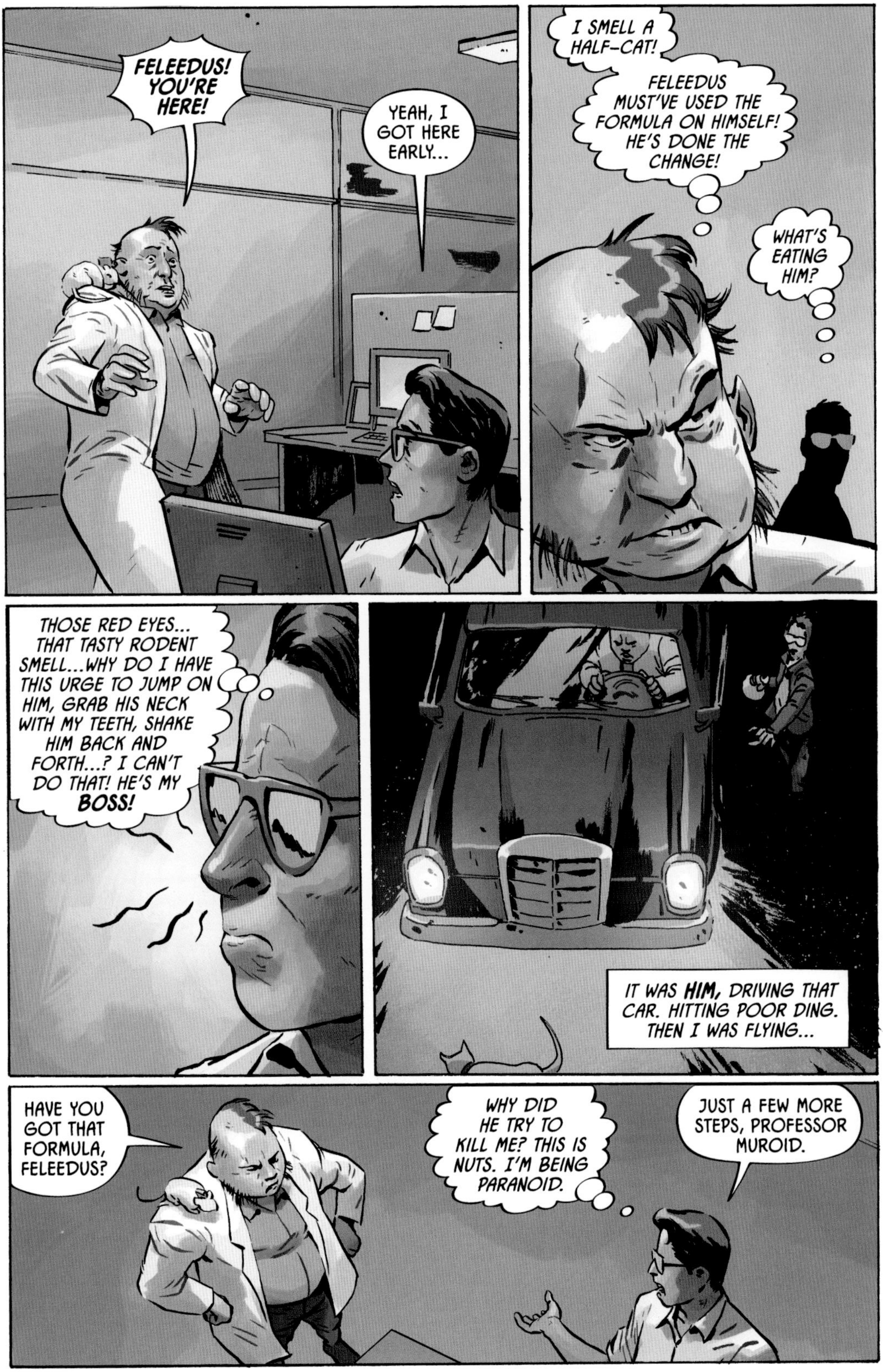
FELEEDUS! YOU'RE HERE!
YEAH, I GOT HERE EARLY...
I SMELL A HALF-CAT!
FELEEDUS MUST'VE USED THE FORMULA ON HIMSELF! HE'S DONE THE CHANGE!
WHAT'S EATING HIM?
THOSE RED EYES... THAT TASTY RODENT SMELL...WHY DO I HAVE THIS URGE TO JUMP ON HIM, GRAB HIS NECK WITH MY TEETH, SHAKE HIM BACK AND FORTH...? I CAN'T DO THAT! HE'S MY BOSS!
IT WAS HIM, DRIVING THAT CAR. HITTING POOR DING. THEN I WAS FLYING...
HAVE YOU GOT THAT FORMULA, FELEEDUS?
WHY DID HE TRY TO KILL ME? THIS IS NUTS. I'M BEING PARANOID.
JUST A FEW MORE STEPS, PROFESSOR MUROID.

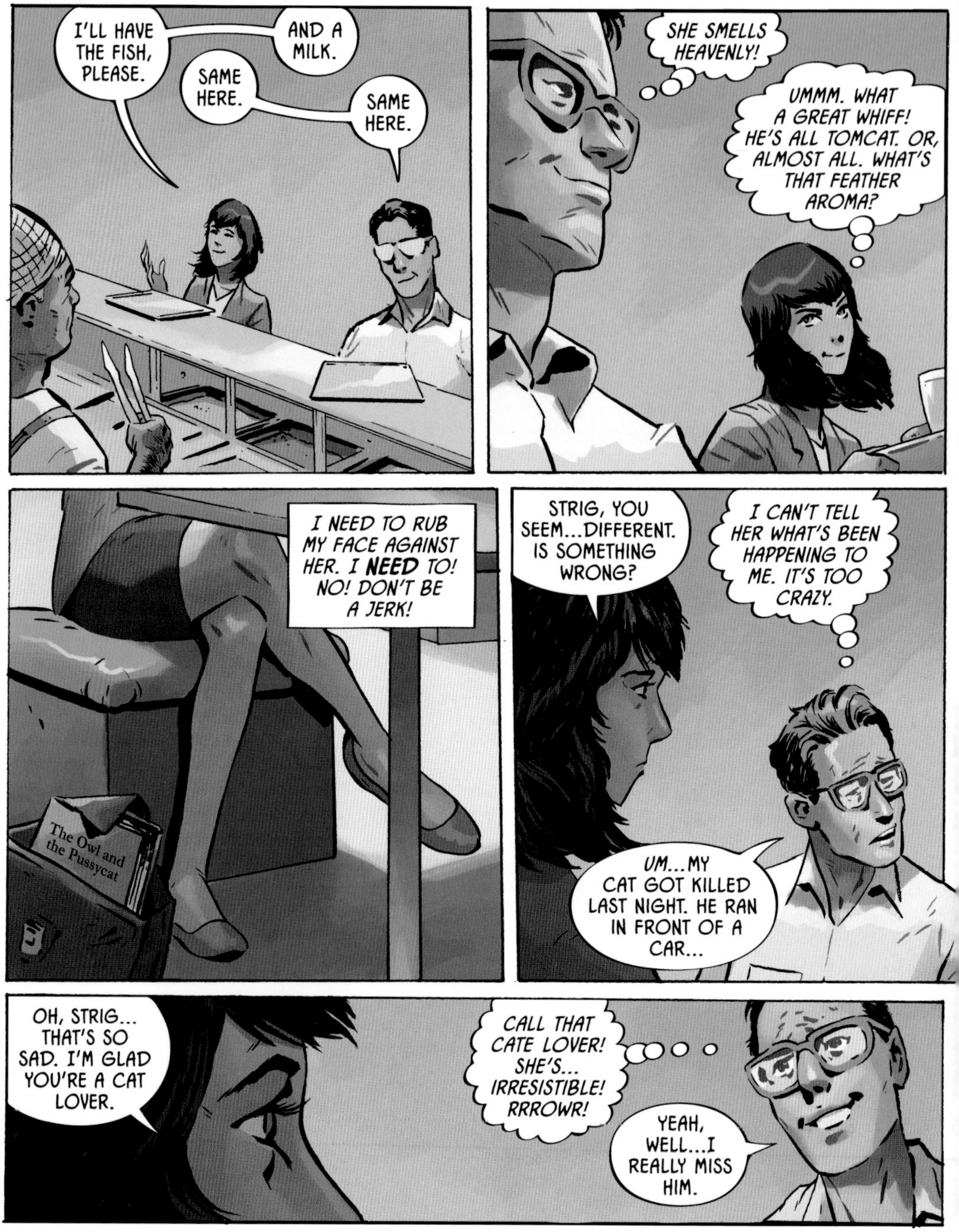
I'LL HAVE THE FISH, PLEASE.
AND A MILK.
SAME HERE.
SAME HERE.
SHE SMELLS HEAVENLY!
UMMM. WHAT A GREAT WHIFF! HE'S ALL TOMCAT. OR, ALMOST ALL. WHAT'S THAT FEATHER AROMA?
I NEED TO RUB MY FACE AGAINST HER. I **NEED** TO! NO! DON'T BE A JERK!
The Owl and the Pussycat
STRIG, YOU SEEM...DIFFERENT. IS SOMETHING WRONG?
I CAN'T TELL HER WHAT'S BEEN HAPPENING TO ME. IT'S TOO CRAZY.
UM...MY CAT GOT KILLED LAST NIGHT. HE RAN IN FRONT OF A CAR...
OH, STRIG... THAT'S SO SAD. I'M GLAD YOU'RE A CAT LOVER.
CALL THAT CATE LOVER! SHE'S... IRRESISTIBLE! RRROWR!
YEAH, WELL...I REALLY MISS HIM.

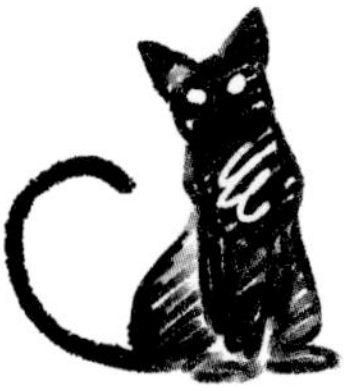

CATS SMELL WELL!

A cat's sense of smell is 14 times stronger than a human's, and it does a lot more than help them find mice—it helps them communicate with other cats. When your cat rubs up against you, she's using her glands to make a scent tattoo that says, "Mine!"

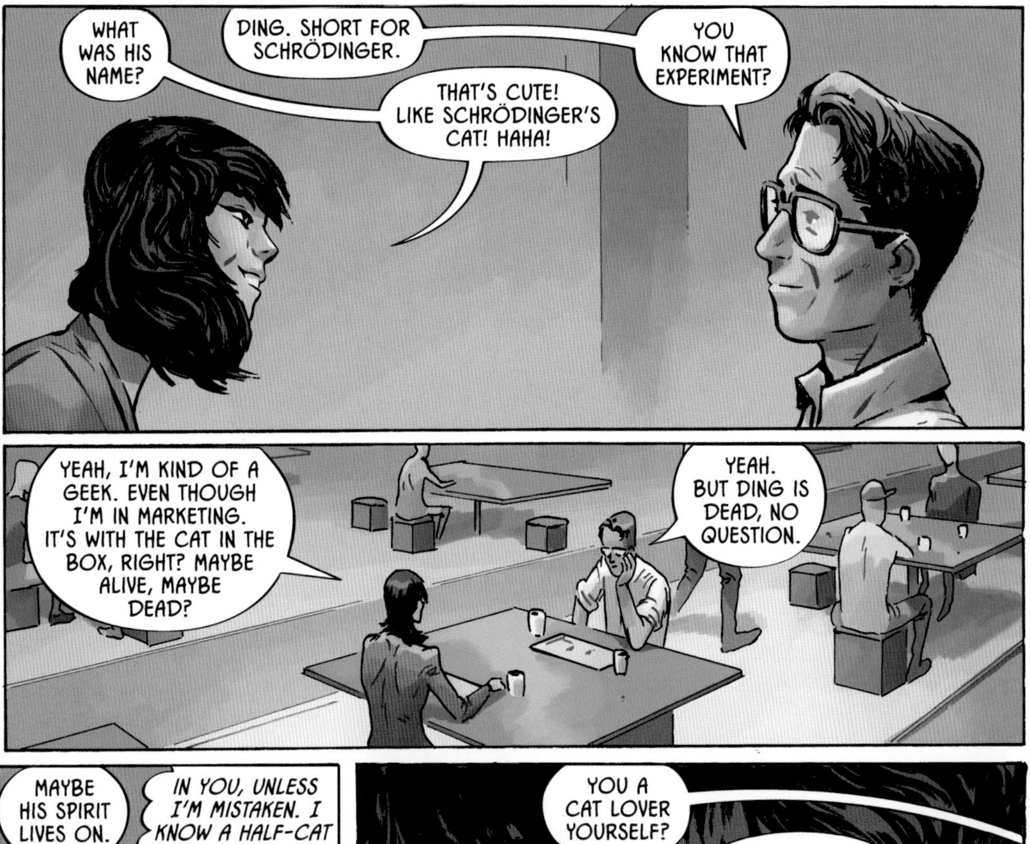
WHAT WAS HIS NAME?
DING. SHORT FOR SCHRÖDINGER.
THAT'S CUTE! LIKE SCHRÖDINGER'S CAT! HAHA!
YOU KNOW THAT EXPERIMENT?
YEAH, I'M KIND OF A GEEK. EVEN THOUGH I'M IN MARKETING. IT'S WITH THE CAT IN THE BOX, RIGHT? MAYBE ALIVE, MAYBE DEAD?
YEAH. BUT DING IS DEAD, NO QUESTION.
MAYBE HIS SPIRIT LIVES ON.
IN YOU, UNLESS I'M MISTAKEN. I KNOW A HALF-CAT WHEN I SMELL ONE.
YOU A CAT LOVER YOURSELF?
STRIG...I AM A CAT. SOME OF THE TIME. AND SO ARE YOU. WE'RE HALF-CATS, STRIG. WE CAN CHANGE OURSELVES.

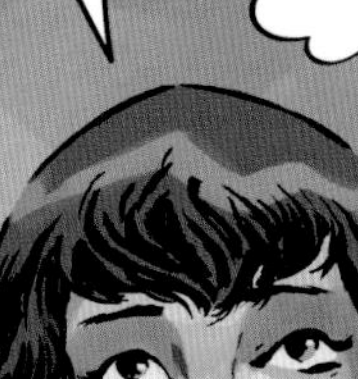

DEAD OR ALIVE?

Shelter statistics from the US, Canada, and the UK: 30% of lost dogs are returned to their owners, but only 5% of cats are. Sadly, many of those lost cats are probably dead, having been hit by a car or mauled by an animal. Identifying your cats with a microchip or tattoo increases their chances of being returned home. www.catsandbirds.ca/about

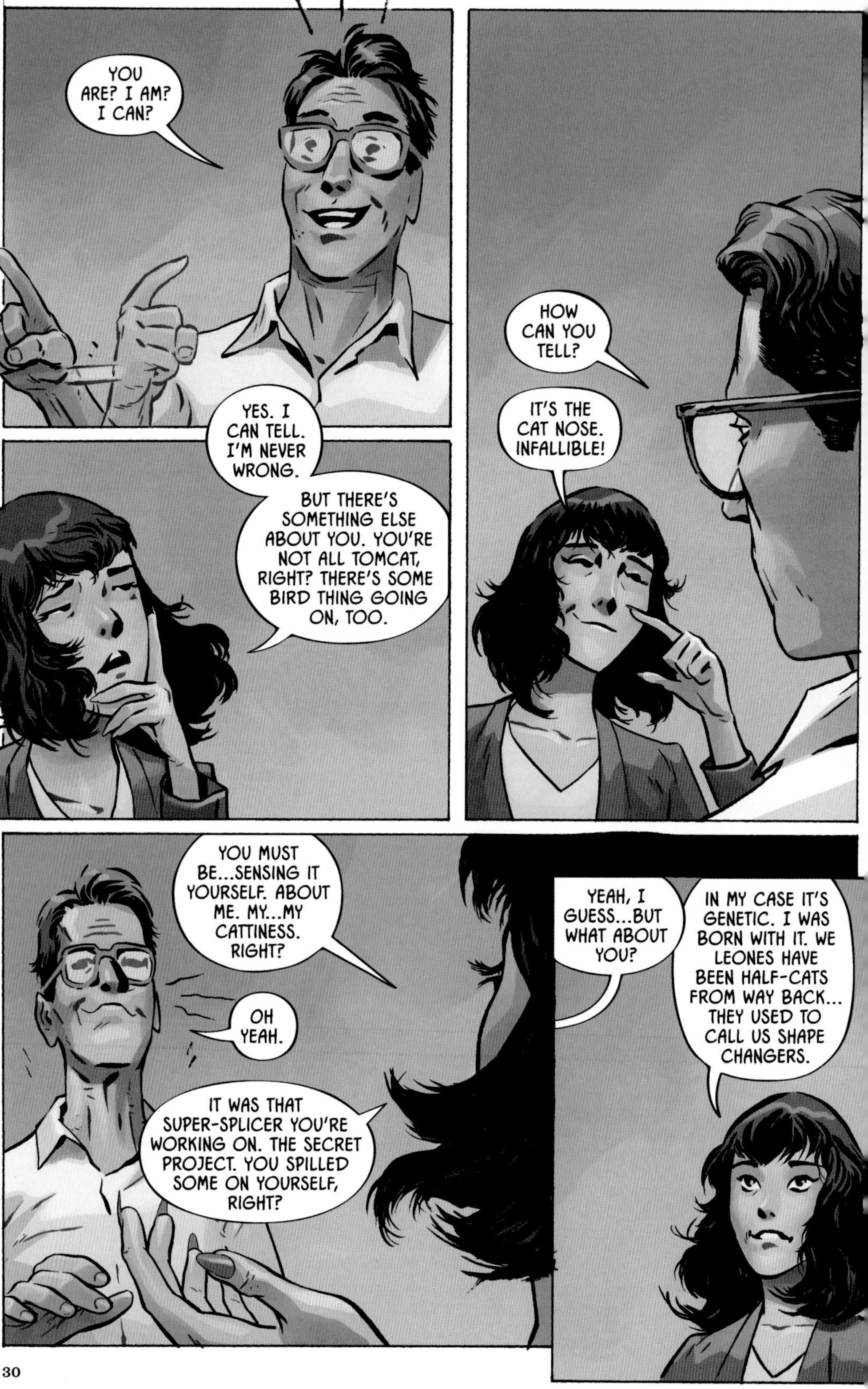
YOU ARE? I AM? I CAN?
HOW CAN YOU TELL?
YES. I CAN TELL. I'M NEVER WRONG.
BUT THERE'S SOMETHING ELSE ABOUT YOU. YOU'RE NOT ALL TOMCAT, RIGHT? THERE'S SOME BIRD THING GOING ON, TOO.
IT'S THE CAT NOSE. INFALLIBLE!
YOU MUST BE...SENSING IT YOURSELF. ABOUT ME. MY...MY CATTINESS. RIGHT?
OH YEAH.
IT WAS THAT SUPER-SPLICER YOU'RE WORKING ON. THE SECRET PROJECT. YOU SPILLED SOME ON YOURSELF, RIGHT?
YEAH, I GUESS...BUT WHAT ABOUT YOU?
IN MY CASE IT'S GENETIC. I WAS BORN WITH IT. WE LEONES HAVE BEEN HALF-CATS FROM WAY BACK... THEY USED TO CALL US SHAPE CHANGERS.

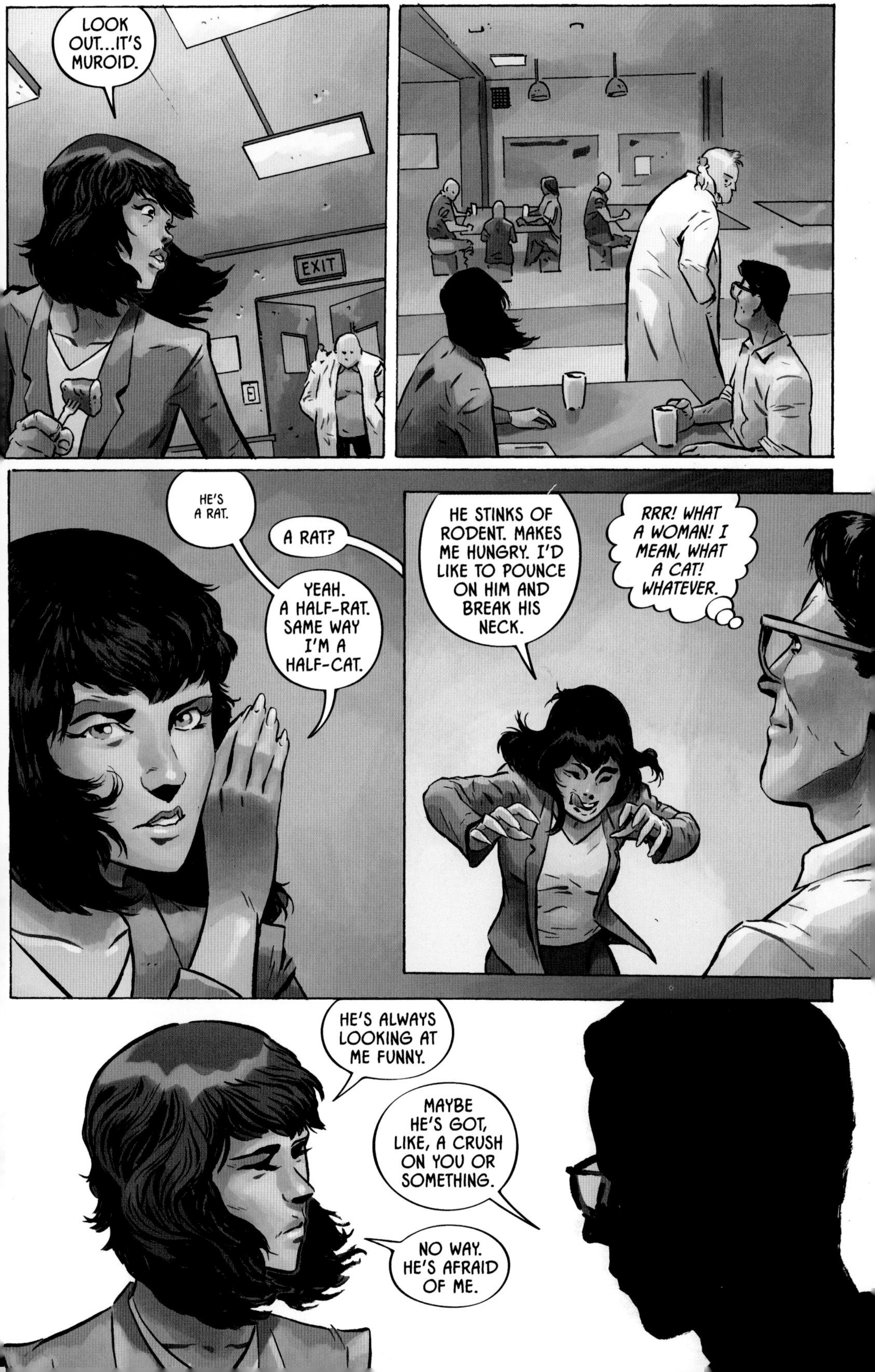
LOOK OUT...IT'S MUROID.
EXIT
HE'S A RAT.
A RAT?
YEAH. A HALF-RAT. SAME WAY I'M A HALF-CAT.
HE STINKS OF RODENT. MAKES ME HUNGRY. I'D LIKE TO POUNCE ON HIM AND BREAK HIS NECK.
RRR! WHAT A WOMAN! I MEAN, WHAT A CAT! WHATEVER.
HE'S ALWAYS LOOKING AT ME FUNNY.
MAYBE HE'S GOT, LIKE, A CRUSH ON YOU OR SOMETHING.
NO WAY. HE'S AFRAID OF ME.

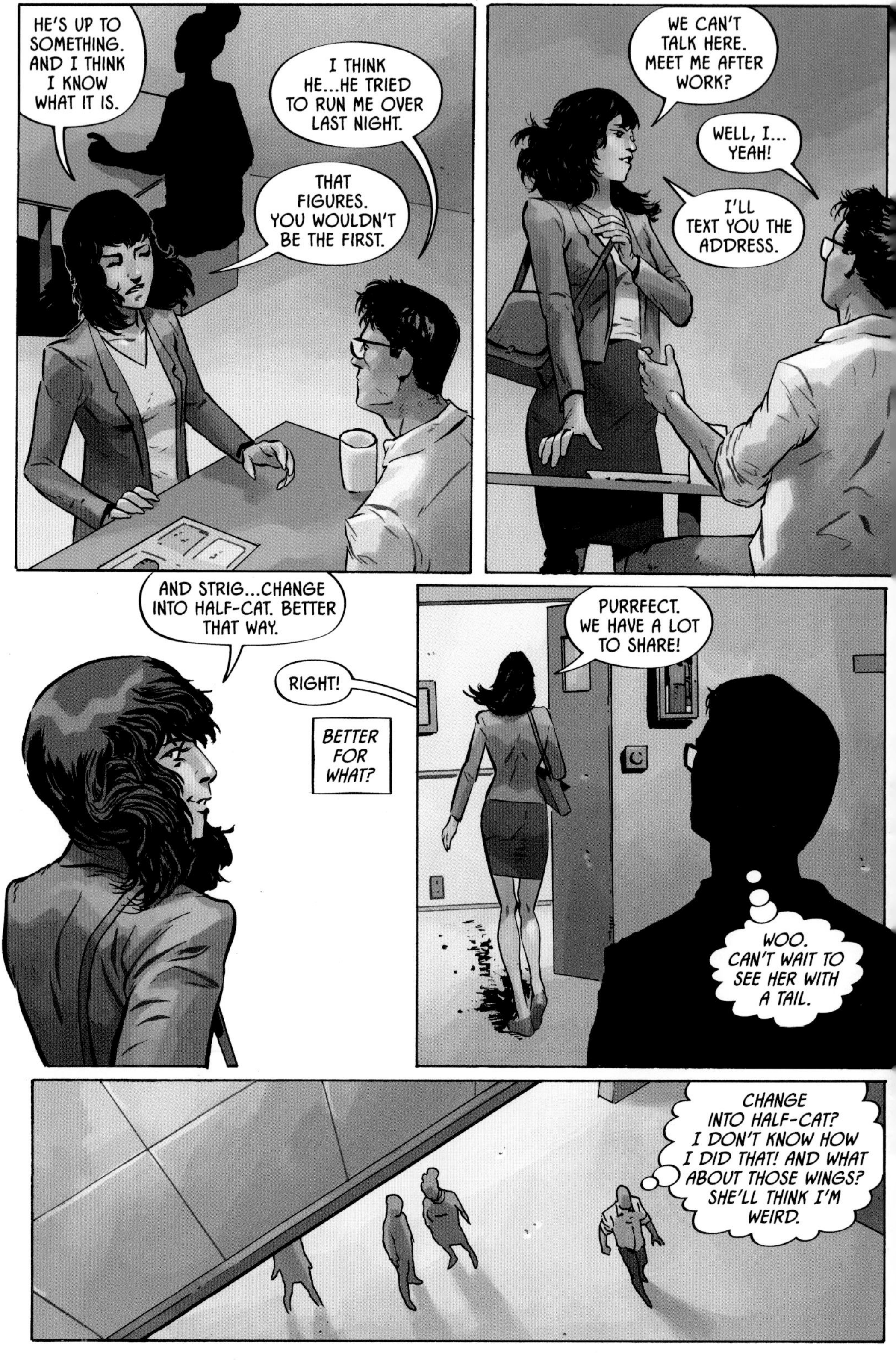
HE'S UP TO SOMETHING. AND I THINK I KNOW WHAT IT IS.
I THINK HE...HE TRIED TO RUN ME OVER LAST NIGHT.
THAT FIGURES. YOU WOULDN'T BE THE FIRST.
WE CAN'T TALK HERE. MEET ME AFTER WORK?
WELL, I... YEAH!
I'LL TEXT YOU THE ADDRESS.
AND STRIG...CHANGE INTO HALF-CAT. BETTER THAT WAY.
RIGHT!
BETTER FOR WHAT?
PURRFECT. WE HAVE A LOT TO SHARE!
WOO. CAN'T WAIT TO SEE HER WITH A TAIL.
CHANGE INTO HALF-CAT? I DON'T KNOW HOW I DID THAT! AND WHAT ABOUT THOSE WINGS? SHE'LL THINK I'M WEIRD.

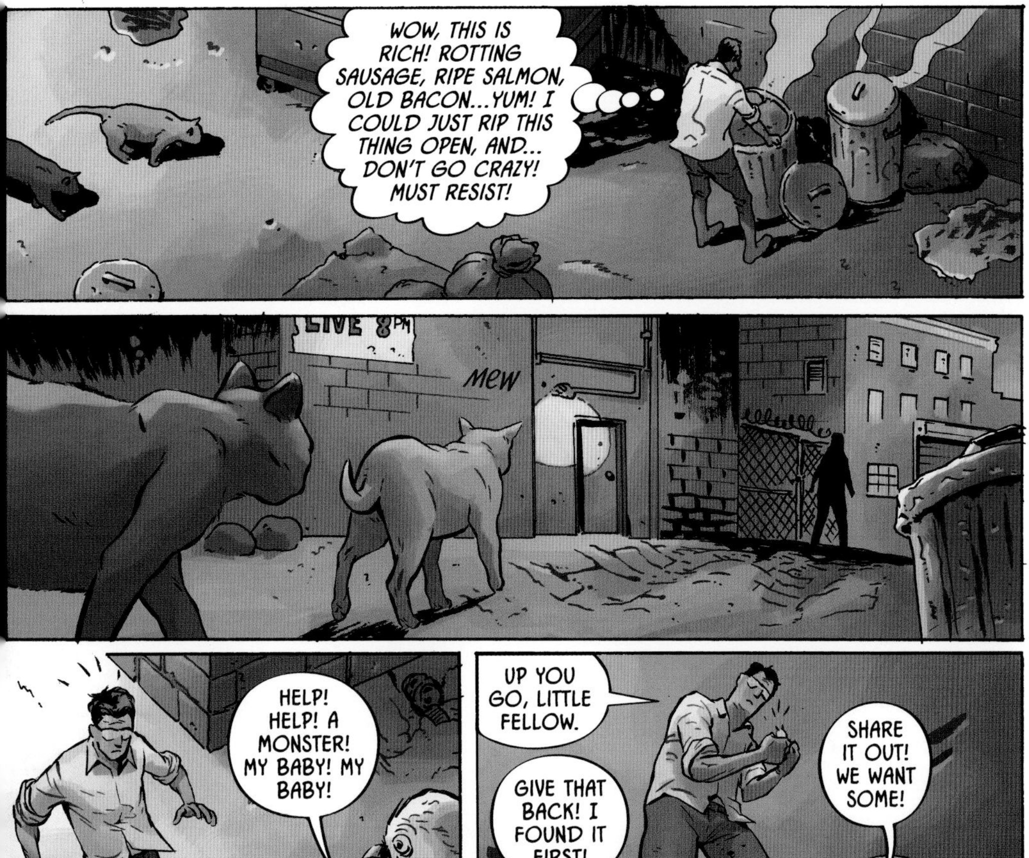
WOW, THIS IS RICH! ROTTING SAUSAGE, RIPE SALMON, OLD BACON...YUM! I COULD JUST RIP THIS THING OPEN, AND... DON'T GO CRAZY! MUST RESIST!
LIVE 8PM
MEW
HELP! HELP! A MONSTER! MY BABY! MY BABY!
FLAP FLAP
UP YOU GO, LITTLE FELLOW.
GIVE THAT BACK! I FOUND IT FIRST!
SHARE IT OUT! WE WANT SOME!
DO I RESCUE IT, OR EAT IT?
THANK YOU! THANK YOU! PUT HIM BACK IN THE NEST!

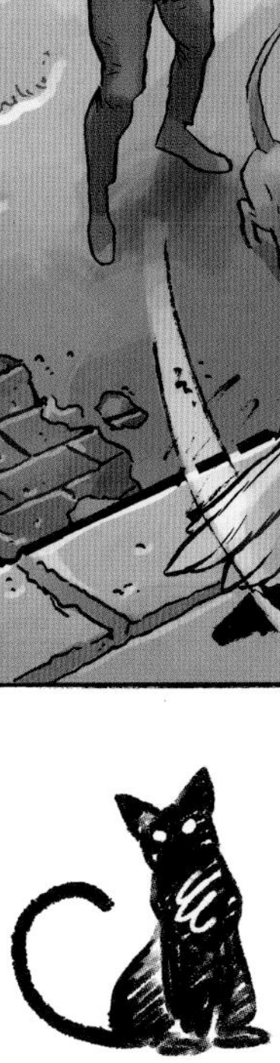

CAT-BIRD MATH, Part I

Cats are estimated to kill 200 million birds a year in Canada. In the US, the figure is roughly 2.6 billion, and in the UK, about 55 million. Feral and stray cats are thought to be the cause of more than 60% of those estimated fatalities, despite the fact that their population is smaller than that of pet cats. Protect your cat—save birds! www.catsandbirds.ca/research/estimated-number-of-birds-killed-by-house-cats/

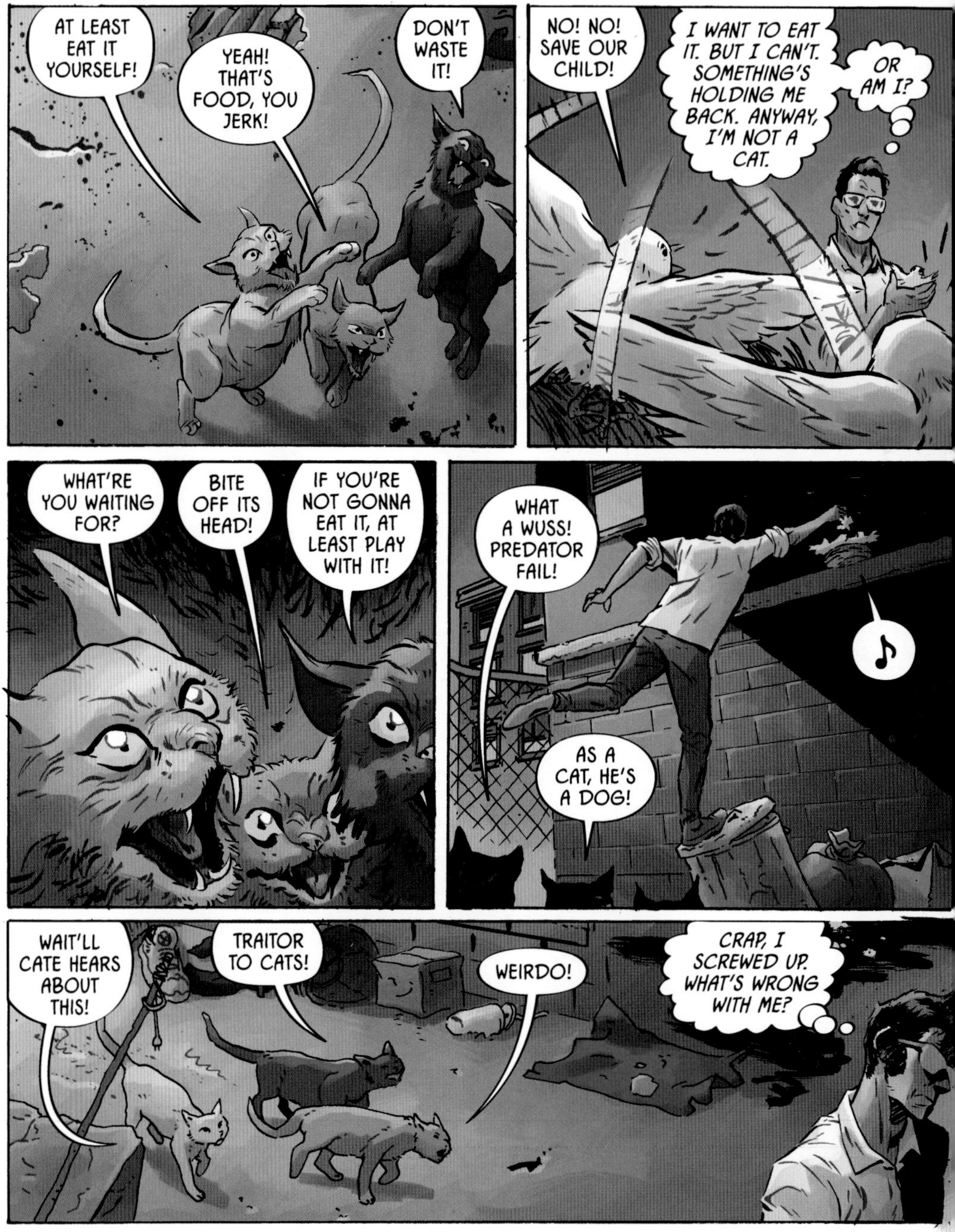
AT LEAST EAT IT YOURSELF!
YEAH! THAT'S FOOD, YOU JERK!
DON'T WASTE IT!
NO! NO! SAVE OUR CHILD!
I WANT TO EAT IT. BUT I CAN'T. SOMETHING'S HOLDING ME BACK. ANYWAY, I'M NOT A CAT.
OR AM I?
WHAT'RE YOU WAITING FOR?
BITE OFF ITS HEAD!
IF YOU'RE NOT GONNA EAT IT, AT LEAST PLAY WITH IT!
WHAT A WUSS! PREDATOR FAIL!
♪
AS A CAT, HE'S A DOG!
WAIT'LL CATE HEARS ABOUT THIS!
TRAITOR TO CATS!
WEIRDO!
CRAP, I SCREWED UP. WHAT'S WRONG WITH ME?

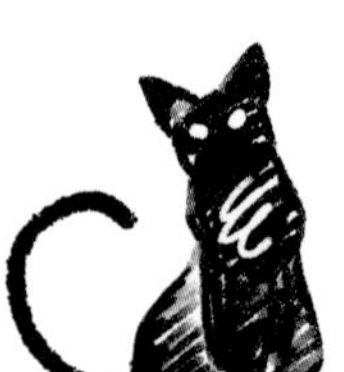

CAT-BIRD MATH, Part II

Pet cats kill fewer birds per cat than their feral cousins, but even well-fed pet cats still hunt. Canada's 10 million pet cats cause an estimated 80 million bird deaths each year. For pet cats, hunting is entertainment, providing stimulation and exercise. But play is an excellent substitute for hunting. Help your cat play! http://catsandbirds.wiseworkbench.com/research/safe-happy-cat/

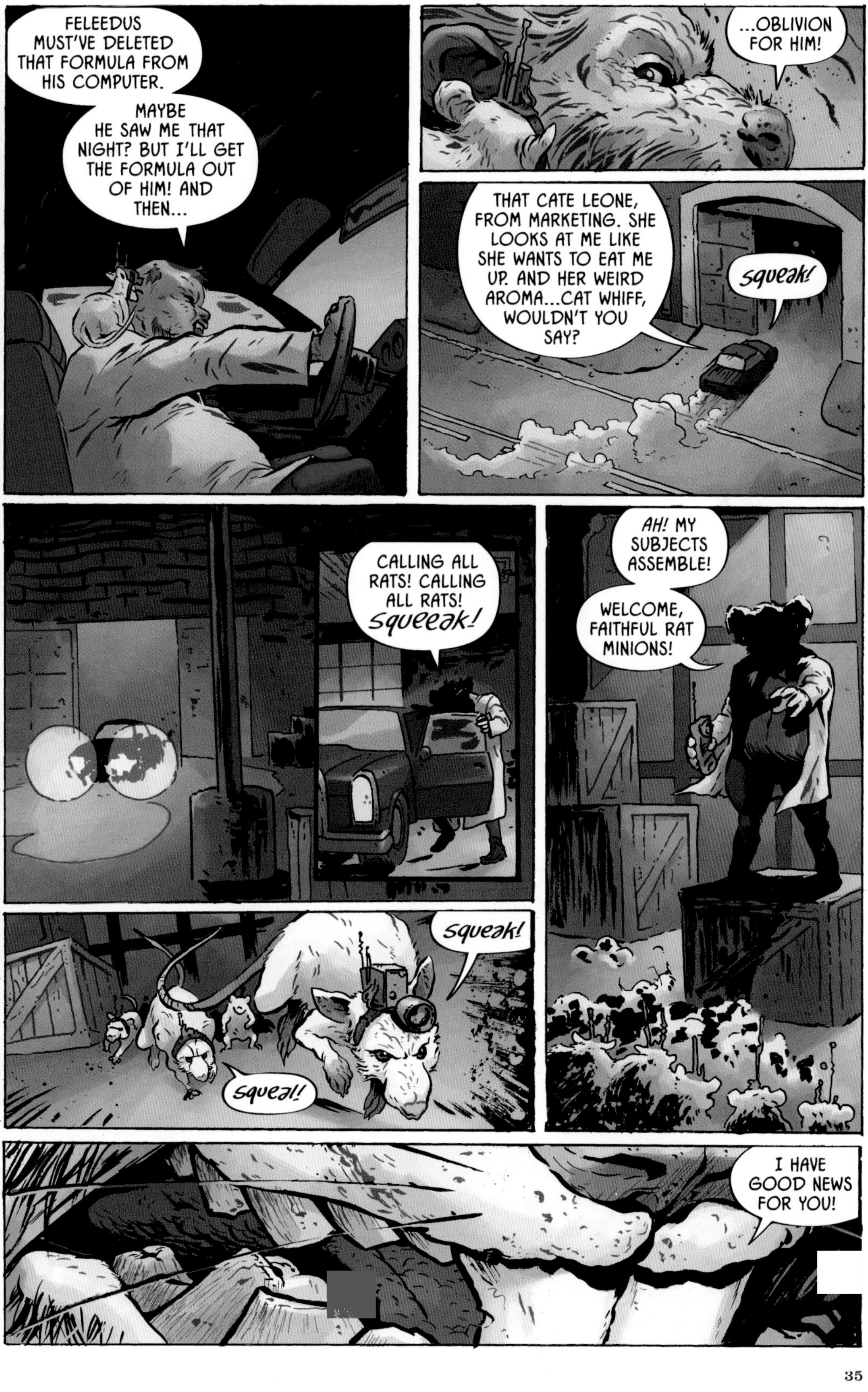
FELEEDUS MUST'VE DELETED THAT FORMULA FROM HIS COMPUTER.
MAYBE HE SAW ME THAT NIGHT? BUT I'LL GET THE FORMULA OUT OF HIM! AND THEN...
...OBLIVION FOR HIM!
THAT CATE LEONE, FROM MARKETING. SHE LOOKS AT ME LIKE SHE WANTS TO EAT ME UP. AND HER WEIRD AROMA...CAT WHIFF, WOULDN'T YOU SAY?
squeak!
CALLING ALL RATS! CALLING ALL RATS! squeeak!
AH! MY SUBJECTS ASSEMBLE!
WELCOME, FAITHFUL RAT MINIONS!
squeak!
squeal!
I HAVE GOOD NEWS FOR YOU!

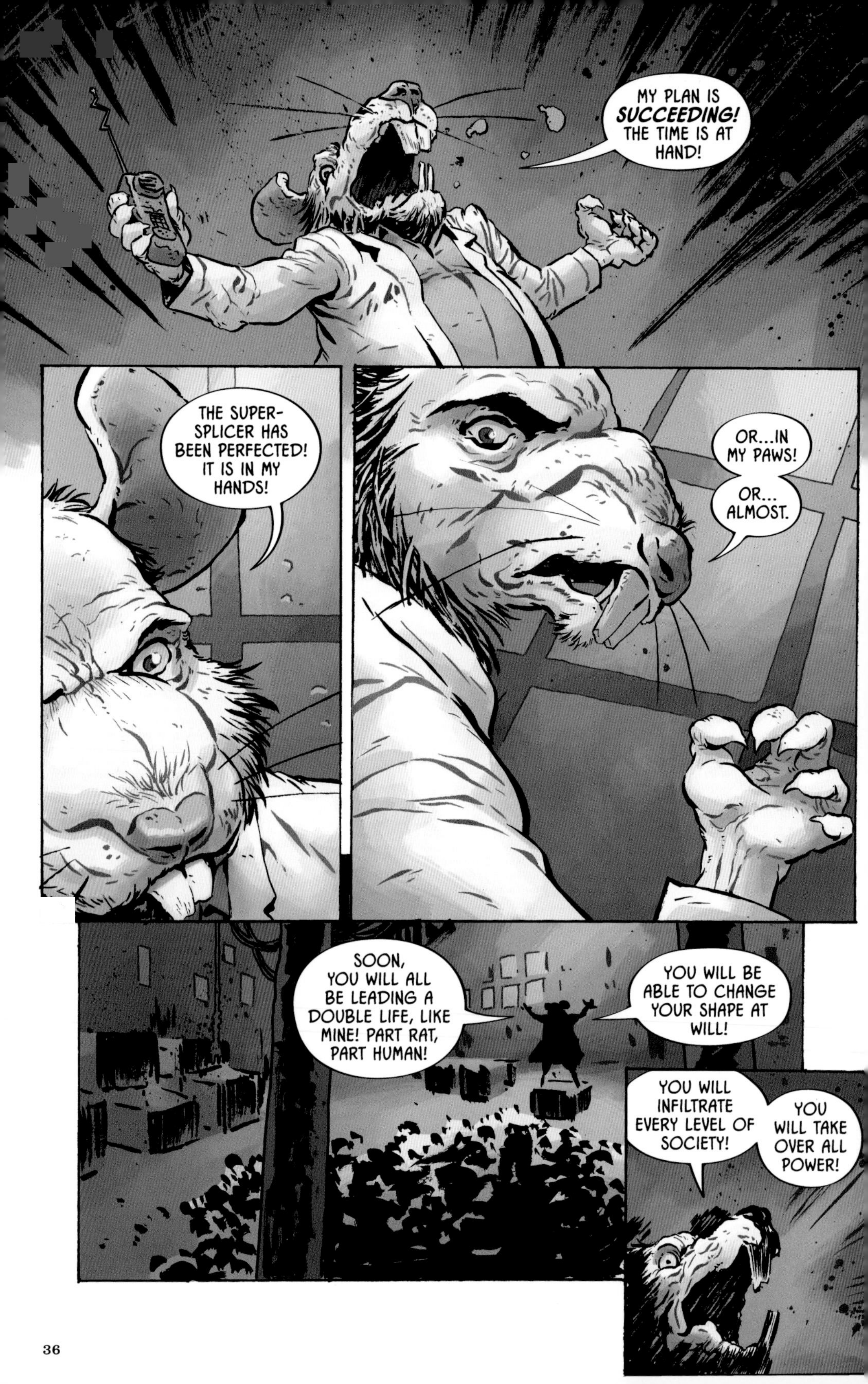
MY PLAN IS SUCCEEDING! THE TIME IS AT HAND!
THE SUPER-SPLICER HAS BEEN PERFECTED! IT IS IN MY HANDS!
OR...IN MY PAWS!
OR... ALMOST.
SOON, YOU WILL ALL BE LEADING A DOUBLE LIFE, LIKE MINE! PART RAT, PART HUMAN!
YOU WILL BE ABLE TO CHANGE YOUR SHAPE AT WILL!
YOU WILL INFILTRATE EVERY LEVEL OF SOCIETY!
YOU WILL TAKE OVER ALL POWER!

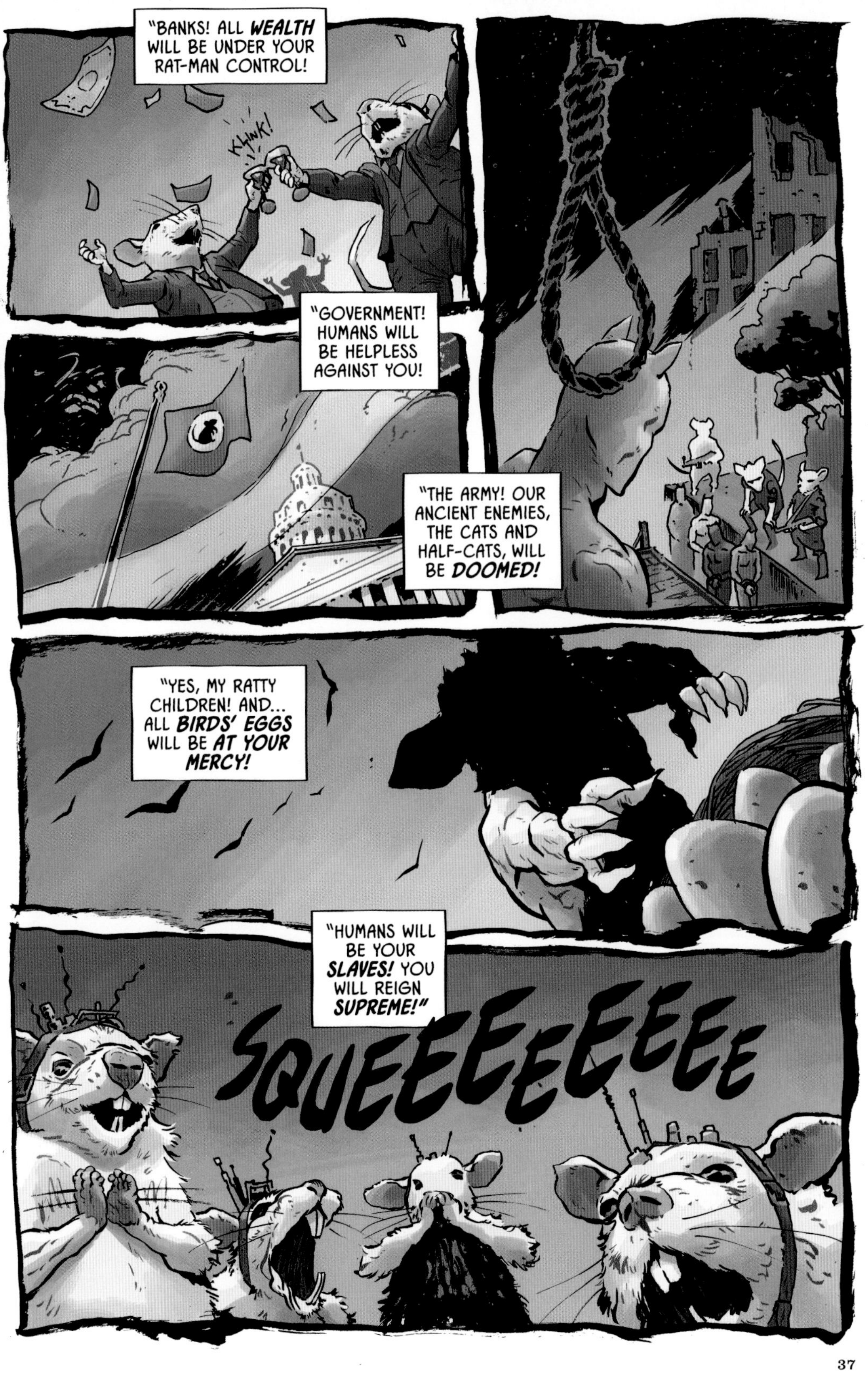
"BANKS! ALL WEALTH WILL BE UNDER YOUR RAT-MAN CONTROL!
KLINK!
"GOVERNMENT! HUMANS WILL BE HELPLESS AGAINST YOU!
"THE ARMY! OUR ANCIENT ENEMIES, THE CATS AND HALF-CATS, WILL BE DOOMED!
"YES, MY RATTY CHILDREN! AND... ALL BIRDS' EGGS WILL BE AT YOUR MERCY!
"HUMANS WILL BE YOUR SLAVES! YOU WILL REIGN SUPREME!"
SQUEEEEEEEEE

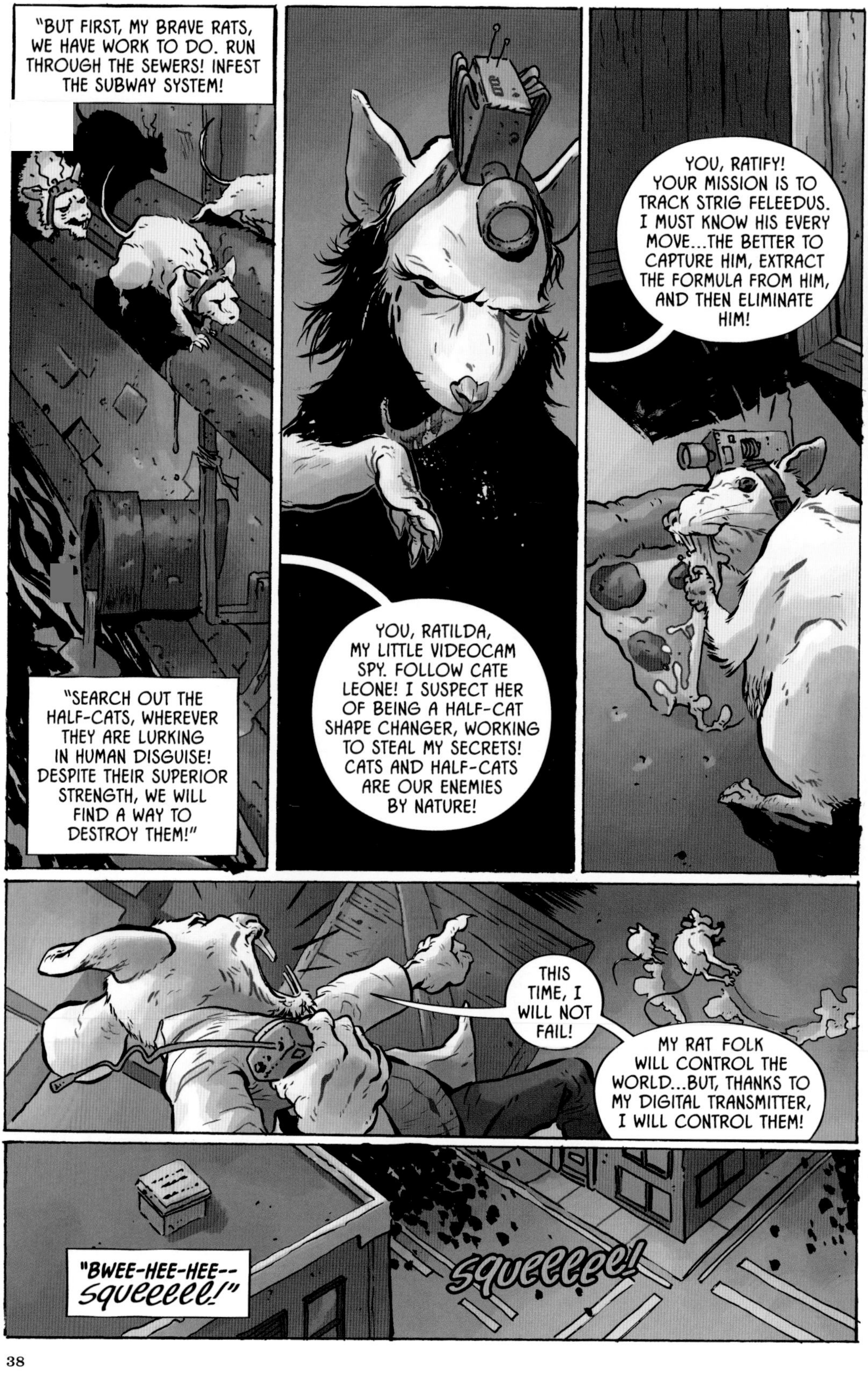

"BUT FIRST, MY BRAVE RATS, WE HAVE WORK TO DO. RUN THROUGH THE SEWERS! INFEST THE SUBWAY SYSTEM!
"SEARCH OUT THE HALF-CATS, WHEREVER THEY ARE LURKING IN HUMAN DISGUISE! DESPITE THEIR SUPERIOR STRENGTH, WE WILL FIND A WAY TO DESTROY THEM!"
YOU, RATILDA, MY LITTLE VIDEOCAM SPY. FOLLOW CATE LEONE! I SUSPECT HER OF BEING A HALF-CAT SHAPE CHANGER, WORKING TO STEAL MY SECRETS! CATS AND HALF-CATS ARE OUR ENEMIES BY NATURE!
YOU, RATIFY! YOUR MISSION IS TO TRACK STRIG FELEEDUS. I MUST KNOW HIS EVERY MOVE...THE BETTER TO CAPTURE HIM, EXTRACT THE FORMULA FROM HIM, AND THEN ELIMINATE HIM!
THIS TIME, I WILL NOT FAIL!
MY RAT FOLK WILL CONTROL THE WORLD...BUT, THANKS TO MY DIGITAL TRANSMITTER, I WILL CONTROL THEM!
"BWEE-HEE-HEE--SQUEEEEL!"
SQUEEEEE!

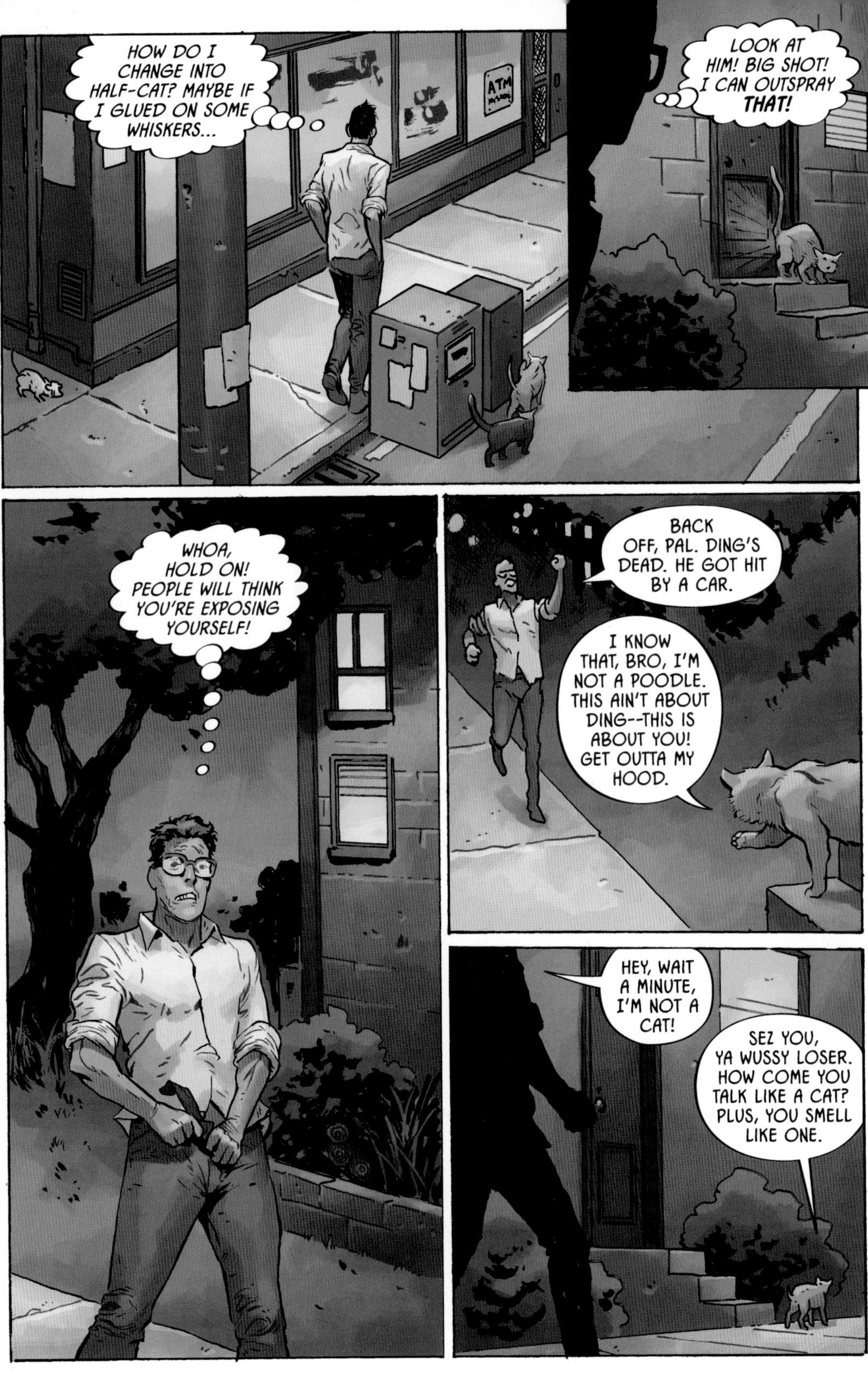
HOW DO I CHANGE INTO HALF-CAT? MAYBE IF I GLUED ON SOME WHISKERS...
LOOK AT HIM! BIG SHOT! I CAN OUTSPRAY **THAT!**
WHOA, HOLD ON! PEOPLE WILL THINK YOU'RE EXPOSING YOURSELF!
BACK OFF, PAL. DING'S DEAD. HE GOT HIT BY A CAR.
I KNOW THAT, BRO, I'M NOT A POODLE. THIS AIN'T ABOUT DING--THIS IS ABOUT YOU! GET OUTTA MY HOOD.
HEY, WAIT A MINUTE, I'M NOT A CAT!
SEZ YOU, YA WUSSY LOSER. HOW COME YOU TALK LIKE A CAT? PLUS, YOU SMELL LIKE ONE.

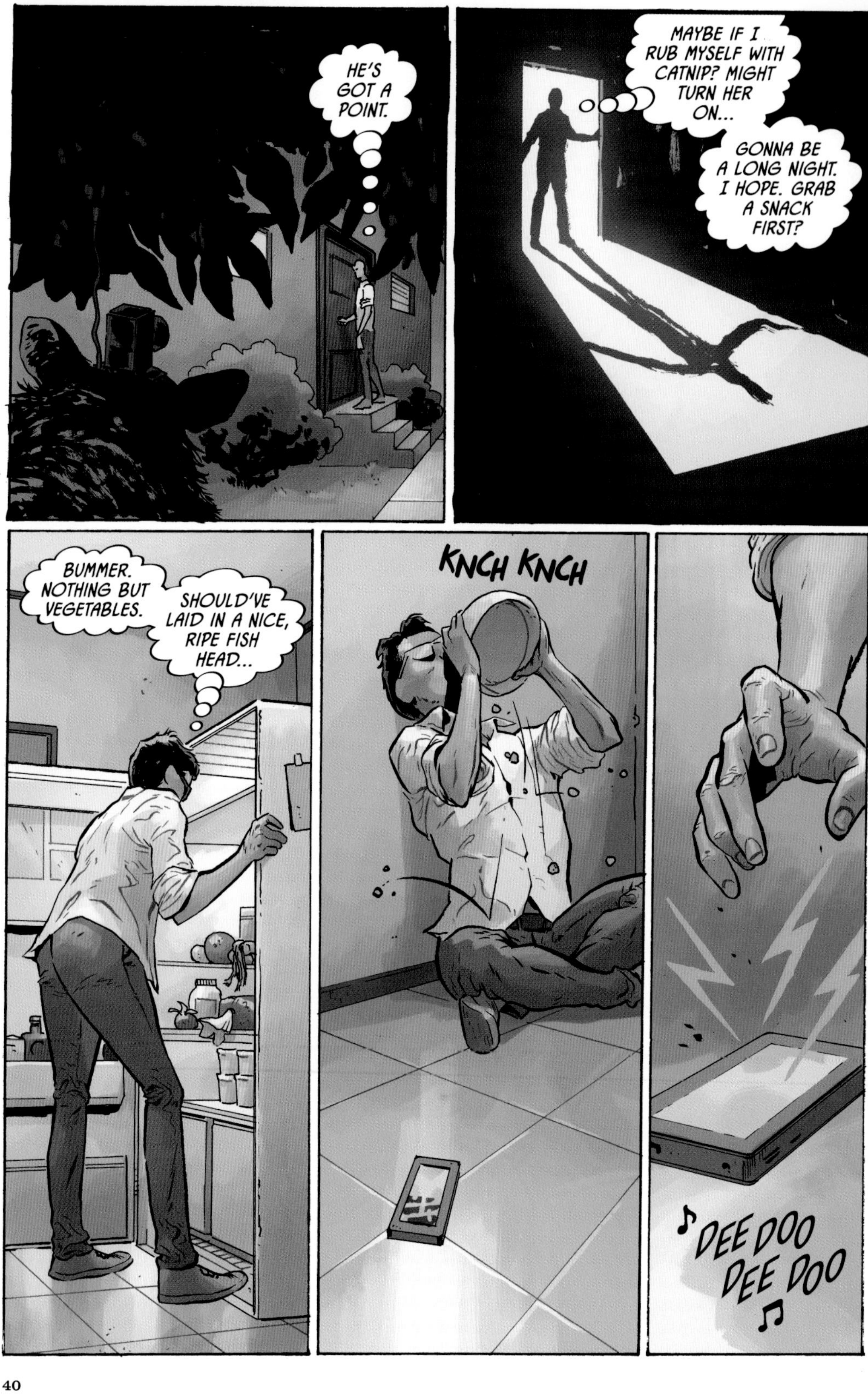
HE'S GOT A POINT.
MAYBE IF I RUB MYSELF WITH CATNIP? MIGHT TURN HER ON...
GONNA BE A LONG NIGHT. I HOPE. GRAB A SNACK FIRST?
BUMMER. NOTHING BUT VEGETABLES.
SHOULD'VE LAID IN A NICE, RIPE FISH HEAD...
KNCH KNCH
DEE DOO DEE DOO

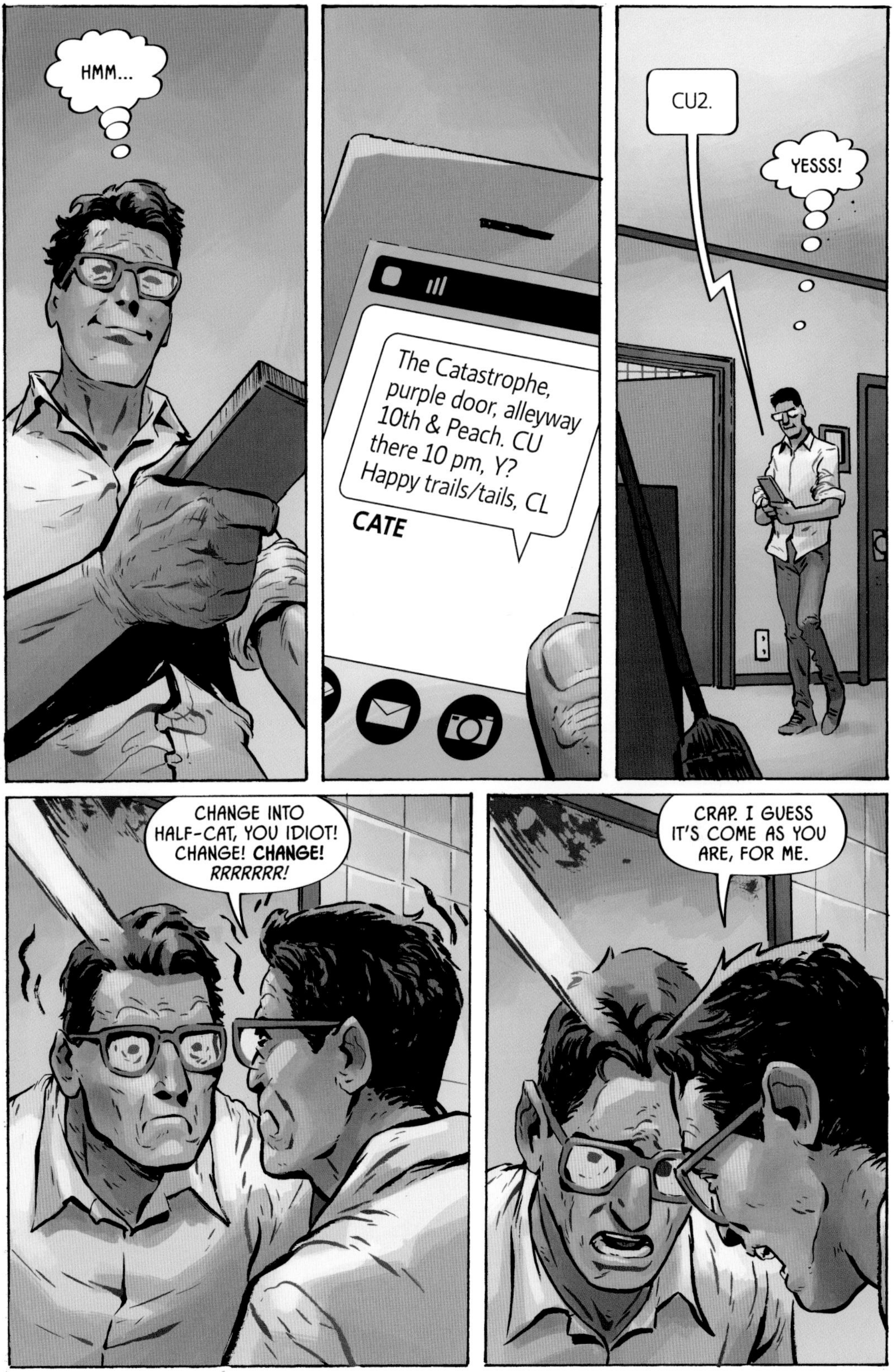
HMM...
The Catastrophe, purple door, alleyway 10th & Peach. CU there 10 pm, Y? Happy trails/tails, CL
CATE
CU2.
YESSS!
CHANGE INTO HALF-CAT, YOU IDIOT! CHANGE! **CHANGE!** *RRRRRRR!*
CRAP. I GUESS IT'S COME AS YOU ARE, FOR ME.

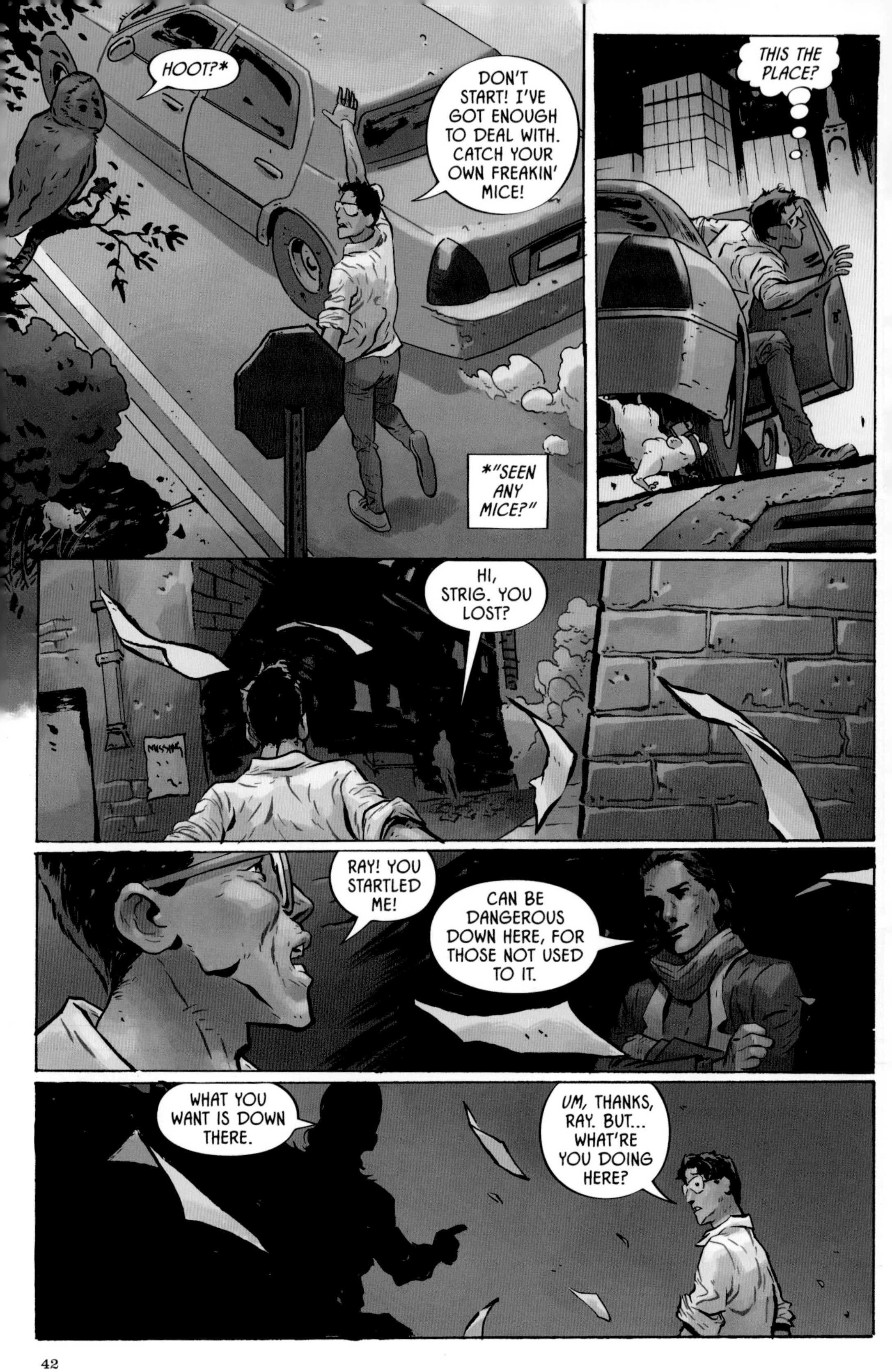
HOOT?*
DON'T START! I'VE GOT ENOUGH TO DEAL WITH. CATCH YOUR OWN FREAKIN' MICE!
*"SEEN ANY MICE?"
THIS THE PLACE?
HI, STRIG. YOU LOST?
RAY! YOU STARTLED ME!
CAN BE DANGEROUS DOWN HERE, FOR THOSE NOT USED TO IT.
WHAT YOU WANT IS DOWN THERE.
UM, THANKS, RAY. BUT... WHAT'RE YOU DOING HERE?

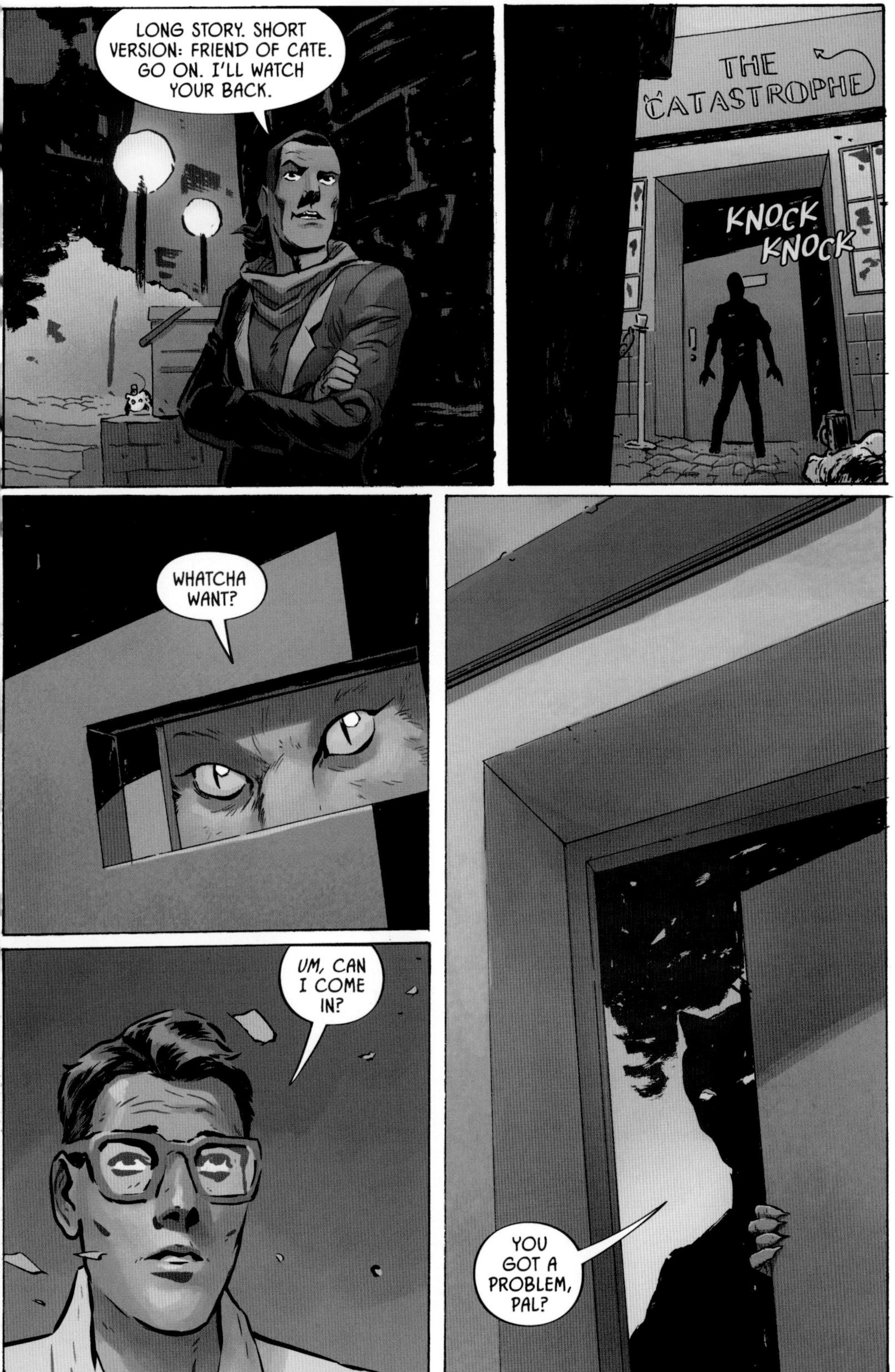
LONG STORY. SHORT VERSION: FRIEND OF CATE. GO ON. I'LL WATCH YOUR BACK.
THE CATASTROPHE
KNOCK KNOCK
WHATCHA WANT?
UM, CAN I COME IN?
YOU GOT A PROBLEM, PAL?

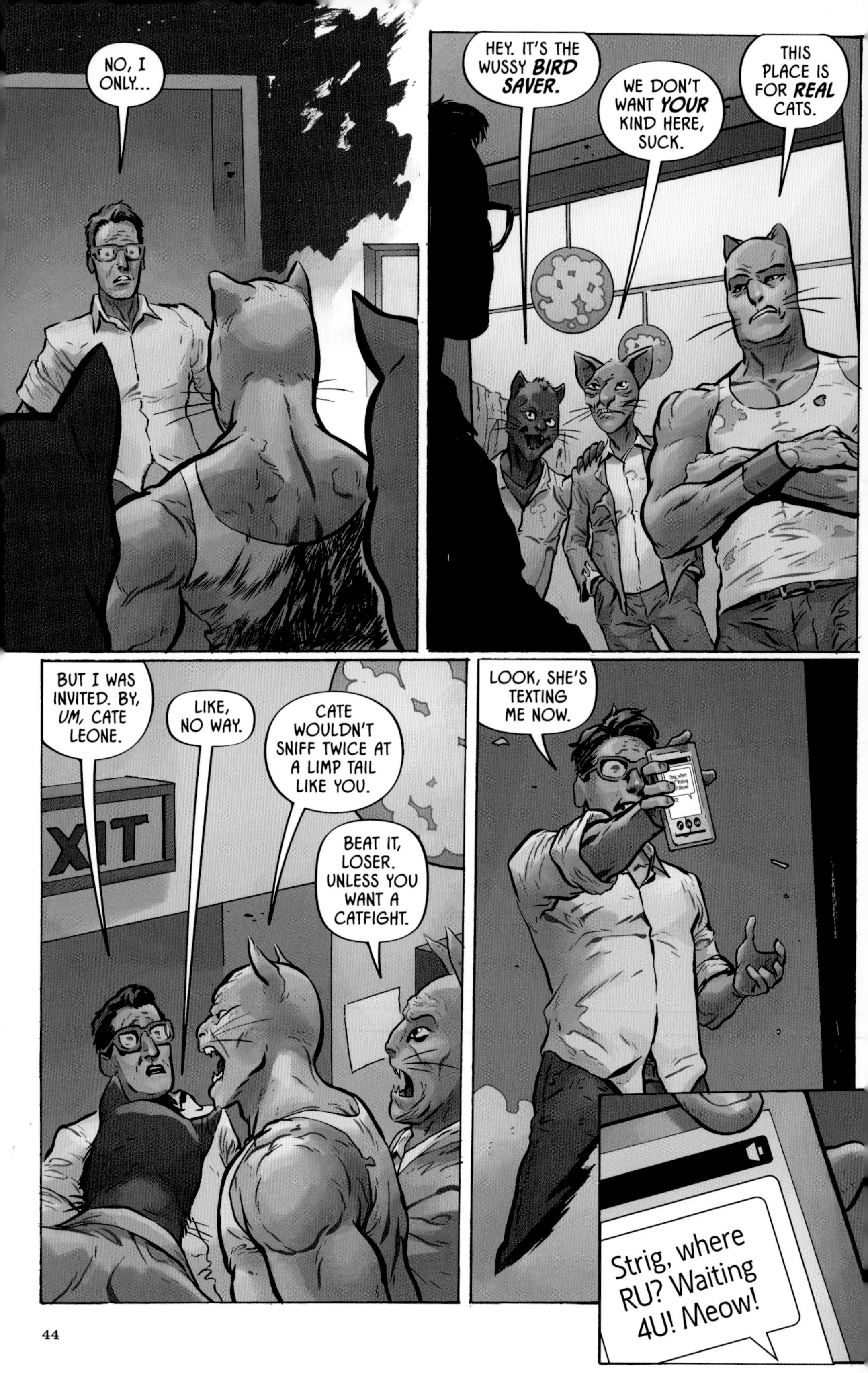
NO, I ONLY...
HEY. IT'S THE WUSSY **BIRD SAVER.**
WE DON'T WANT ***YOUR*** KIND HERE, SUCK.
THIS PLACE IS FOR ***REAL*** CATS.
BUT I WAS INVITED. BY, *UM*, CATE LEONE.
LIKE, NO WAY.
CATE WOULDN'T SNIFF TWICE AT A LIMP TAIL LIKE YOU.
BEAT IT, LOSER. UNLESS YOU WANT A CATFIGHT.
EXIT
LOOK, SHE'S TEXTING ME NOW.
Strig, where RU? Waiting 4U! Meow!

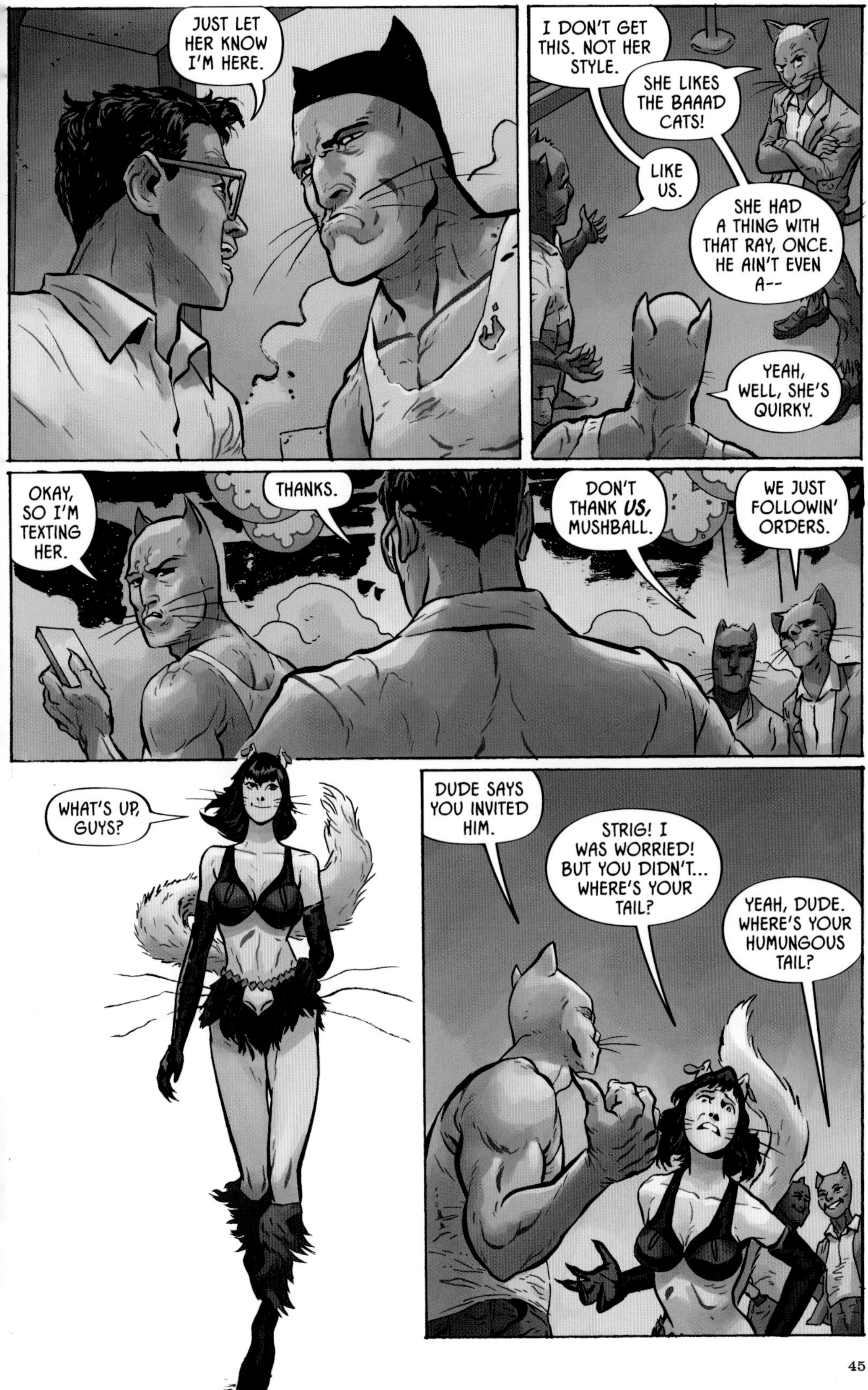
JUST LET HER KNOW I'M HERE.
I DON'T GET THIS. NOT HER STYLE.
SHE LIKES THE BAAAD CATS!
LIKE US.
SHE HAD A THING WITH THAT RAY, ONCE. HE AIN'T EVEN A--
YEAH, WELL, SHE'S QUIRKY.
OKAY, SO I'M TEXTING HER.
THANKS.
DON'T THANK *US,* MUSHBALL.
WE JUST FOLLOWIN' ORDERS.
WHAT'S UP, GUYS?
DUDE SAYS YOU INVITED HIM.
STRIG! I WAS WORRIED! BUT YOU DIDN'T... WHERE'S YOUR TAIL?
YEAH, DUDE. WHERE'S YOUR HUMUNGOUS TAIL?

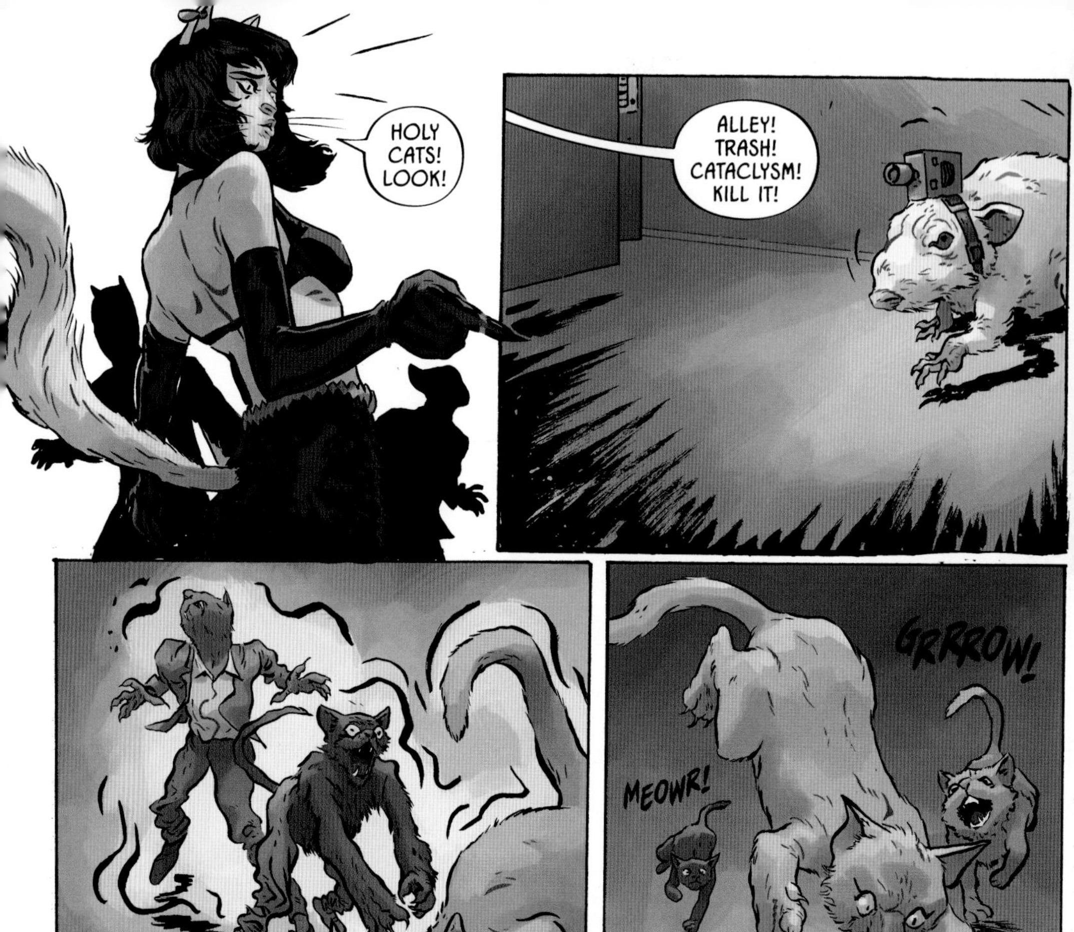
HOLY CATS! LOOK!
ALLEY! TRASH! CATACLYSM! KILL IT!
ROWR!
GRRROW!
MEOWR!
squeeek
SLNRP

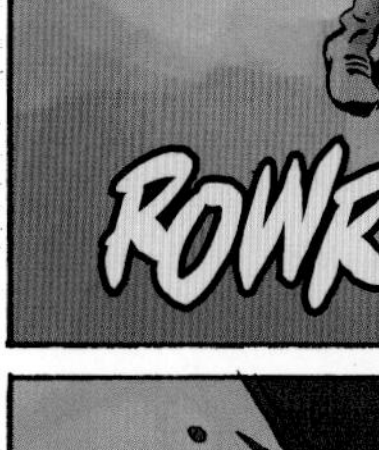

CATS ARE NATURAL HUNTERS

Hunting is a natural cat instinct. It's also "natural" for dogs to hunt cats, but we don't let them do it! Cats and dogs have been domesticated for thousands of years. They're pets, not wild animals.

www.catsandbirds.ca/blog/isnt-it-natural-for-my-cat-to-hunt/

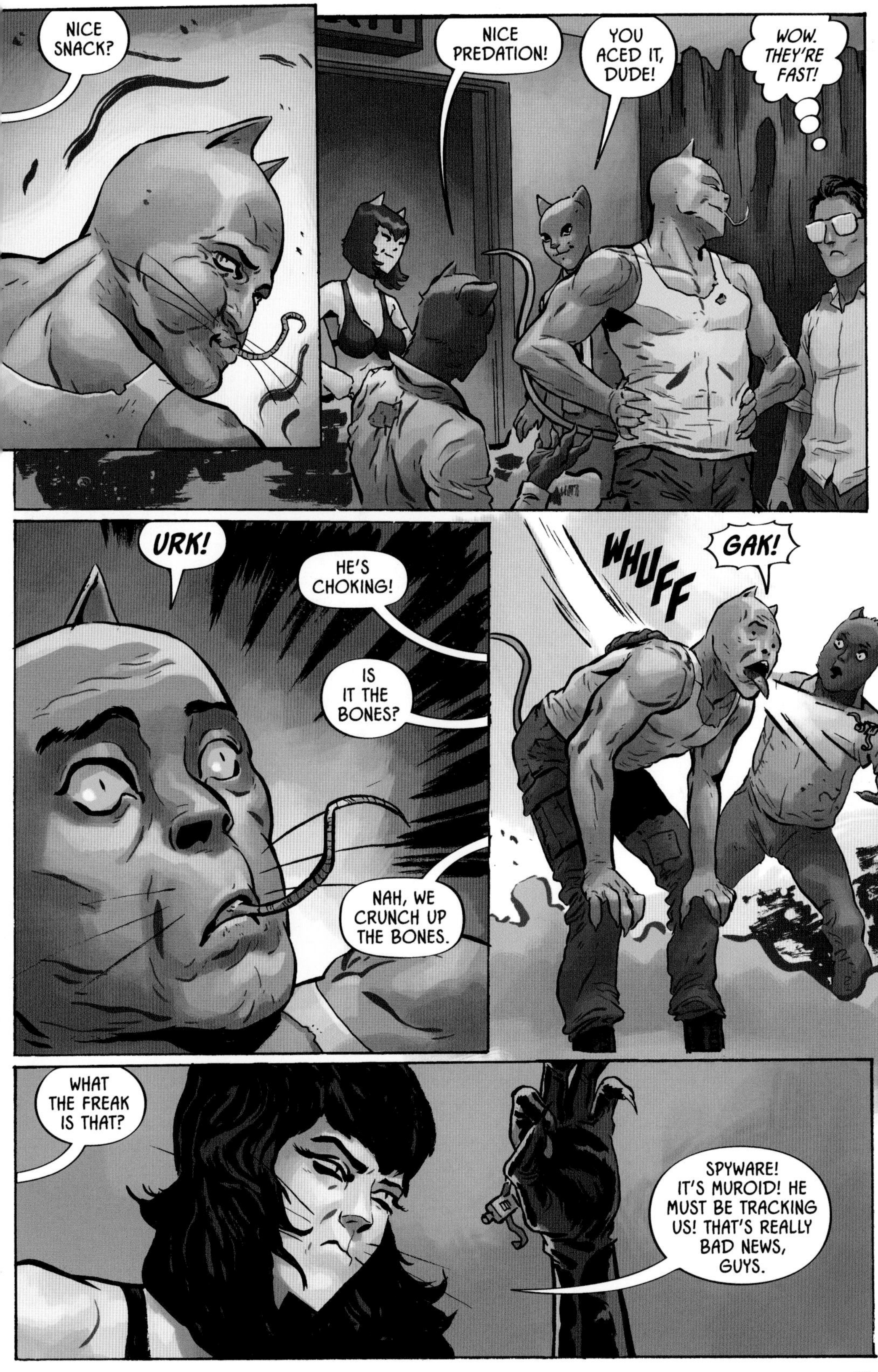
NICE SNACK?
NICE PREDATION!
YOU ACED IT, DUDE!
WOW. THEY'RE FAST!
URK!
HE'S CHOKING!
IS IT THE BONES?
NAH, WE CRUNCH UP THE BONES.
WHUFF
GAK!
WHAT THE FREAK IS THAT?
SPYWARE! IT'S MUROID! HE MUST BE TRACKING US! THAT'S REALLY BAD NEWS, GUYS.

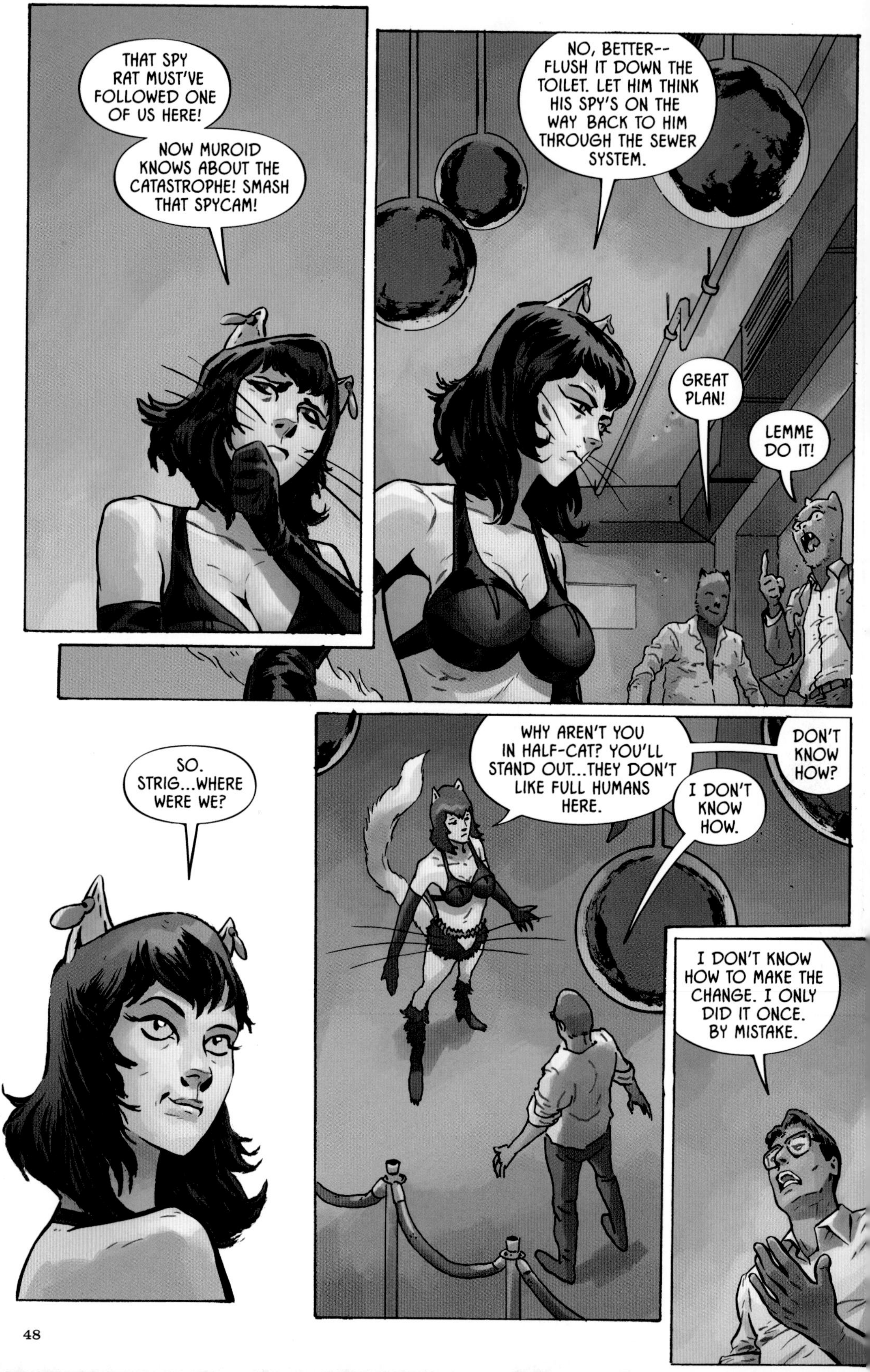

THAT SPY RAT MUST'VE FOLLOWED ONE OF US HERE!
NOW MUROID KNOWS ABOUT THE CATASTROPHE! SMASH THAT SPYCAM!
NO, BETTER-- FLUSH IT DOWN THE TOILET. LET HIM THINK HIS SPY'S ON THE WAY BACK TO HIM THROUGH THE SEWER SYSTEM.
GREAT PLAN!
LEMME DO IT!
SO. STRIG...WHERE WERE WE?
WHY AREN'T YOU IN HALF-CAT? YOU'LL STAND OUT...THEY DON'T LIKE FULL HUMANS HERE.
I DON'T KNOW HOW.
DON'T KNOW HOW?
I DON'T KNOW HOW TO MAKE THE CHANGE. I ONLY DID IT ONCE. BY MISTAKE.

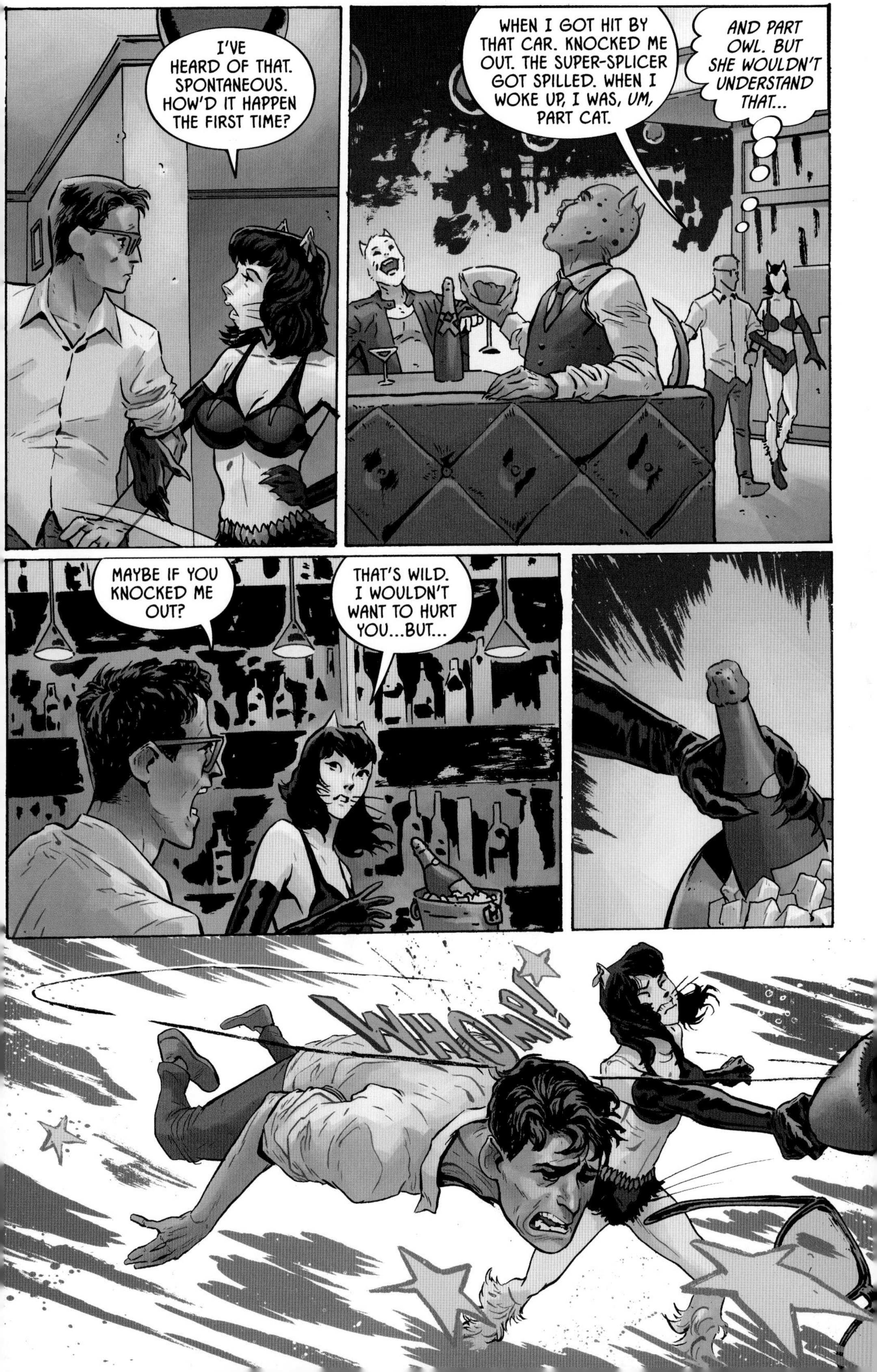
I'VE HEARD OF THAT. SPONTANEOUS. HOW'D IT HAPPEN THE FIRST TIME?
WHEN I GOT HIT BY THAT CAR. KNOCKED ME OUT. THE SUPER-SPLICER GOT SPILLED. WHEN I WOKE UP, I WAS, *UM*, PART CAT.
AND PART OWL. BUT SHE WOULDN'T UNDERSTAND THAT...
MAYBE IF YOU KNOCKED ME OUT?
THAT'S WILD. I WOULDN'T WANT TO HURT YOU...BUT...
WHOM!

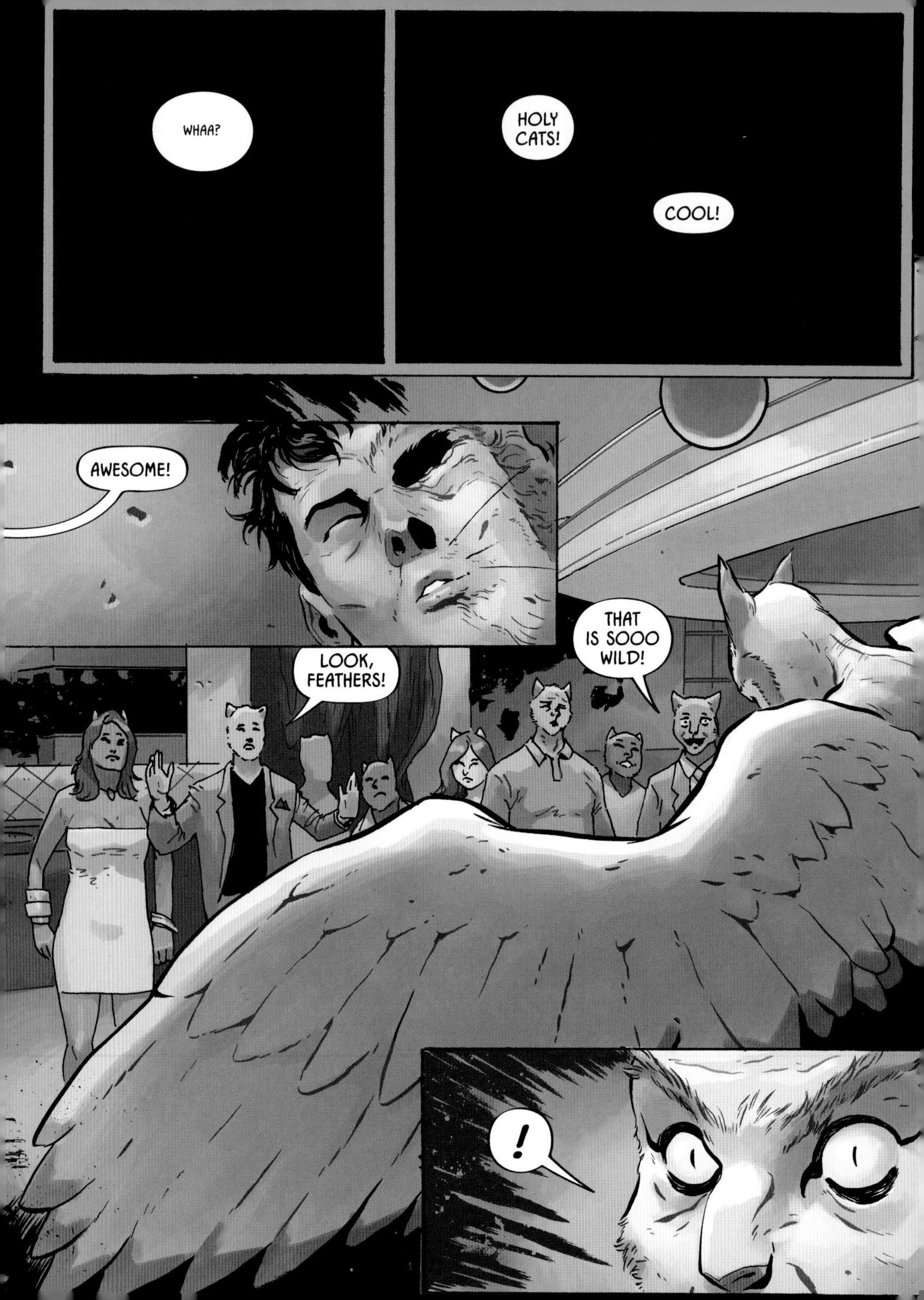
WHAA?
HOLY CATS!
COOL!
AWESOME!
THAT IS SOOO WILD!
LOOK, FEATHERS!
!

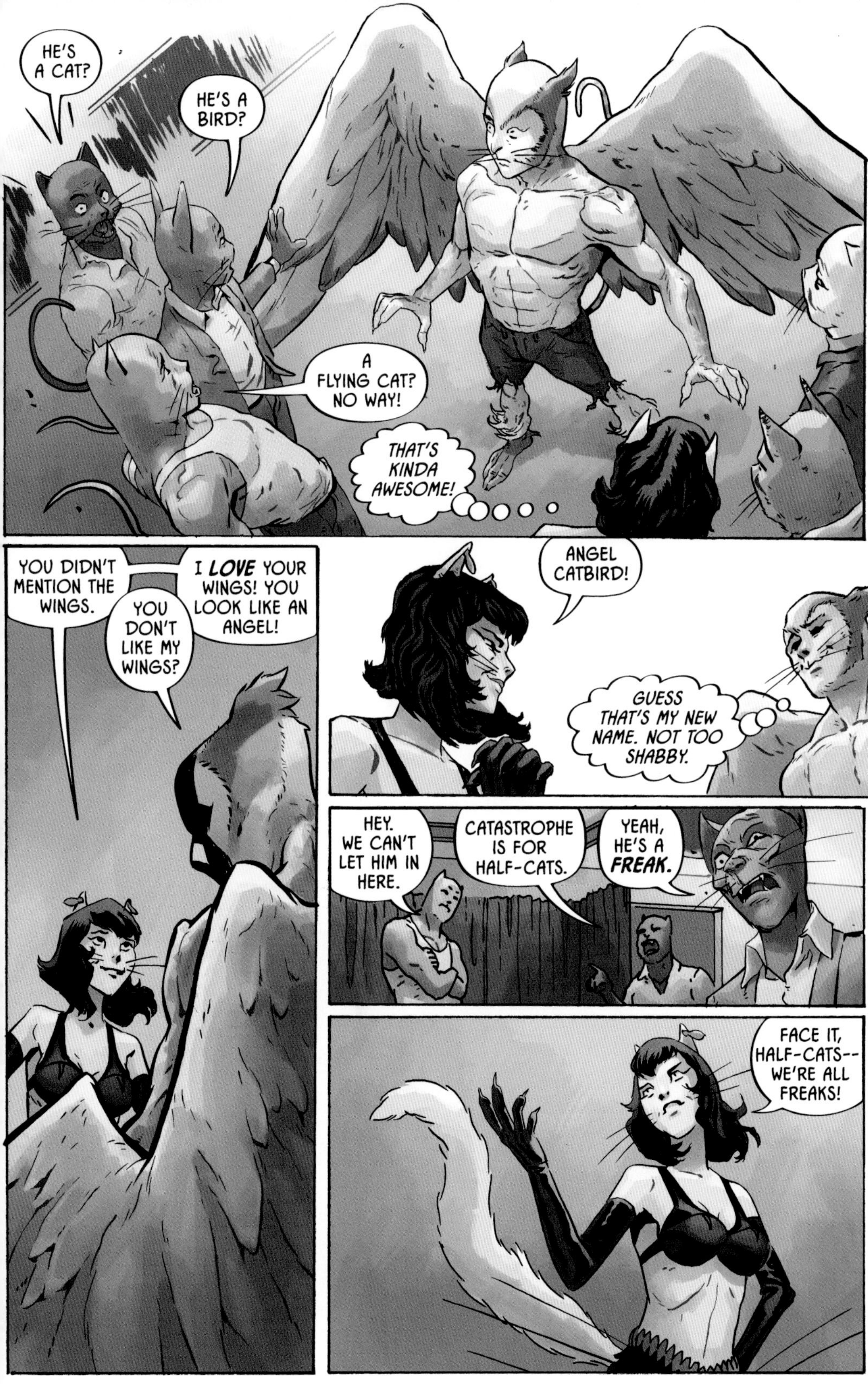
HE'S A CAT?
HE'S A BIRD?
A FLYING CAT? NO WAY!
THAT'S KINDA AWESOME!
YOU DIDN'T MENTION THE WINGS.
YOU DON'T LIKE MY WINGS?
I LOVE YOUR WINGS! YOU LOOK LIKE AN ANGEL!
ANGEL CATBIRD!
GUESS THAT'S MY NEW NAME. NOT TOO SHABBY.
HEY. WE CAN'T LET HIM IN HERE.
CATASTROPHE IS FOR HALF-CATS.
YEAH, HE'S A FREAK.
FACE IT, HALF-CATS--WE'RE ALL FREAKS!

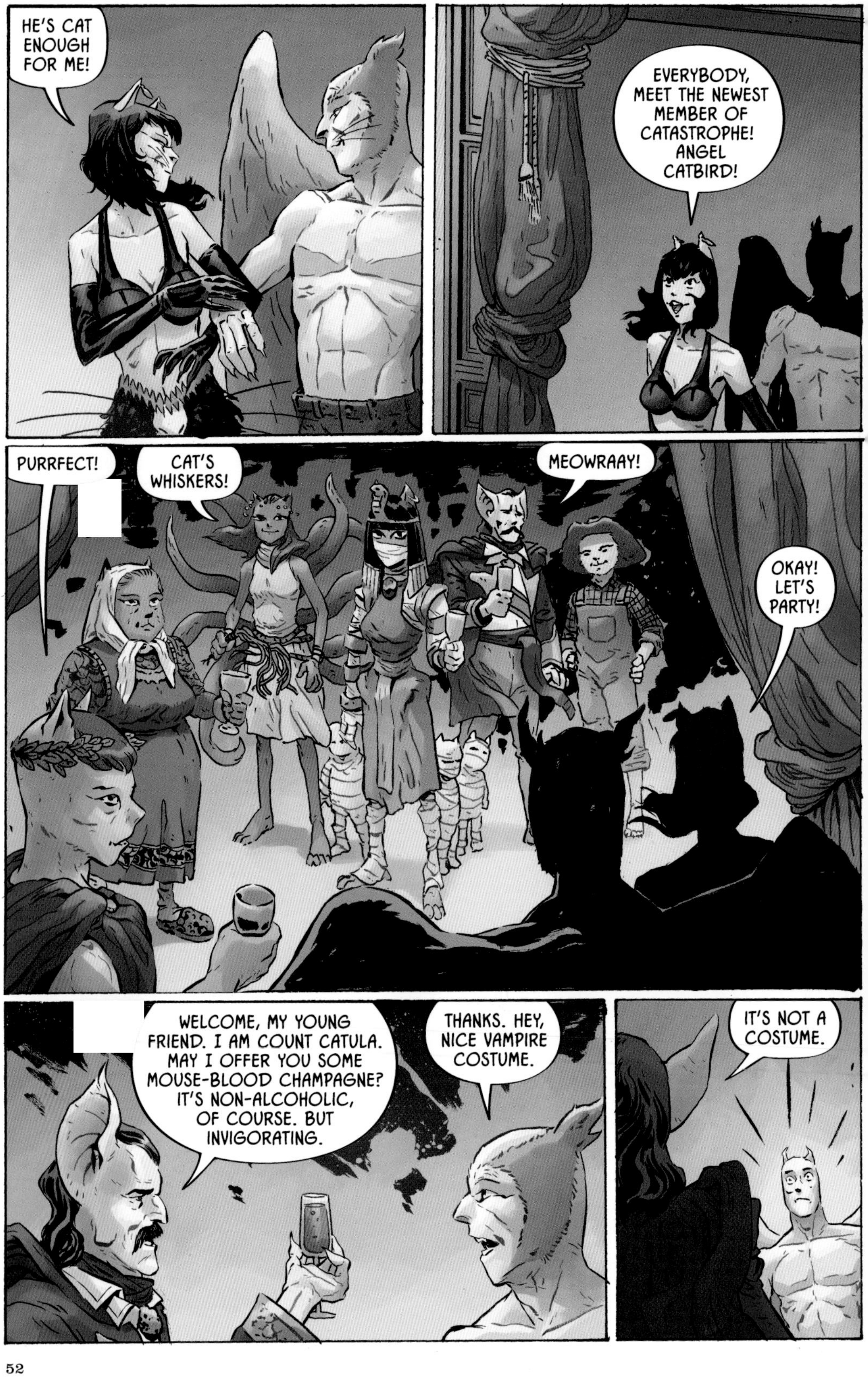
HE'S CAT ENOUGH FOR ME!
EVERYBODY, MEET THE NEWEST MEMBER OF CATASTROPHE! ANGEL CATBIRD!
PURRFECT!
CAT'S WHISKERS!
MEOWRAAY!
OKAY! LET'S PARTY!
WELCOME, MY YOUNG FRIEND. I AM COUNT CATULA. MAY I OFFER YOU SOME MOUSE-BLOOD CHAMPAGNE? IT'S NON-ALCOHOLIC, OF COURSE. BUT INVIGORATING.
THANKS. HEY, NICE VAMPIRE COSTUME.
IT'S NOT A COSTUME.

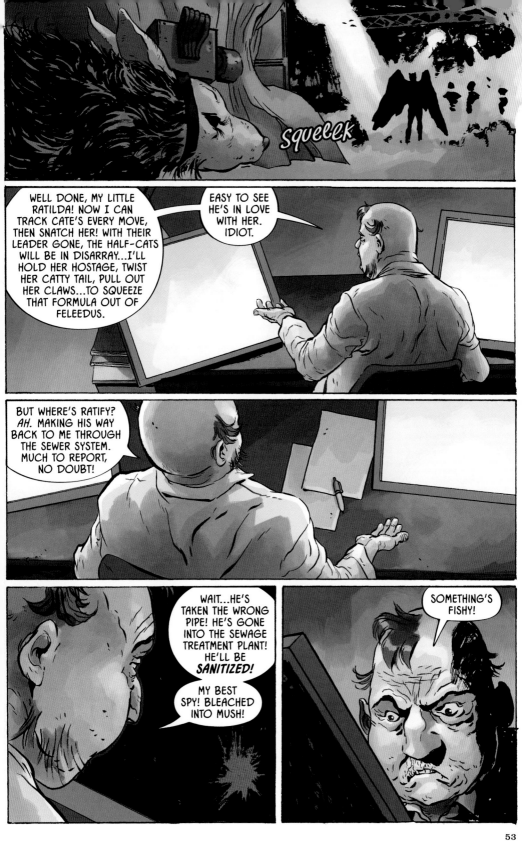

SQUEEEK

WELL DONE, MY LITTLE RATILDA! NOW I CAN TRACK CATE'S EVERY MOVE, THEN SNATCH HER! WITH THEIR LEADER GONE, THE HALF-CATS WILL BE IN DISARRAY...I'LL HOLD HER HOSTAGE, TWIST HER CATTY TAIL, PULL OUT HER CLAWS...TO SQUEEZE THAT FORMULA OUT OF FELEEDUS.

EASY TO SEE HE'S IN LOVE WITH HER. IDIOT.

BUT WHERE'S RATIFY? AH. MAKING HIS WAY BACK TO ME THROUGH THE SEWER SYSTEM. MUCH TO REPORT, NO DOUBT!

WAIT...HE'S TAKEN THE WRONG PIPE! HE'S GONE INTO THE SEWAGE TREATMENT PLANT! HE'LL BE **SANITIZED!**

MY BEST SPY! BLEACHED INTO MUSH!

SOMETHING'S FISHY!

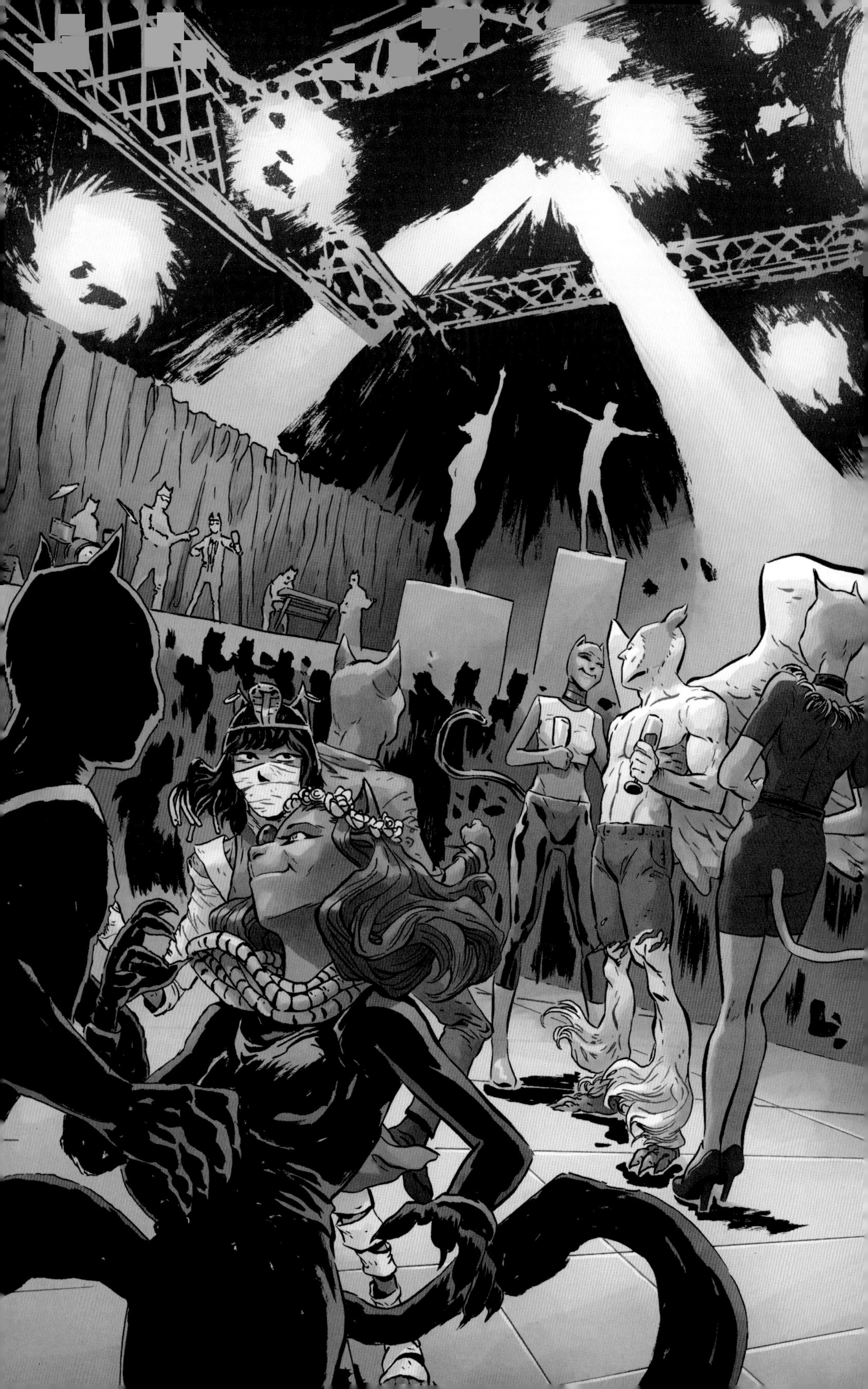

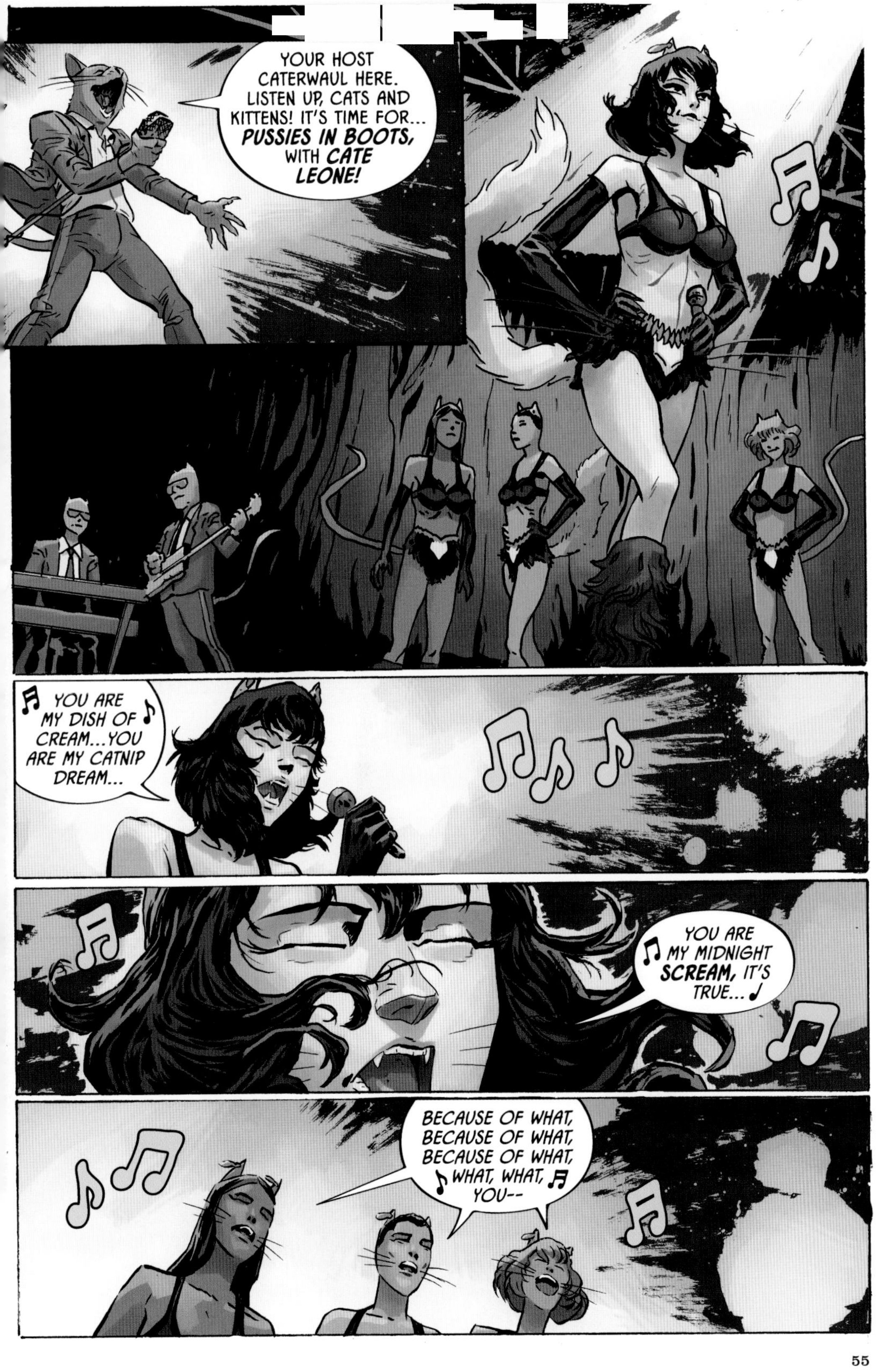
YOUR HOST CATERWAUL HERE. LISTEN UP, CATS AND KITTENS! IT'S TIME FOR... **PUSSIES IN BOOTS,** WITH **CATE LEONE!**
YOU ARE MY DISH OF CREAM...YOU ARE MY CATNIP DREAM...
YOU ARE MY MIDNIGHT **SCREAM,** IT'S TRUE...
BECAUSE OF WHAT, BECAUSE OF WHAT, BECAUSE OF WHAT, WHAT, WHAT, YOU--

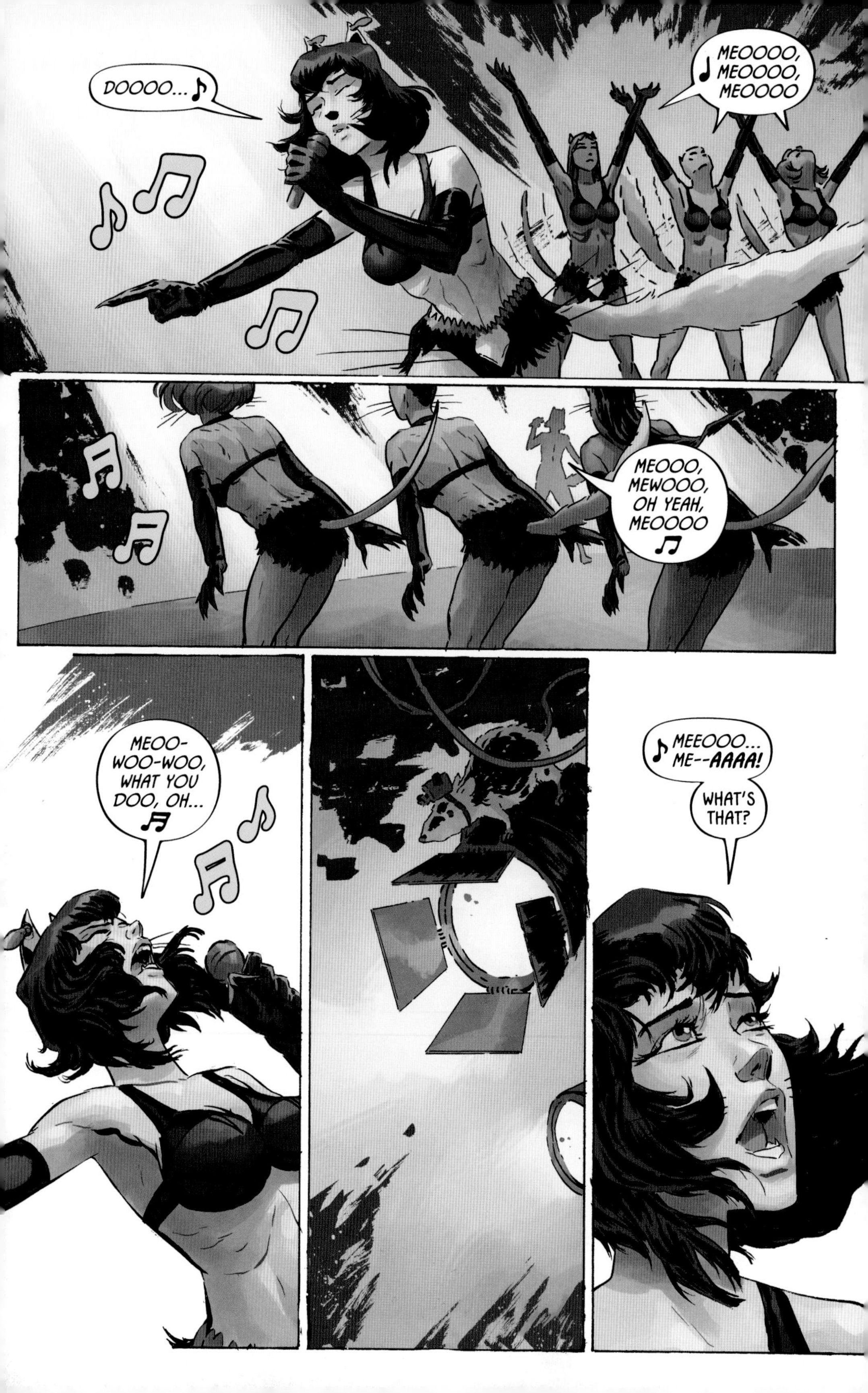
DOOOO... ♪
♩ MEOOOO, MEOOOO, MEOOOO
MEOOO, MEWOOO, OH YEAH, MEOOOO ♫
MEOO-WOO-WOO, WHAT YOU DOO, OH... ♫
♪ MEEOOO... ME--AAAA!
WHAT'S THAT?

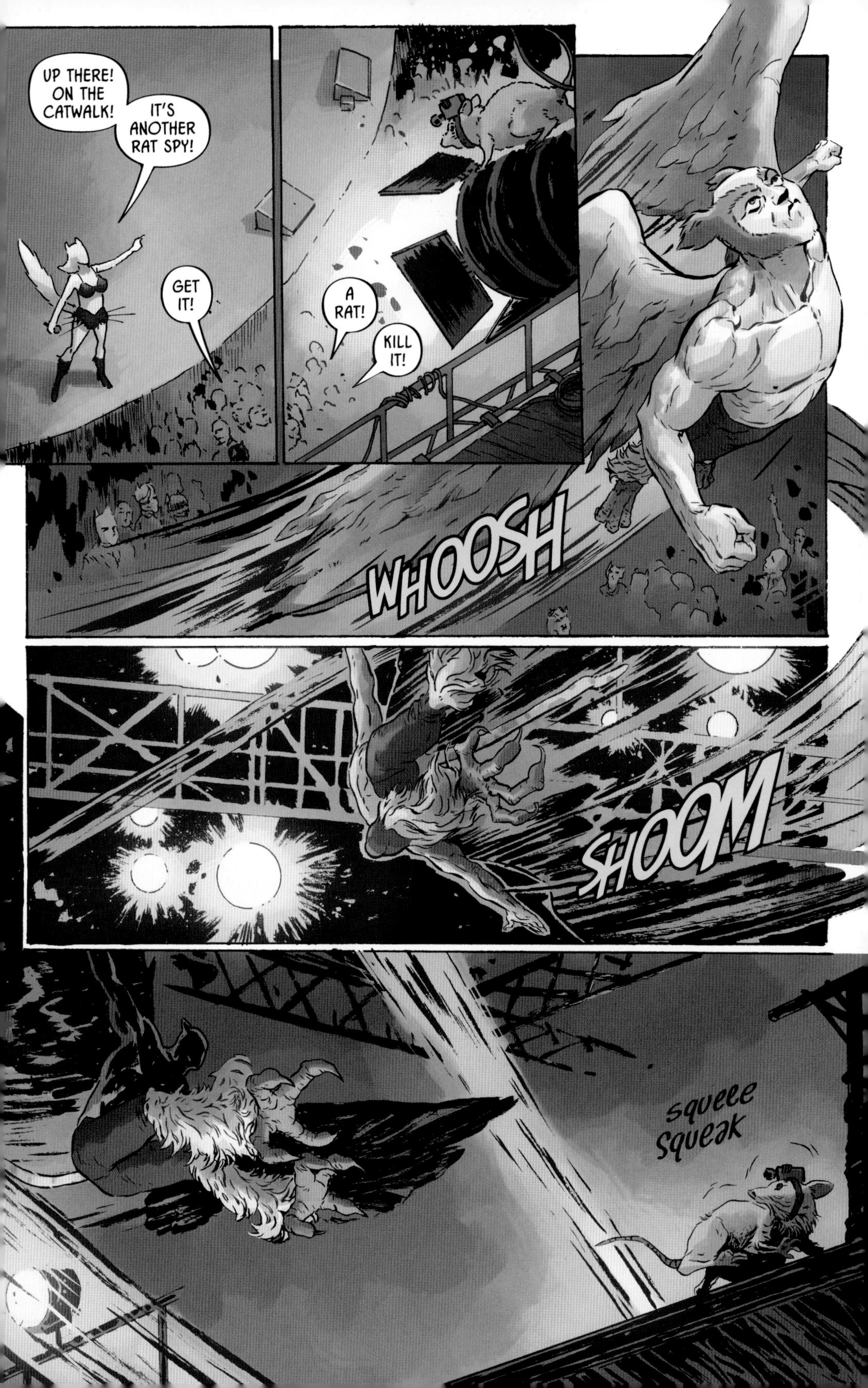
UP THERE! ON THE CATWALK!
IT'S ANOTHER RAT SPY!
GET IT!
A RAT!
KILL IT!
WHOOSH
SHOOM
squeee
Squeak

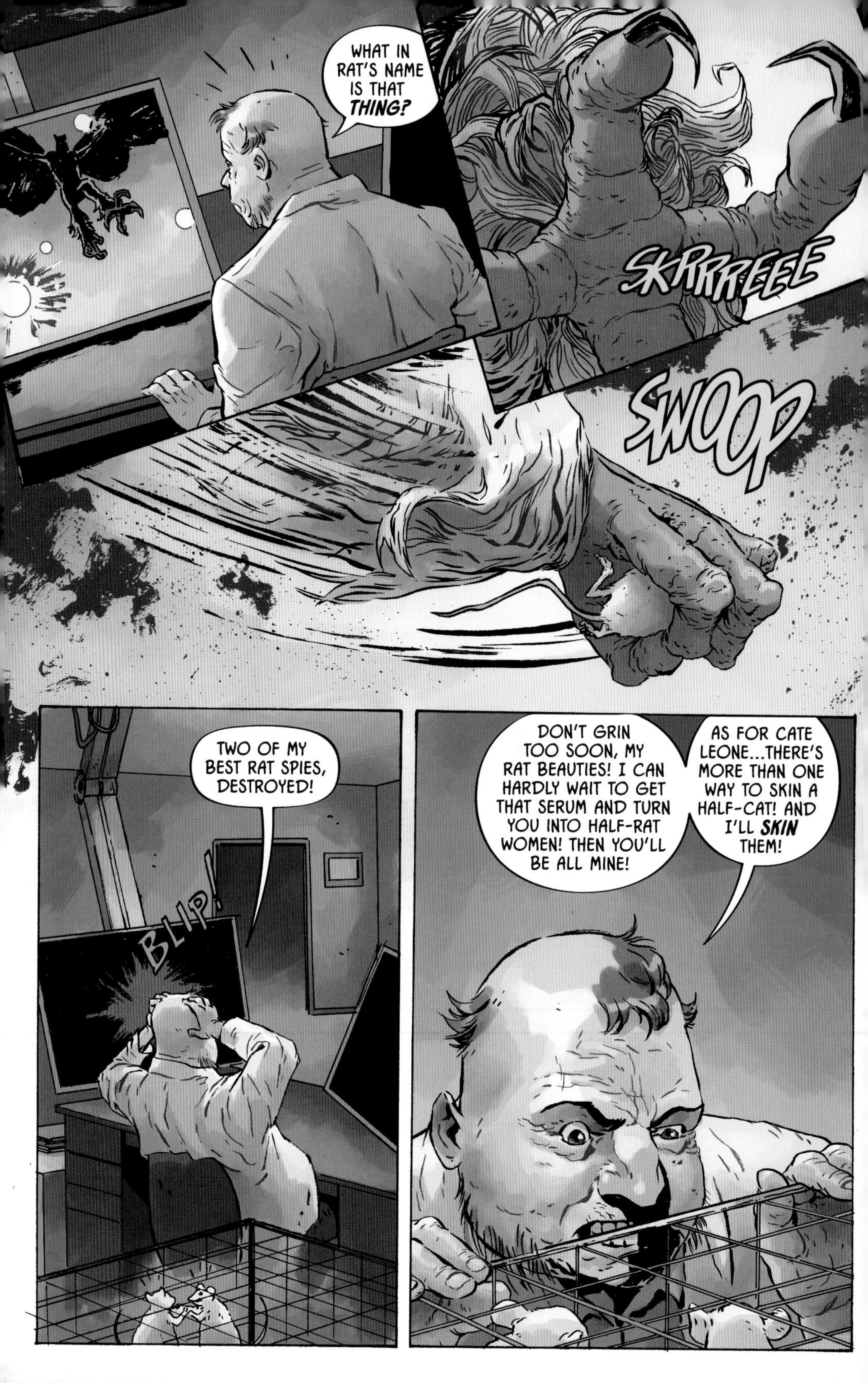
WHAT IN RAT'S NAME IS THAT THING?
SKRRRREEEE
SWOOP
TWO OF MY BEST RAT SPIES, DESTROYED!
BLIP!
DON'T GRIN TOO SOON, MY RAT BEAUTIES! I CAN HARDLY WAIT TO GET THAT SERUM AND TURN YOU INTO HALF-RAT WOMEN! THEN YOU'LL BE ALL MINE!
AS FOR CATE LEONE...THERE'S MORE THAN ONE WAY TO SKIN A HALF-CAT! AND I'LL SKIN THEM!

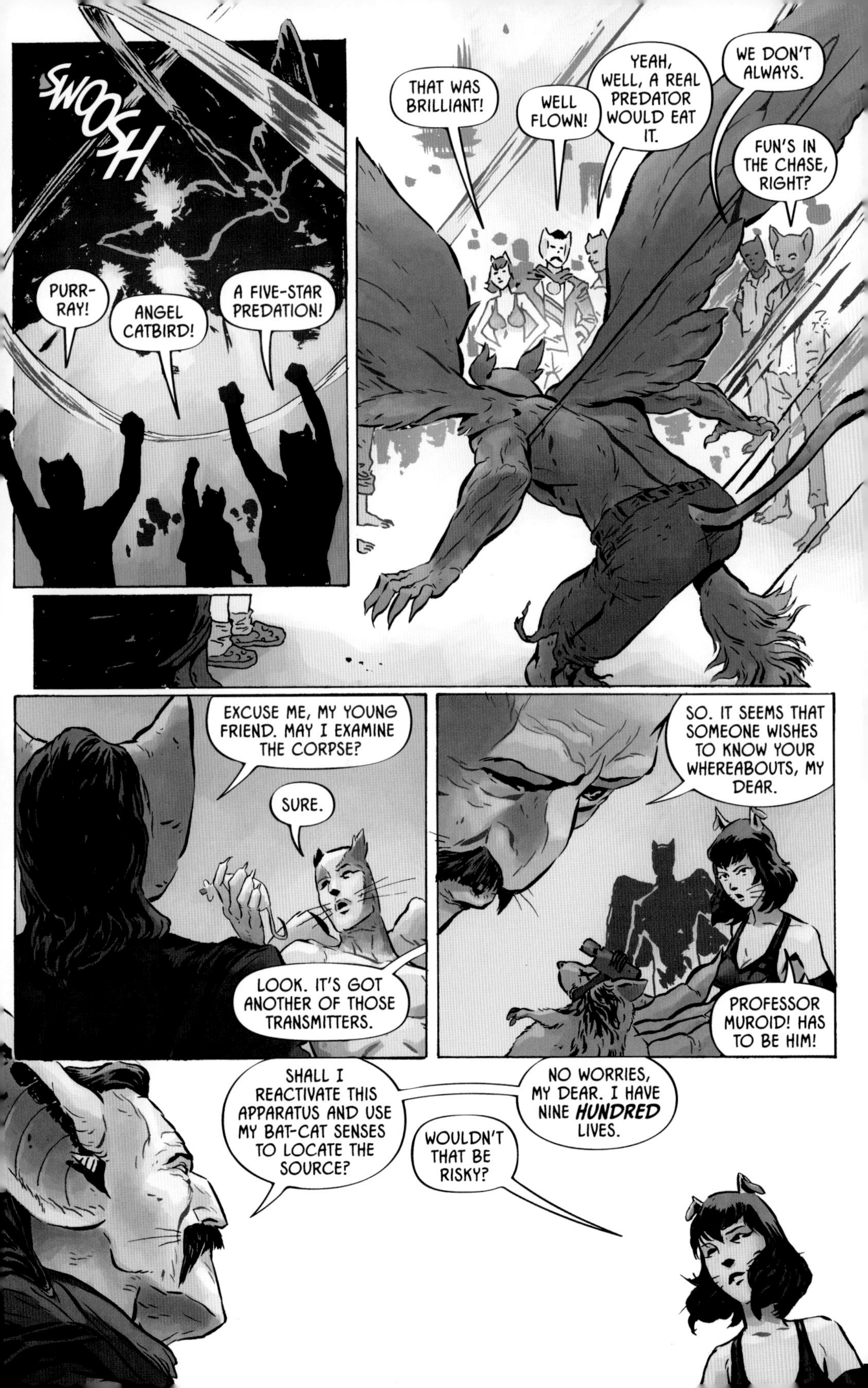
SWOOSH
PURR-RAY!
ANGEL CATBIRD!
A FIVE-STAR PREDATION!
THAT WAS BRILLIANT!
WELL FLOWN!
YEAH, WELL, A REAL PREDATOR WOULD EAT IT.
WE DON'T ALWAYS.
FUN'S IN THE CHASE, RIGHT?
EXCUSE ME, MY YOUNG FRIEND. MAY I EXAMINE THE CORPSE?
SURE.
LOOK. IT'S GOT ANOTHER OF THOSE TRANSMITTERS.
SO. IT SEEMS THAT SOMEONE WISHES TO KNOW YOUR WHEREABOUTS, MY DEAR.
PROFESSOR MUROID! HAS TO BE HIM!
SHALL I REACTIVATE THIS APPARATUS AND USE MY BAT-CAT SENSES TO LOCATE THE SOURCE?
WOULDN'T THAT BE RISKY?
NO WORRIES, MY DEAR. I HAVE NINE HUNDRED LIVES.

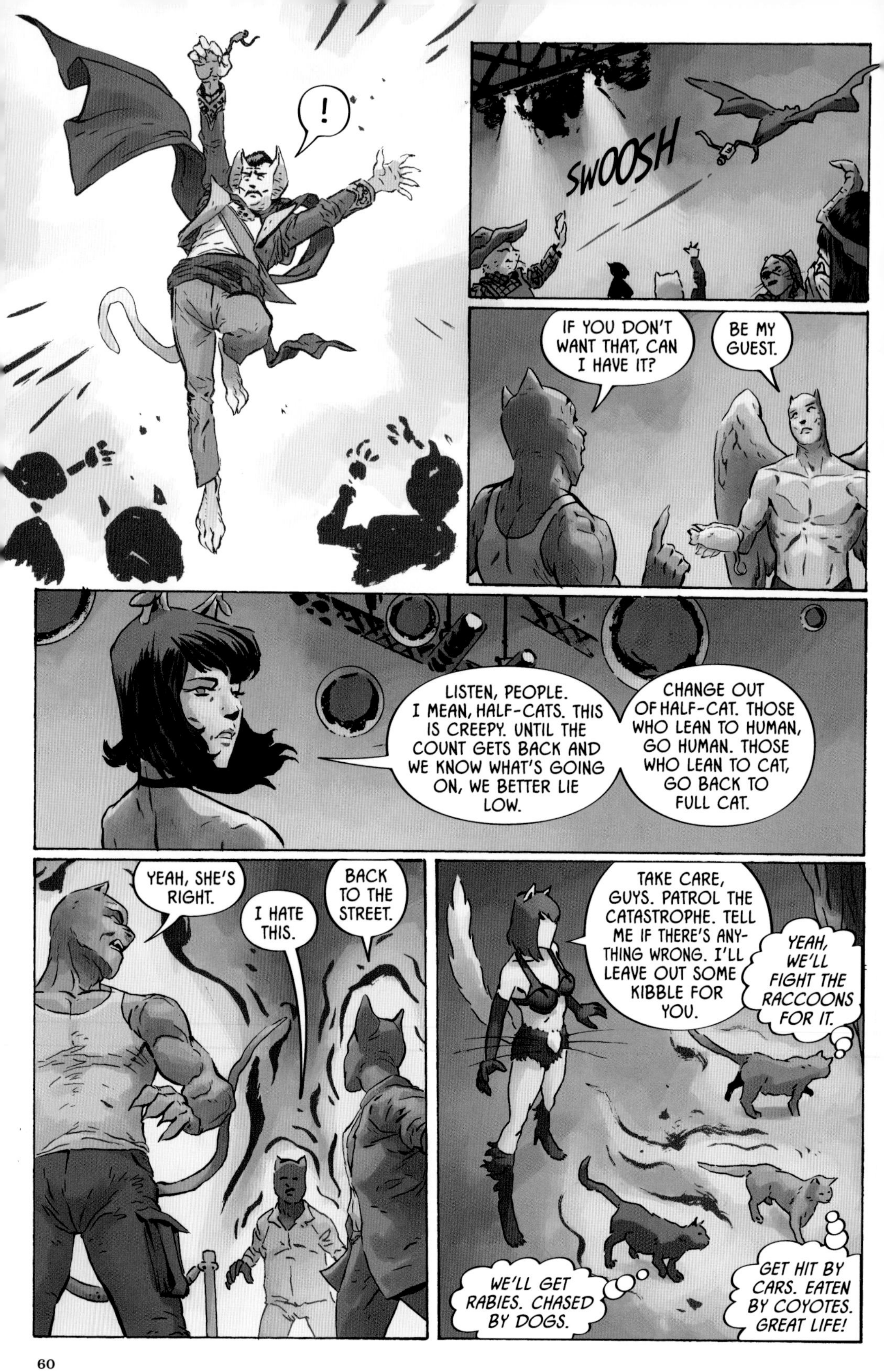
!
SWOOSH
IF YOU DON'T WANT THAT, CAN I HAVE IT?
BE MY GUEST.
LISTEN, PEOPLE. I MEAN, HALF-CATS. THIS IS CREEPY. UNTIL THE COUNT GETS BACK AND WE KNOW WHAT'S GOING ON, WE BETTER LIE LOW.
CHANGE OUT OF HALF-CAT. THOSE WHO LEAN TO HUMAN, GO HUMAN. THOSE WHO LEAN TO CAT, GO BACK TO FULL CAT.
YEAH, SHE'S RIGHT.
I HATE THIS.
BACK TO THE STREET.
TAKE CARE, GUYS. PATROL THE CATASTROPHE. TELL ME IF THERE'S ANYTHING WRONG. I'LL LEAVE OUT SOME KIBBLE FOR YOU.
YEAH, WE'LL FIGHT THE RACCOONS FOR IT.
WE'LL GET RABIES. CHASED BY DOGS.
GET HIT BY CARS. EATEN BY COYOTES. GREAT LIFE!

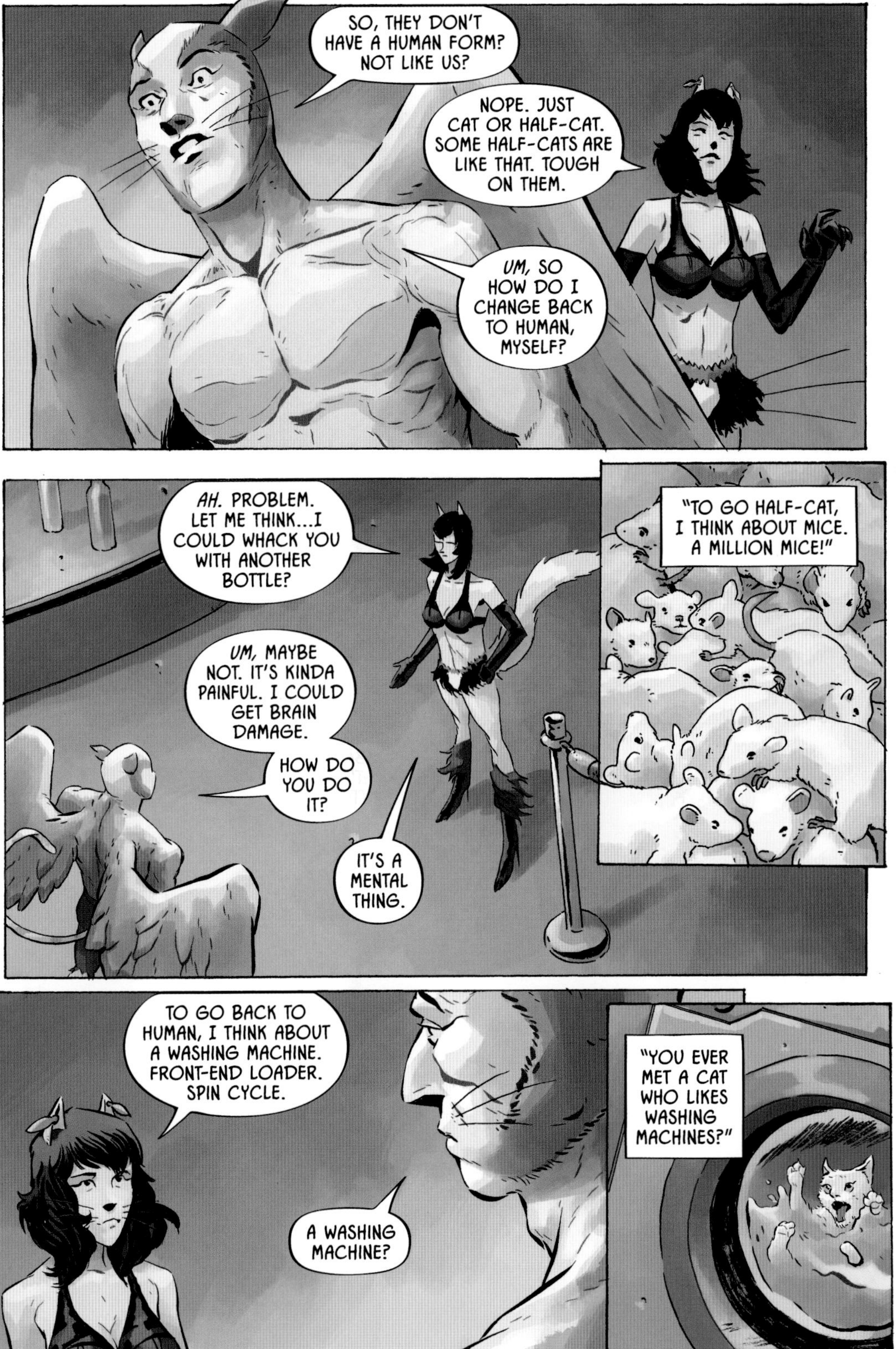
SO, THEY DON'T HAVE A HUMAN FORM? NOT LIKE US?
NOPE. JUST CAT OR HALF-CAT. SOME HALF-CATS ARE LIKE THAT. TOUGH ON THEM.
UM, SO HOW DO I CHANGE BACK TO HUMAN, MYSELF?
AH. PROBLEM. LET ME THINK...I COULD WHACK YOU WITH ANOTHER BOTTLE?
UM, MAYBE NOT. IT'S KINDA PAINFUL. I COULD GET BRAIN DAMAGE.
HOW DO YOU DO IT?
IT'S A MENTAL THING.
"TO GO HALF-CAT, I THINK ABOUT MICE. A MILLION MICE!"
TO GO BACK TO HUMAN, I THINK ABOUT A WASHING MACHINE. FRONT-END LOADER. SPIN CYCLE.
A WASHING MACHINE?
"YOU EVER MET A CAT WHO LIKES WASHING MACHINES?"

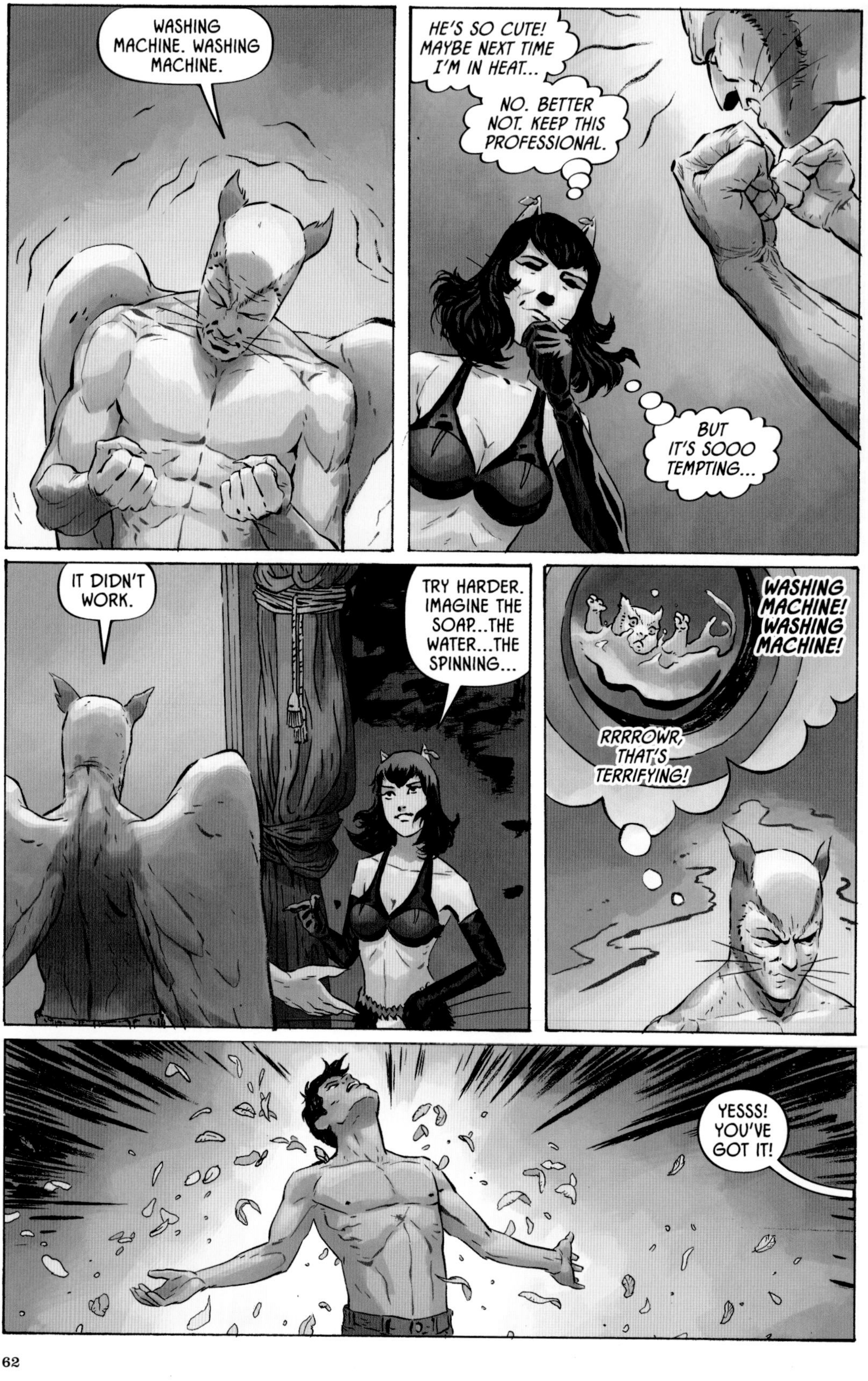
WASHING MACHINE. WASHING MACHINE.
HE'S SO CUTE! MAYBE NEXT TIME I'M IN HEAT...
NO. BETTER NOT. KEEP THIS PROFESSIONAL.
BUT IT'S SOOO TEMPTING...
IT DIDN'T WORK.
TRY HARDER. IMAGINE THE SOAP...THE WATER...THE SPINNING...
WASHING MACHINE! WASHING MACHINE!
RRRROWR, THAT'S TERRIFYING!
YESSS! YOU'VE GOT IT!

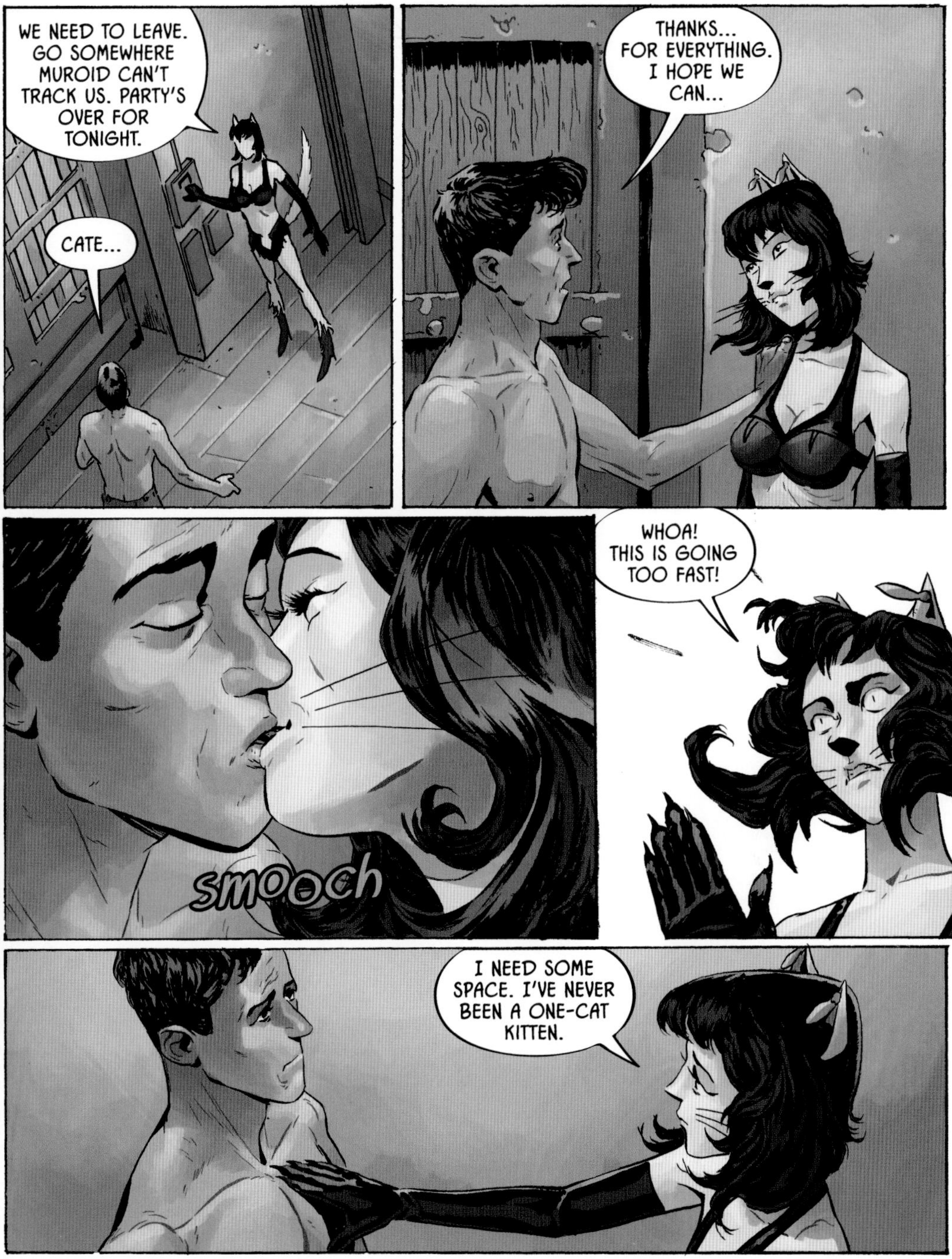
WE NEED TO LEAVE. GO SOMEWHERE MUROID CAN'T TRACK US. PARTY'S OVER FOR TONIGHT.
CATE...
THANKS... FOR EVERYTHING. I HOPE WE CAN...
SMOOCH
WHOA! THIS IS GOING TOO FAST!
I NEED SOME SPACE. I'VE NEVER BEEN A ONE-CAT KITTEN.

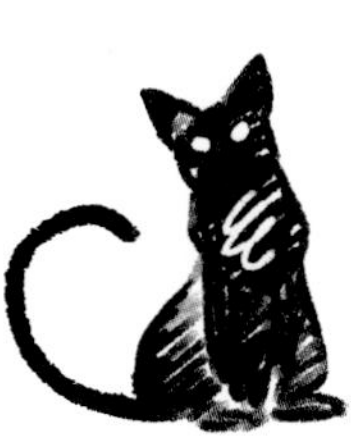

CAT-BIRD MATH, Part III

A female cat has an average of 1.4 litters per year, up to 3 in warm climates—with an average of 3 kittens per litter. At that rate, it takes only 3 1/2 years for your cat and her kittens to produce more than a thousand cats! Fix your cat! www.catsandbirds.ca/blog/the-importance-of-fixing-your-cat/

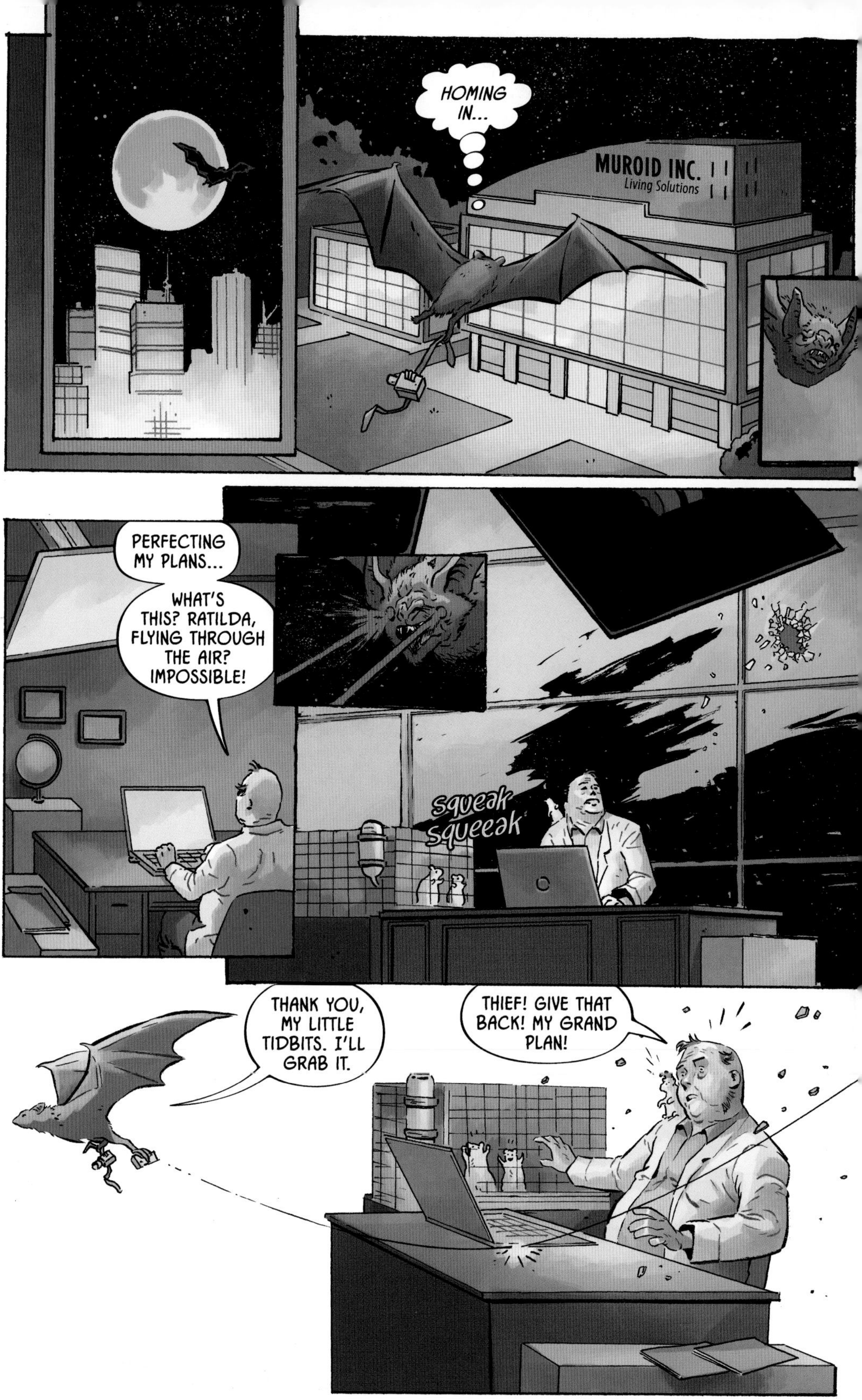
HOMING IN...
MUROID INC.
Living Solutions
PERFECTING MY PLANS...
WHAT'S THIS? RATILDA, FLYING THROUGH THE AIR? IMPOSSIBLE!
squeak squeeak
THANK YOU, MY LITTLE TIDBITS. I'LL GRAB IT.
THIEF! GIVE THAT BACK! MY GRAND PLAN!

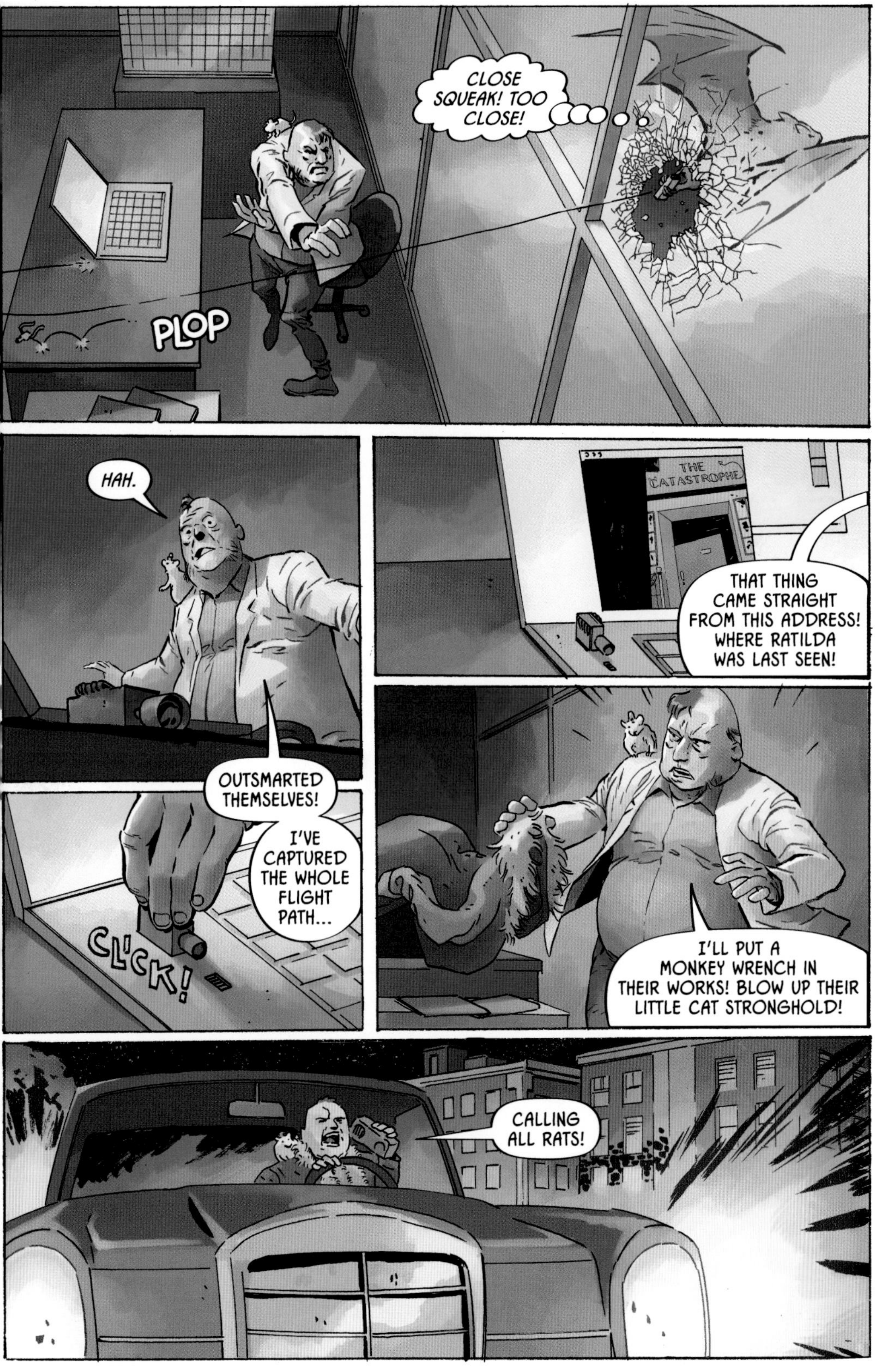
CLOSE SQUEAK! TOO CLOSE!
PLOP
HAH.
THE CATASTROPHE
THAT THING CAME STRAIGHT FROM THIS ADDRESS! WHERE RATILDA WAS LAST SEEN!
OUTSMARTED THEMSELVES!
I'VE CAPTURED THE WHOLE FLIGHT PATH...
CLICK!
I'LL PUT A MONKEY WRENCH IN THEIR WORKS! BLOW UP THEIR LITTLE CAT STRONGHOLD!
CALLING ALL RATS!

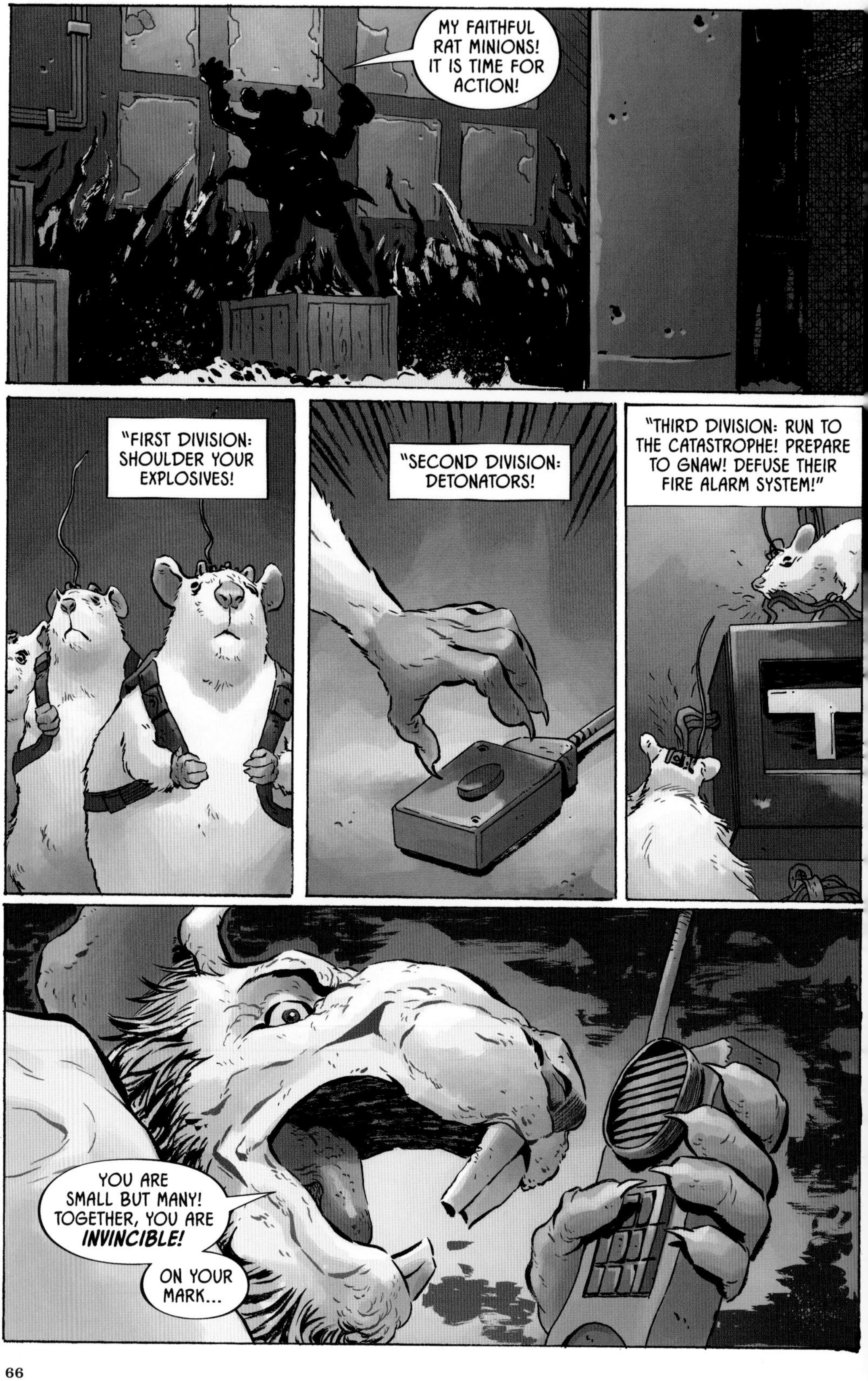
MY FAITHFUL RAT MINIONS! IT IS TIME FOR ACTION!
"FIRST DIVISION: SHOULDER YOUR EXPLOSIVES!
"SECOND DIVISION: DETONATORS!
"THIRD DIVISION: RUN TO THE CATASTROPHE! PREPARE TO GNAW! DEFUSE THEIR FIRE ALARM SYSTEM!"
YOU ARE SMALL BUT MANY! TOGETHER, YOU ARE *INVINCIBLE!*
ON YOUR MARK...

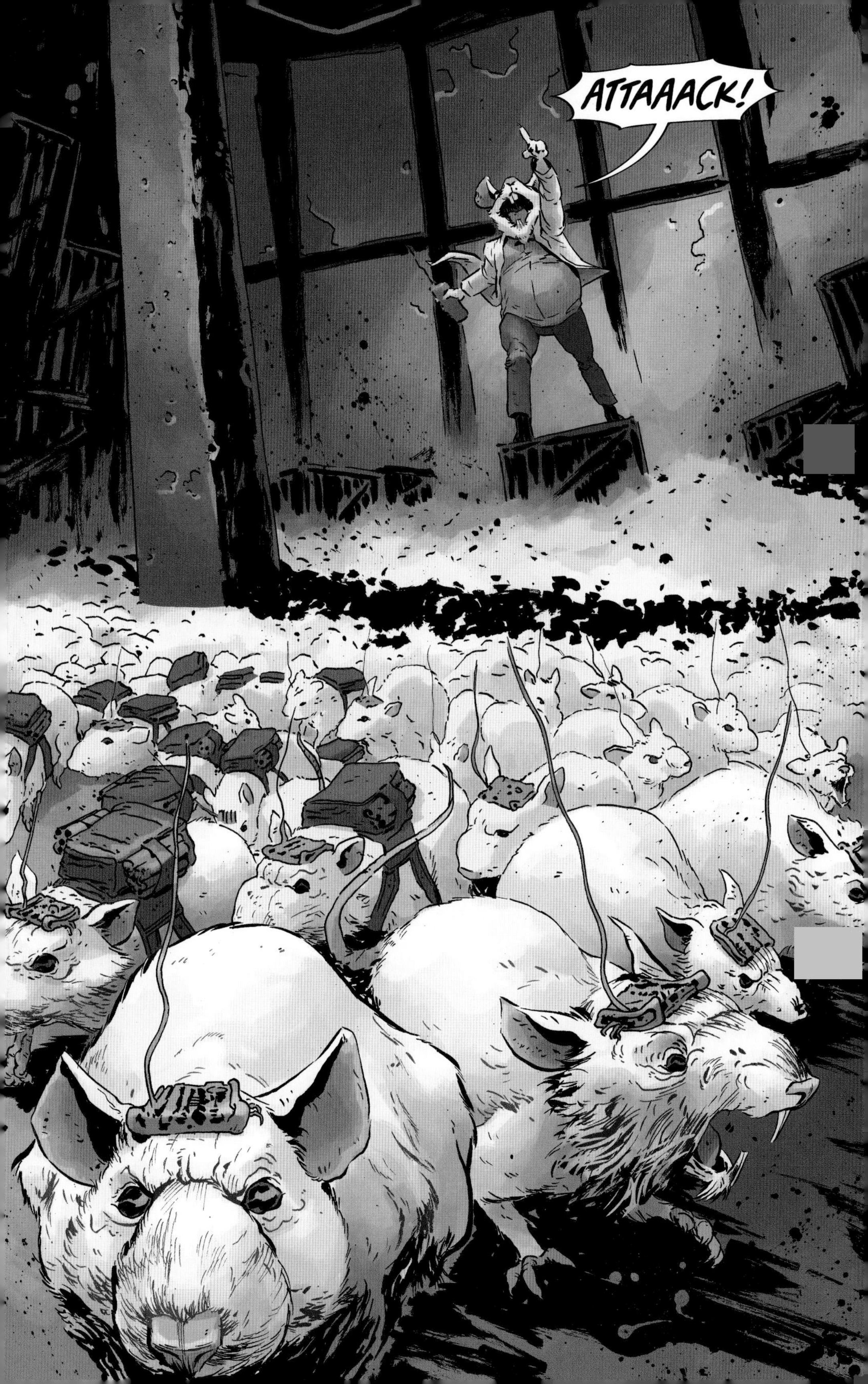
ATTAAACK!

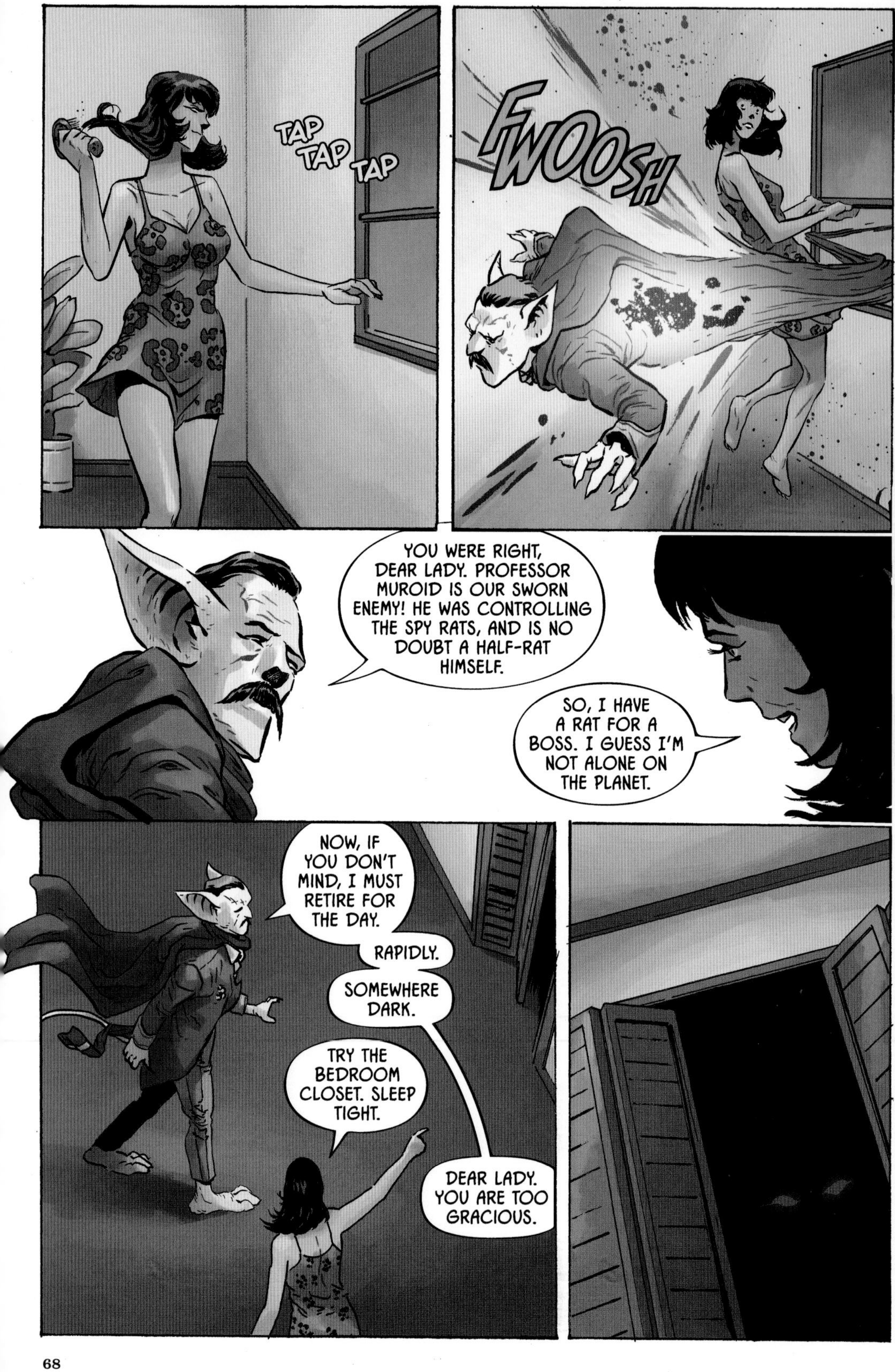
TAP TAP TAP
FWOOSH
YOU WERE RIGHT, DEAR LADY. PROFESSOR MUROID IS OUR SWORN ENEMY! HE WAS CONTROLLING THE SPY RATS, AND IS NO DOUBT A HALF-RAT HIMSELF.
SO, I HAVE A RAT FOR A BOSS. I GUESS I'M NOT ALONE ON THE PLANET.
NOW, IF YOU DON'T MIND, I MUST RETIRE FOR THE DAY.
RAPIDLY.
SOMEWHERE DARK.
TRY THE BEDROOM CLOSET. SLEEP TIGHT.
DEAR LADY. YOU ARE TOO GRACIOUS.

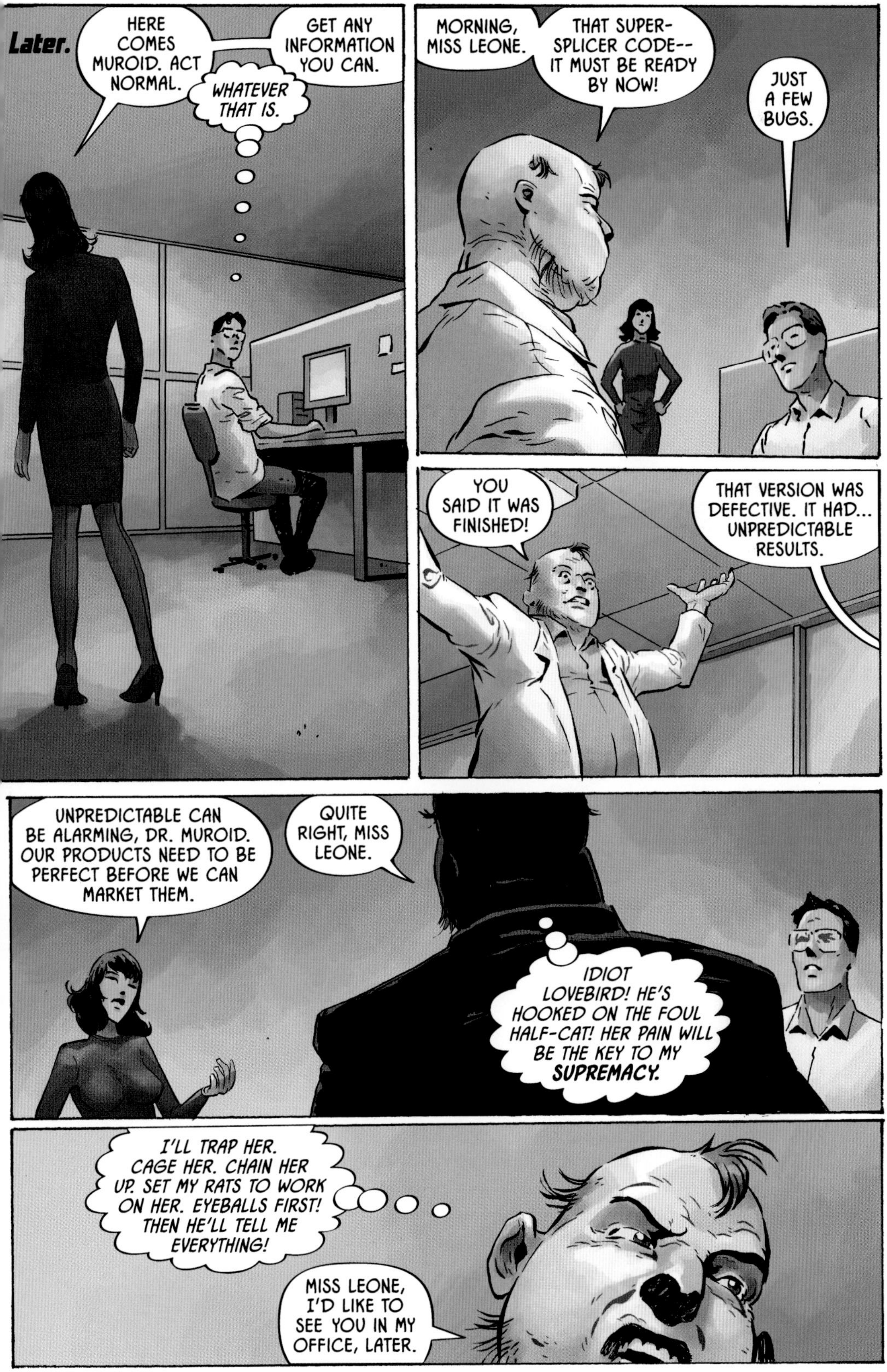
Later.
HERE COMES MUROID. ACT NORMAL.
GET ANY INFORMATION YOU CAN.
WHATEVER THAT IS.
MORNING, MISS LEONE.
THAT SUPER-SPLICER CODE-- IT MUST BE READY BY NOW!
JUST A FEW BUGS.
YOU SAID IT WAS FINISHED!
THAT VERSION WAS DEFECTIVE. IT HAD... UNPREDICTABLE RESULTS.
UNPREDICTABLE CAN BE ALARMING, DR. MUROID. OUR PRODUCTS NEED TO BE PERFECT BEFORE WE CAN MARKET THEM.
QUITE RIGHT, MISS LEONE.
IDIOT LOVEBIRD! HE'S HOOKED ON THE FOUL HALF-CAT! HER PAIN WILL BE THE KEY TO MY SUPREMACY.
I'LL TRAP HER. CAGE HER. CHAIN HER UP. SET MY RATS TO WORK ON HER. EYEBALLS FIRST! THEN HE'LL TELL ME EVERYTHING!
MISS LEONE, I'D LIKE TO SEE YOU IN MY OFFICE, LATER.

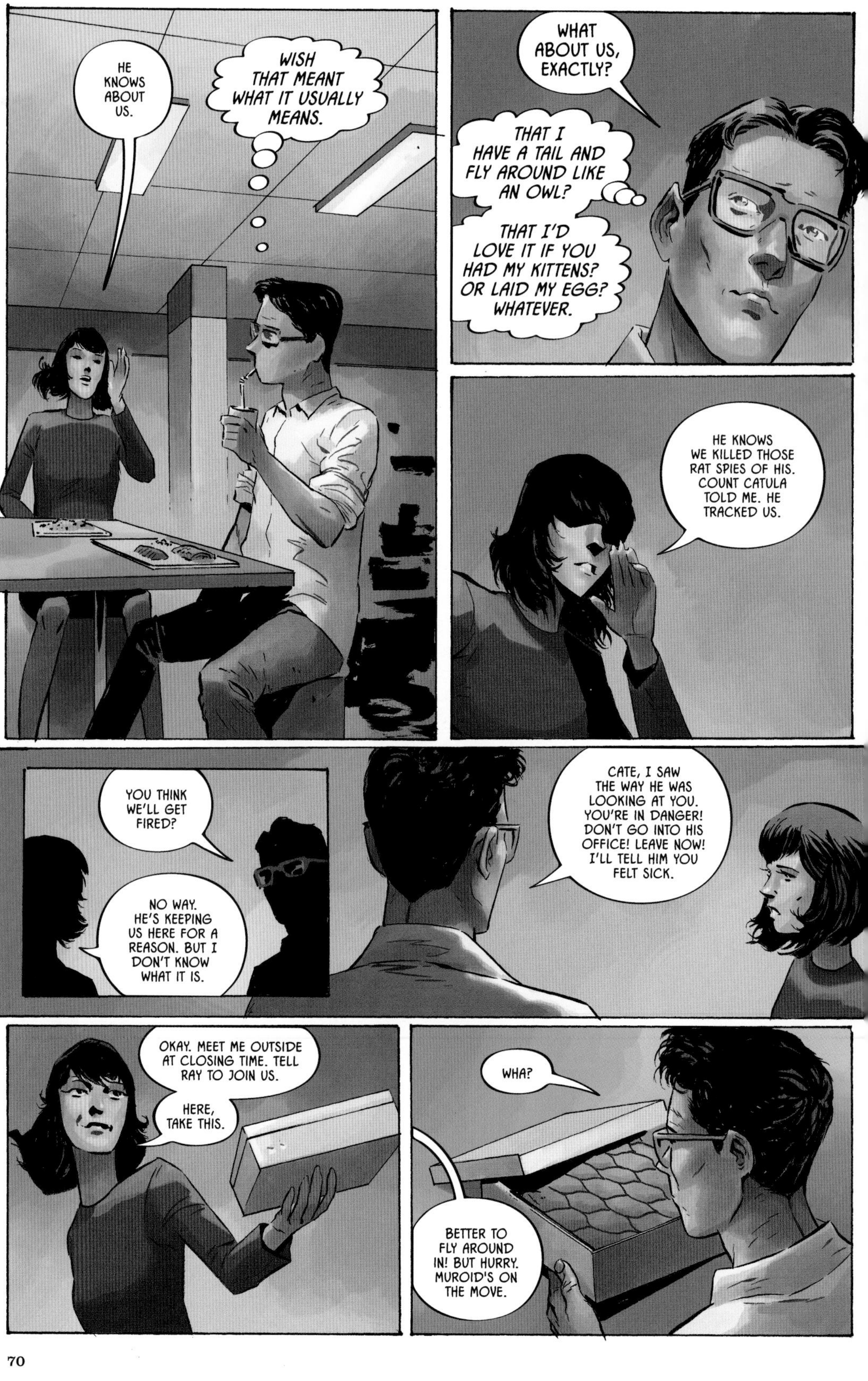
HE KNOWS ABOUT US.
WISH THAT MEANT WHAT IT USUALLY MEANS.
WHAT ABOUT US, EXACTLY?
THAT I HAVE A TAIL AND FLY AROUND LIKE AN OWL?
THAT I'D LOVE IT IF YOU HAD MY KITTENS? OR LAID MY EGG? WHATEVER.
HE KNOWS WE KILLED THOSE RAT SPIES OF HIS. COUNT CATULA TOLD ME. HE TRACKED US.
YOU THINK WE'LL GET FIRED?
NO WAY. HE'S KEEPING US HERE FOR A REASON. BUT I DON'T KNOW WHAT IT IS.
CATE, I SAW THE WAY HE WAS LOOKING AT YOU. YOU'RE IN DANGER! DON'T GO INTO HIS OFFICE! LEAVE NOW! I'LL TELL HIM YOU FELT SICK.
OKAY. MEET ME OUTSIDE AT CLOSING TIME. TELL RAY TO JOIN US.
HERE, TAKE THIS.
WHA?
BETTER TO FLY AROUND IN! BUT HURRY. MUROID'S ON THE MOVE.

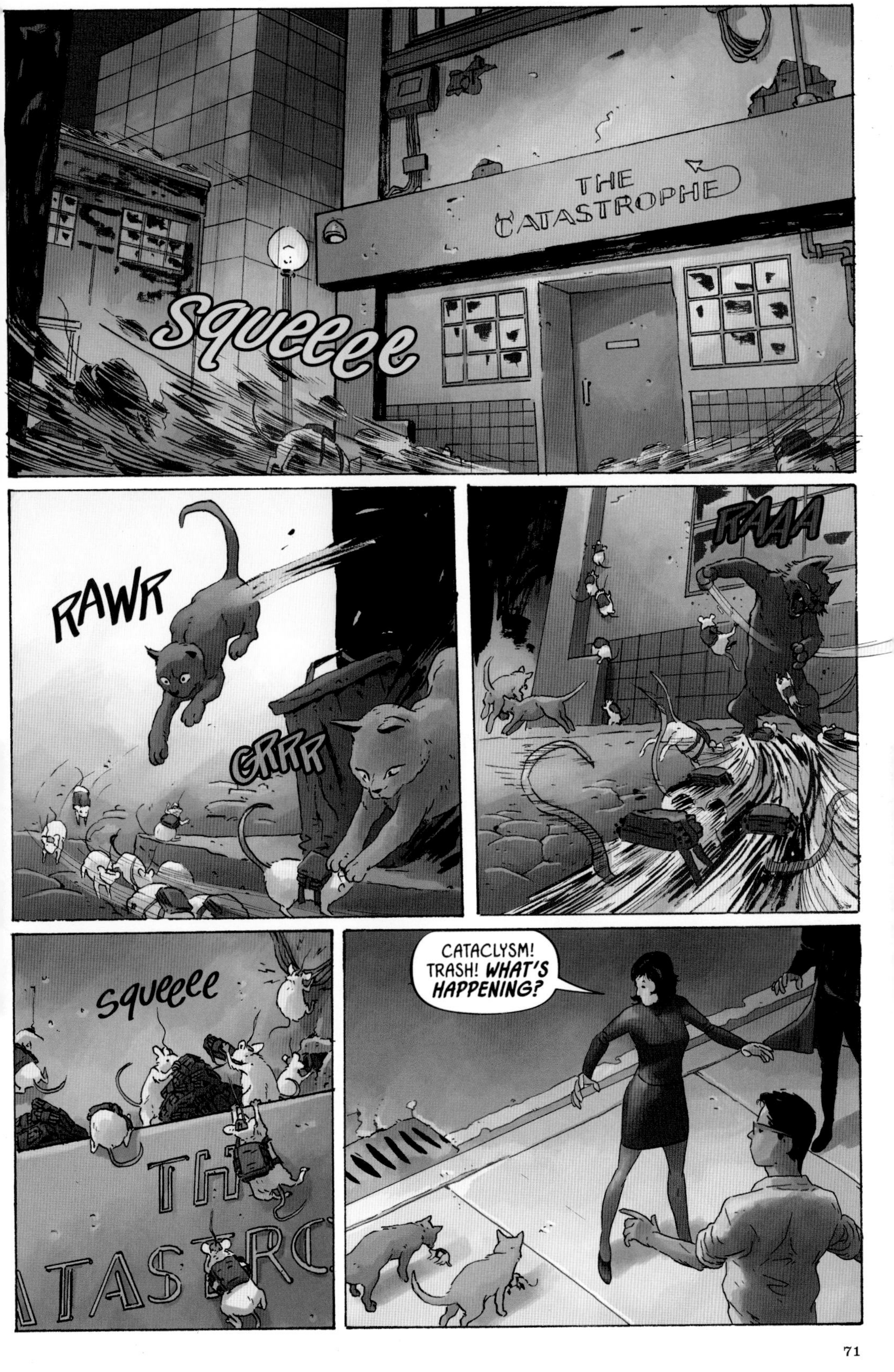
THE CATASTROPHE
Squeeee
RAWR
GRRR
RAAA
squeeee
CATACLYSM! TRASH! **WHAT'S HAPPENING?**

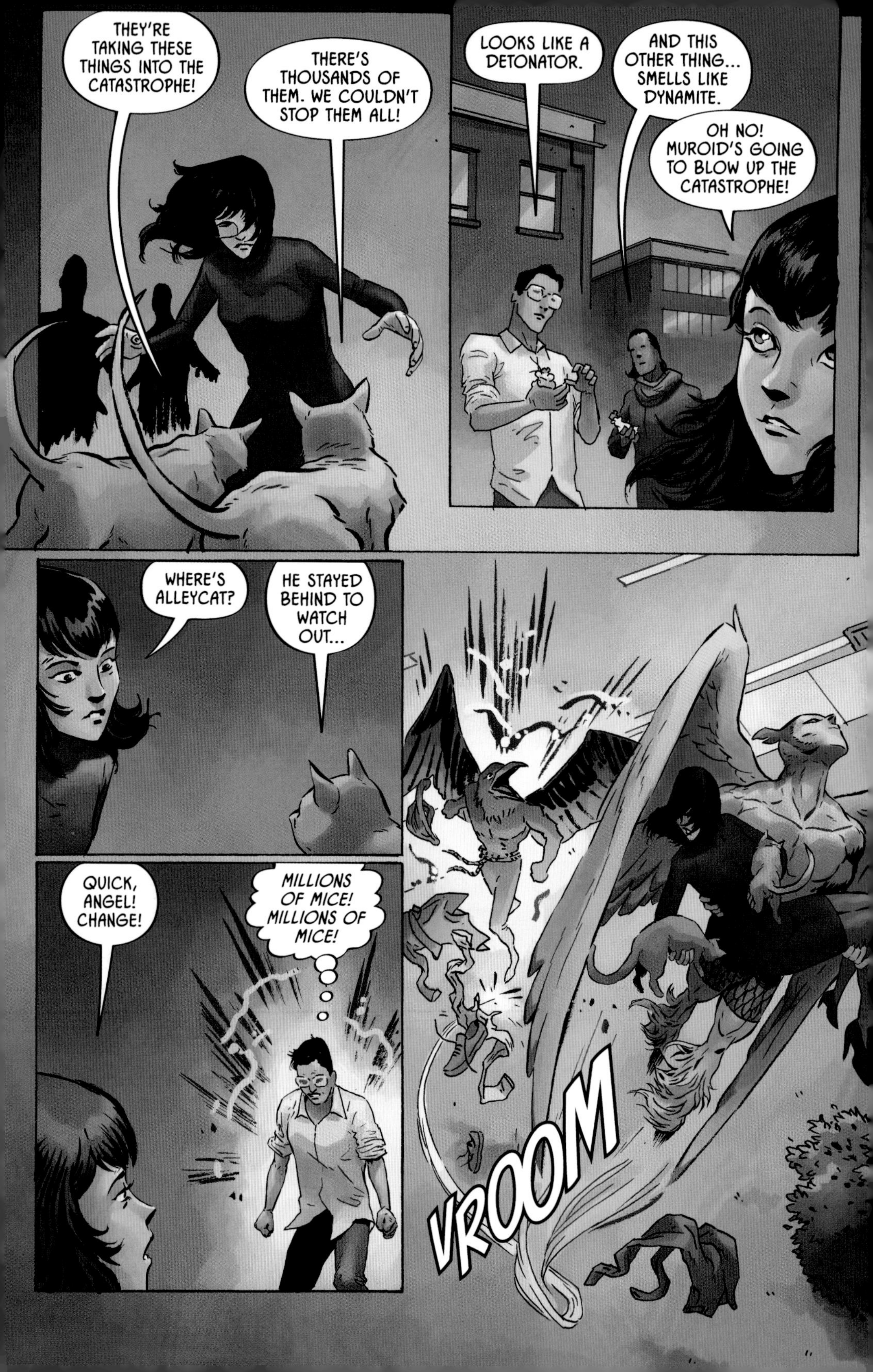
THEY'RE TAKING THESE THINGS INTO THE CATASTROPHE!
THERE'S THOUSANDS OF THEM. WE COULDN'T STOP THEM ALL!
LOOKS LIKE A DETONATOR.
AND THIS OTHER THING... SMELLS LIKE DYNAMITE.
OH NO! MUROID'S GOING TO BLOW UP THE CATASTROPHE!
WHERE'S ALLEYCAT?
HE STAYED BEHIND TO WATCH OUT...
QUICK, ANGEL! CHANGE!
MILLIONS OF MICE! MILLIONS OF MICE!
VROOM

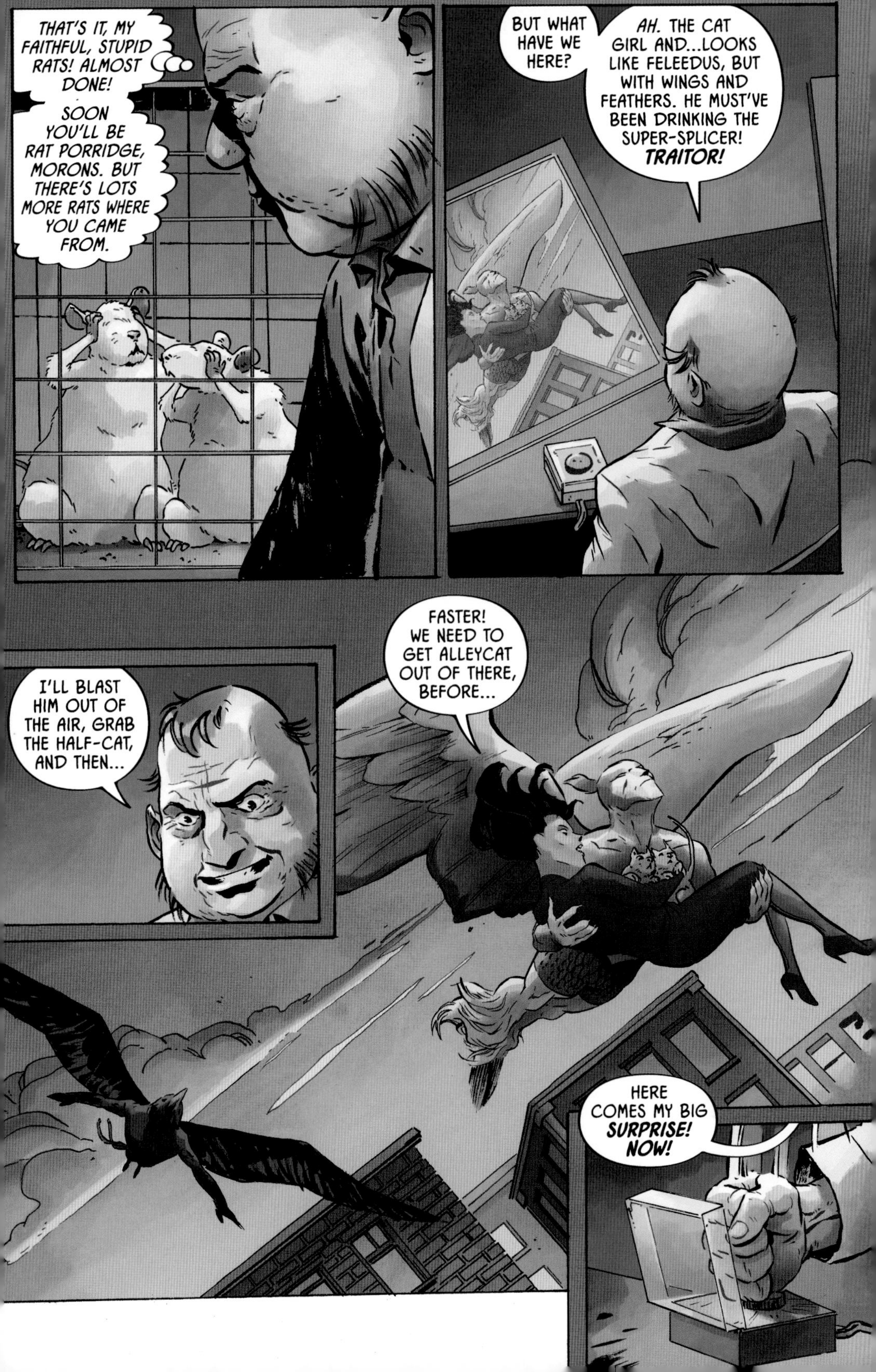
THAT'S IT, MY FAITHFUL, STUPID RATS! ALMOST DONE!
SOON YOU'LL BE RAT PORRIDGE, MORONS. BUT THERE'S LOTS MORE RATS WHERE YOU CAME FROM.
BUT WHAT HAVE WE HERE?
AH. THE CAT GIRL AND...LOOKS LIKE FELEEDUS, BUT WITH WINGS AND FEATHERS. HE MUST'VE BEEN DRINKING THE SUPER-SPLICER! TRAITOR!
I'LL BLAST HIM OUT OF THE AIR, GRAB THE HALF-CAT, AND THEN...
FASTER! WE NEED TO GET ALLEYCAT OUT OF THERE, BEFORE...
HERE COMES MY BIG SURPRISE! NOW!

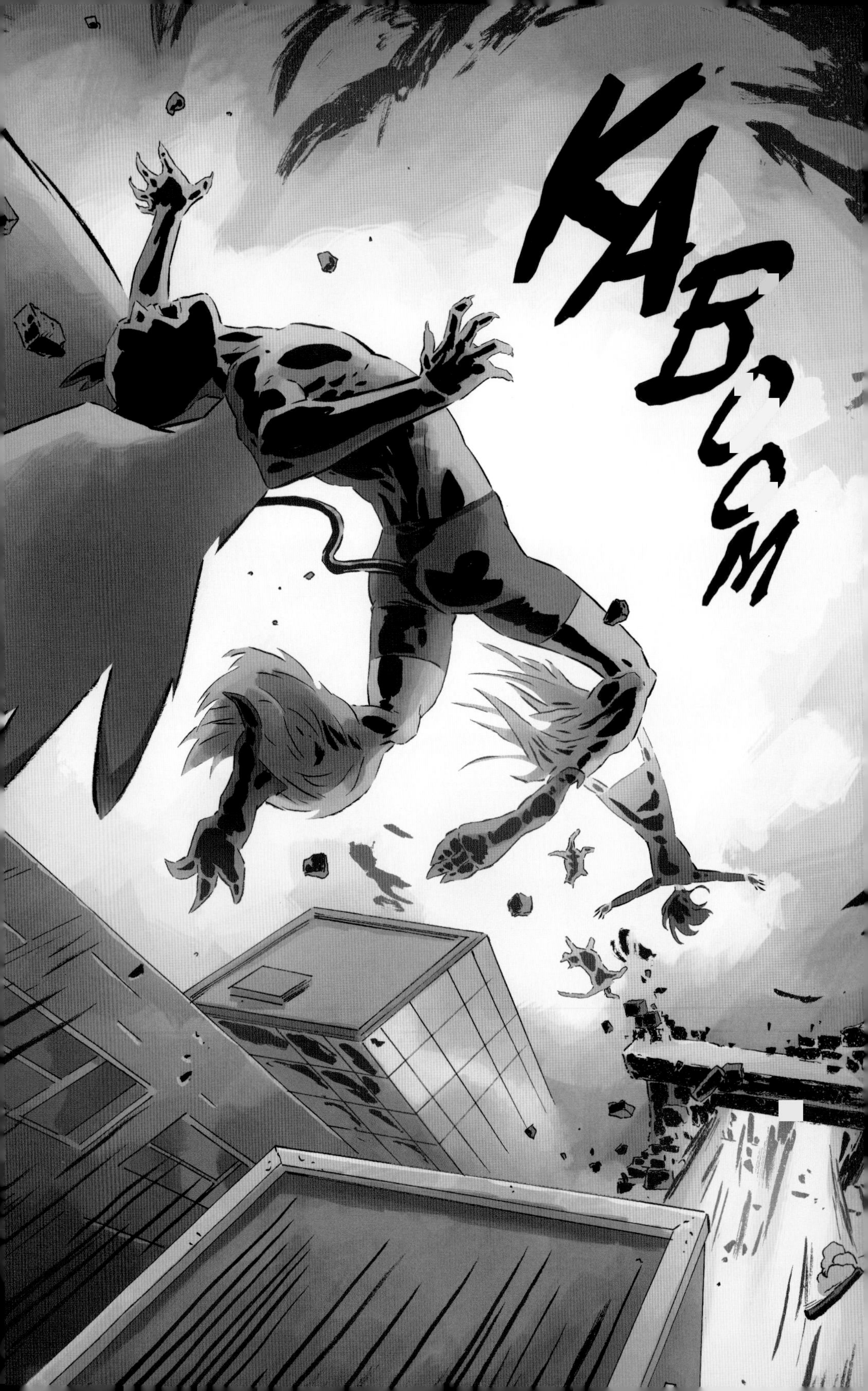
KABLOOM

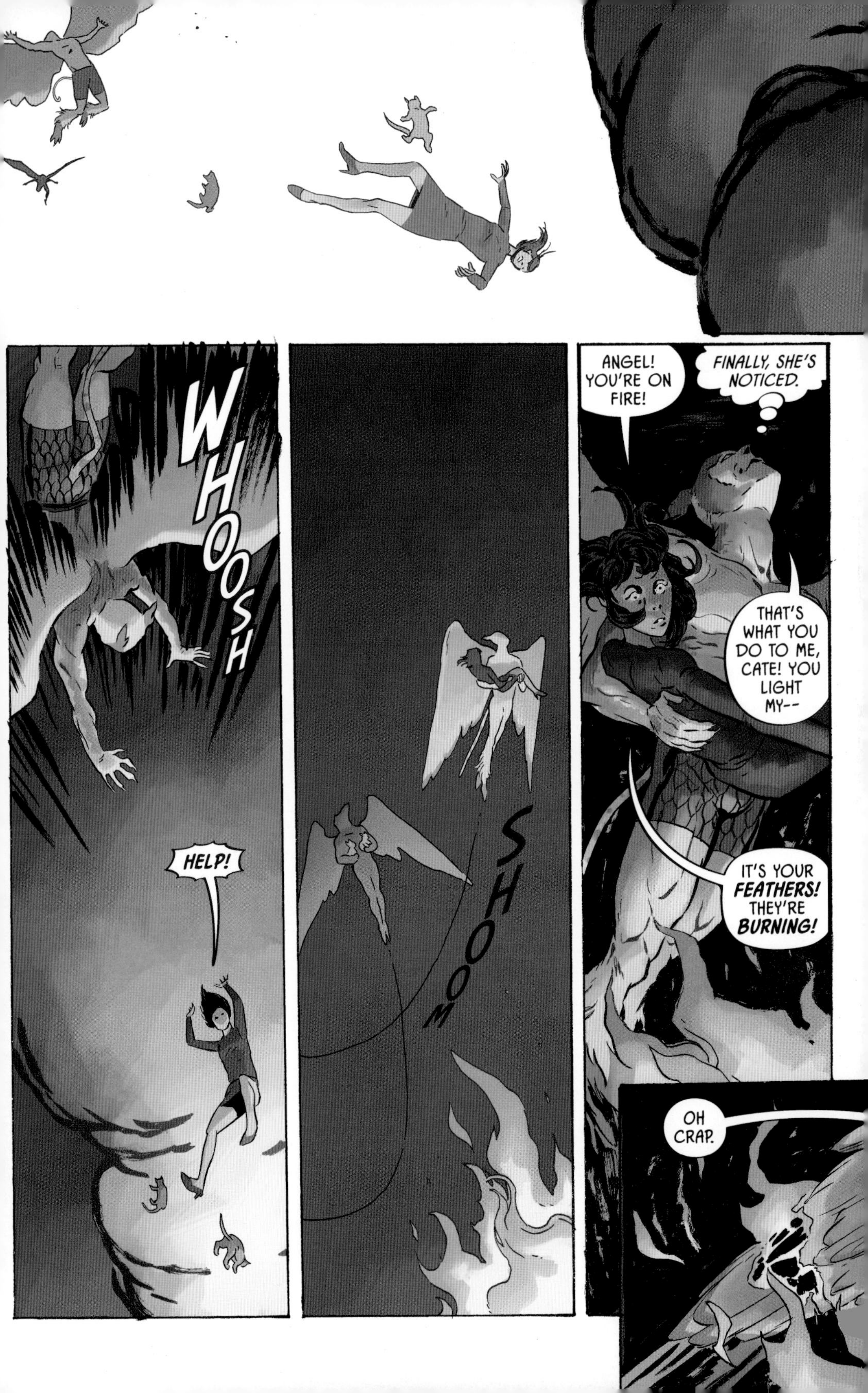
WHOOOSH
HELP!
SHOOOOM
ANGEL! YOU'RE ON FIRE!
FINALLY, SHE'S NOTICED.
THAT'S WHAT YOU DO TO ME, CATE! YOU LIGHT MY--
IT'S YOUR FEATHERS! THEY'RE BURNING!
OH CRAP.

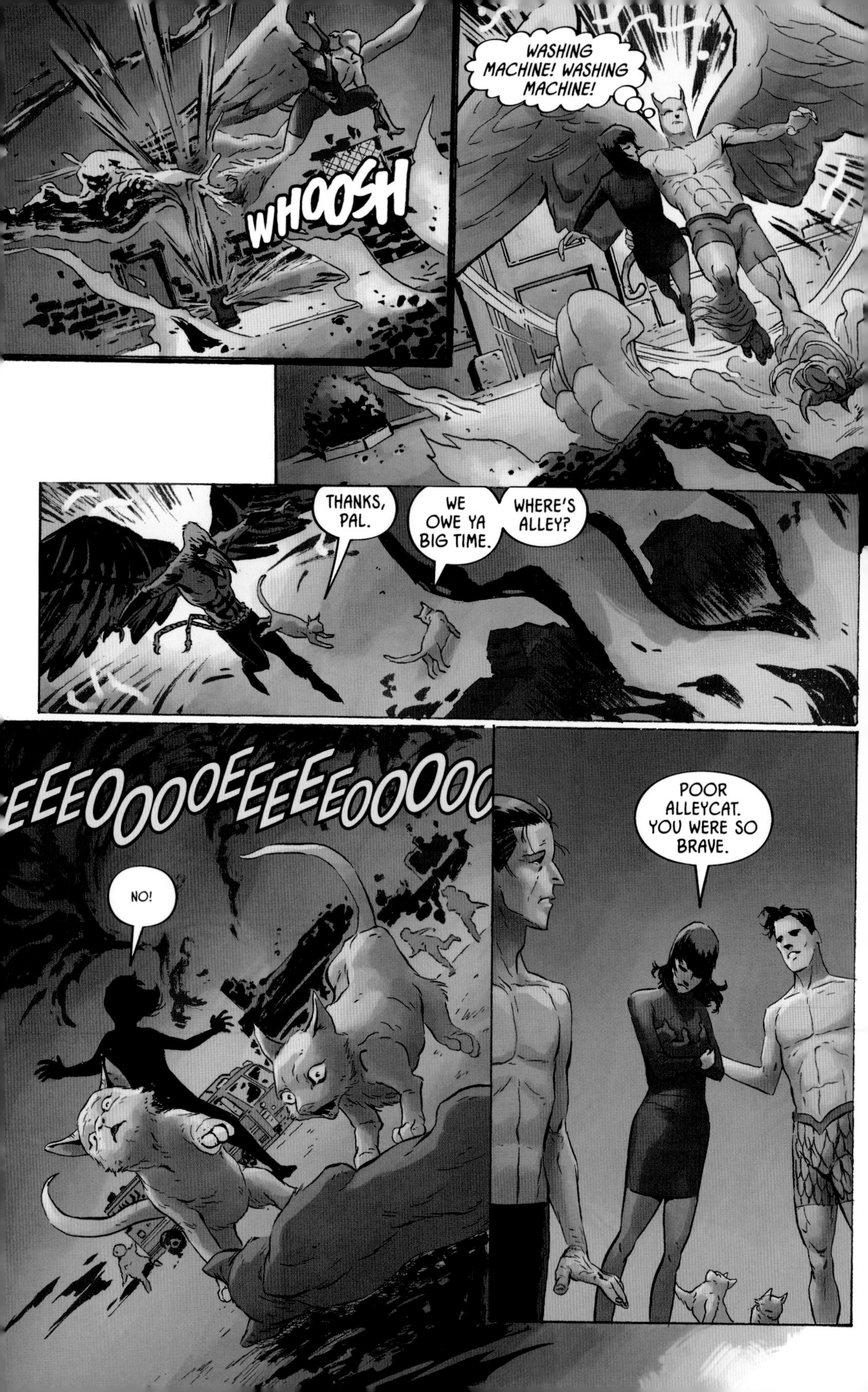
WHOOSH
WASHING MACHINE! WASHING MACHINE!
THANKS, PAL.
WE OWE YA BIG TIME.
WHERE'S ALLEY?
EEEOOOOEEEEEOOOOO
NO!
POOR ALLEYCAT. YOU WERE SO BRAVE.

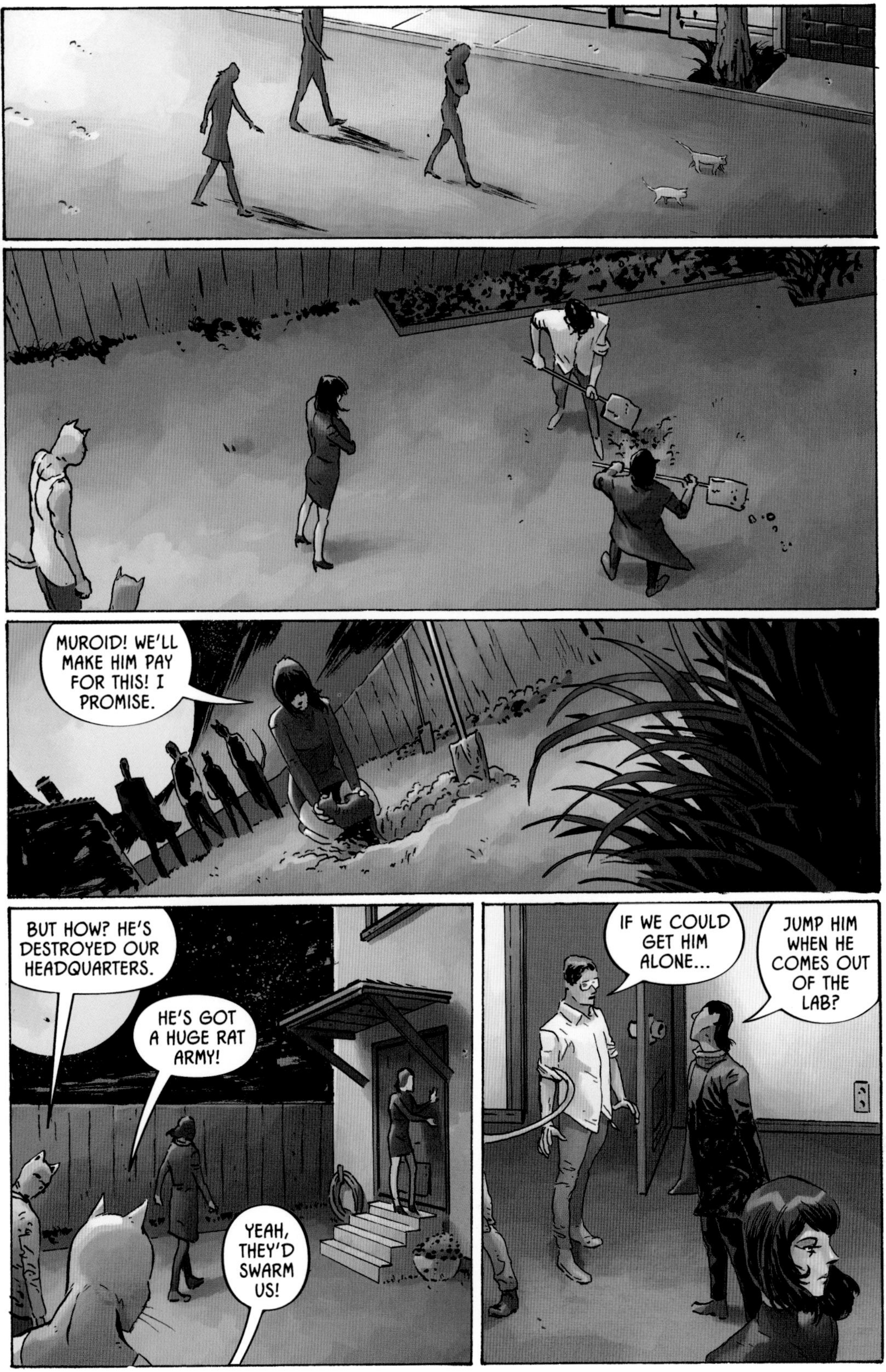
MUROID! WE'LL MAKE HIM PAY FOR THIS! I PROMISE.
BUT HOW? HE'S DESTROYED OUR HEADQUARTERS.
HE'S GOT A HUGE RAT ARMY!
YEAH, THEY'D SWARM US!
IF WE COULD GET HIM ALONE...
JUMP HIM WHEN HE COMES OUT OF THE LAB?

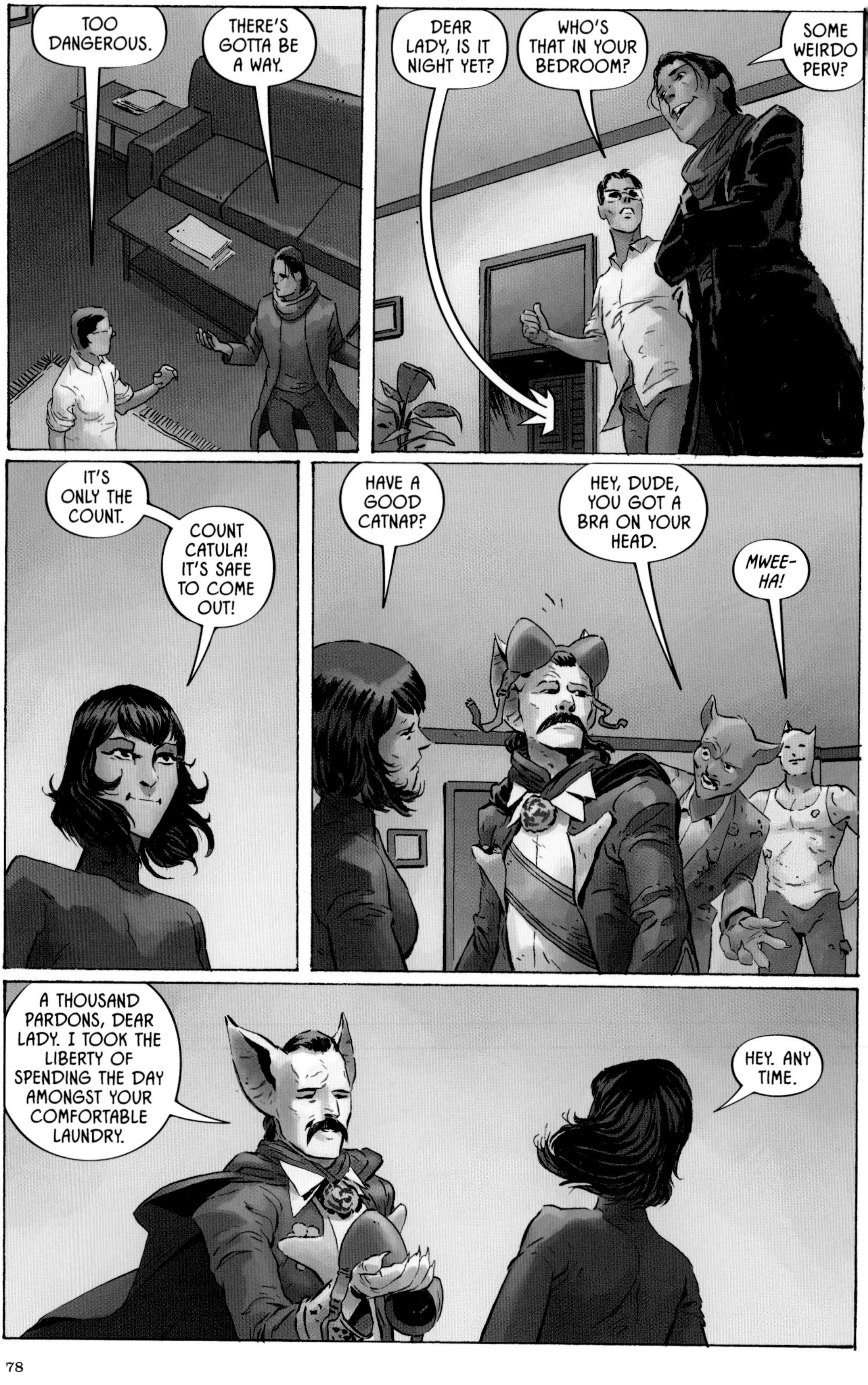
TOO DANGEROUS.
THERE'S GOTTA BE A WAY.
DEAR LADY, IS IT NIGHT YET?
WHO'S THAT IN YOUR BEDROOM?
SOME WEIRDO PERV?
IT'S ONLY THE COUNT.
COUNT CATULA! IT'S SAFE TO COME OUT!
HAVE A GOOD CATNAP?
HEY, DUDE, YOU GOT A BRA ON YOUR HEAD.
MWEE-HA!
A THOUSAND PARDONS, DEAR LADY. I TOOK THE LIBERTY OF SPENDING THE DAY AMONGST YOUR COMFORTABLE LAUNDRY.
HEY. ANY TIME.

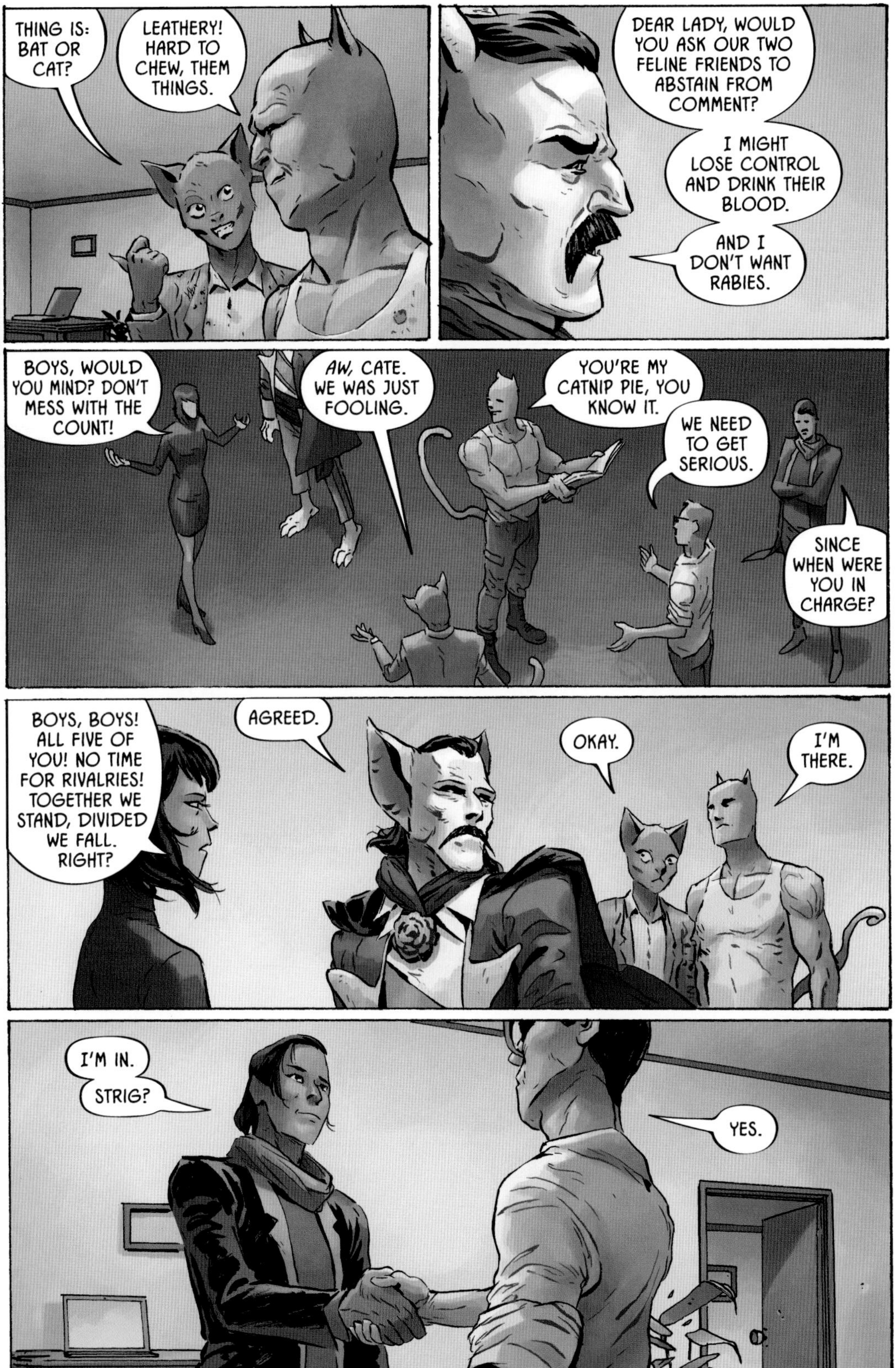
THING IS: BAT OR CAT?
LEATHERY! HARD TO CHEW, THEM THINGS.
DEAR LADY, WOULD YOU ASK OUR TWO FELINE FRIENDS TO ABSTAIN FROM COMMENT?
I MIGHT LOSE CONTROL AND DRINK THEIR BLOOD.
AND I DON'T WANT RABIES.
BOYS, WOULD YOU MIND? DON'T MESS WITH THE COUNT!
AW, CATE. WE WAS JUST FOOLING.
YOU'RE MY CATNIP PIE, YOU KNOW IT.
WE NEED TO GET SERIOUS.
SINCE WHEN WERE YOU IN CHARGE?
BOYS, BOYS! ALL FIVE OF YOU! NO TIME FOR RIVALRIES! TOGETHER WE STAND, DIVIDED WE FALL. RIGHT?
AGREED.
OKAY.
I'M THERE.
I'M IN.
STRIG?
YES.

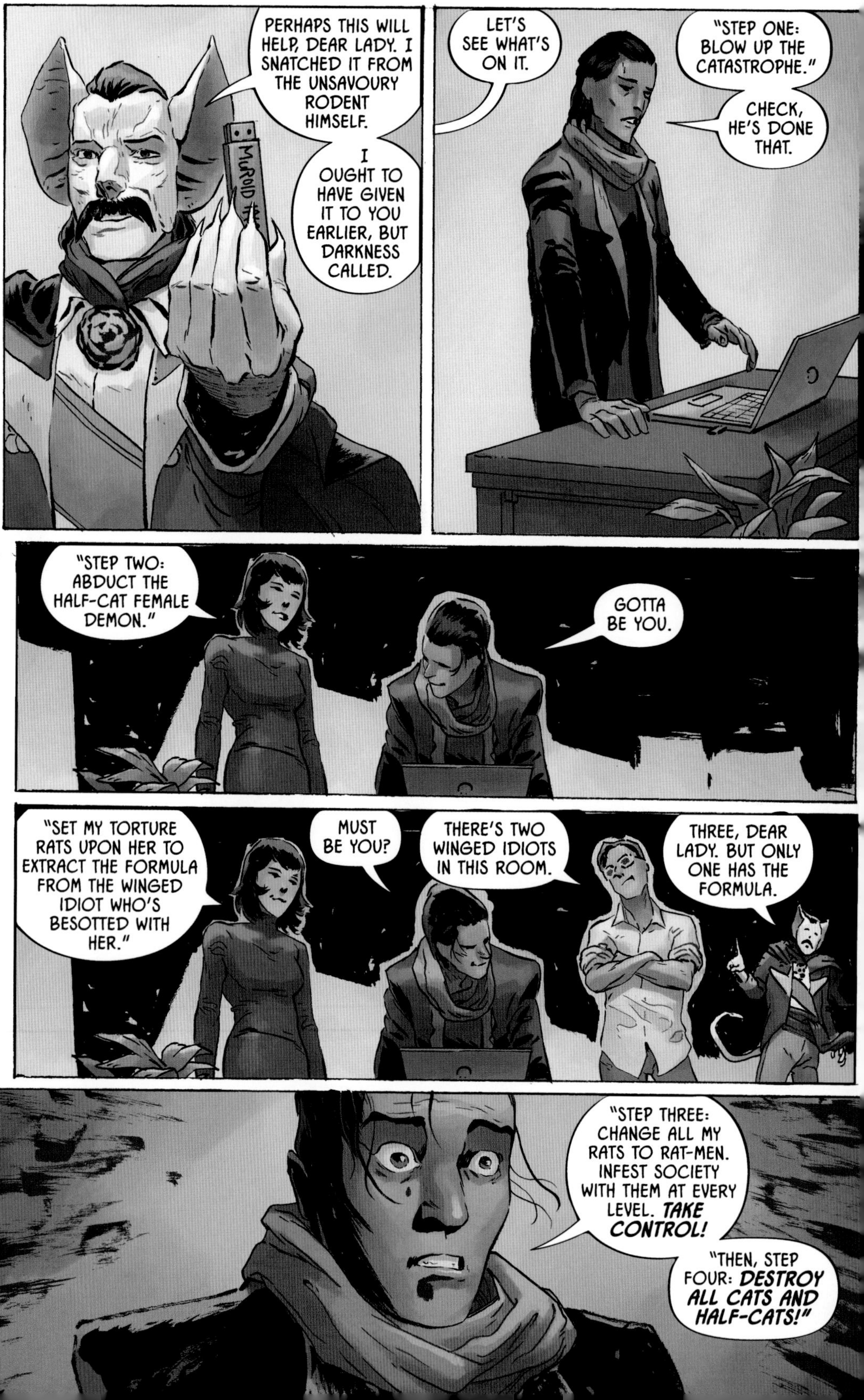
PERHAPS THIS WILL HELP, DEAR LADY. I SNATCHED IT FROM THE UNSAVOURY RODENT HIMSELF.
I OUGHT TO HAVE GIVEN IT TO YOU EARLIER, BUT DARKNESS CALLED.
LET'S SEE WHAT'S ON IT.
"STEP ONE: BLOW UP THE CATASTROPHE."
CHECK, HE'S DONE THAT.
"STEP TWO: ABDUCT THE HALF-CAT FEMALE DEMON."
GOTTA BE YOU.
"SET MY TORTURE RATS UPON HER TO EXTRACT THE FORMULA FROM THE WINGED IDIOT WHO'S BESOTTED WITH HER."
MUST BE YOU?
THERE'S TWO WINGED IDIOTS IN THIS ROOM.
THREE, DEAR LADY. BUT ONLY ONE HAS THE FORMULA.
"STEP THREE: CHANGE ALL MY RATS TO RAT-MEN. INFEST SOCIETY WITH THEM AT EVERY LEVEL. *TAKE CONTROL!*
"THEN, STEP FOUR: *DESTROY ALL CATS AND HALF-CATS!*"

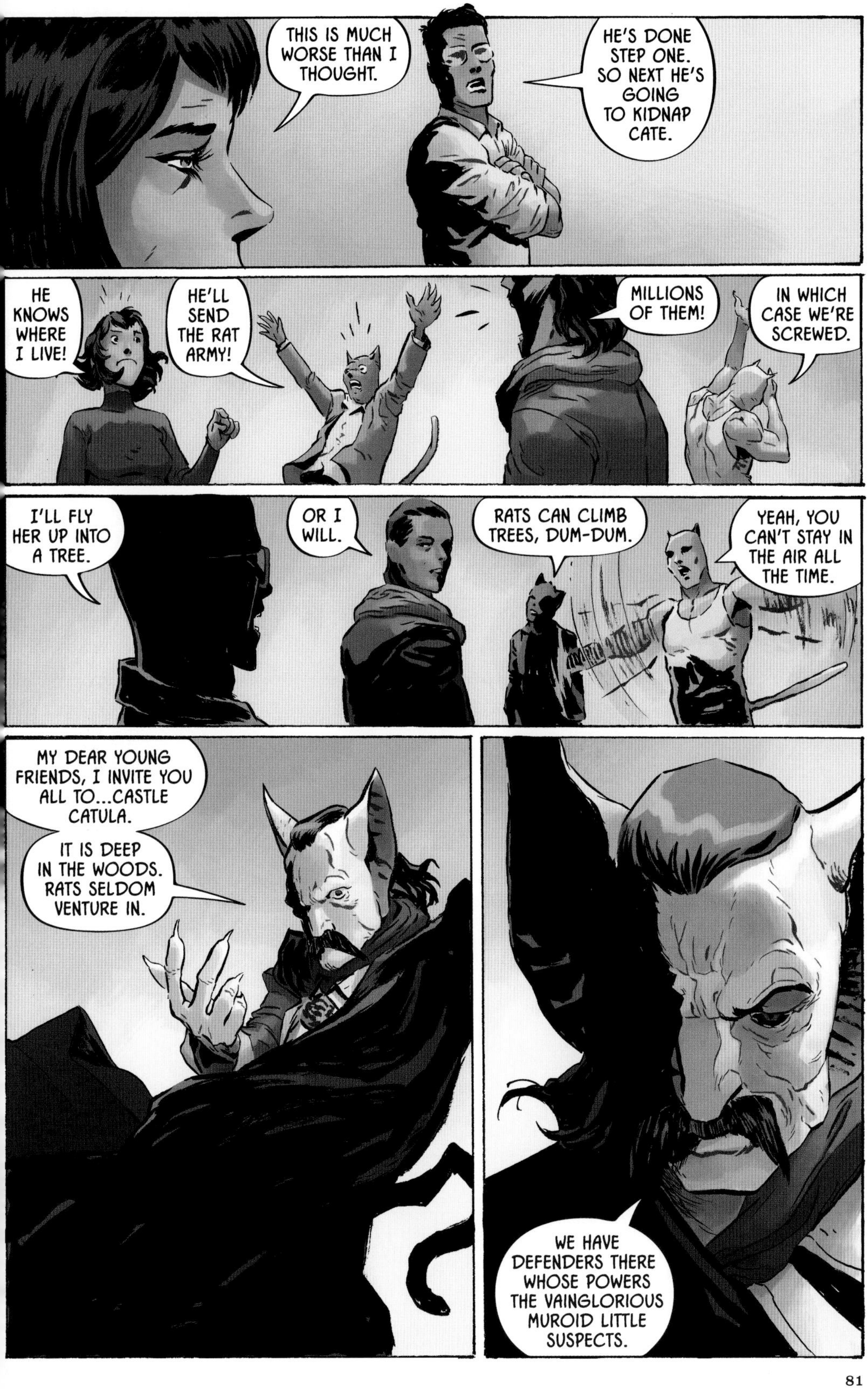

THIS IS MUCH WORSE THAN I THOUGHT.
HE'S DONE STEP ONE. SO NEXT HE'S GOING TO KIDNAP CATE.
HE KNOWS WHERE I LIVE!
HE'LL SEND THE RAT ARMY!
MILLIONS OF THEM!
IN WHICH CASE WE'RE SCREWED.
I'LL FLY HER UP INTO A TREE.
OR I WILL.
RATS CAN CLIMB TREES, DUM-DUM.
YEAH, YOU CAN'T STAY IN THE AIR ALL THE TIME.
MY DEAR YOUNG FRIENDS, I INVITE YOU ALL TO...CASTLE CATULA.
IT IS DEEP IN THE WOODS. RATS SELDOM VENTURE IN.
WE HAVE DEFENDERS THERE WHOSE POWERS THE VAINGLORIOUS MUROID LITTLE SUSPECTS.

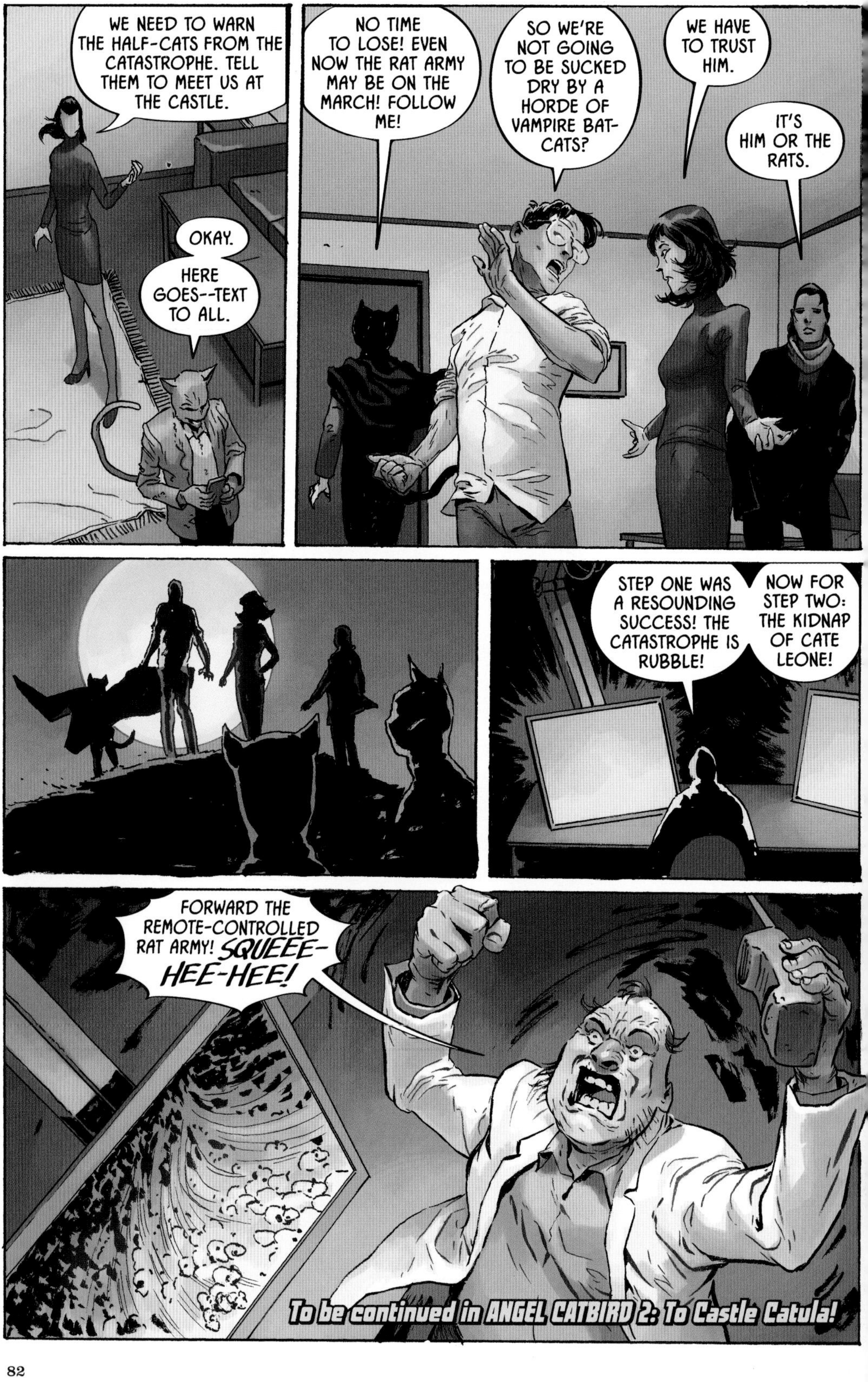
WE NEED TO WARN THE HALF-CATS FROM THE CATASTROPHE. TELL THEM TO MEET US AT THE CASTLE.
OKAY.
HERE GOES--TEXT TO ALL.
NO TIME TO LOSE! EVEN NOW THE RAT ARMY MAY BE ON THE MARCH! FOLLOW ME!
SO WE'RE NOT GOING TO BE SUCKED DRY BY A HORDE OF VAMPIRE BAT-CATS?
WE HAVE TO TRUST HIM.
IT'S HIM OR THE RATS.
STEP ONE WAS A RESOUNDING SUCCESS! THE CATASTROPHE IS RUBBLE!
NOW FOR STEP TWO: THE KIDNAP OF CATE LEONE!
FORWARD THE REMOTE-CONTROLLED RAT ARMY! SQUEEE-HEE-HEE!
To be continued in ANGEL CATBIRD 2: To Castle Catula!

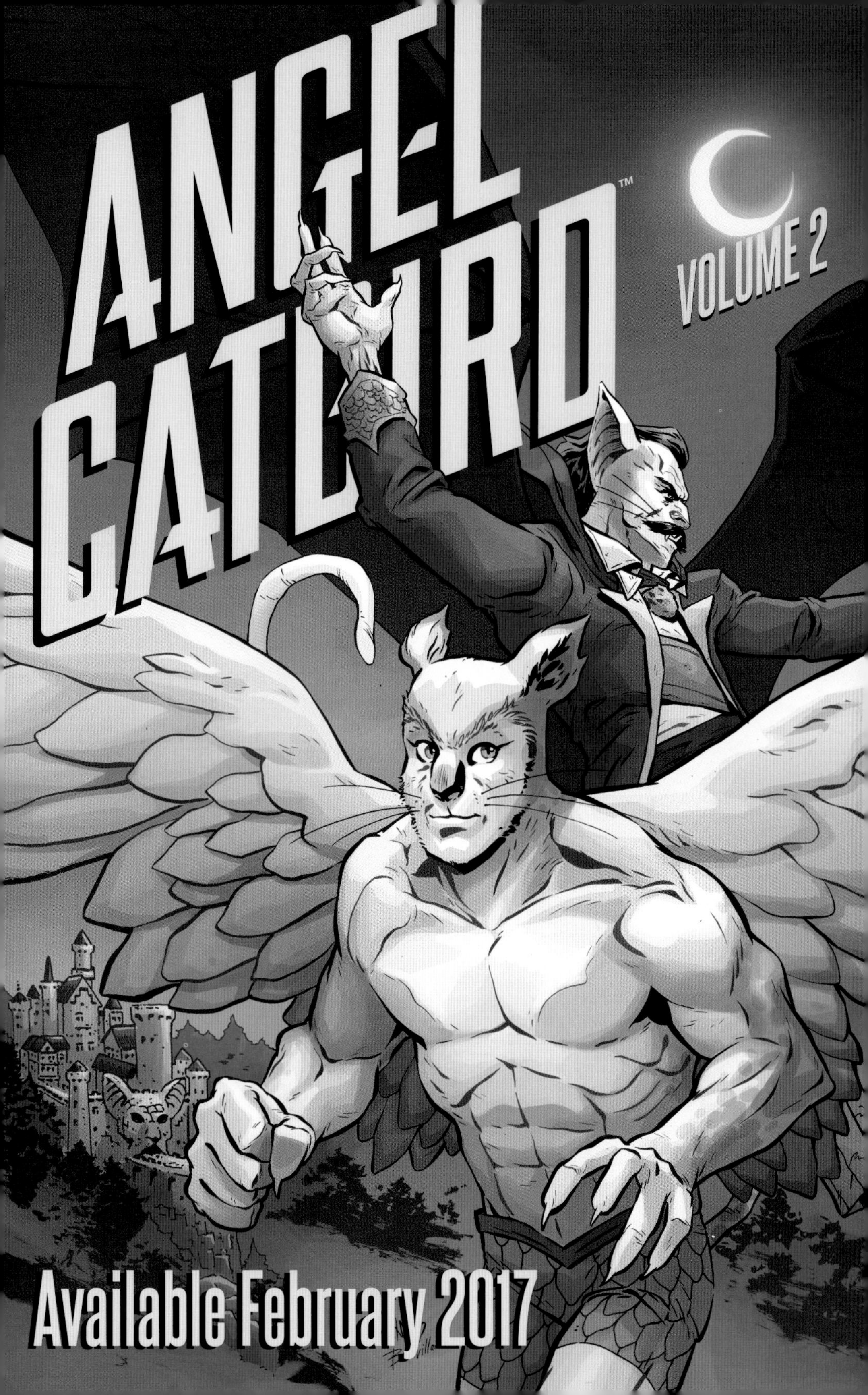
ANGEL CATBIRD™
VOLUME 2
Available February 2017

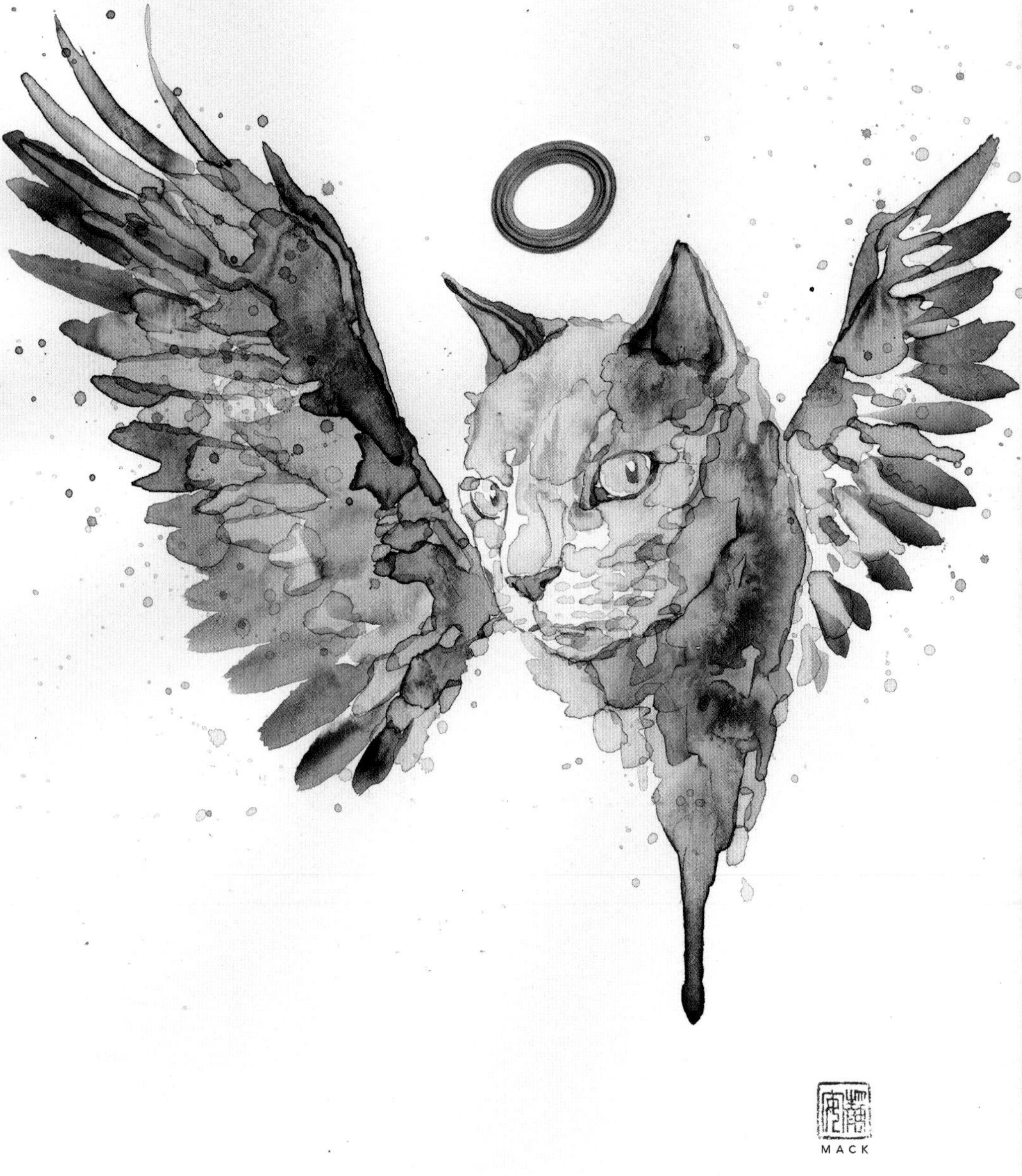
MACK

Art by
DAVID MACK

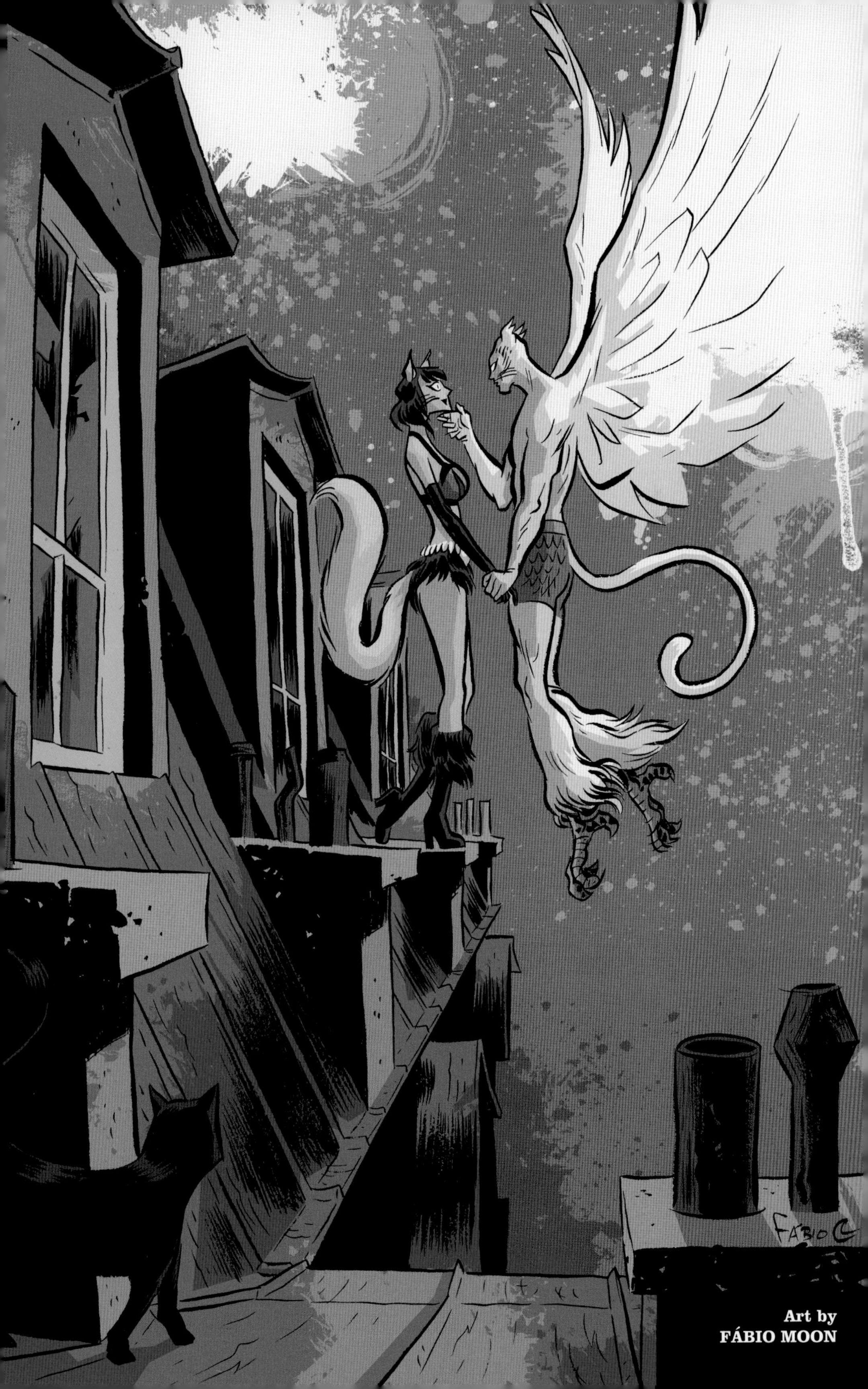

Art by
FÁBIO MOON

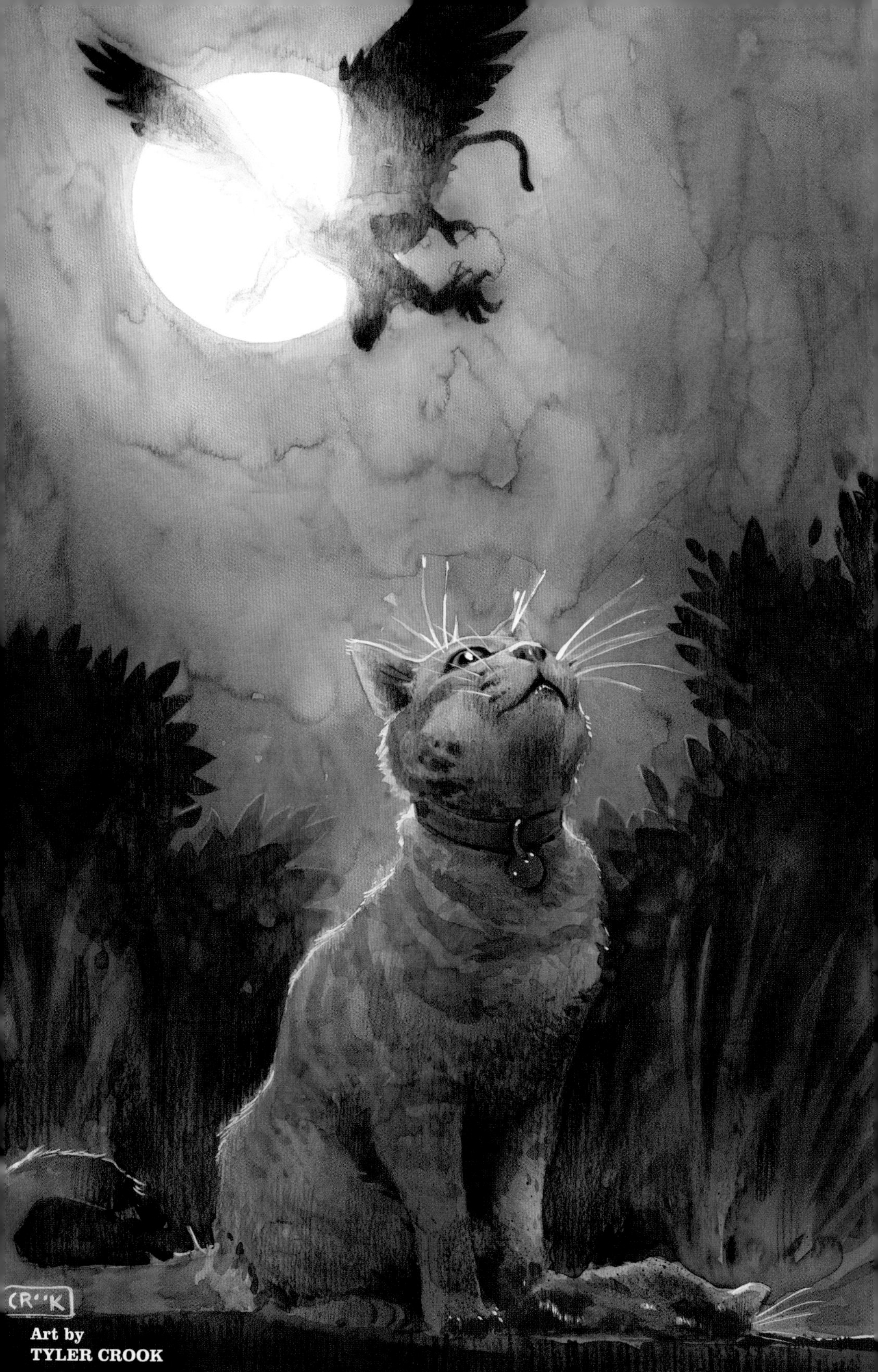
CROOK

Art by
TYLER CROOK

BEWARE! THE CLAWS OF ANGEL...
CAT-BIRD
WHO DARES CAGE THE ULTIMATE HYBRID OF CAT AND BIRD!?
Art by
MATT KINDT

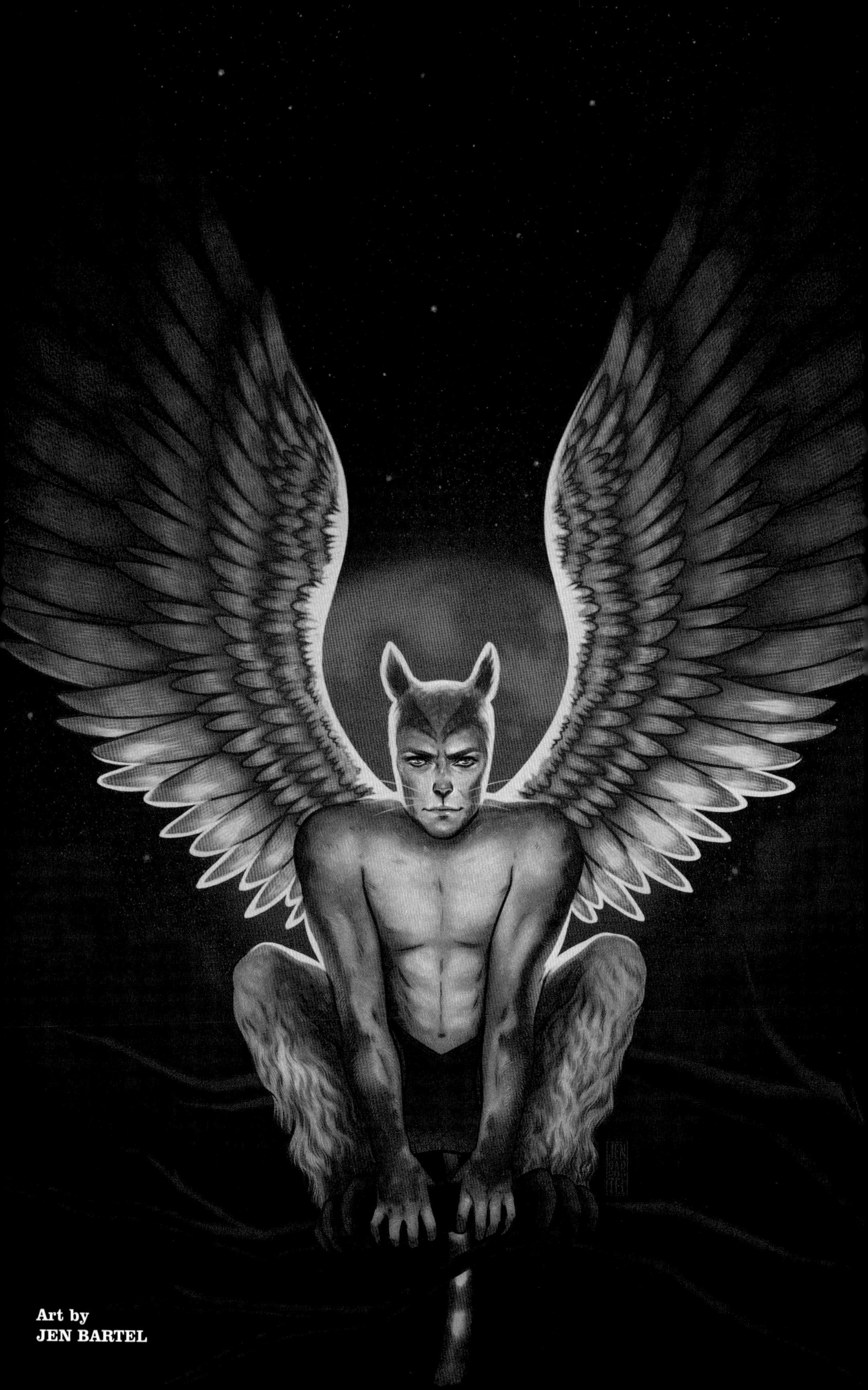

Art by
JEN BARTEL

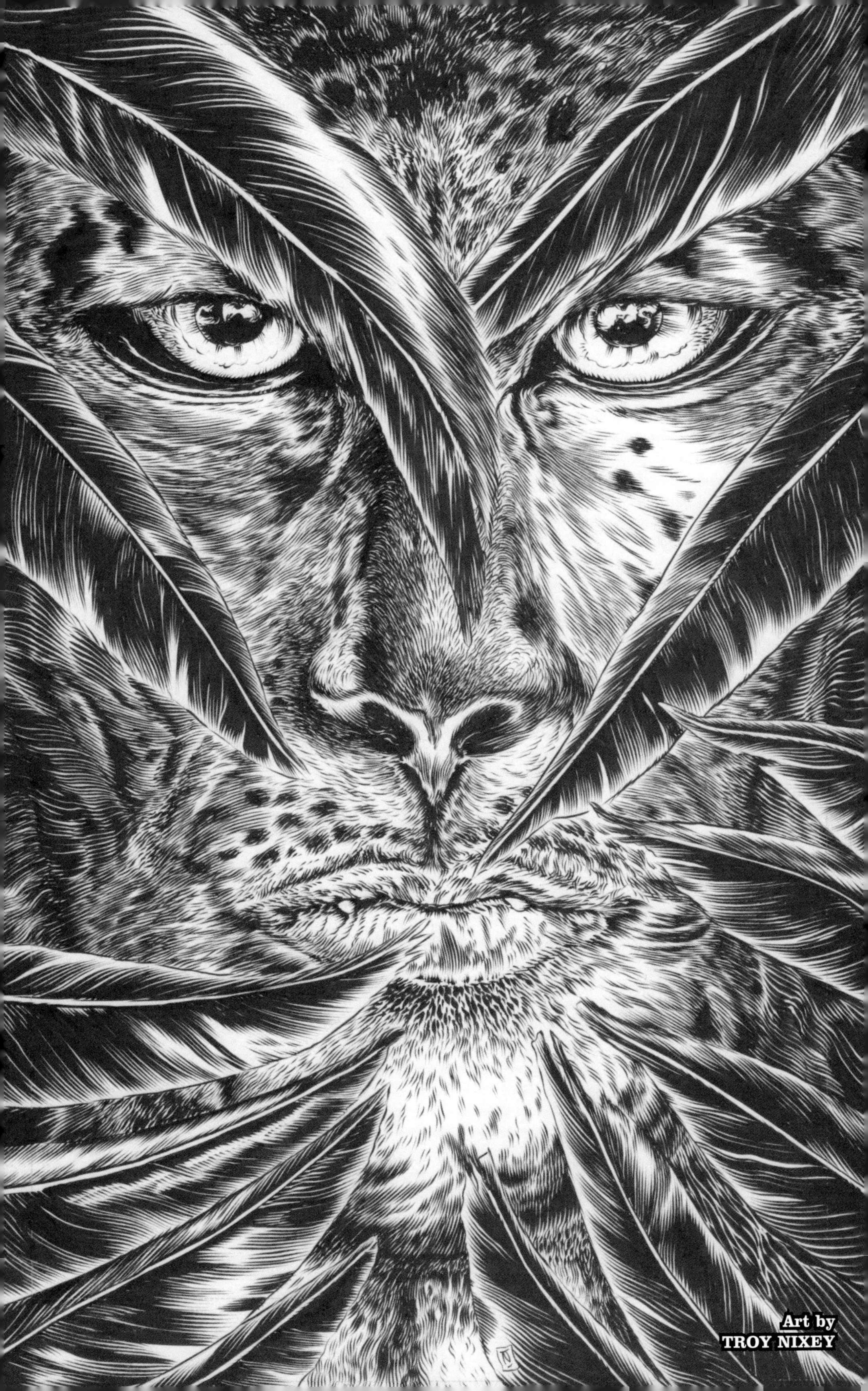

Art by
TROY NIXEY

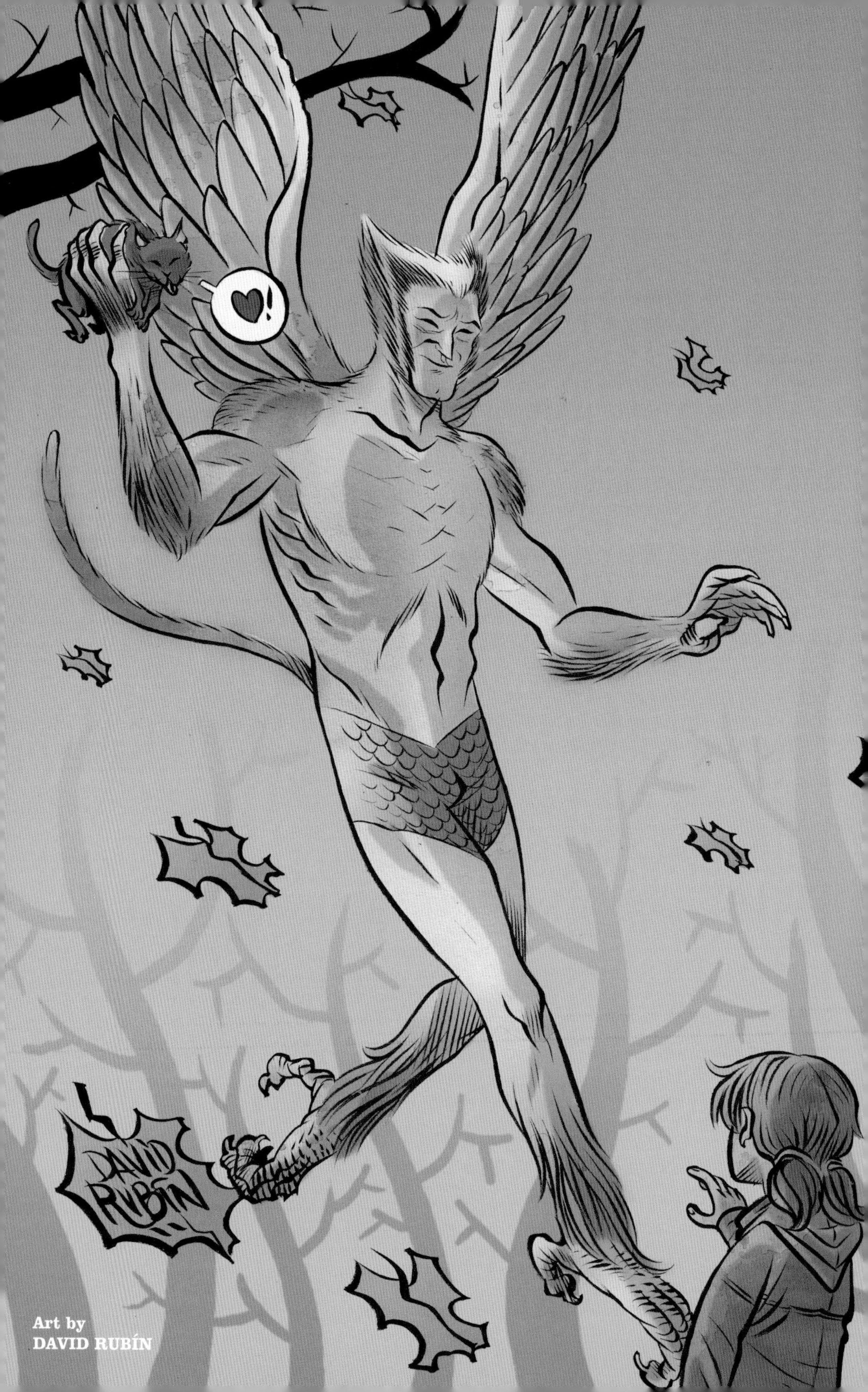
DAVID RUBÍN

Art by
DAVID RUBÍN

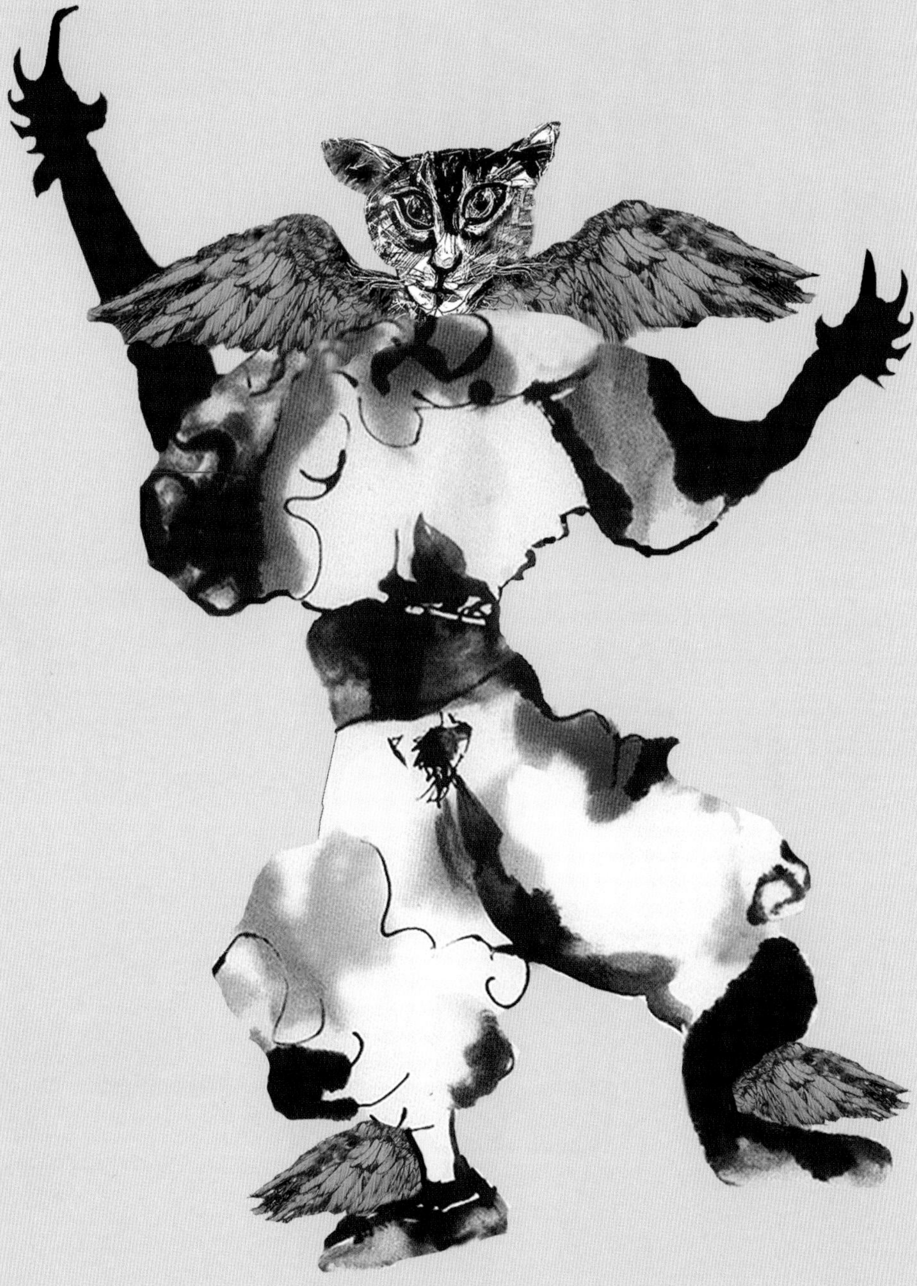

Art by
CHARLIE PACHTER

ANGEL CATBIRD

SKETCHBOOK

Notes by
Johnnie Christmas

STRIG
(HUMAN FORM)

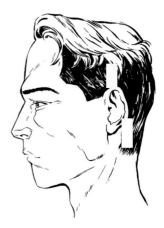

STRIG W/ GLASSES

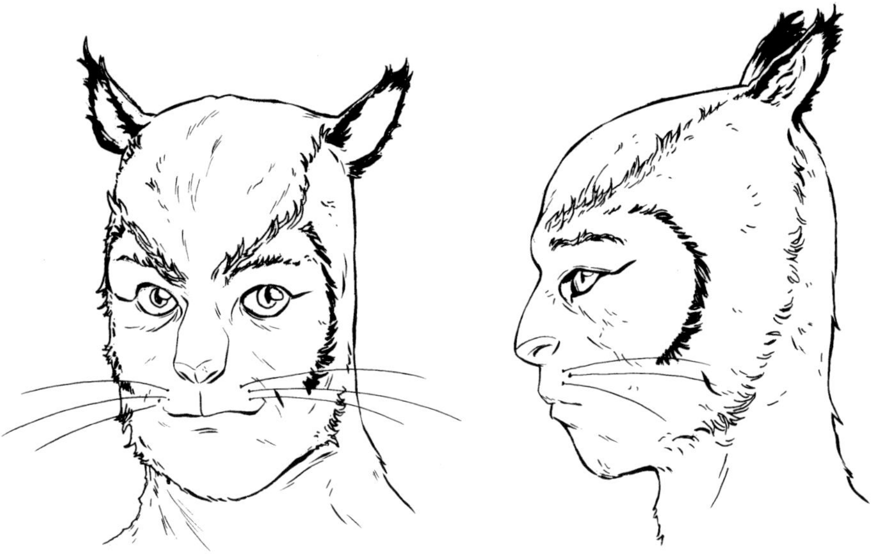

ANGEL CATBIRD

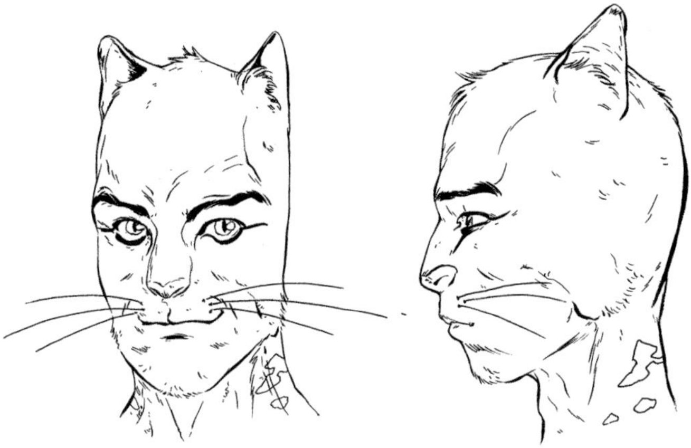

The first passes at Angel Catbird's head were too "cat" and needed a bit more "bird."

ANGEL CATBIRD (HAIR VERSION)

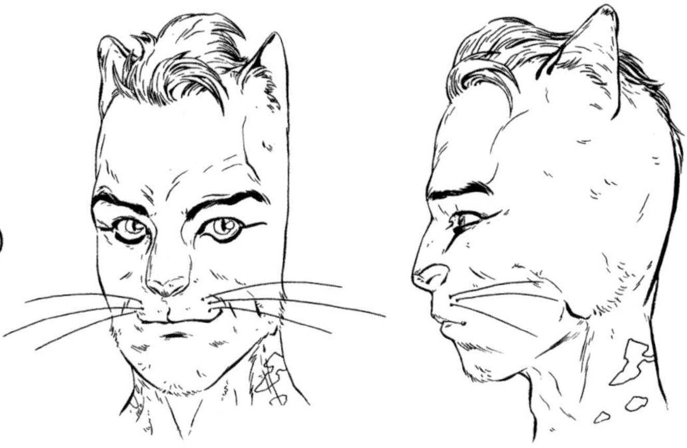

I sort of like the look of Angel Catbird with a coif. But ultimately the streamlined look without human hair works best.

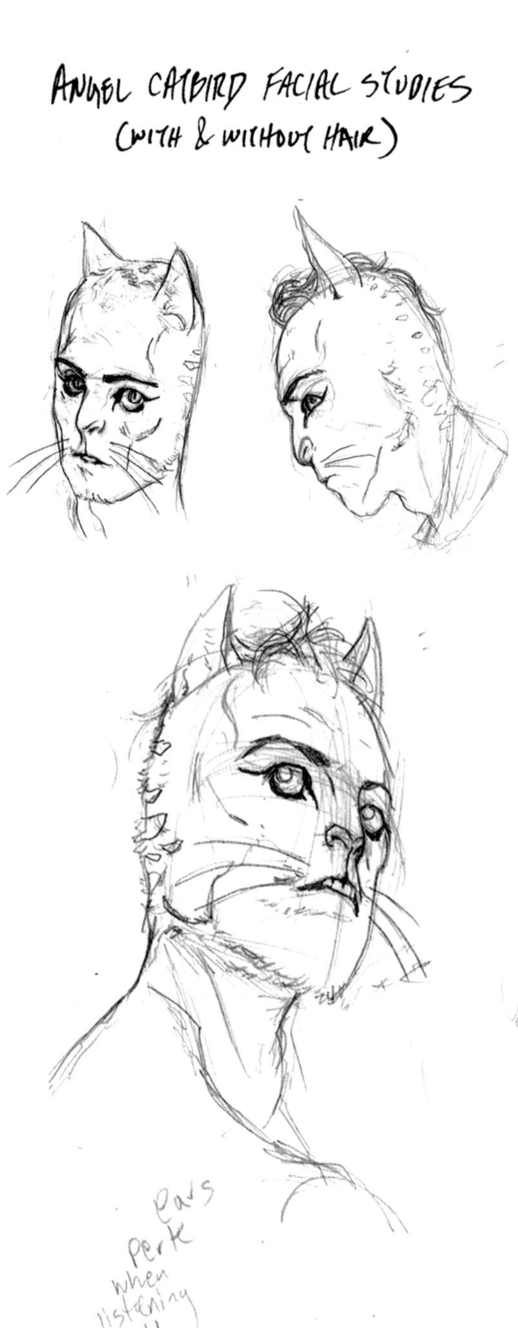
ANGEL CATBIRD FACIAL STUDIES
(WITH & WITHOUT HAIR)
ears perk when listening intently

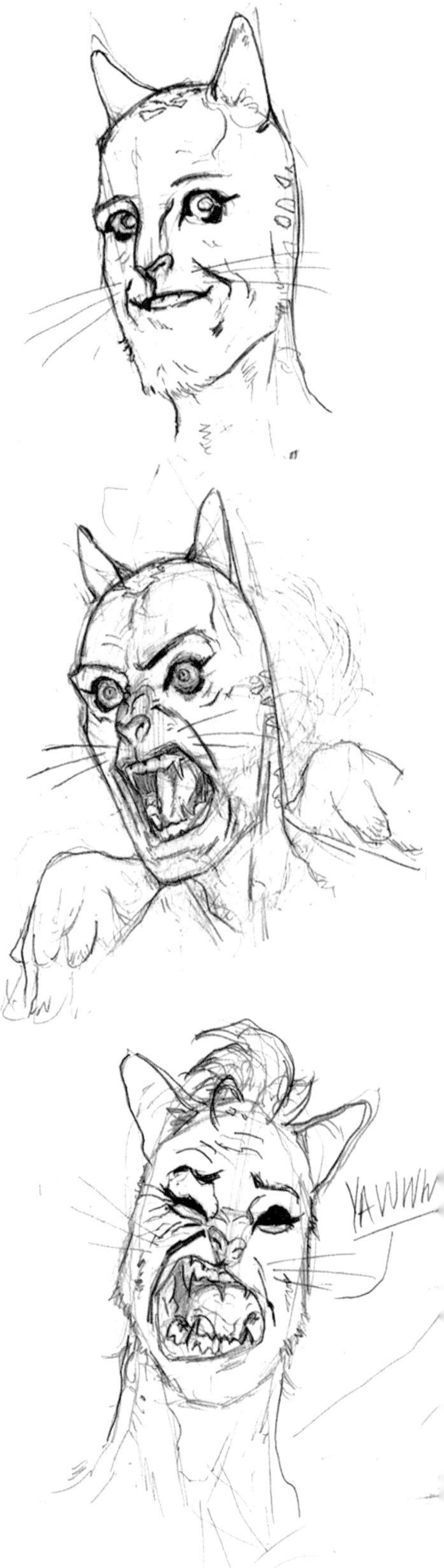
YAWWN

Here are some more very cat-like visuals of
Angel Catbird with different facial expressions.

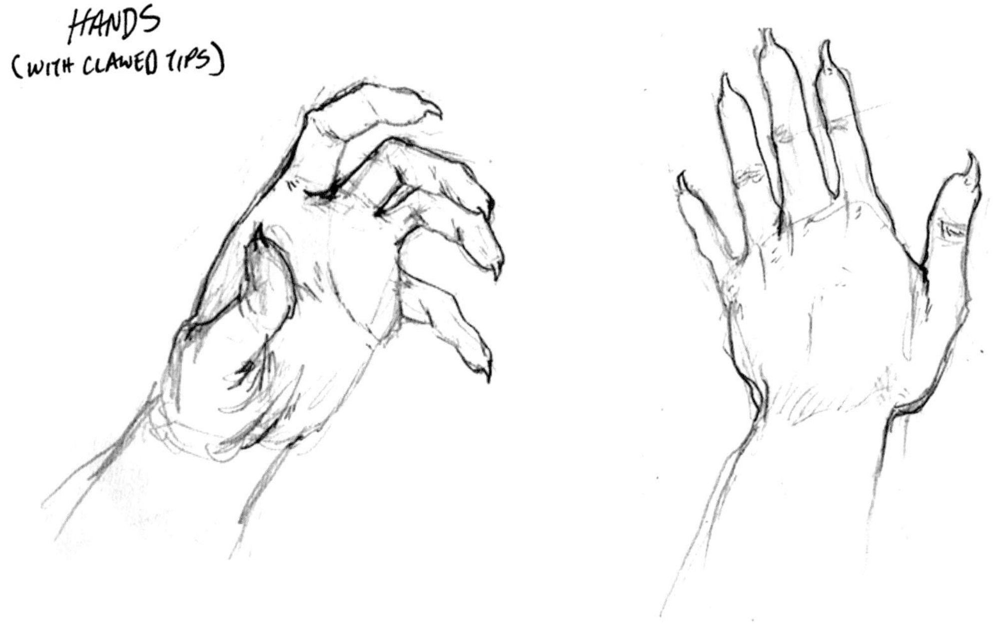
HANDS
(WITH CLAWED TIPS)

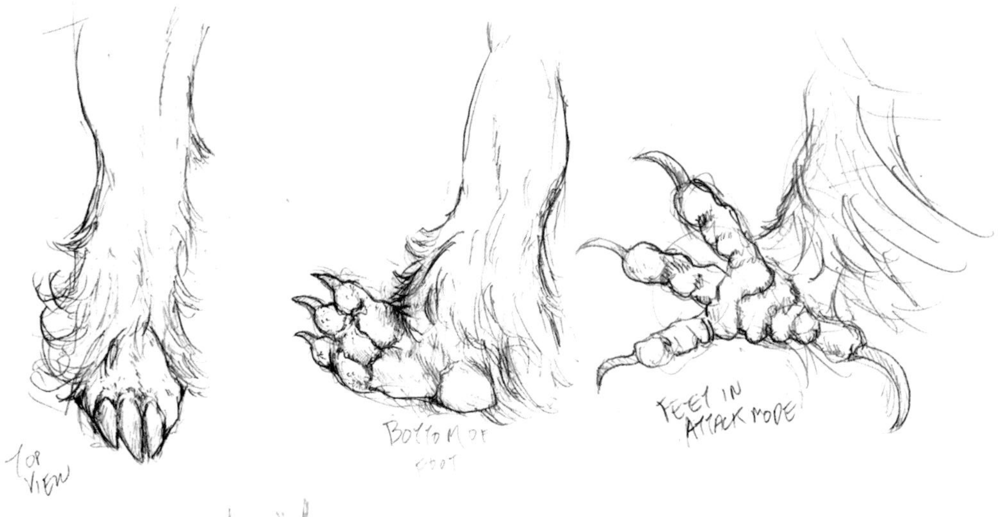
TOP VIEW
BOTTOM OF FOOT
FEET IN ATTACK MODE

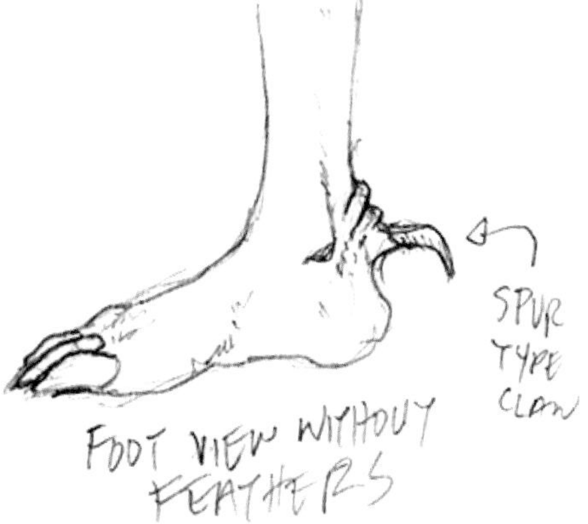
SPUR TYPE CLAW
FOOT VIEW WITHOUT FEATHERS

I wanted Angel Catbird's feet to have a friendlier aspect when he's strolling around. I like the contrast between that and the fierce appearance of his talons when he attacks.

WINGS

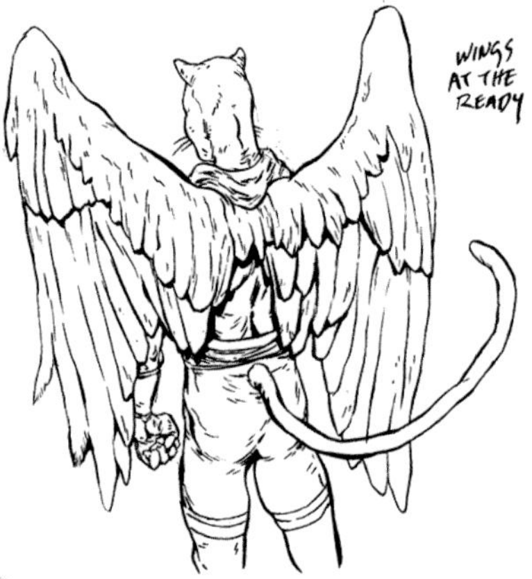
WINGS
AT THE
READY

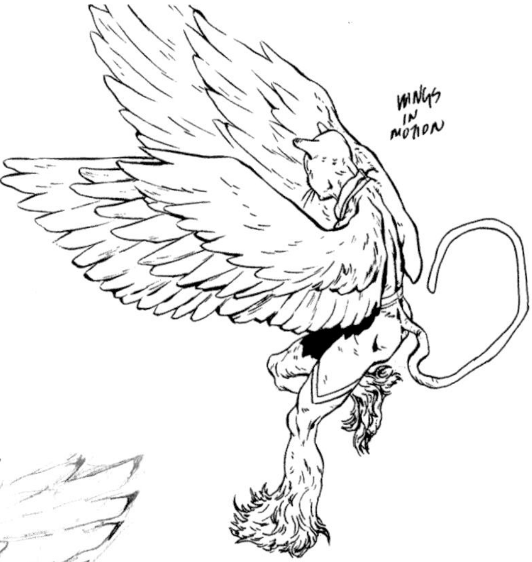
WINGS
IN
MOTION

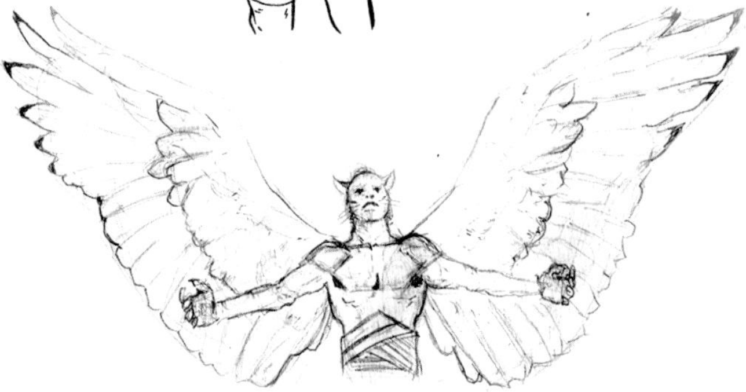

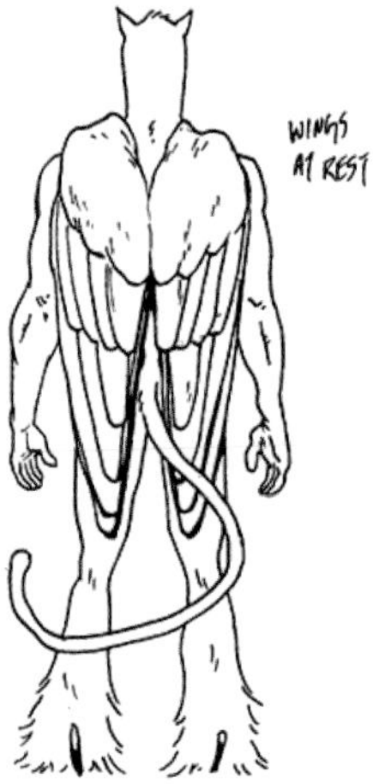
WINGS
AT REST

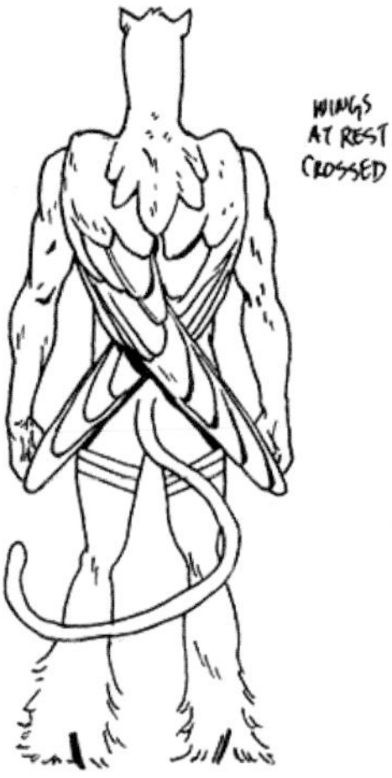
WINGS
AT REST
CROSSED

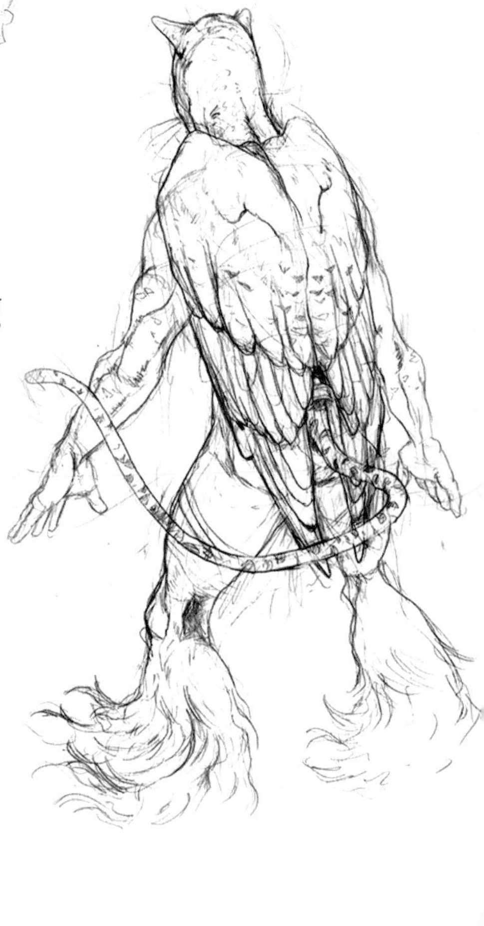

I love drawing Angel's wings.

ANGEL CATBIRD COSTUME OPTIONS

COMBINATION

FIGHTER

AERODYNAMIC SUPERHERO

INUIT INSPIRED

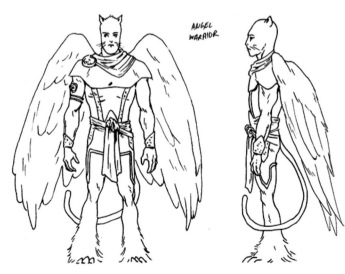
ANGEL WARRIOR

At the beginning of our talks about Angel Catbird I wasn't sure of the specific threats he might encounter. So I wanted to give Margaret lots of costume options.

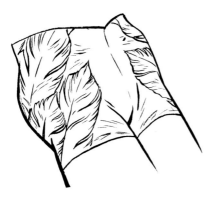
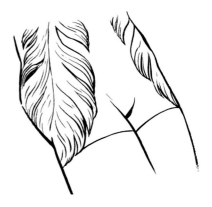
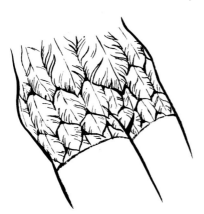
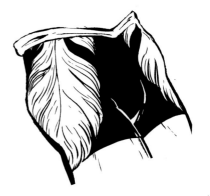
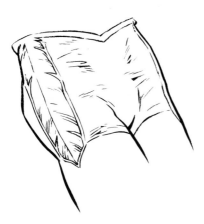
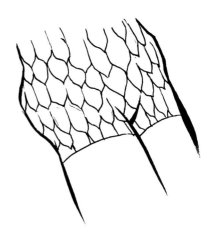

After we settled on him wearing shorts, there were more options still.
The clothes make the owl-cat-man.

SNOWY OWL PATTERN
WITH THE COLOUR OF AN ORANGE TABBY CAT

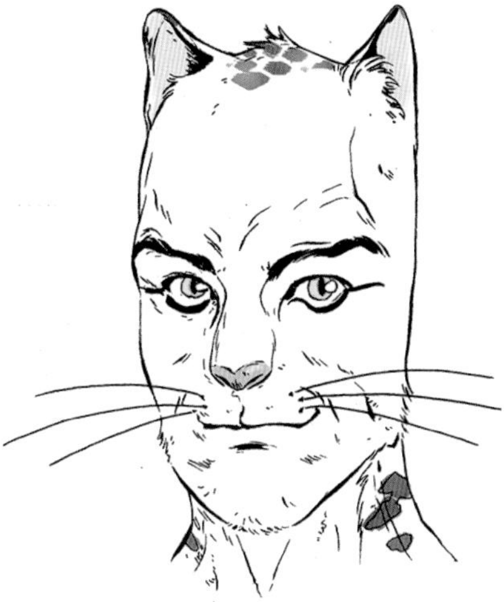

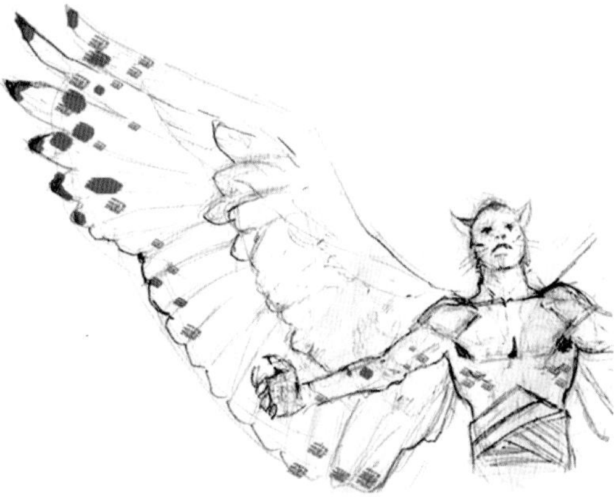

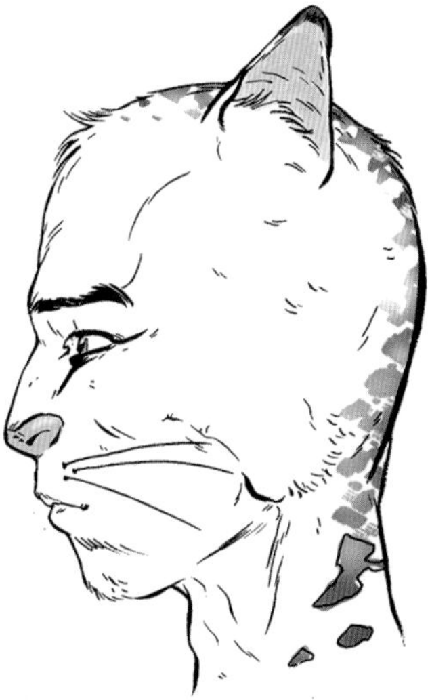

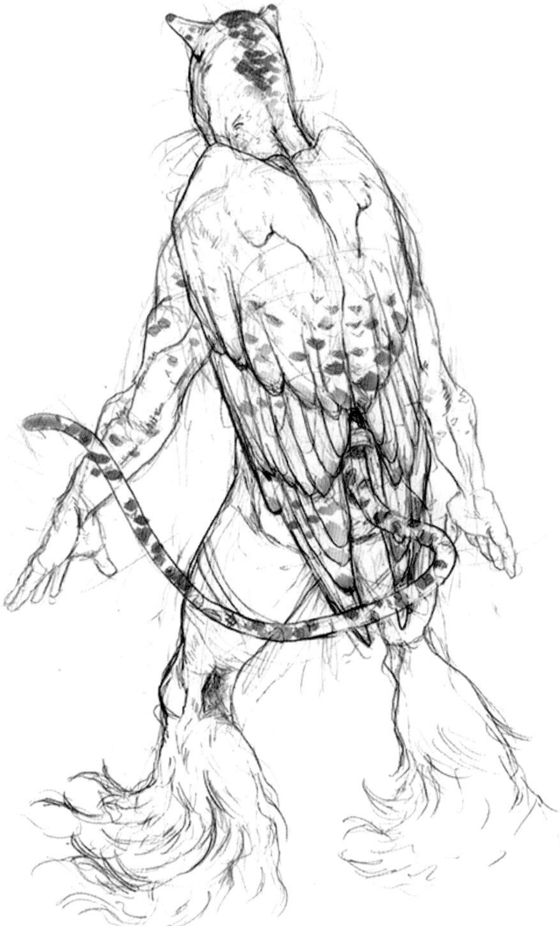

I wanted the snowy owl spots to have the coloring of Strig's cat, Ding. Another way to visually tie together Strig's mix.

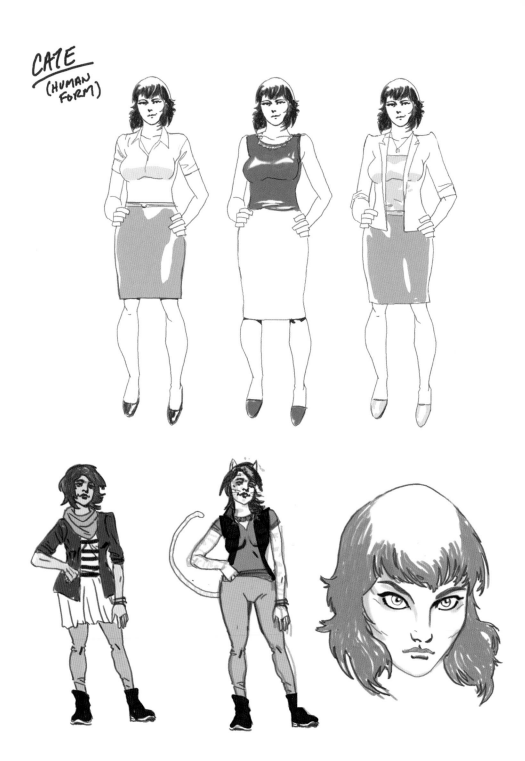

CATE
(HUMAN FORM)

There was a longer road to finding our Cate. I haven't drawn too many characters with sex appeal in my career, so Margaret kept encouraging me to go further in trying to find a visual way to depict a primal appeal. Finally Margaret sharpened her pencil and designed Cate's nightclub outfit herself. It's really cool seeing Margaret's drawings.

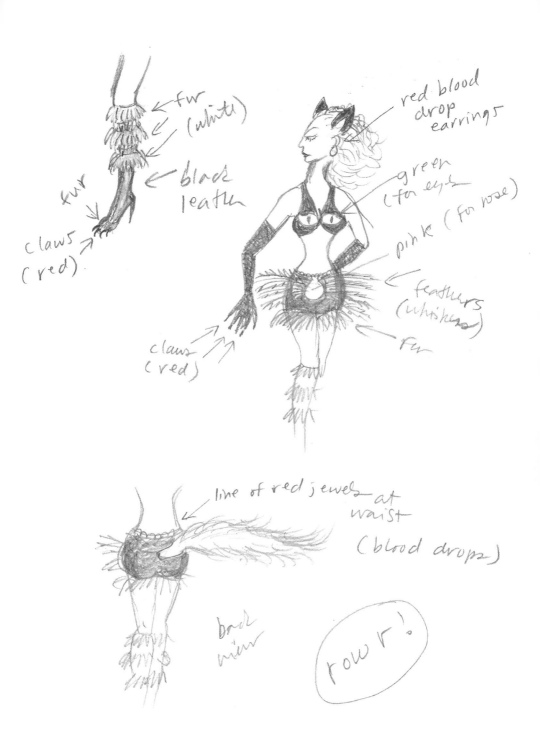

fur (white)

fur

black leather

claws (red)

red blood drop earrings

green (for eyes)

pink (for nose)

feathers (whiskers)

fur

claws (red)

line of red jewels at waist

(blood drops)

back view

rowr!

Margaret Atwood: I designed the nightclub outfit to go with the band name: Pussies in Boots. So there are boots, of course. The tops are cat eyes, the bottoms have cat noses and whiskers. And gloves with claws that are even longer than their real claws. Blood-drop earrings. I'm kinda literal minded.

CATE
CAT FORM

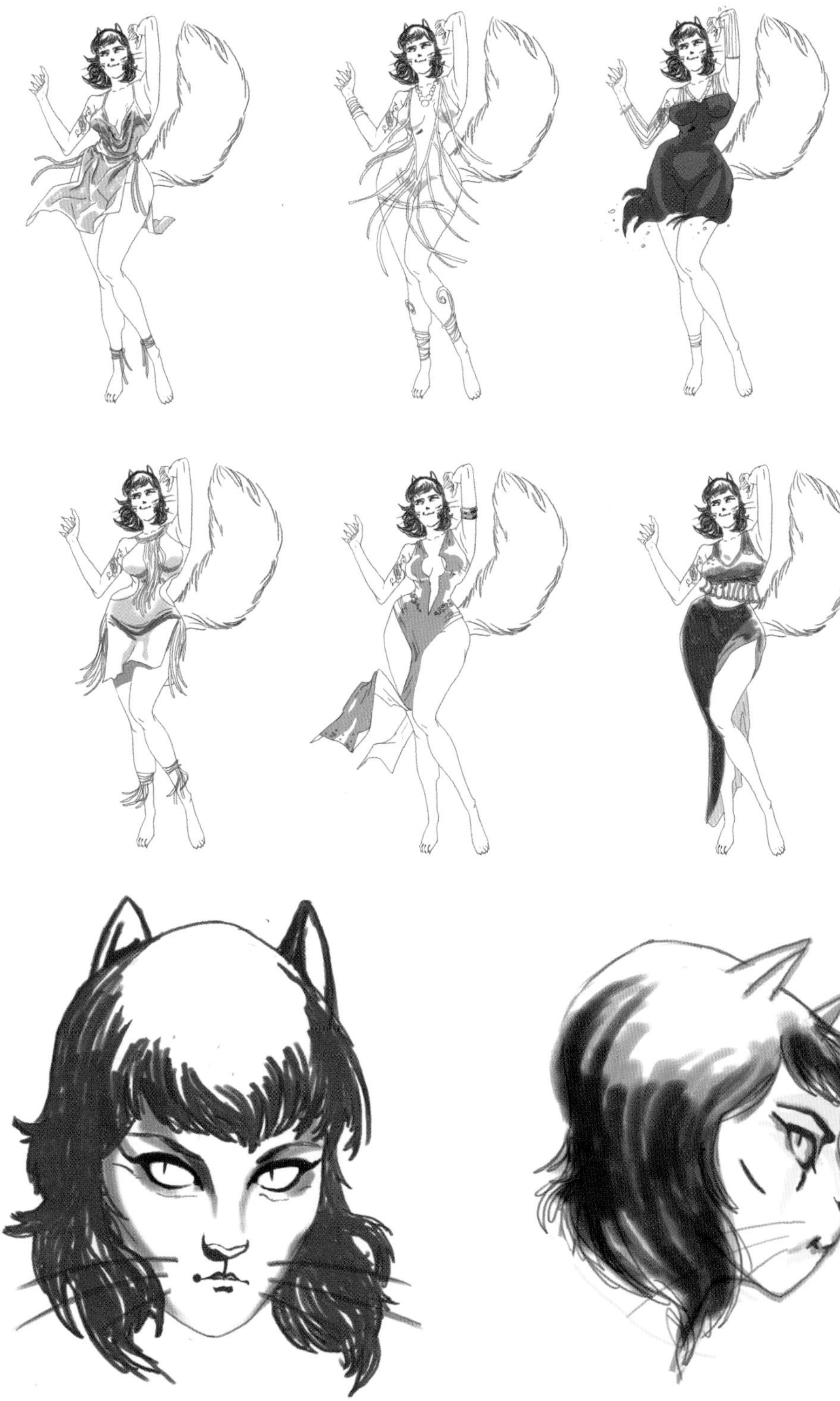

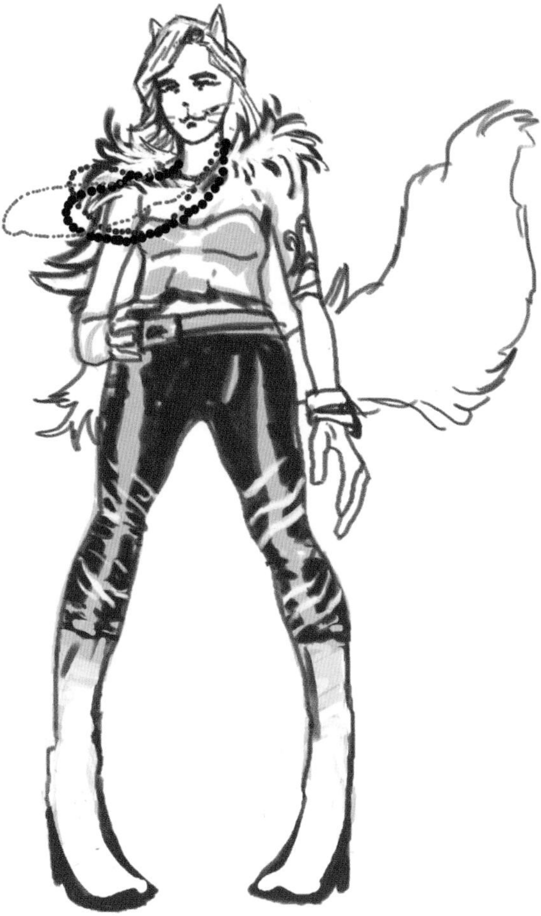
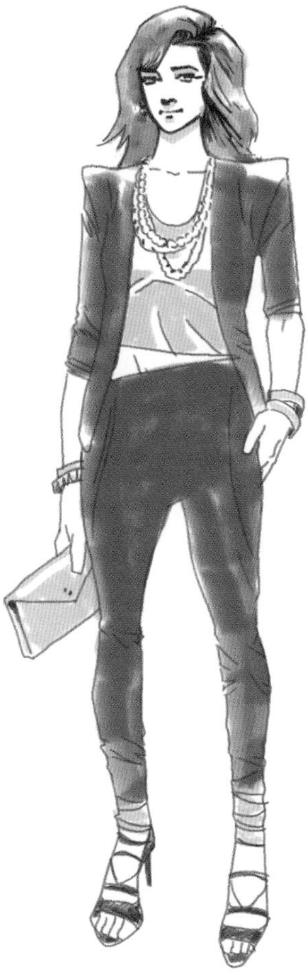
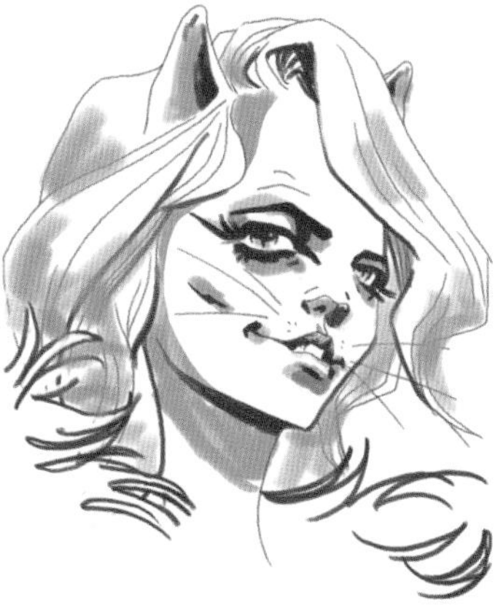
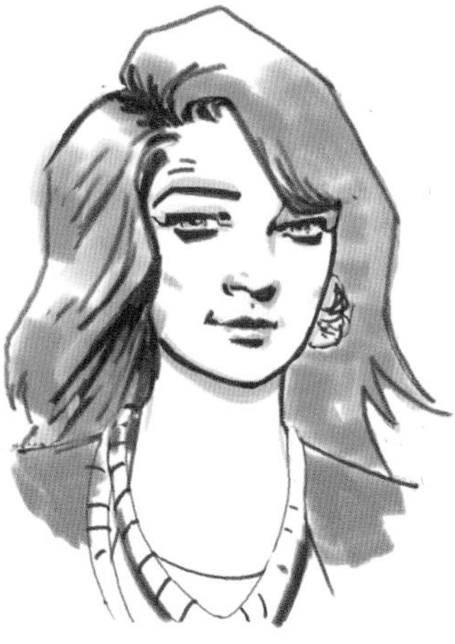

DR. MUROID

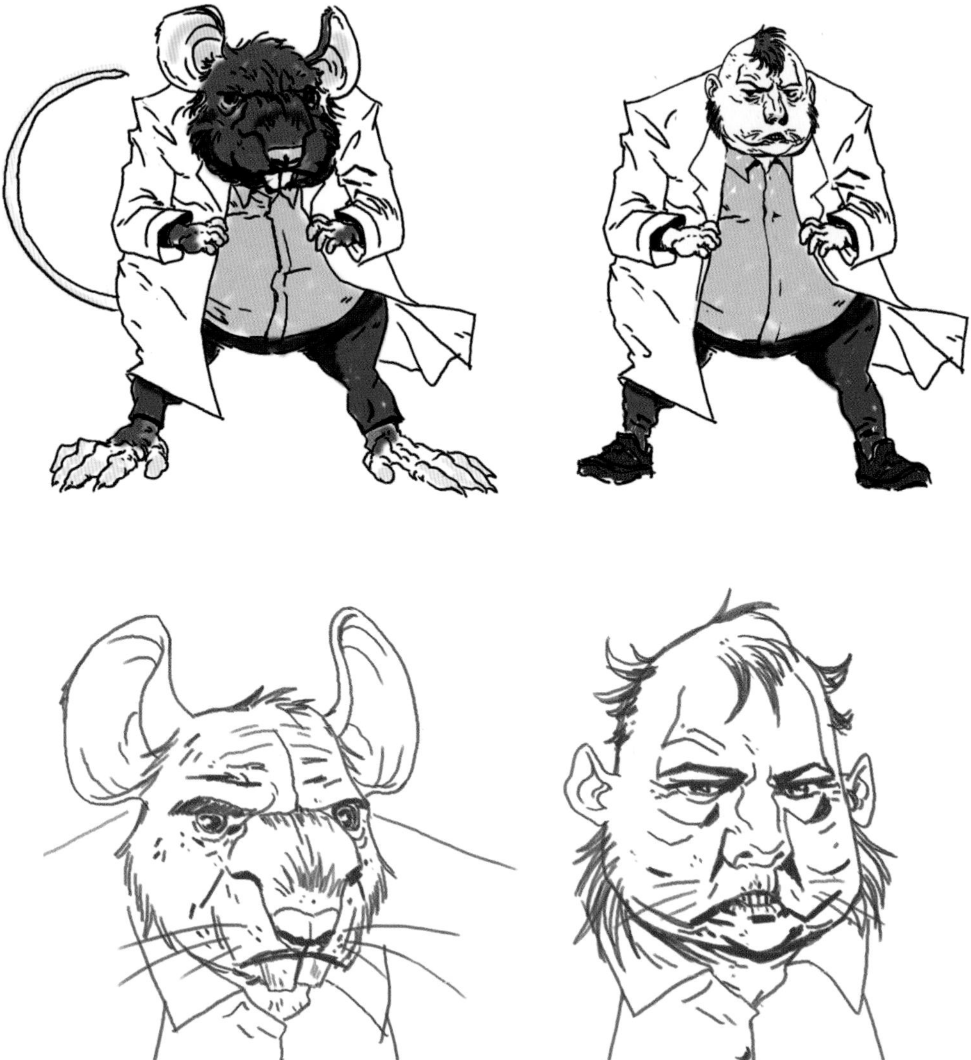

Villains are very fun to draw, and Muroid is no exception. Drawing his menacingly evil facial expressions is a highlight when I'm at the drawing board.

RAY

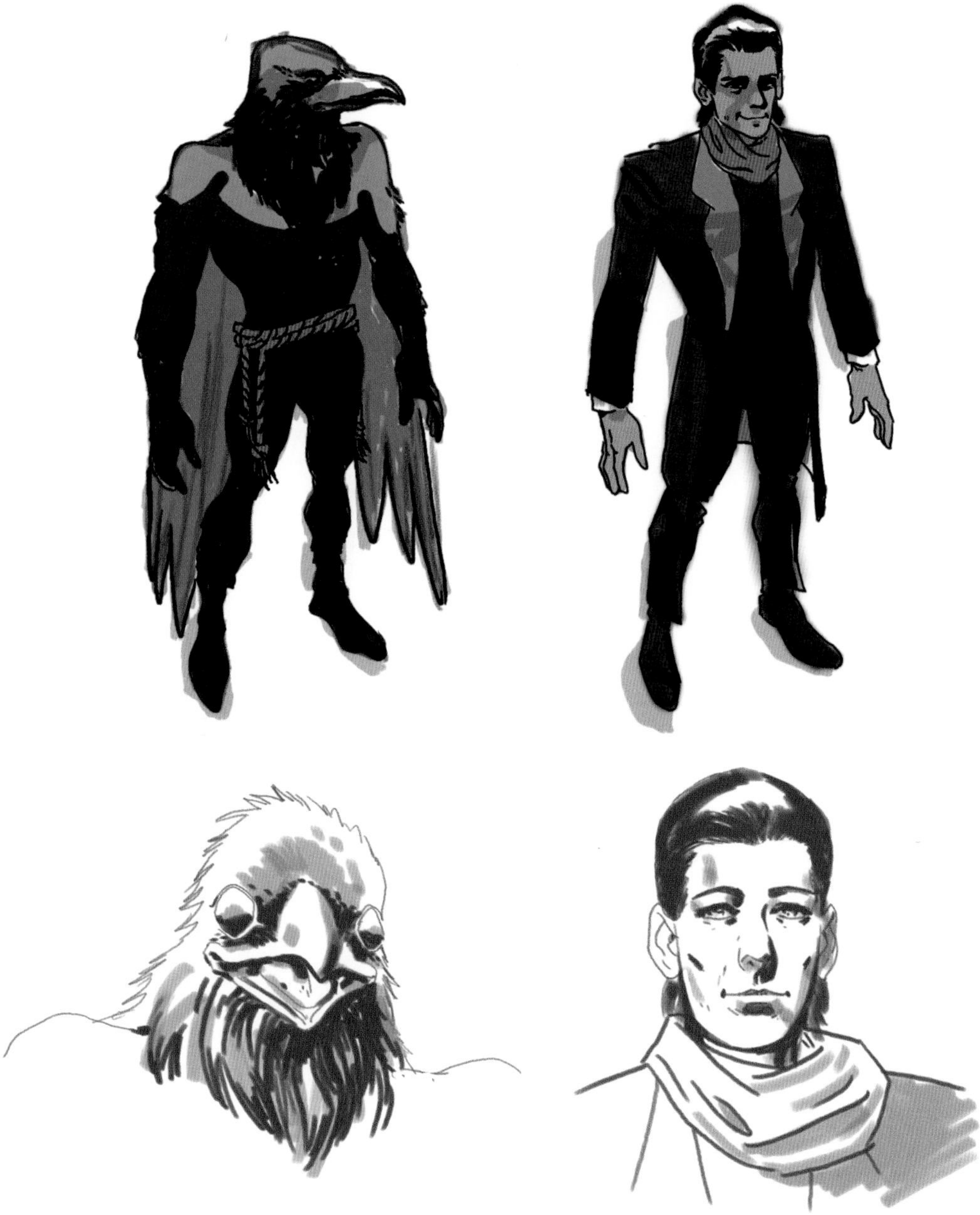

As a potential romantic rival for Cate's affections, Ray is quite fun too. He is Anishinaabe, the First Nations people of the area in which Margaret grew up.

COUNT CATULA

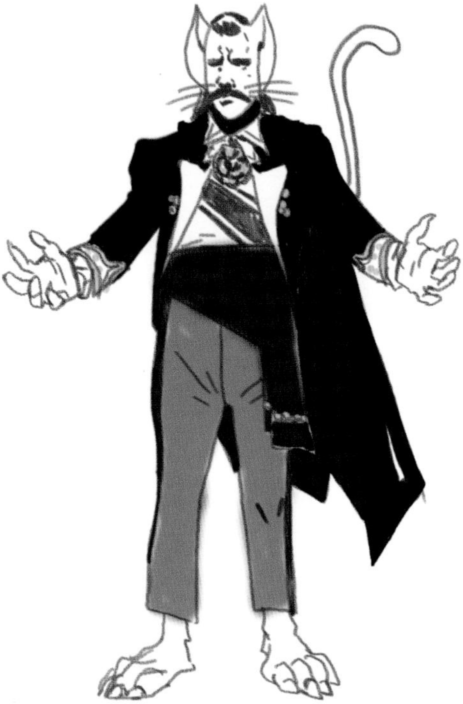

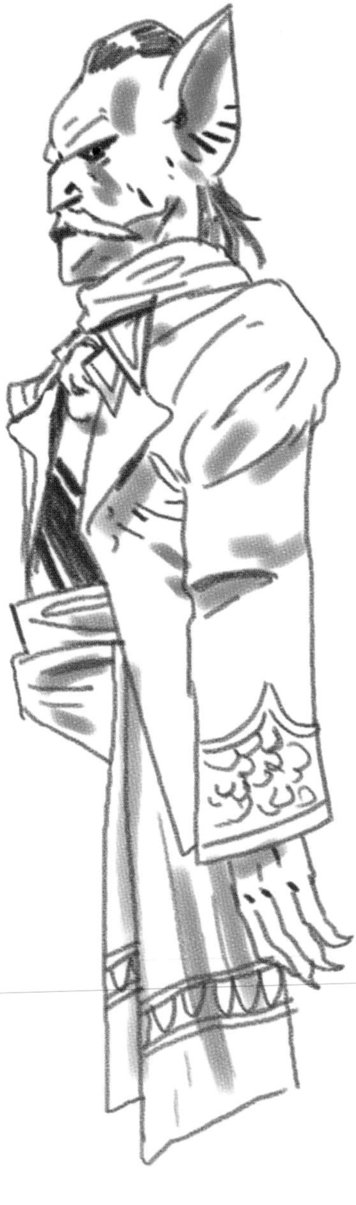

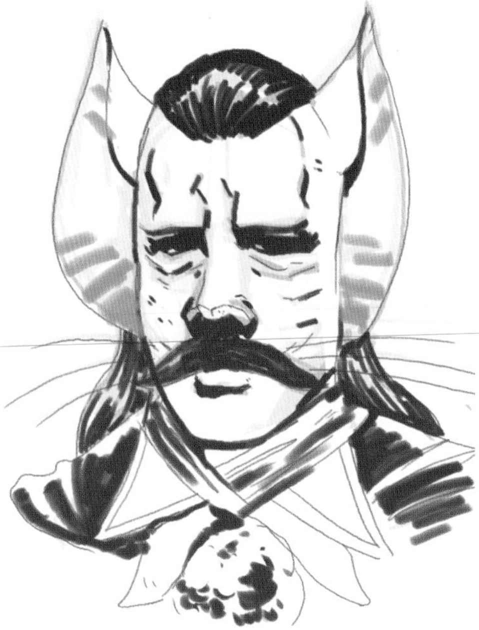

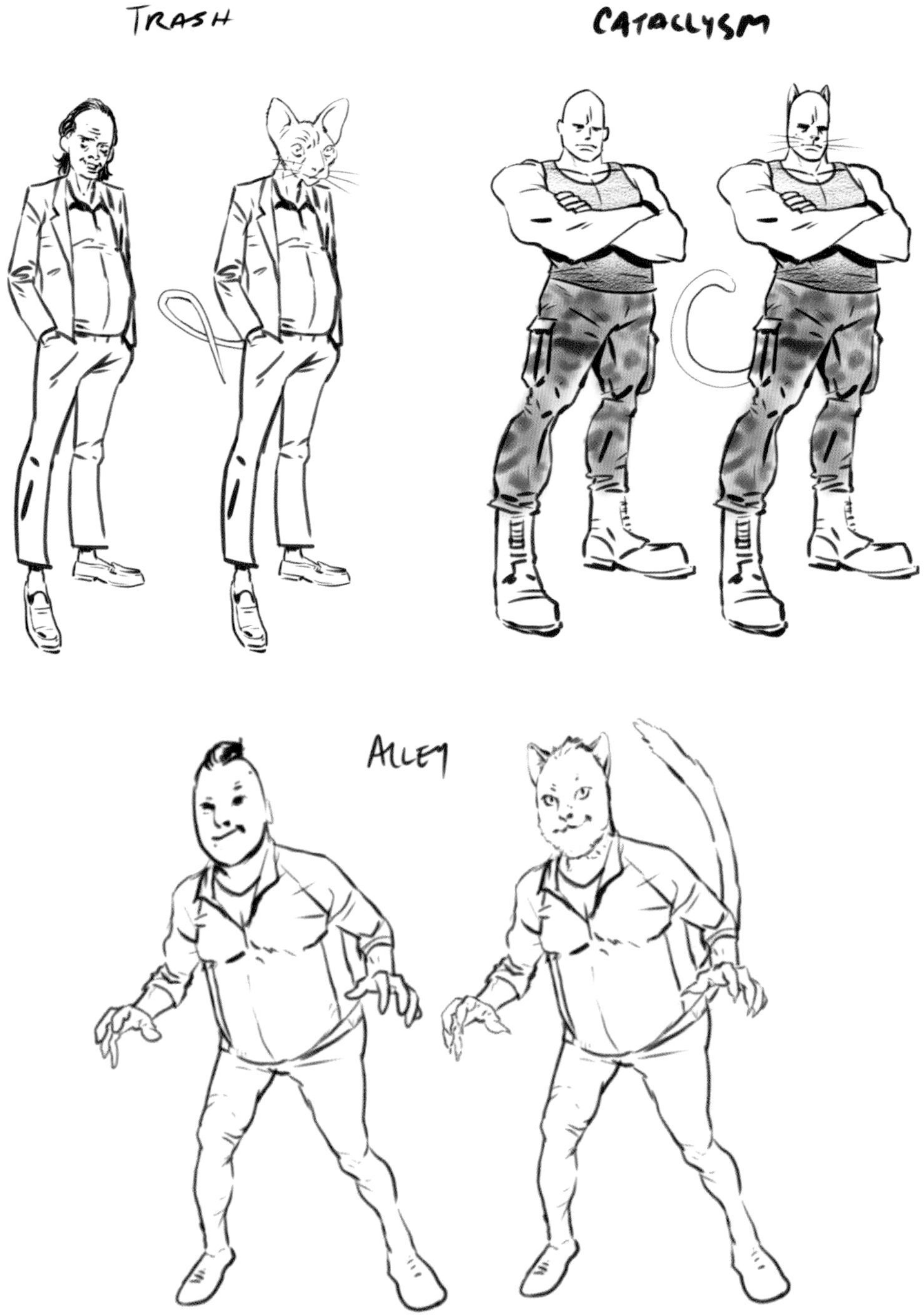
TRASH
CATACLYSM
ALLEY

I gave these half-cats human versions before realizing that some half-cats don't have human versions!

Bubastis

CATFISH

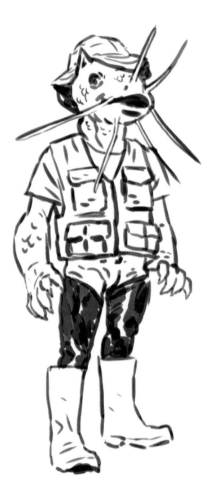

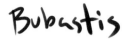

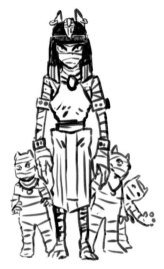

HANSEL & CATTYL

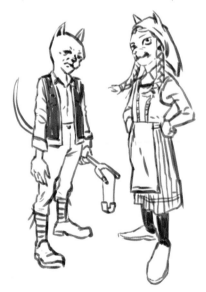

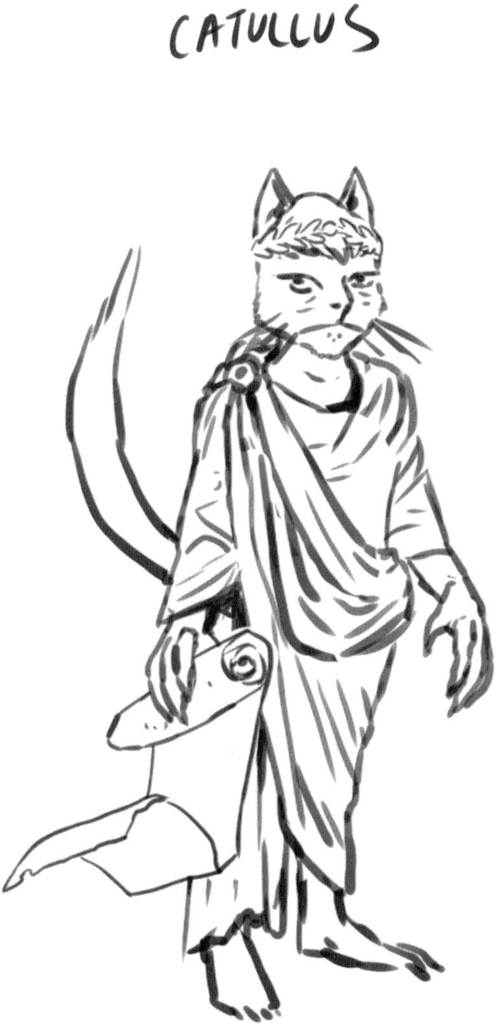
CATULLUS

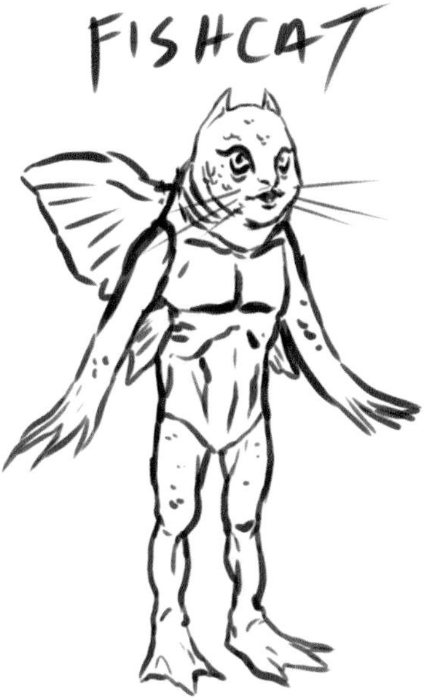
FISHCAT

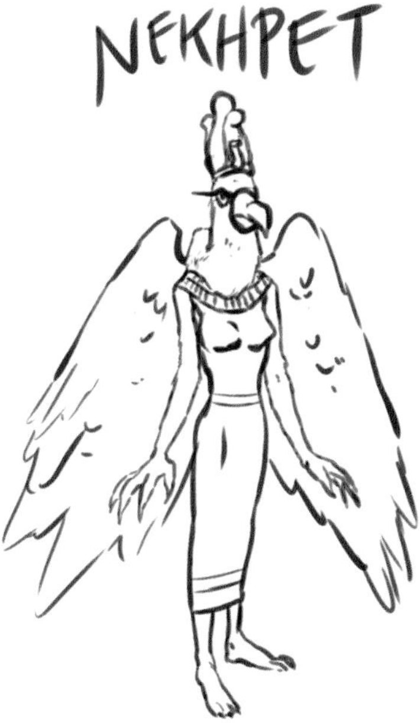
NEKHPET

Cats and cats and cats.

BABUSHKAT

CAT O'NINETALES

CAT O'NINETALES

BARNBORN

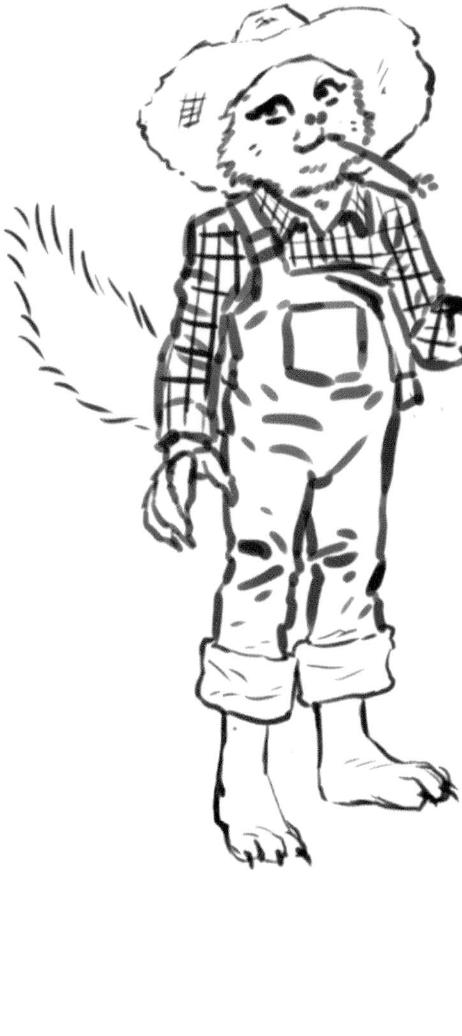

OCTOPUSS

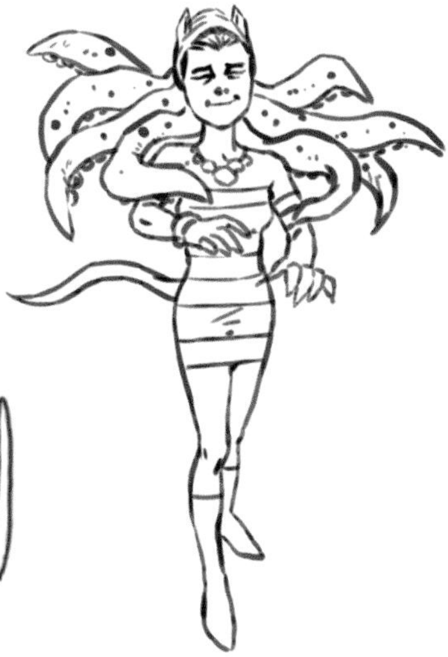

OCTOPUSS

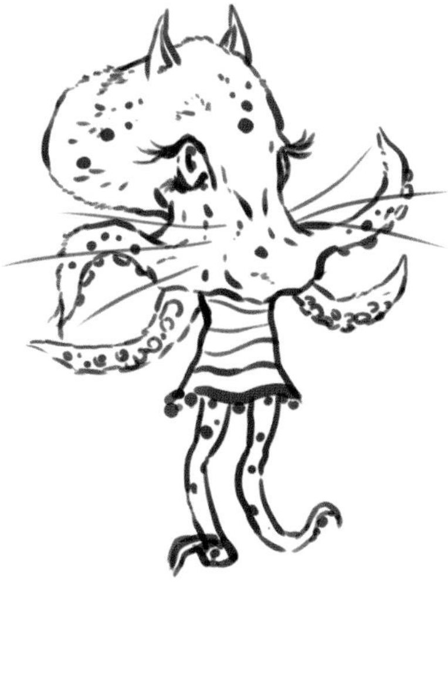

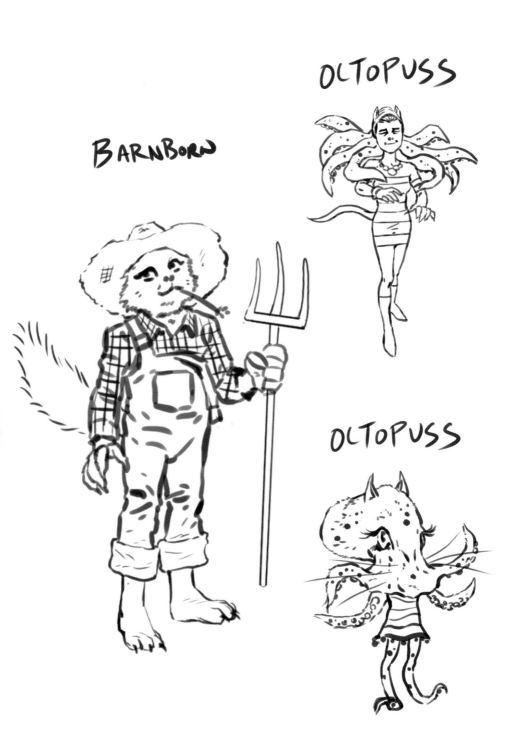

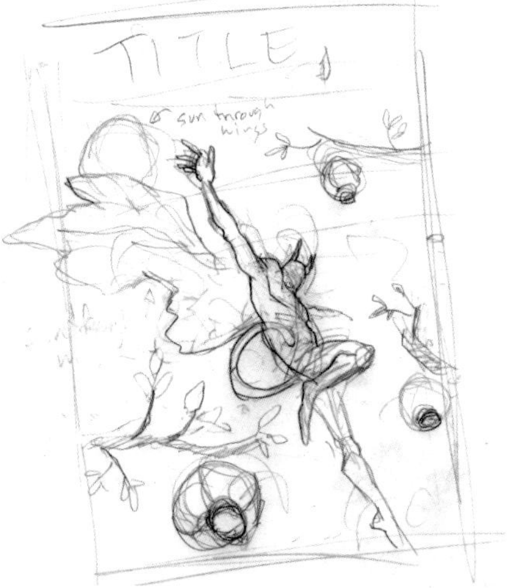
TITLE
sun through wings

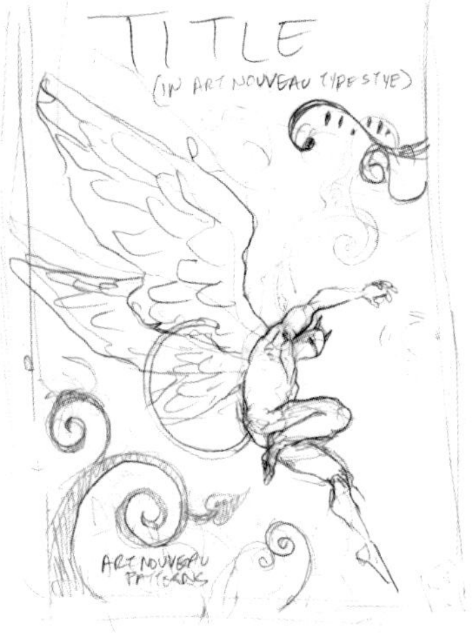
TITLE
(IN ART NOUVEAU TYPE STYLE)
ART NOUVEAU PATTERNS

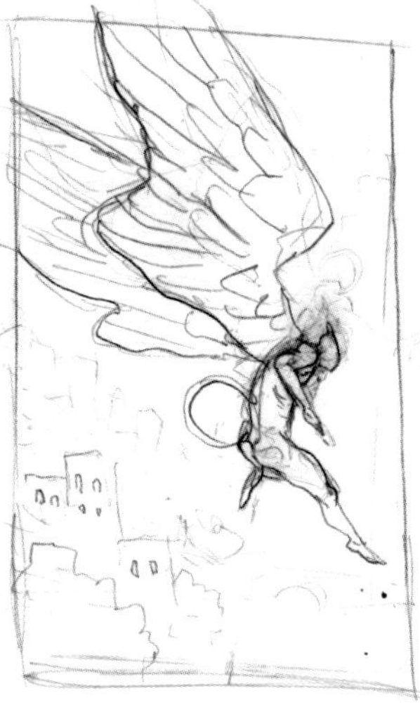

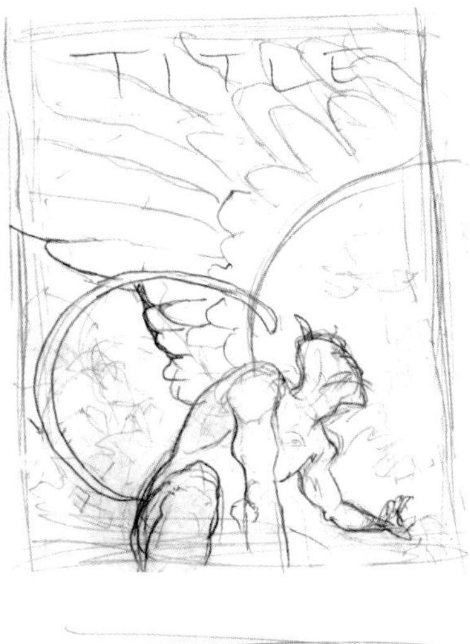
TITLE

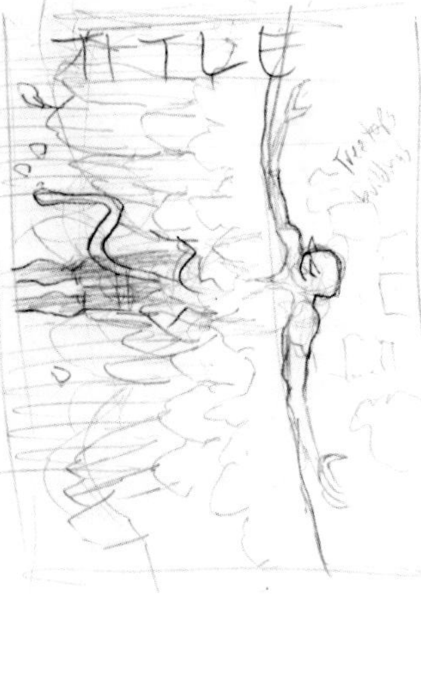
TITLE

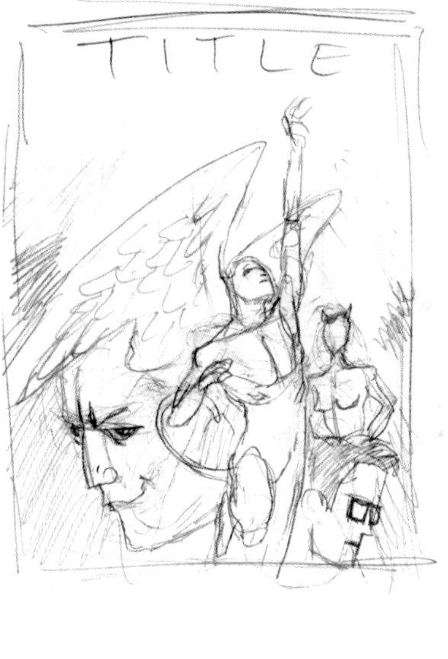
TITLE

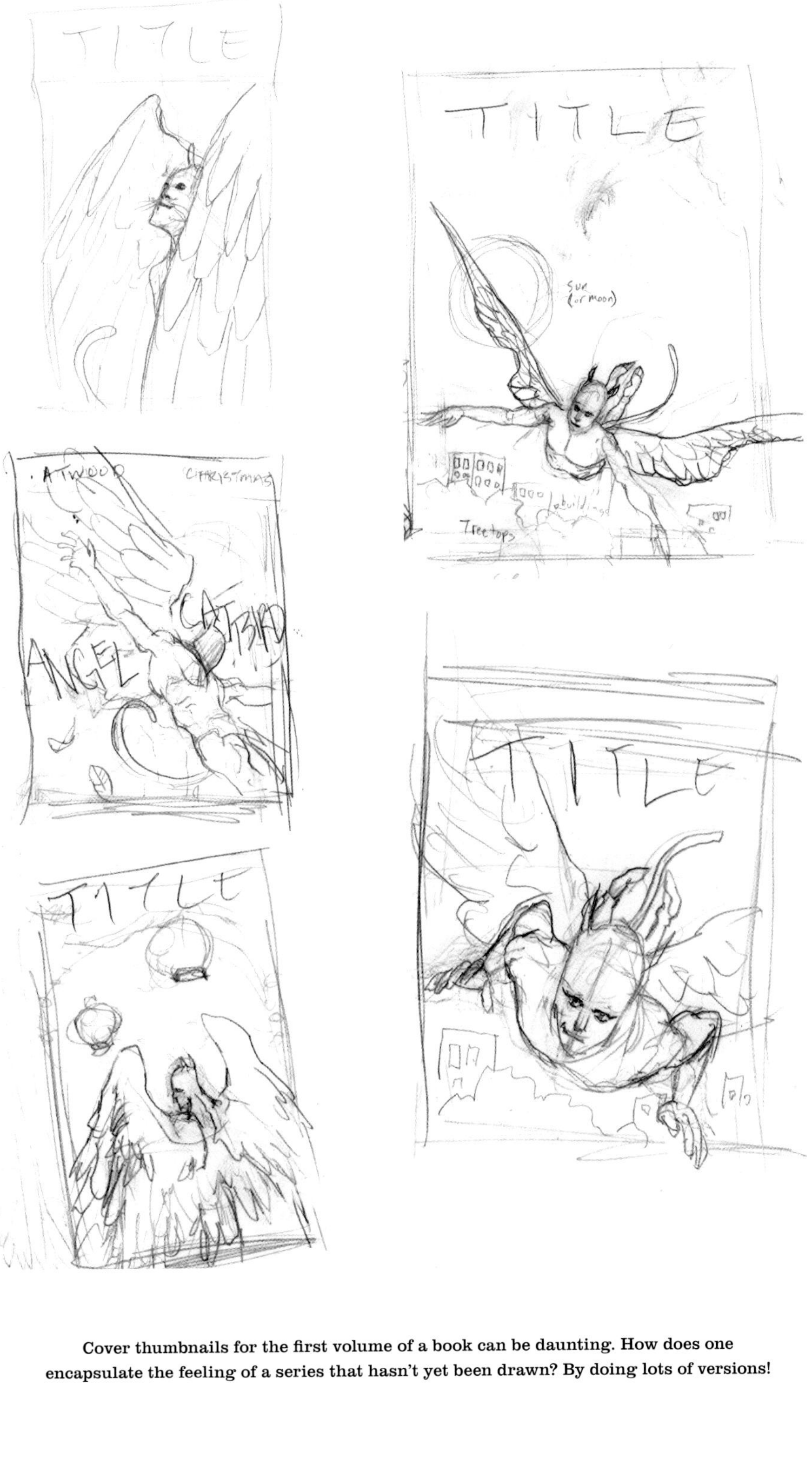
TITLE
TITLE
Sun (or moon)
buildings
Treetops
ATWOOD
CHRISTMAS
CATBIRD
ANGEL
TITLE
TITLE

Cover thumbnails for the first volume of a book can be daunting. How does one encapsulate the feeling of a series that hasn't yet been drawn? By doing lots of versions!

COLOR PROCESS by TAMRA BONVILLAIN

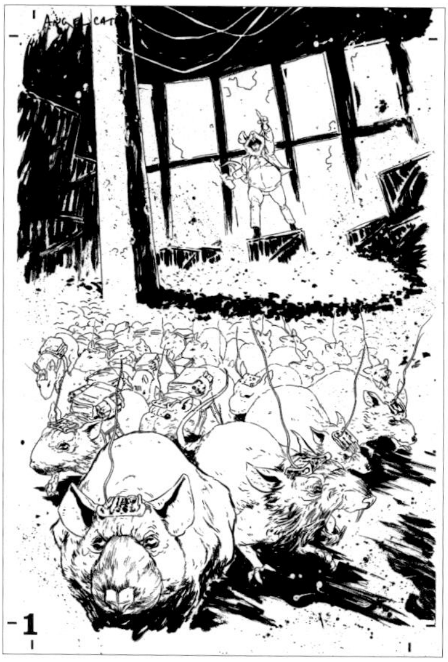
1

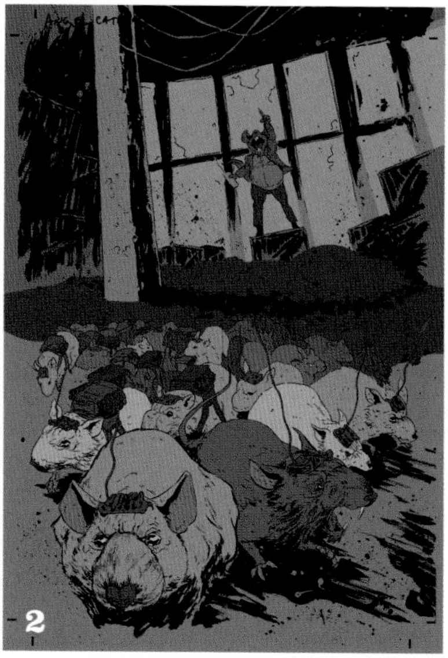
2

1. First, I start with the black-and-white line art from Johnnie.
2. I send the pages off to a flatter. A flatter is an assistant that helps colorists by separating all the different parts of the page for easy selection. Final color choices are made by the colorist; the flats have no bearing on those decisions. These flats are by Fernando Argüello.

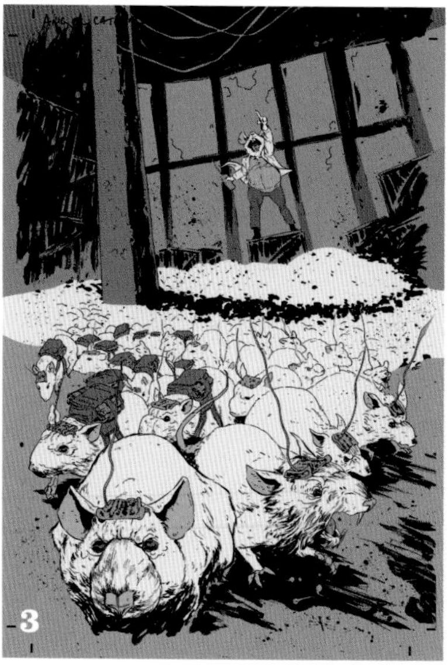
3

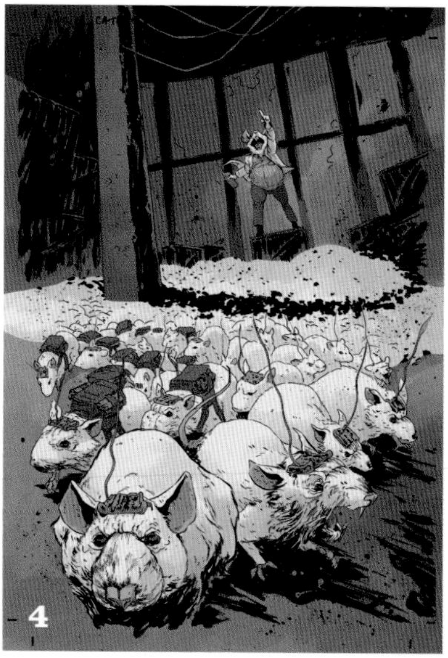
4

3. Using the flats, I adjust the colors to achieve the palette I'm going for. I do the original flats in local colors (the base color of an object, not affected by colored lighting), and then make some adjustments to help shift and/or unify things. The version shown here is after I made it a little warmer and more yellow overall.
4. Next comes the rendering. These next few rendering images are not necessarily shown in the order in which they were applied. In Photoshop, I make rendering layers that apply different effects, and I can jump between them as I'm working. These images show each layer applied one by one. Here, I'm using a saturated magenta shadow layer for the first shadow pass.

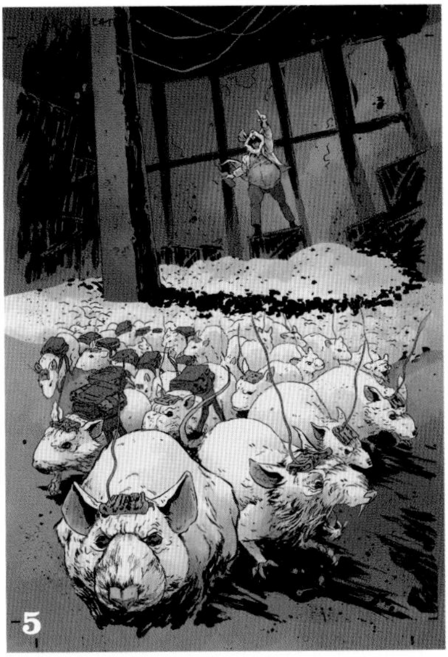
5

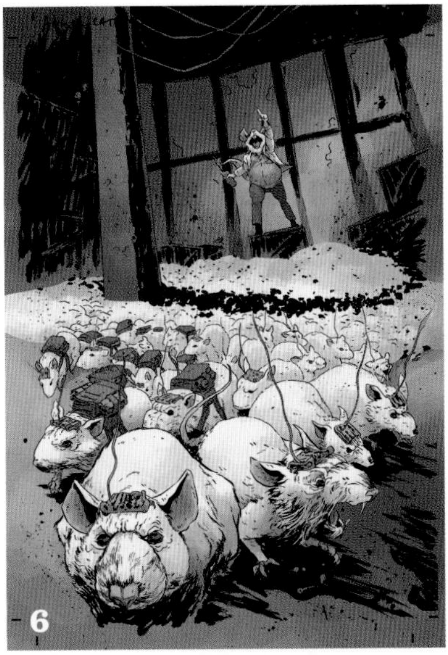
6

5. To tone down the shadow saturation and deepen the shadows to give things more form, I throw another shadow layer on top.
6. To bring focus to some of the areas, I apply a warmer, more saturated light layer.

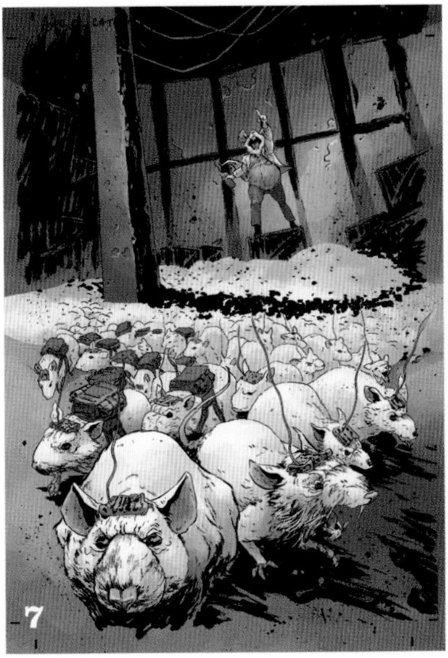
7

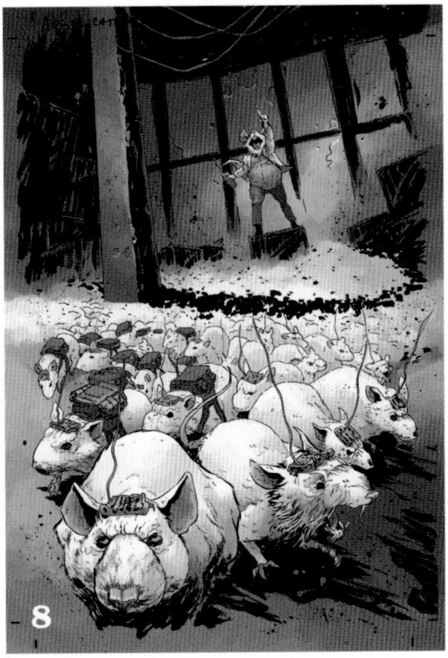
8

7. At this stage I add the final highlights to the lit focal areas.
8. In the final few steps I blend the harsh edges that can't be easily defined from the flatting stage, colorize some of the line art subtly, and then make a small adjustment over everything to increase the contrast a touch.

MARGARET ATWOOD

Photograph by LIAM SHARP

Margaret Atwood was born in 1939 in Ottawa and grew up in northern Ontario, Quebec, and Toronto. She received her undergraduate degree from Victoria College at the University of Toronto and her master's degree from Radcliffe College.

Atwood is the author of more than forty volumes of poetry, children's literature, fiction, and nonfiction, but is best known for her novels, which include *The Edible Woman* (1969), *The Handmaid's Tale* (1985), *The Robber Bride* (1993), *Alias Grace* (1996), and *The Blind Assassin*, which won the prestigious Man Booker Prize in 2000. Her latest work is a book of short stories called *Stone Mattress: Nine Tales* (2014). Her newest novel, *MaddAddam* (2013), is the final volume in a three-book series that began with the Man Booker Prize–nominated *Oryx and Crake* (2003) and continued with *The Year of the Flood* (2009). *The Tent* (mini-fictions) and *Moral Disorder* (short fiction) both appeared in 2006. Her most recent volume of poetry, *The Door*, was published in 2007. *In Other Worlds: SF and the Human Imagination*, a collection of nonfiction essays, appeared in 2011. Her nonfiction book *Payback: Debt and the Shadow Side of Wealth* was adapted for the screen in 2012. Ms. Atwood's work has been published in more than forty languages, including Farsi, Japanese, Turkish, Finnish, Korean, Icelandic, and Estonian.

JOHNNIE CHRISTMAS

Photograph by AVALON MOTT

Johnnie Christmas was born in Río Piedras, Puerto Rico, and raised in Miami, Florida. He attended the Center for Media Arts magnet program at South Miami Senior High School and received a BFA from Pratt Institute in Brooklyn, New York, before going on to a career in graphic design and art direction. In 2013 he entered the world of comics as cocreator of the critically acclaimed Image Comics series *Sheltered*. He's also the creator, writer, and artist of *Firebug*, serialized in *Island*, also published by Image Comics. His work has been translated into multiple languages.

Johnnie makes Vancouver, BC, his home.

TAMRA BONVILLAIN

Tamra Bonvillain is originally from Augusta, Georgia, and took an interest in art and comics at a young age. After graduating from the local Davidson Fine Arts Magnet School in 2000, she majored in art at Augusta State University. She later attended the Joe Kubert School, and upon graduating in 2009, she began working full time as an assistant and designer for Greg Hildebrandt and Jean Scrocco's company, Spiderwebart. During this time, she also began to take on work as a comics colorist, eventually leaving the company to pursue a career in the comics industry full time. In the years since, she has worked for many major comic publishers, including Dark Horse, Dynamite, Boom, Image, and Marvel. She is currently the colorist for *Rat Queens*, *Wayward*, and several other titles.

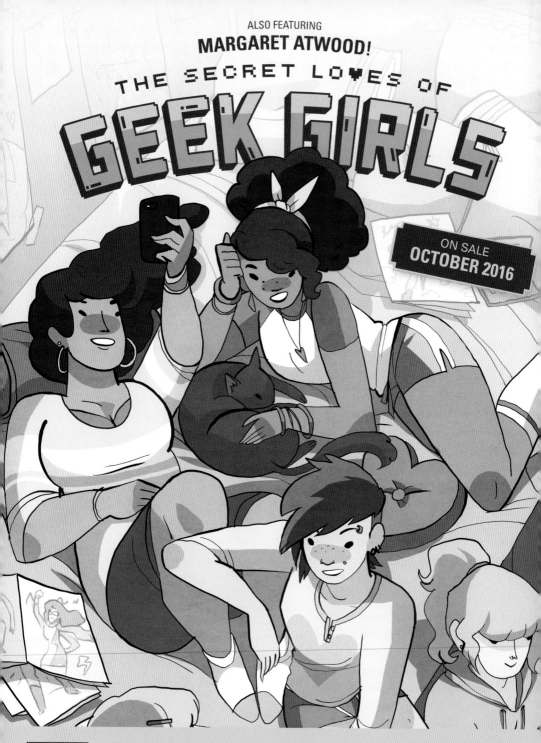

ALSO FEATURING
MARGARET ATWOOD!

THE SECRET LOVES OF

GEEK GIRLS

ON SALE
OCTOBER 2016

The Secret Loves of Geek Girls is a nonfiction anthology mixing prose, comics, and illustrated stories about the lives and loves of an amazing cast of female creators. Featuring work by **Margaret Atwood** (*The Heart Goes Last*), **Mariko Tamaki** (*This One Summer*), **Trina Robbins** (*Wonder Woman*), **Marguerite Bennett** (Marvel's *A-Force*), **Noelle Stevenson** (*Nimona*), **Marjorie Liu** (*Monstress*), **Carla Speed McNeil** (*Finder*), and over fifty more creators, it's a compilation of tales told from both sides of the tables: from the fans who love video games, comics, and sci-fi to those that work behind the scenes as creators and industry insiders.

$14.99 | ISBN 978-1-50670-099-1

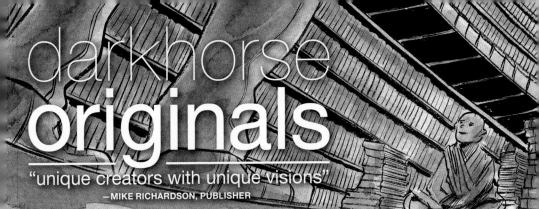

darkhorse originals

"unique creators with unique visions"

—MIKE RICHARDSON, PUBLISHER

3 STORY: THE SECRET HISTORY OF THE GIANT MAN
978-1-59582-356-4 | $19.99

365 SAMURAI AND A FEW BOWLS OF RICE
978-1-59582-412-7 | $16.99

THE ADVENTURES OF BLANCHE
978-1-59582-258-1 | $15.99

APOCALYPTIGIRL: AN ARIA FOR THE END TIMES
978-1-61655-566-5 | $9.99

BEANWORLD
Volume 1: Wahoolazuma!
978-1-59582-240-6 | $19.99
Volume 2: A Gift Comes!
978-1-59582-299-4 | $19.99
Volume 3: Remember Here When You Are There!
978-1-59582-355-7 | $19.99
Volume 3.5: Tales of the Beanworld
978-1-59582-897-2 | $14.99

BLACKSAD
978-1-59582-393-9 | $29.99

BLACKSAD: A SILENT HELL
978-1-59582-931-3 | $19.99

BLOOD SONG: A SILENT BALLAD
978-1-59582-389-2 | $19.99

THE BOOK OF GRICKLE
978-1-59582-430-1 | $17.99

BRODY'S GHOST
Book 1: 978-1-59582-521-6 | $6.99
Book 2: 978-1-59582-665-7 | $6.99
Book 3: 978-1-59582-862-0 | $6.99
Book 4: 978-1-61655-129-2 | $6.99

BUCKO
978-1-59582-973-3 | $19.99

CHANNEL ZERO
978-1-59582-936-8 | $19.99

CHERUBS
978-1-59582-984-9 | $19.99

CHIMICHANGA
978-1-59582-755-5 | $14.99

CITIZEN REX
978-1-59582-556-8 | $19.99

THE COMPLETE PISTOLWHIP
978-1-61655-720-1 | $27.99

CROSSING THE EMPTY QUARTER AND OTHER STORIES
978-1-59582-388-5 | $24.99

DE:TALES
HC: 978-1-59582-557-5 | $19.99
TPB: 978-1-59307-485-2 | $14.99

EVERYBODY GETS IT WRONG! AND OTHER STORIES: DAVID CHELSEA'S 24-HOUR COMICS
978-1-61655-155-1 | $19.99

EXURBIA
978-1-59582-339-7 | $9.99

FLUFFY
978-1-59307-972-7 | $19.99

GREEN RIVER KILLER
978-1-61655-812-3 | $19.99

HEART IN A BOX
978-1-61655-694-5 | $14.99

INSOMNIA CAFÉ
978-1-59582-357-1 | $14.99

THE MIGHTY SKULLBOY ARMY
Volume 2
978-1-59582-872-9 | $14.99

MILK AND CHEESE: DAIRY PRODUCTS GONE BAD
978-1-59582-805-7 | $19.99

MIND MGMT
Volume 1: The Manager
978-1-59582-797-5 | $19.99
Volume 2: The Futurist
978-1-61655-198-8 | $19.99

MOTEL ART IMPROVEMENT SERVICE
978-1-59582-550-6 | $19.99

THE NIGHT OF YOUR LIFE
978-1-59582-183-6 | $15.99

NINGEN'S NIGHTMARES
978-1-59582-859-0 | $12.99

NOIR
978-1-59582-358-8 | $12.99

PIXU: THE MARK OF EVIL
978-1-61655-813-0 | $14.99

RESET
978-1-61655-003-5 | $15.99

SACRIFICE
978-1-59582-985-6 | $19.99

SINFEST: VIVA LA RESISTANCE
978-1-59582-424-0 | $14.99

SPEAK OF THE DEVIL
978-1-59582-193-5 | $19.99

UNCLE SILAS
978-1-59582-566-7 | $9.99

AVAILABLE AT YOUR LOCAL COMICS SHOP OR BOOKSTORE!
To find a comics shop in your area, call 1-888-266-4226

For more information or to order direct:
On the web: DarkHorse.com
E-mail: mailorder@darkhorse.com
Phone: 1-800-862-0052 Mon.–Fri. 9 AM to 5 PM Pacific Time.

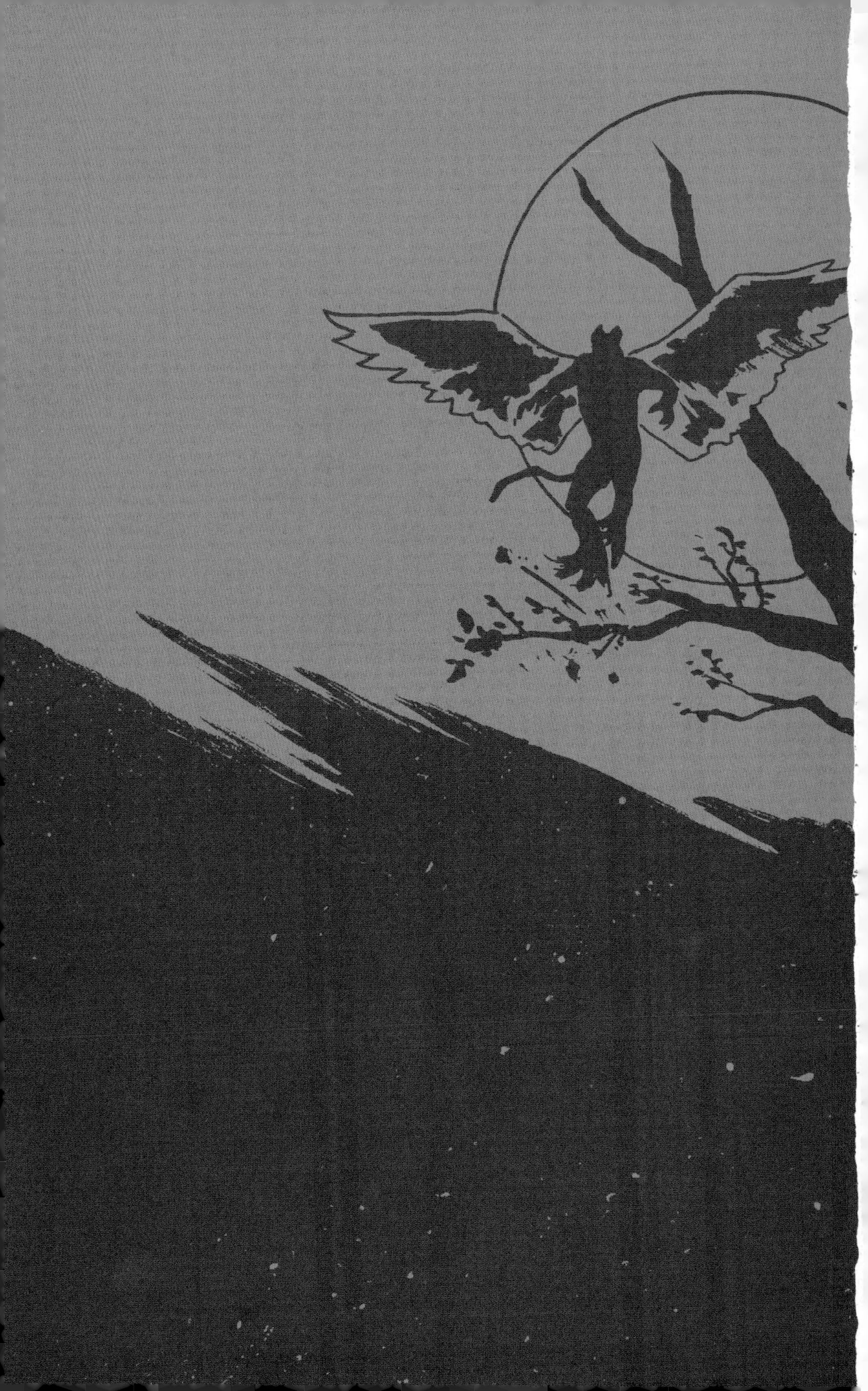